THE **LEGEND** OF **BRIGHTBLADE**

ALSO BY ETHAN M. ALDRIDGE

Estranged
Estranged: The Changeling King

THE LEGEND OF BRIGHTBLADE

ETHAN M. ALDRIDGE

Quill Tree Books

Imprints of HarperCollinsPublishers

HARPER alley

Quill Tree Books is an imprint of HarperCollins Publishers.
HarperAlley is an imprint of HarperCollins Publishers.

The Legend of Brightblade
Copyright © 2022 by Ethan M. Aldridge
All rights reserved. Manufactured in Italy.
No part of this book may be used or reproduced in any manner
whatsoever without written permission except in the case of brief
quotations embodied in critical articles and reviews. For information
address HarperCollins Children's Books, a division of HarperCollins
Publishers, 195 Broadway, New York, NY 10007.
www.harpercollinschildrens.com

ISBN 978-0-06-299552-0 (paperback)
ISBN 978-0-06-299553-7 (hardcover)

The artist used watercolors, ink, and Adobe Photoshop
to create the illustrations for this book.
Typography by Ethan M. Aldridge and Molly Fehr

21 22 23 24 25   RTLO   10 9 8 7 6 5 4 3 2 1
First Edition

R0462048092

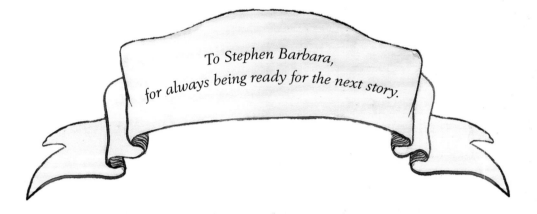

To Stephen Barbara,
for always being ready for the next story.

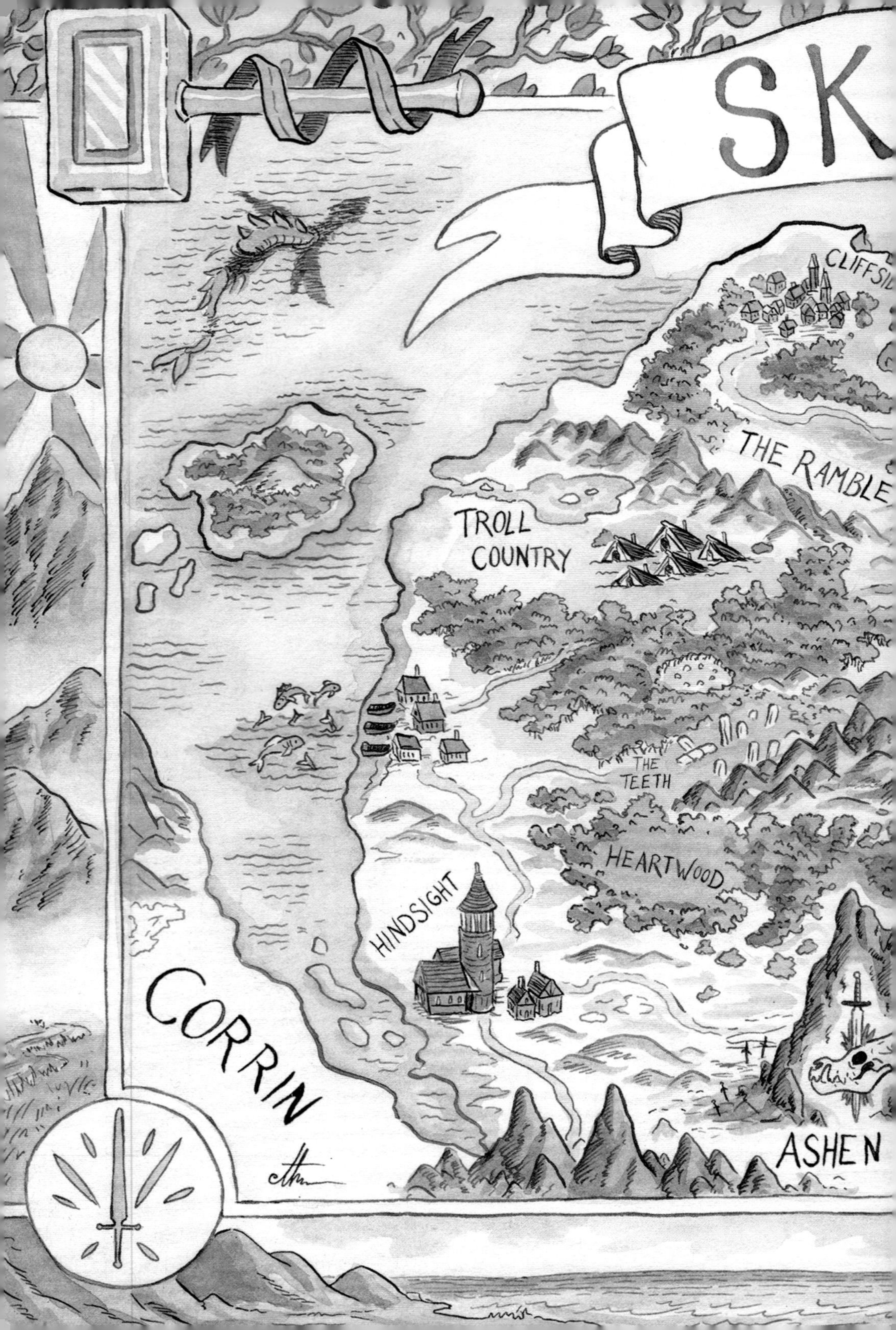
SK
CLIFFSI
THE RAMBLE
TROLL COUNTRY
THE TEETH
HEARTWOOD
HINDSIGHT
CORRIN
ASHEN

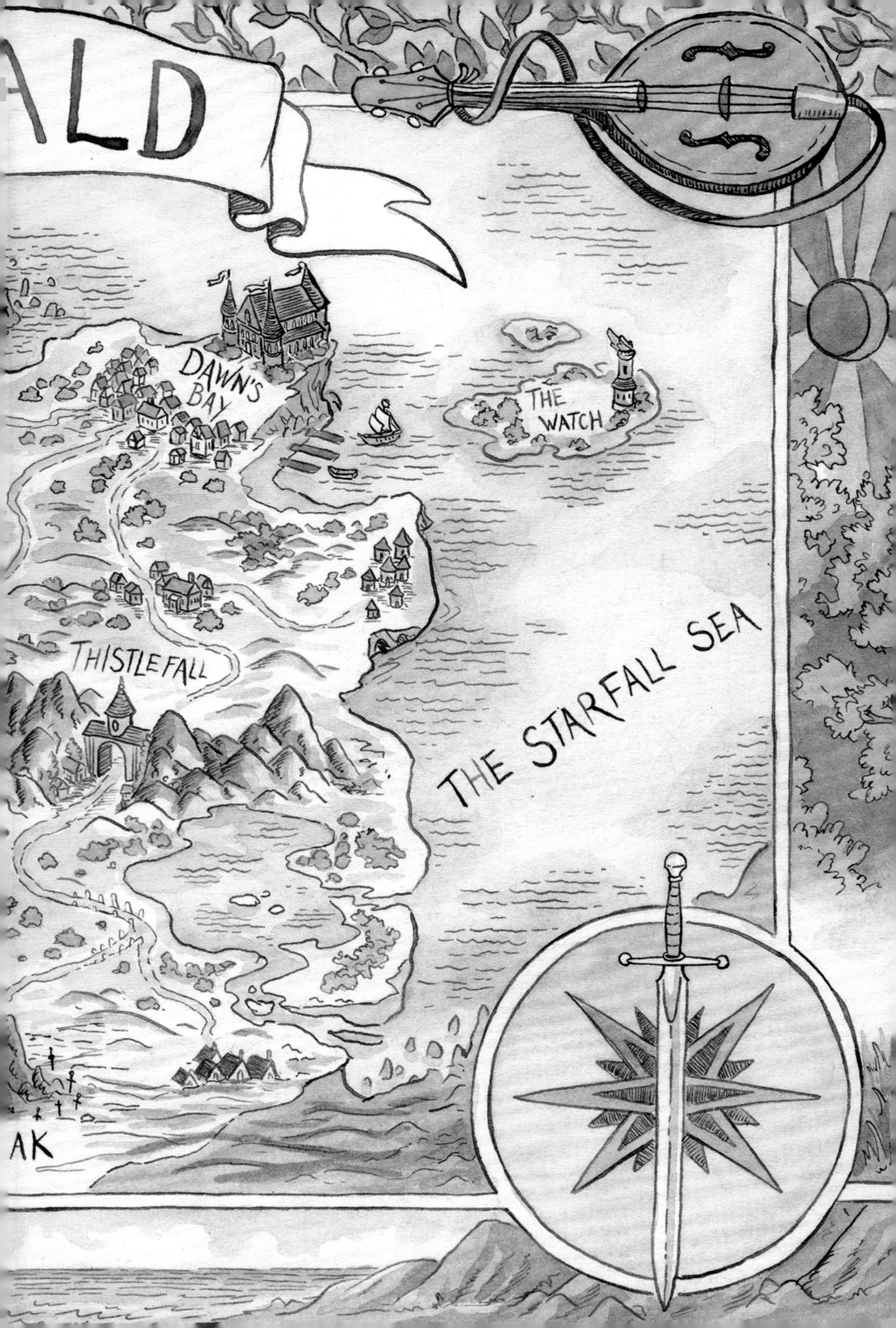
ALD
DAWN'S BAY
THE WATCH
THISTLEFALL
THE STARFALL SEA
AK

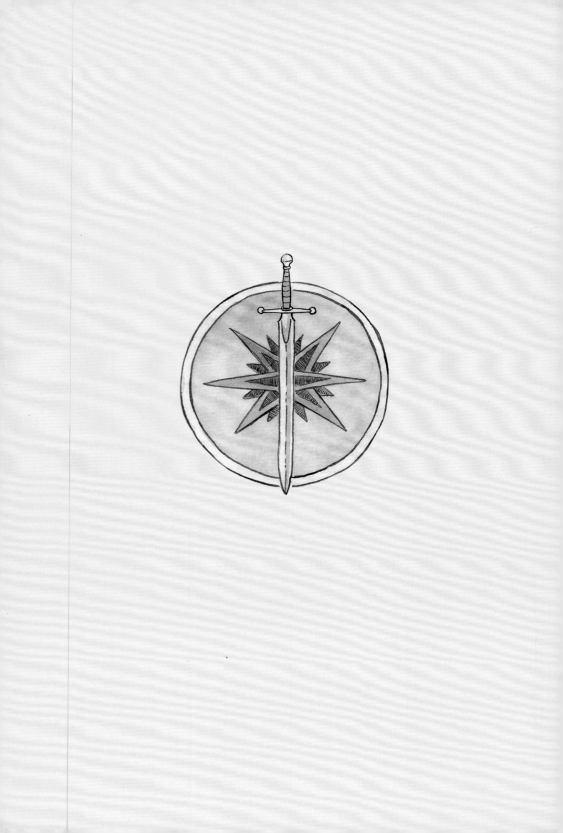

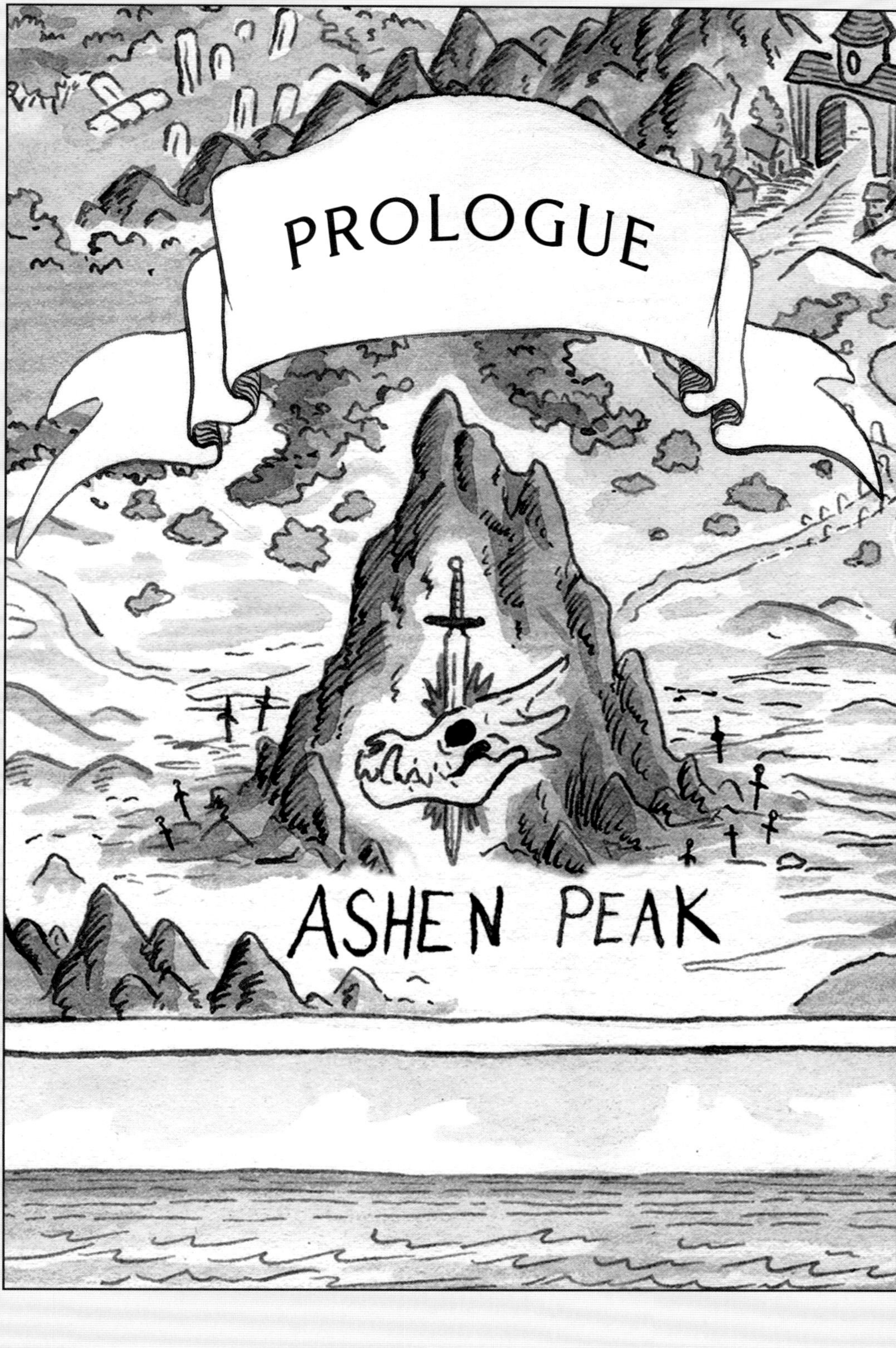
PROLOGUE
ASHEN PEAK

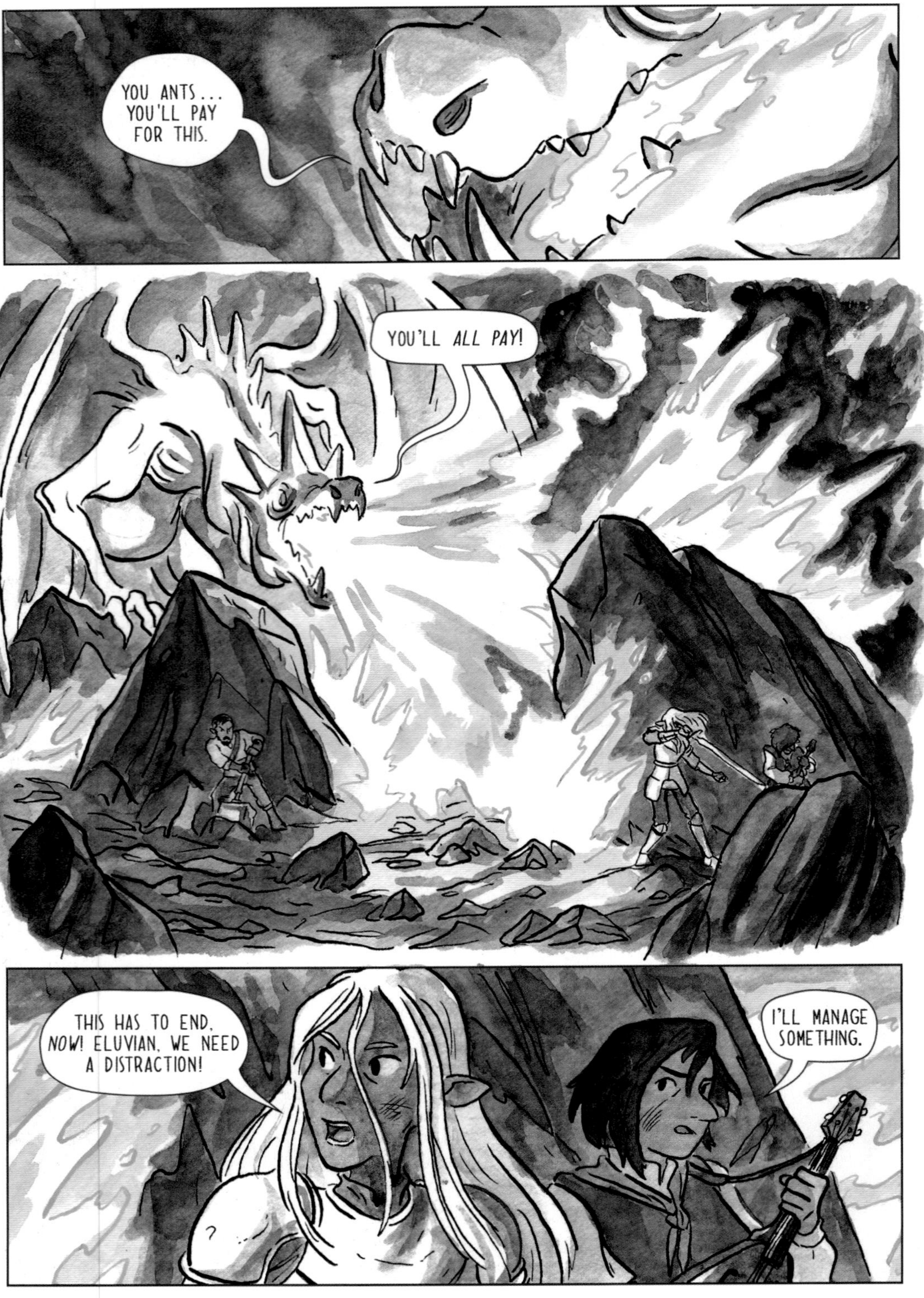

YOU ANTS... YOU'LL PAY FOR THIS.
YOU'LL *ALL PAY*!
THIS HAS TO END, *NOW*! ELUVIAN, WE NEED A DISTRACTION!
I'LL MANAGE SOMETHING.

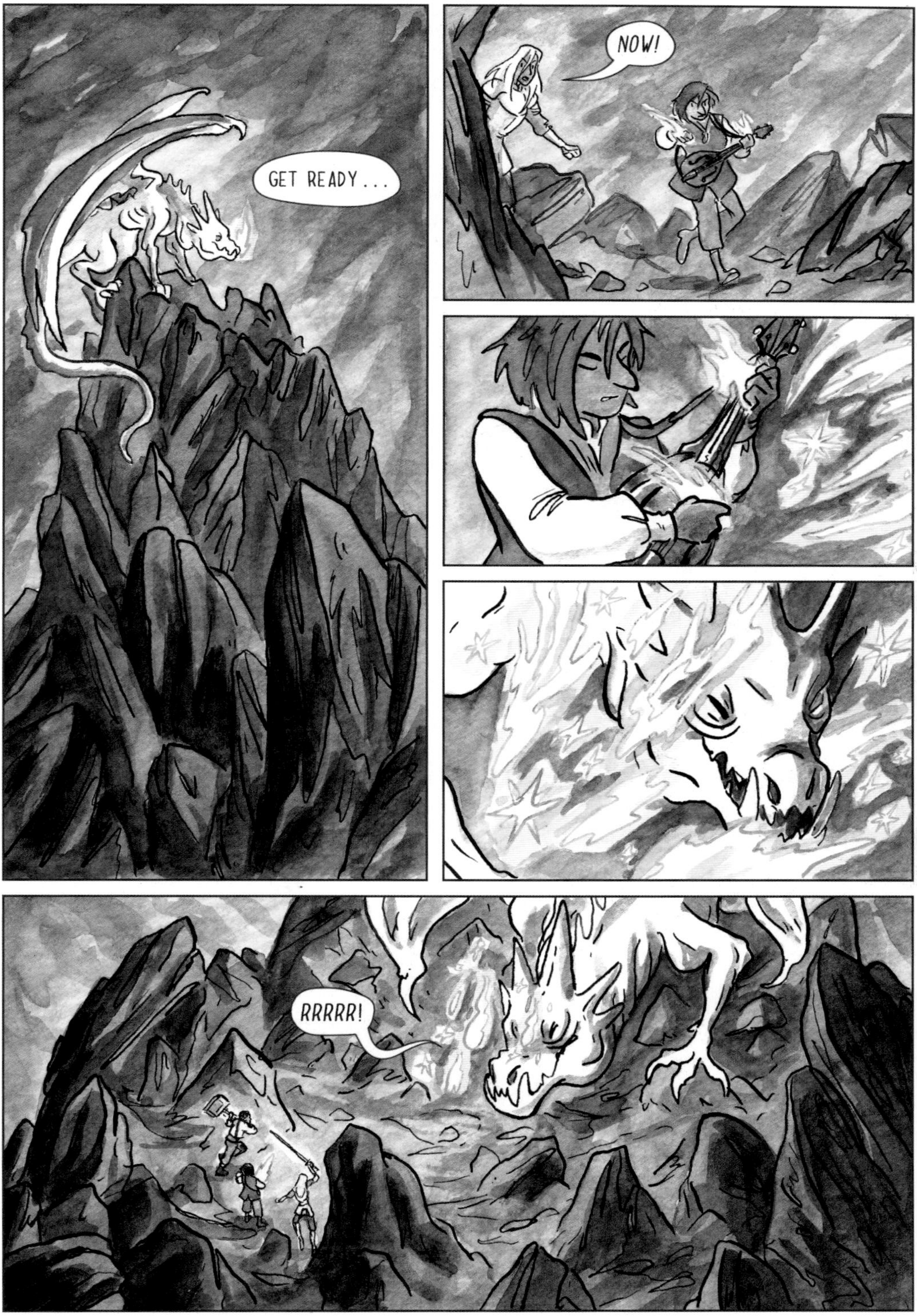
GET READY...
NOW!
RRRRR!

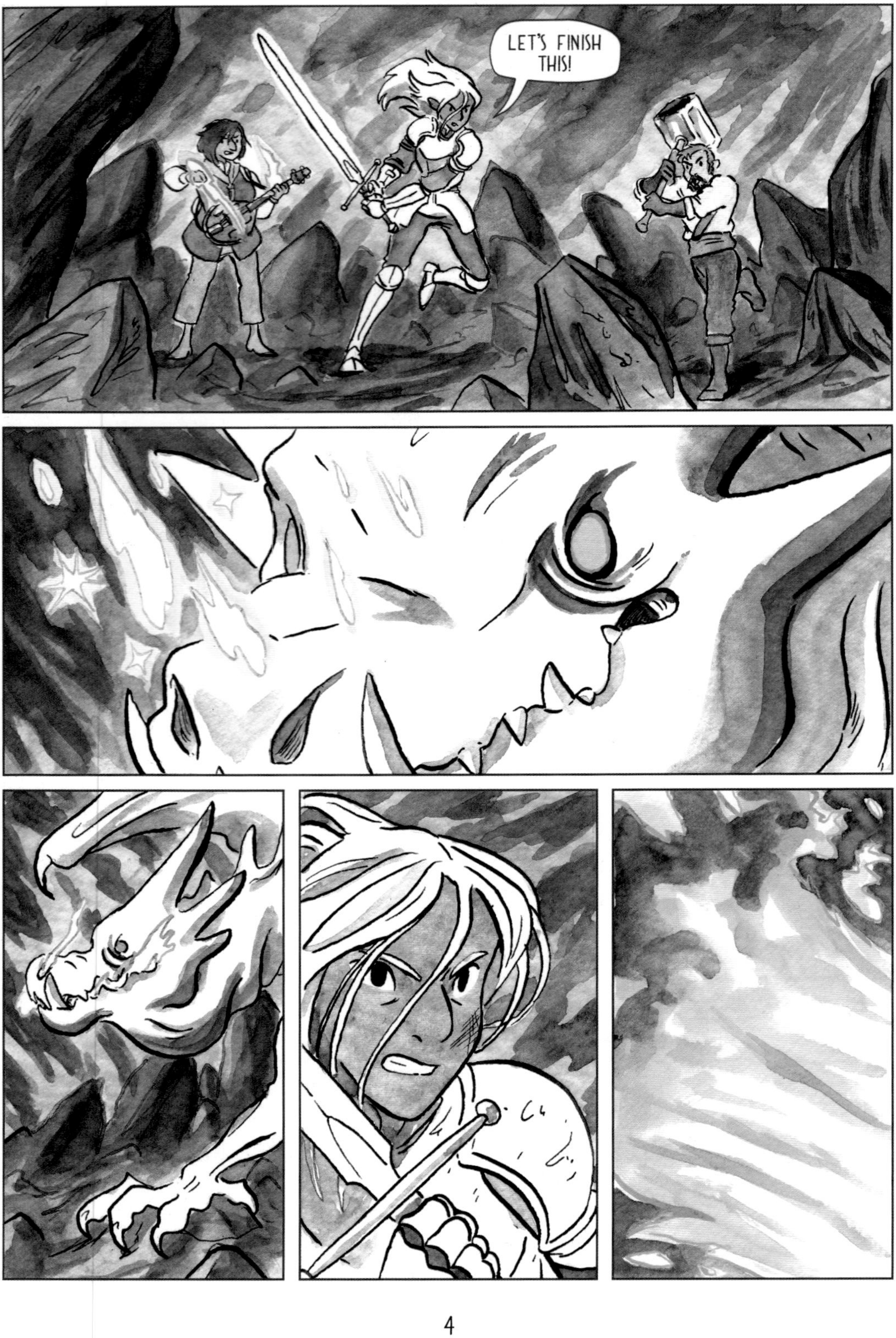
LET'S FINISH THIS!

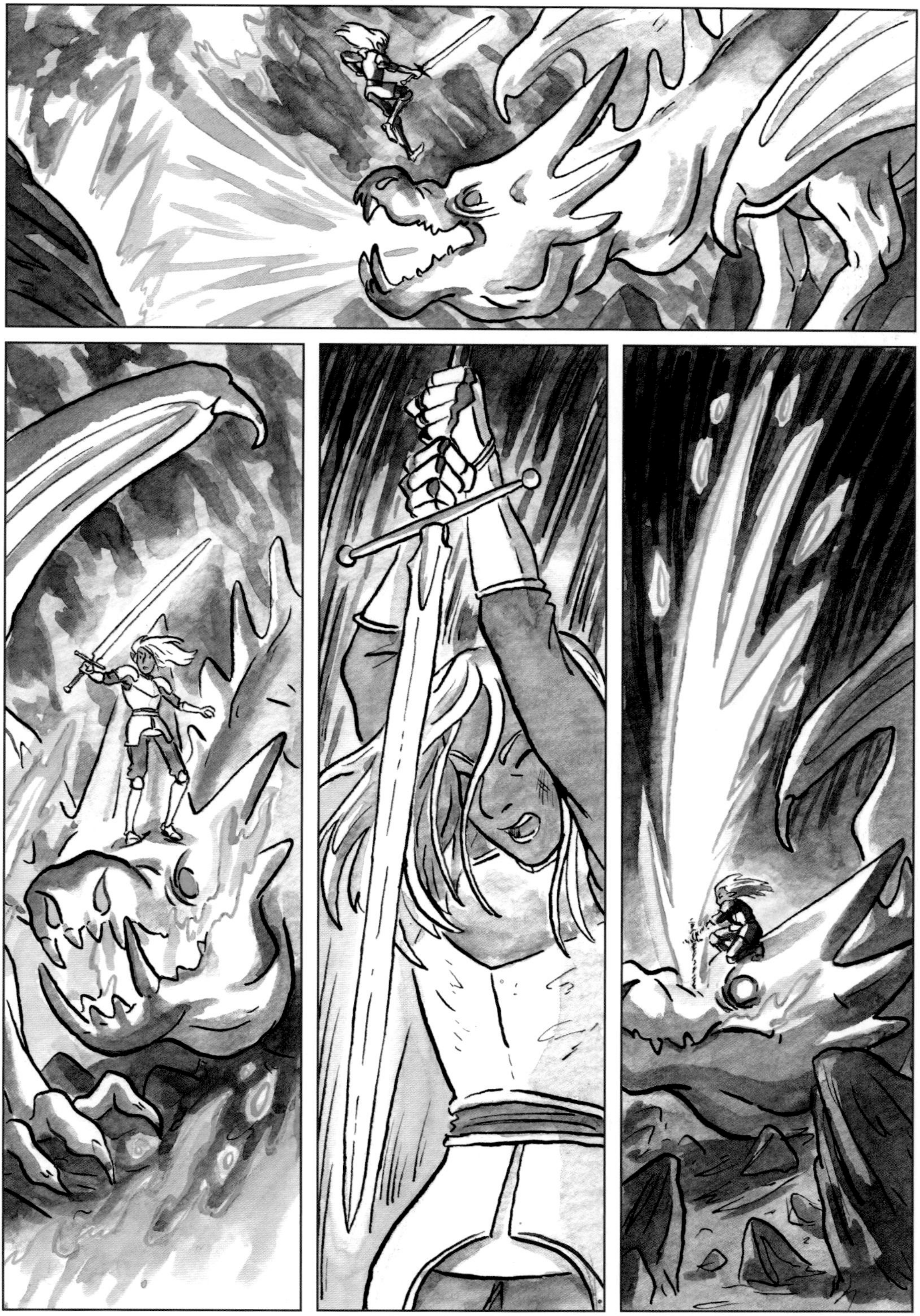

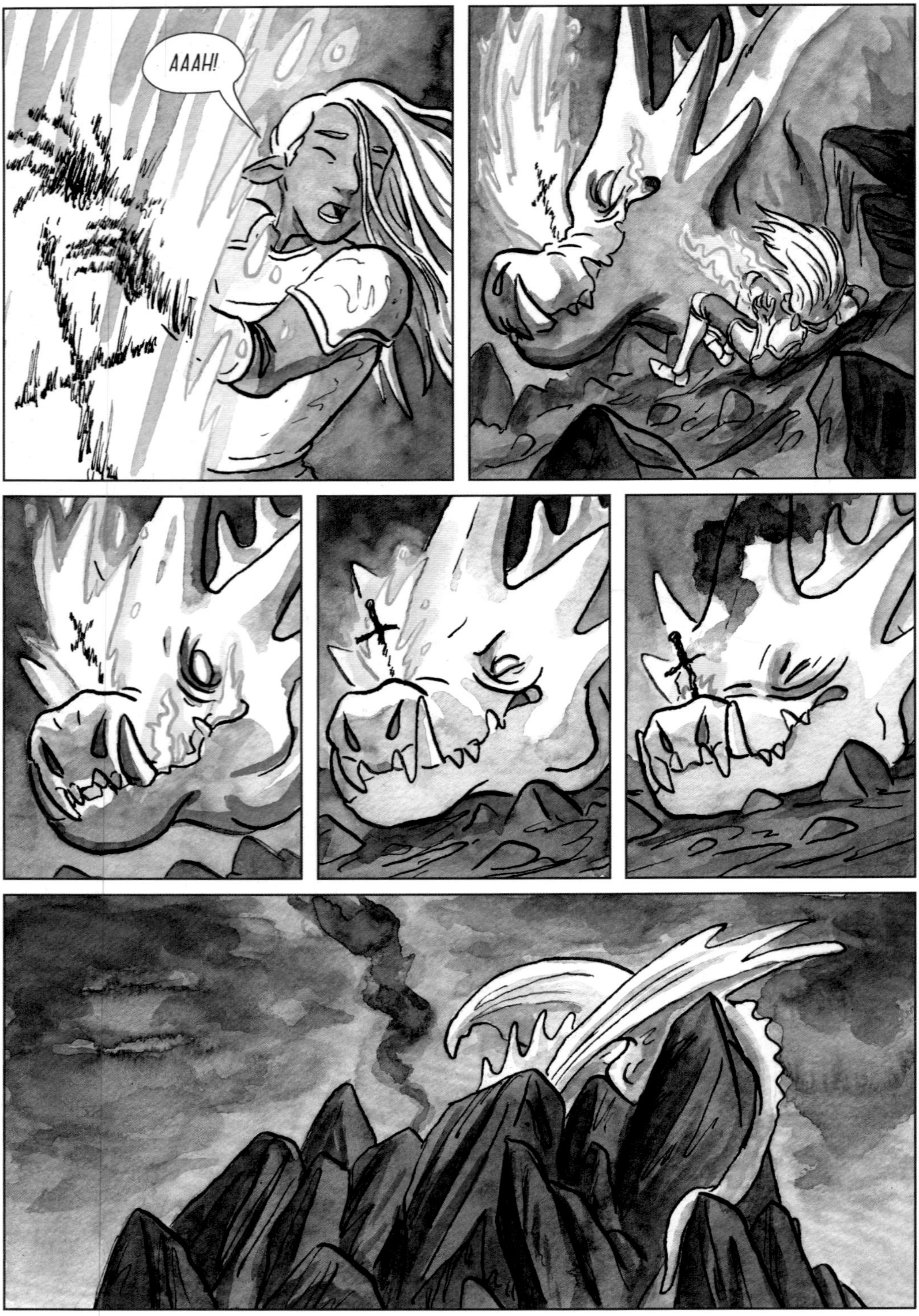
AAAH!

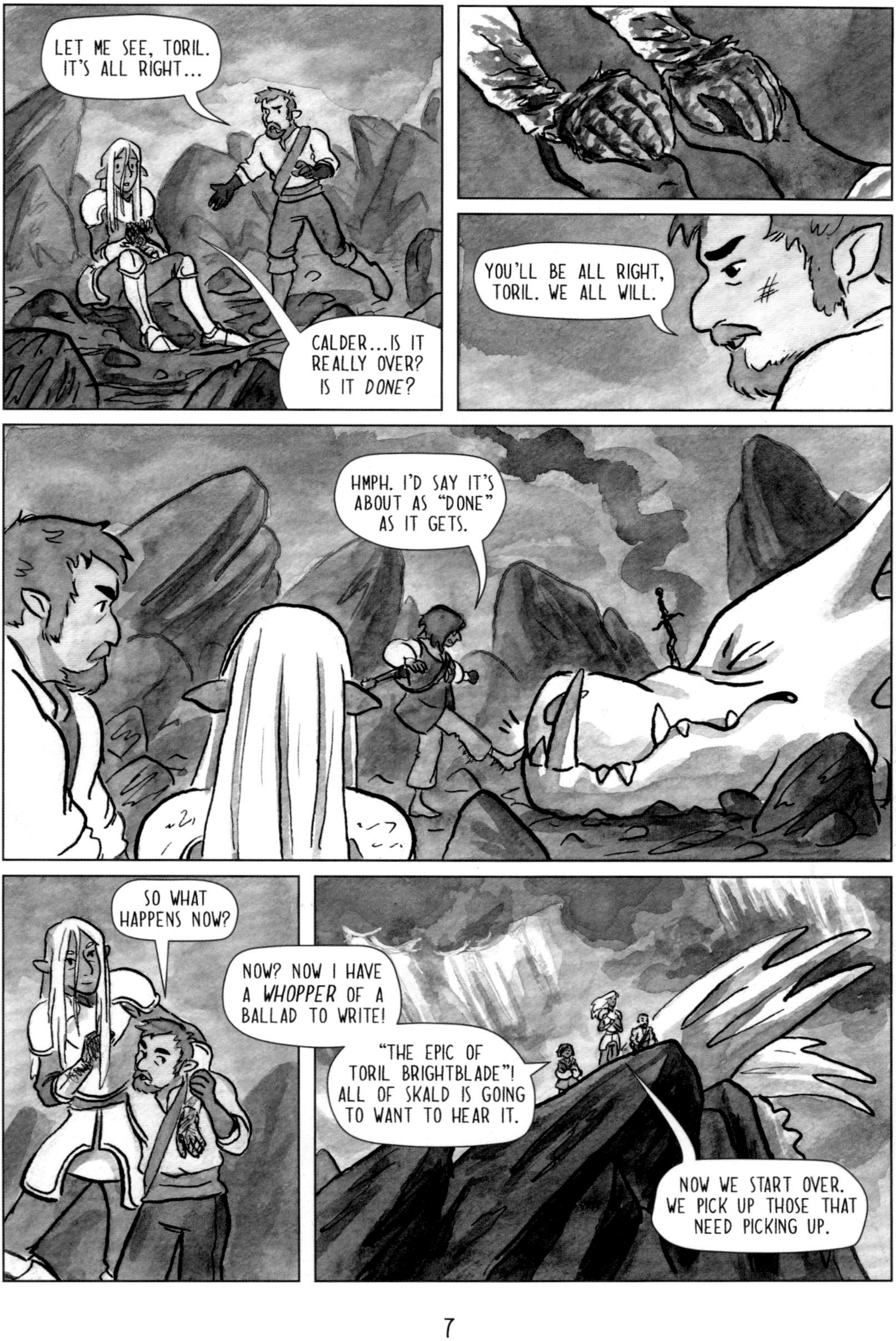
LET ME SEE, TORIL. IT'S ALL RIGHT...
CALDER...IS IT REALLY OVER? IS IT *DONE*?
YOU'LL BE ALL RIGHT, TORIL. WE ALL WILL.
HMPH. I'D SAY IT'S ABOUT AS "DONE" AS IT GETS.
SO WHAT HAPPENS NOW?
NOW? NOW I HAVE A *WHOPPER* OF A BALLAD TO WRITE!
"THE EPIC OF TORIL BRIGHTBLADE"! ALL OF SKALD IS GOING TO WANT TO HEAR IT.
NOW WE START OVER. WE PICK UP THOSE THAT NEED PICKING UP.

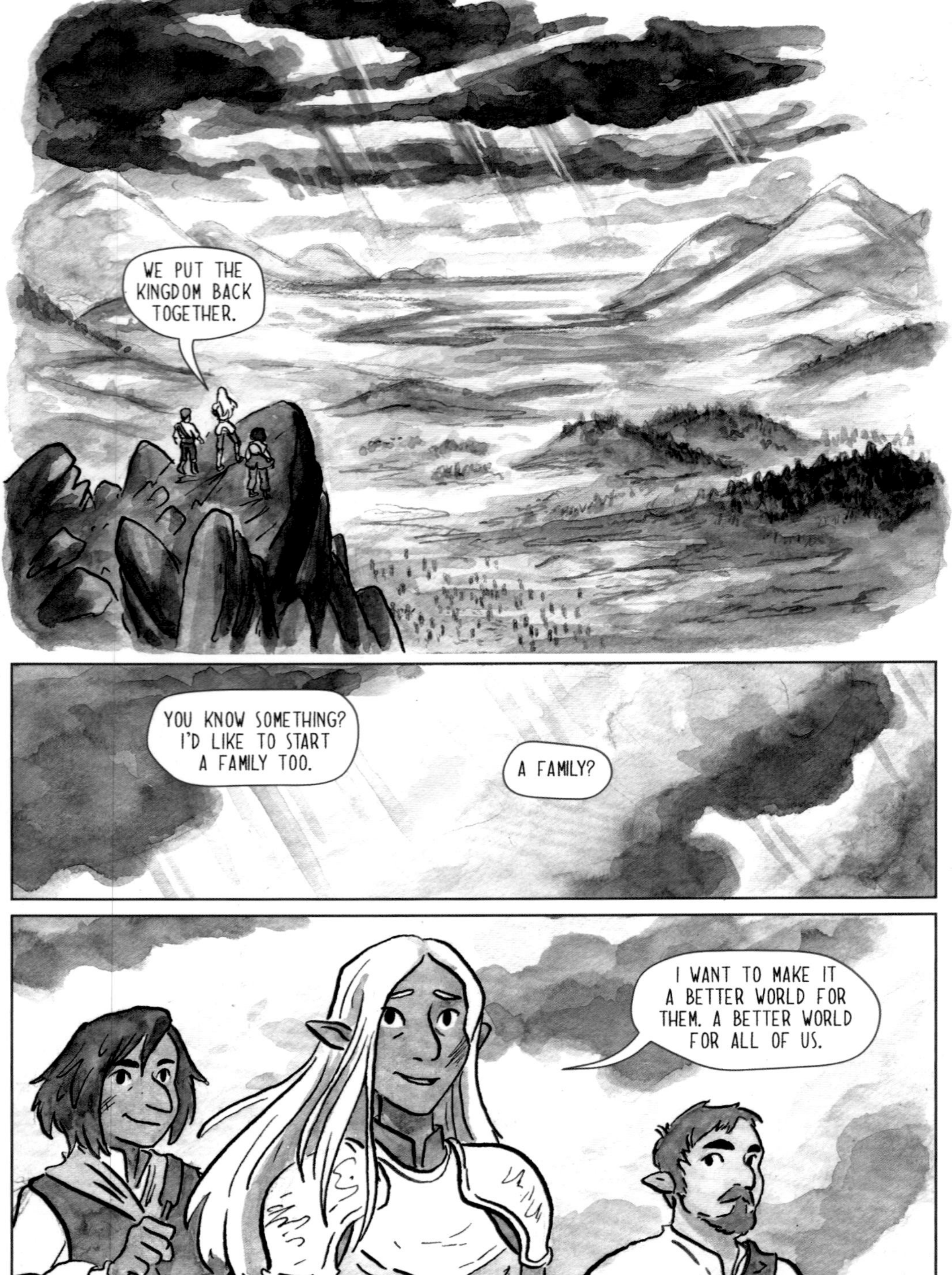
WE PUT THE KINGDOM BACK TOGETHER.
YOU KNOW SOMETHING? I'D LIKE TO START A FAMILY TOO.
A FAMILY?
I WANT TO MAKE IT A BETTER WORLD FOR THEM. A BETTER WORLD FOR ALL OF US.

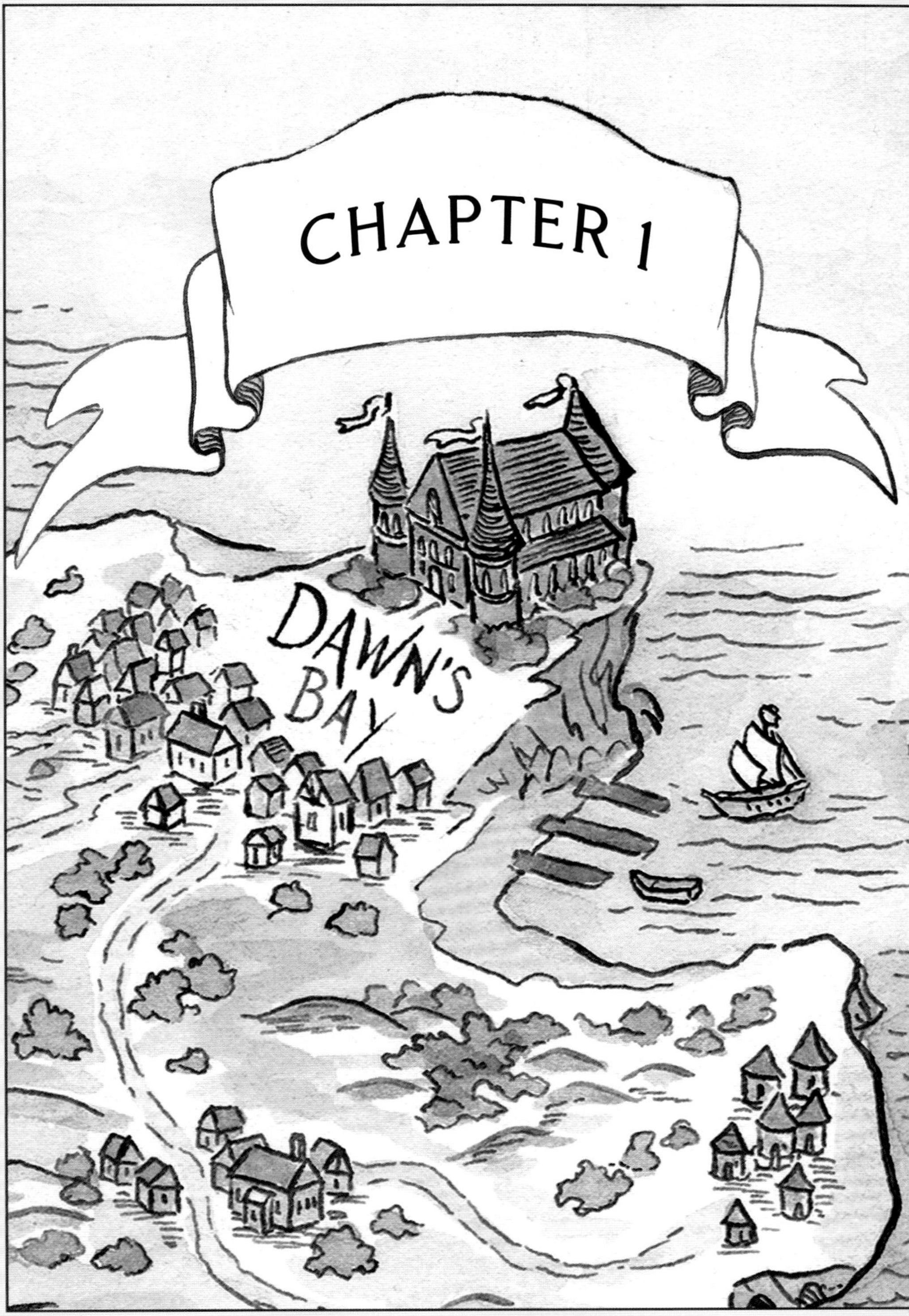
CHAPTER 1
DAWN'S BAY

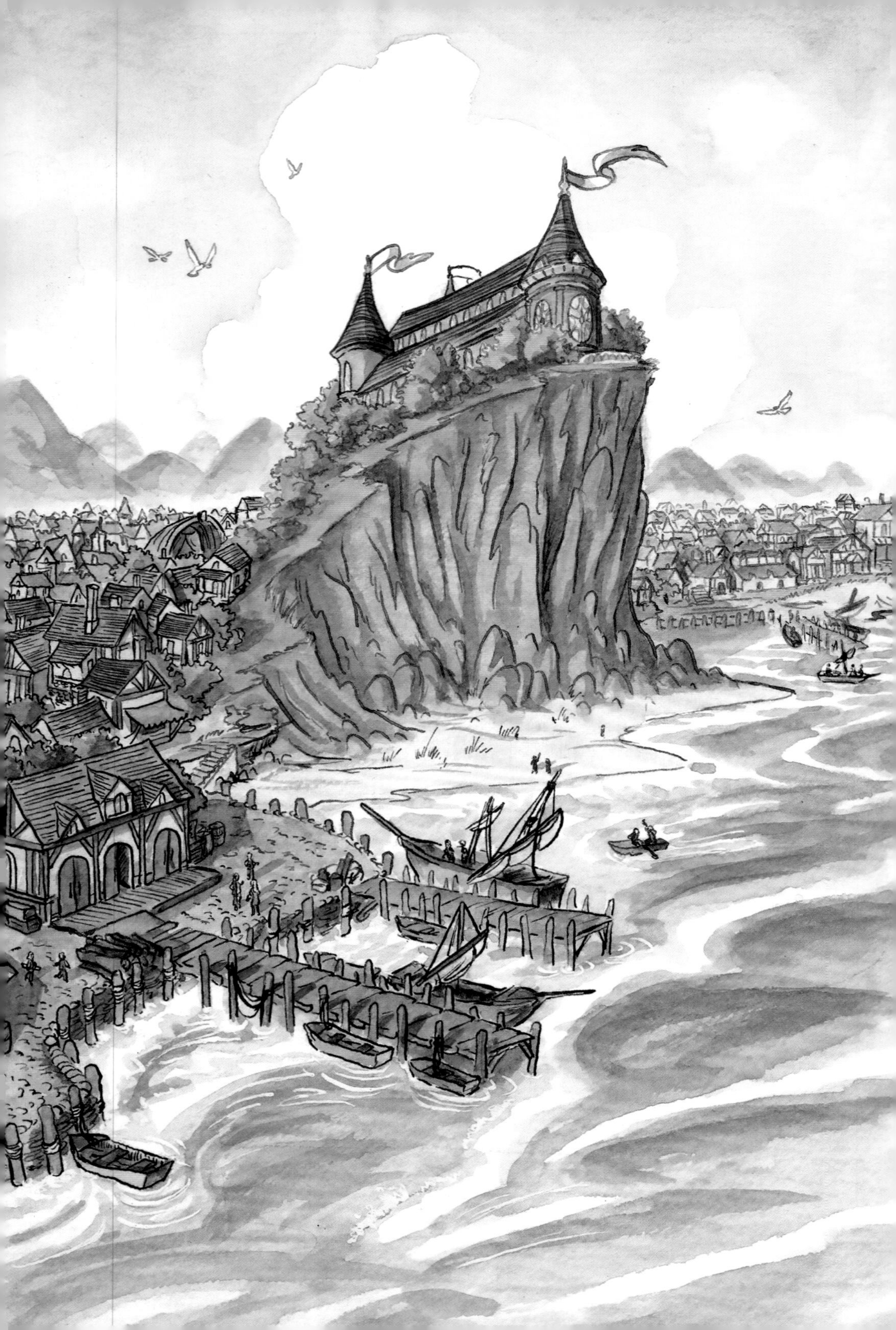

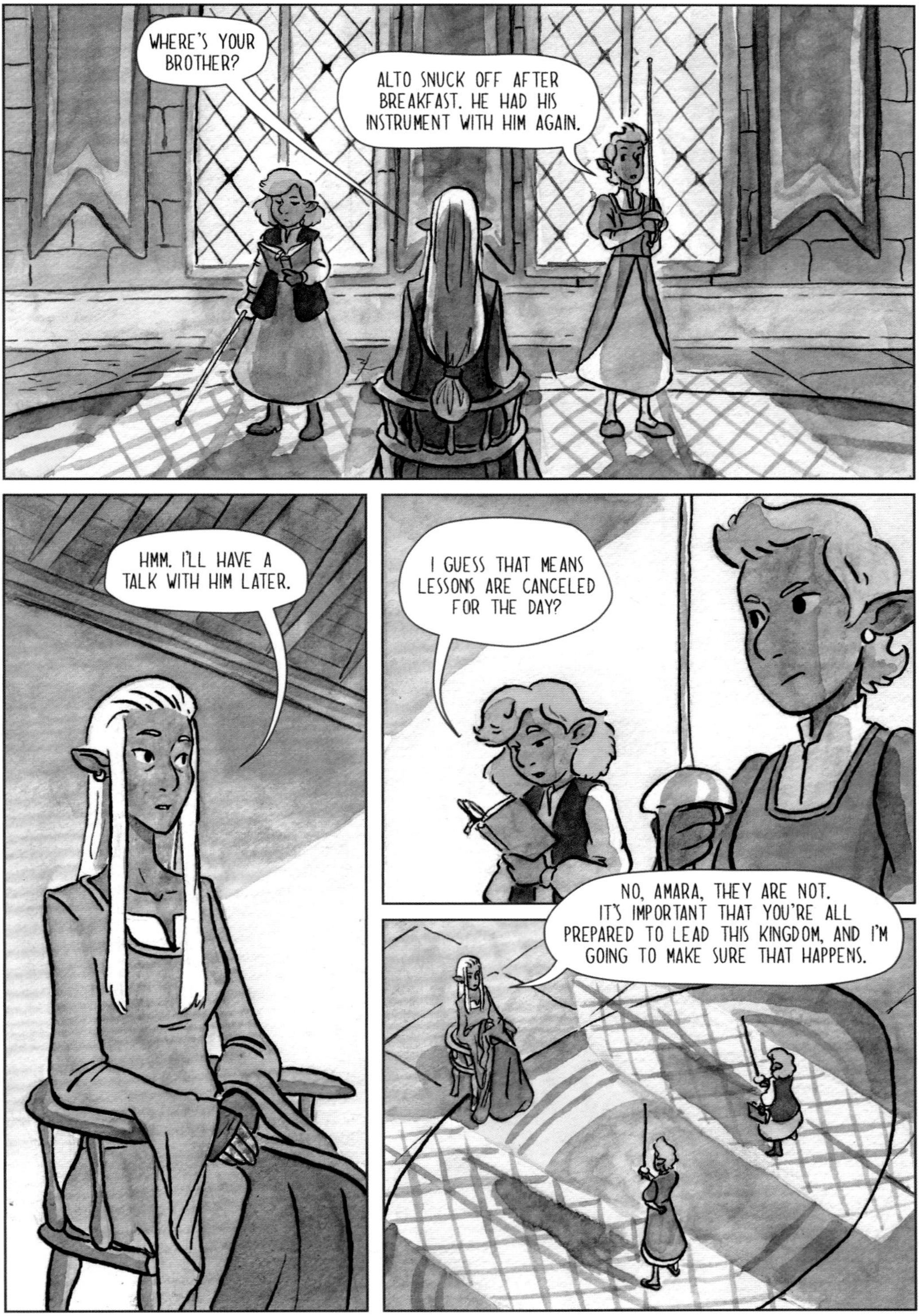
WHERE'S YOUR BROTHER?
ALTO SNUCK OFF AFTER BREAKFAST. HE HAD HIS INSTRUMENT WITH HIM AGAIN.
HMM. I'LL HAVE A TALK WITH HIM LATER.
I GUESS THAT MEANS LESSONS ARE CANCELED FOR THE DAY?
NO, AMARA, THEY ARE NOT. IT'S IMPORTANT THAT YOU'RE ALL PREPARED TO LEAD THIS KINGDOM, AND I'M GOING TO MAKE SURE THAT HAPPENS.

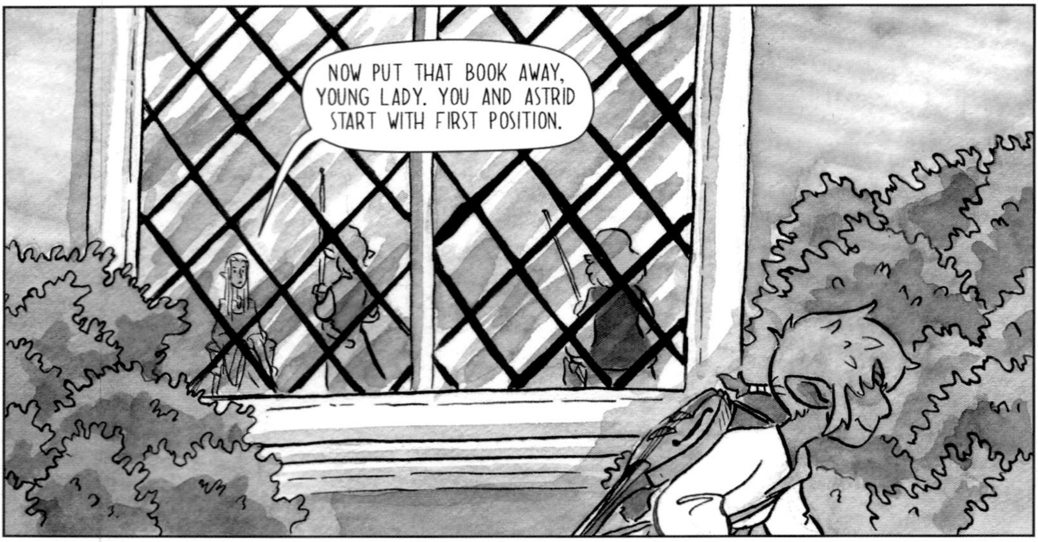
NOW PUT THAT BOOK AWAY, YOUNG LADY. YOU AND ASTRID START WITH FIRST POSITION.

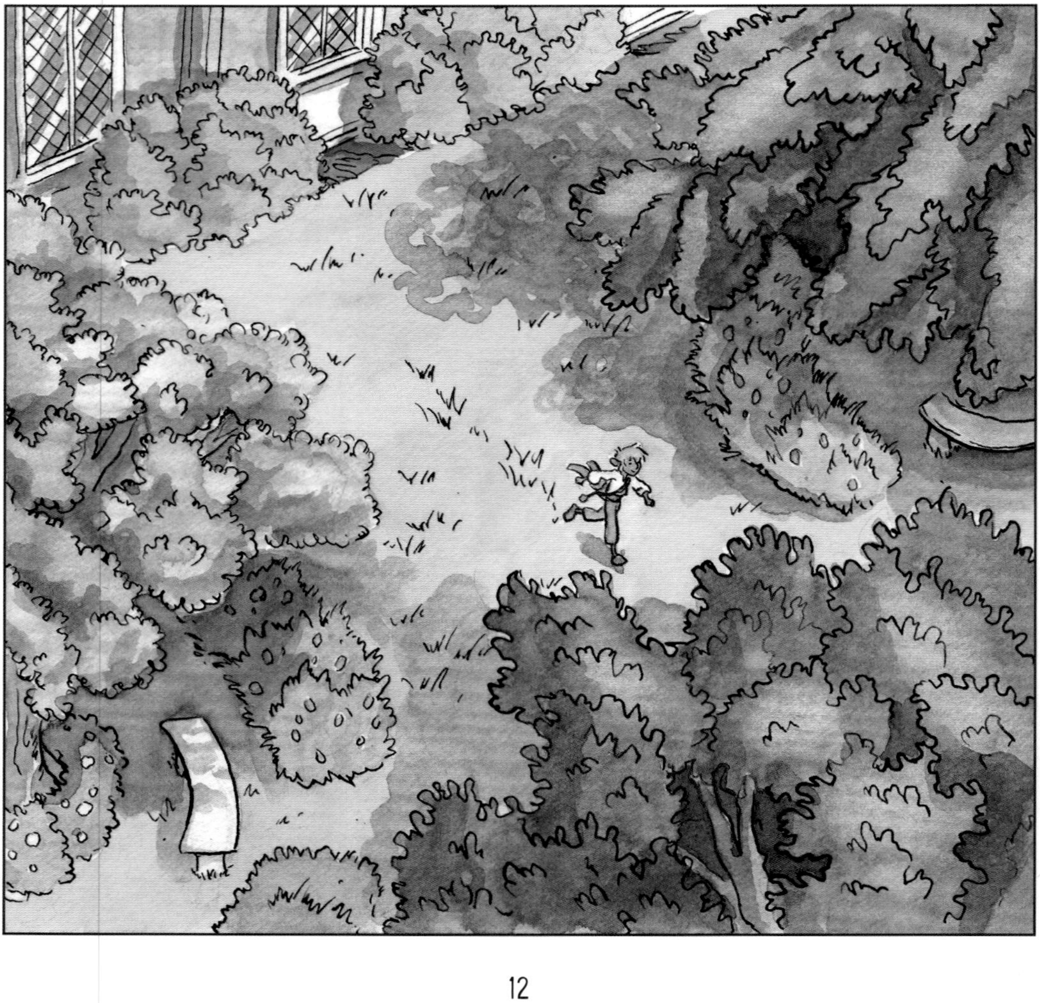

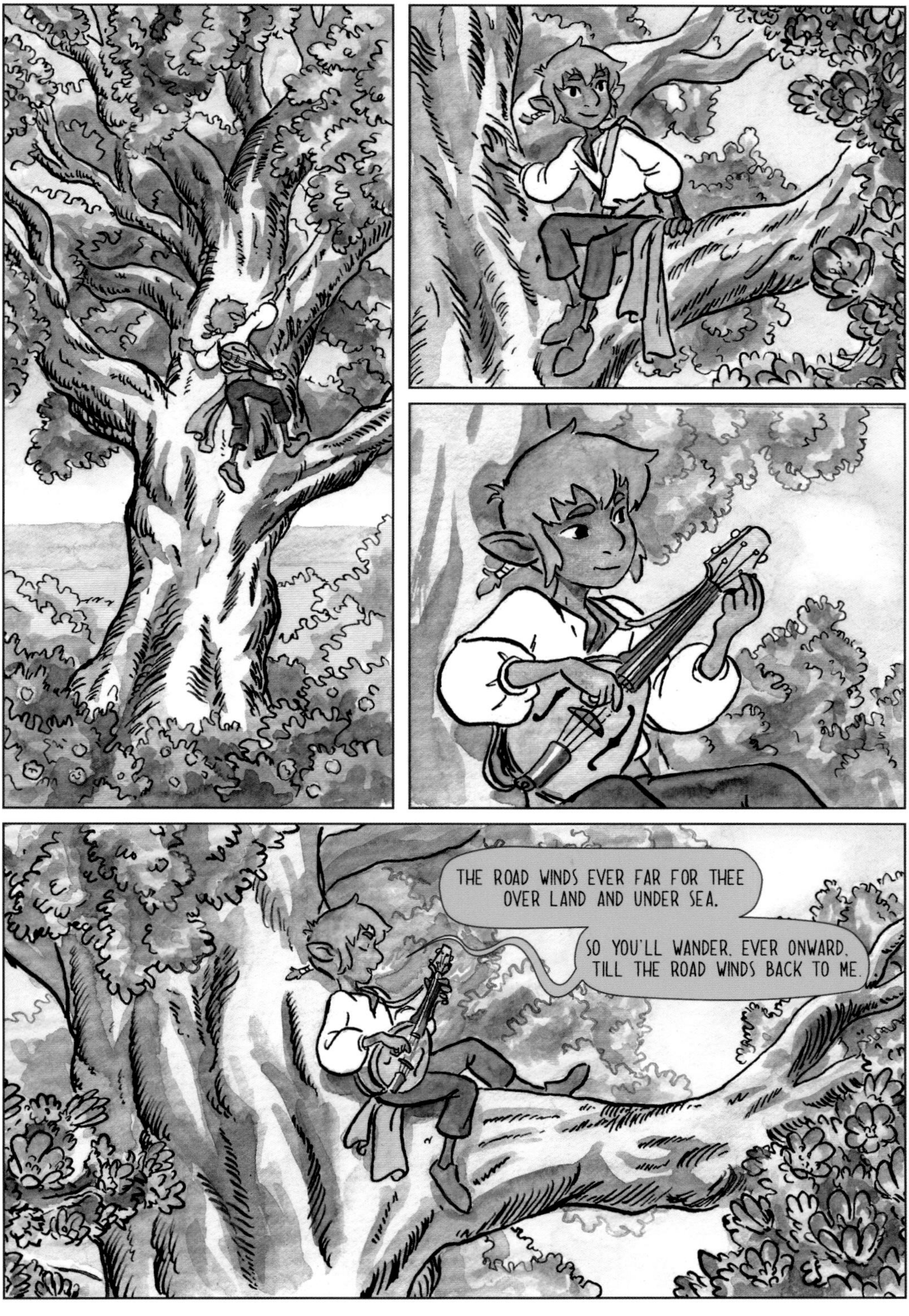
THE ROAD WINDS EVER FAR FOR THEE
OVER LAND AND UNDER SEA.
SO YOU'LL WANDER, EVER ONWARD,
TILL THE ROAD WINDS BACK TO ME.

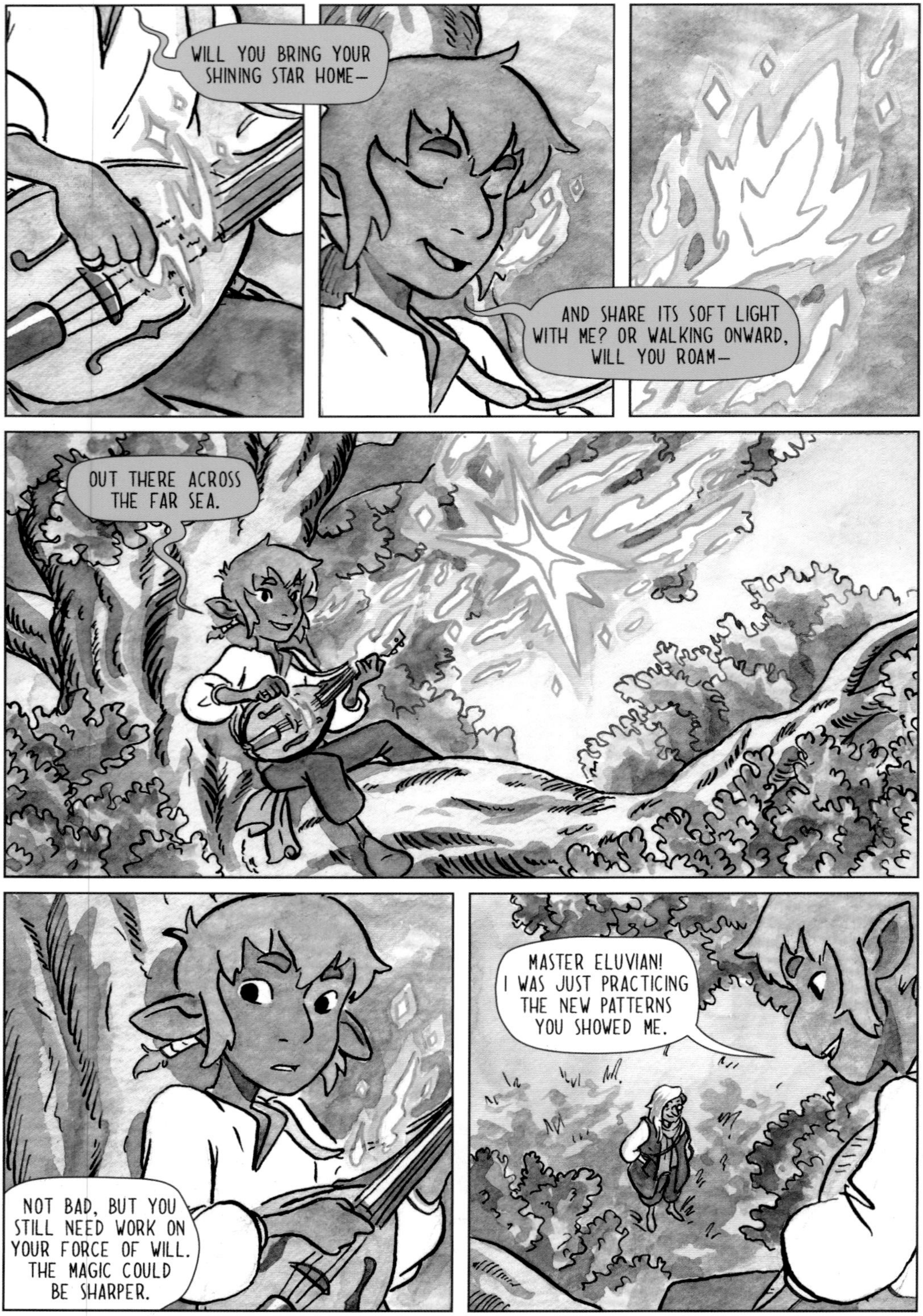
WILL YOU BRING YOUR SHINING STAR HOME—
AND SHARE ITS SOFT LIGHT WITH ME? OR WALKING ONWARD, WILL YOU ROAM—
OUT THERE ACROSS THE FAR SEA.
NOT BAD, BUT YOU STILL NEED WORK ON YOUR FORCE OF WILL. THE MAGIC COULD BE SHARPER.
MASTER ELUVIAN! I WAS JUST PRACTICING THE NEW PATTERNS YOU SHOWED ME.

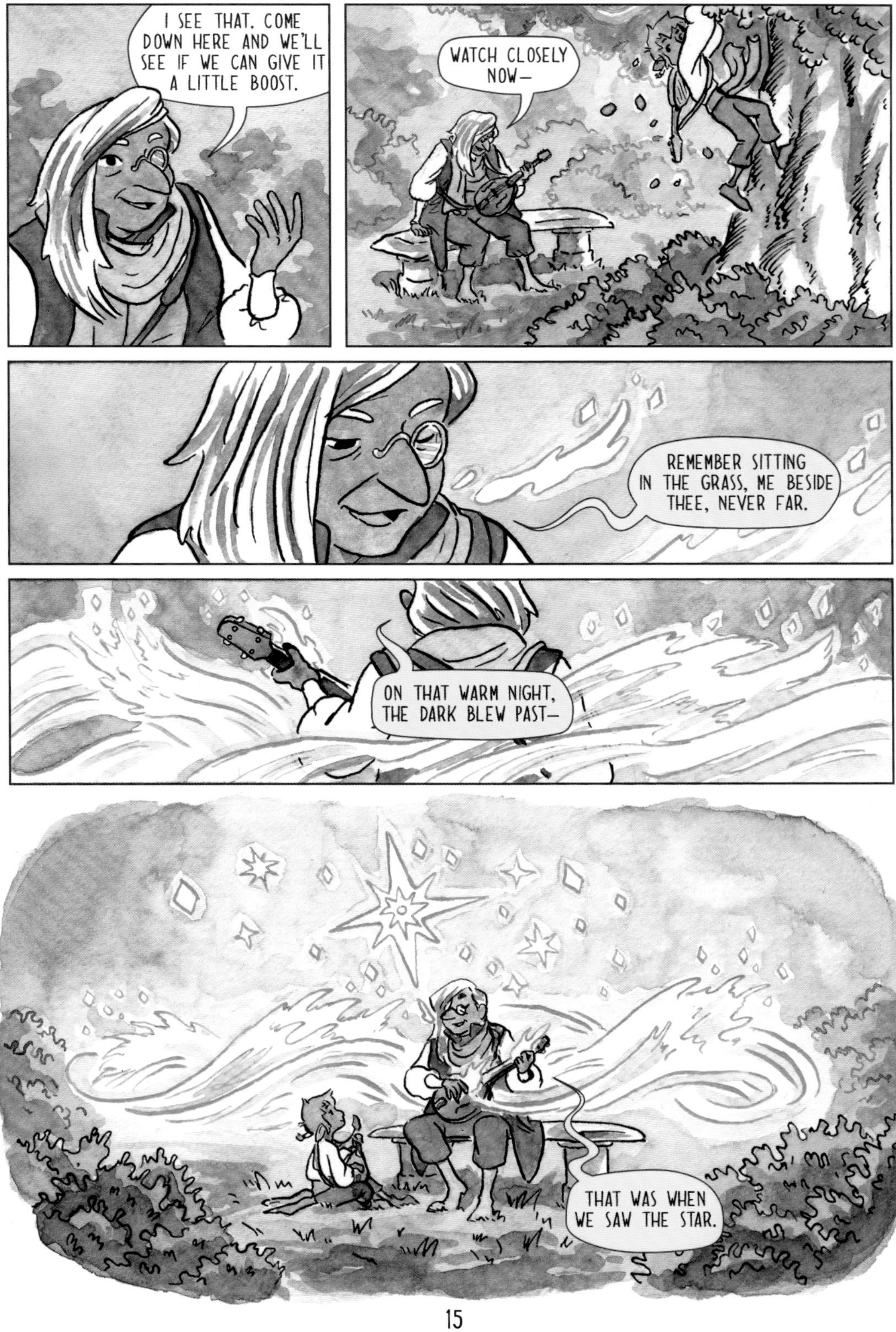
I SEE THAT. COME DOWN HERE AND WE'LL SEE IF WE CAN GIVE IT A LITTLE BOOST.
WATCH CLOSELY NOW—
REMEMBER SITTING IN THE GRASS, ME BESIDE THEE, NEVER FAR.
ON THAT WARM NIGHT, THE DARK BLEW PAST—
THAT WAS WHEN WE SAW THE STAR.

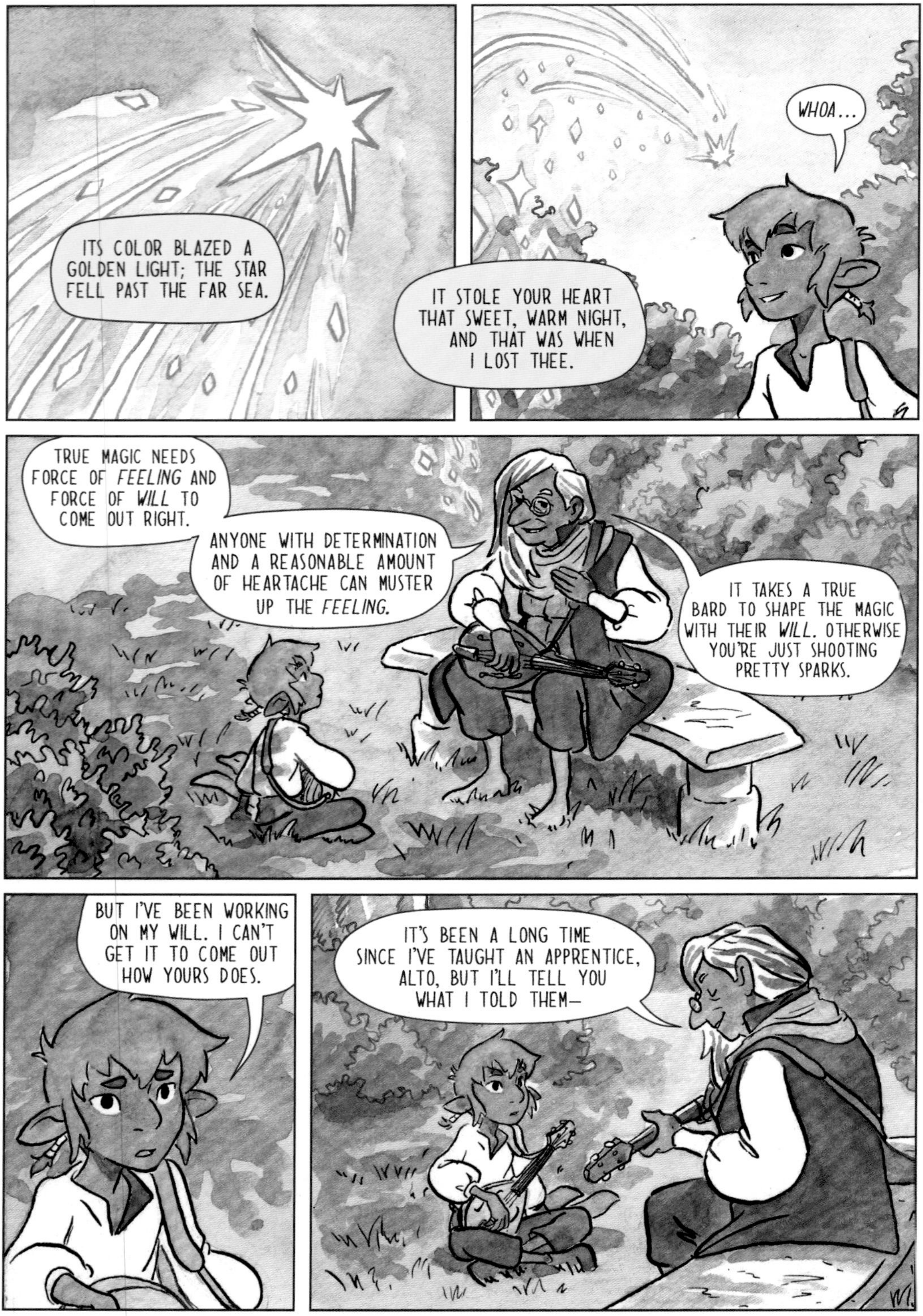
ITS COLOR BLAZED A GOLDEN LIGHT; THE STAR FELL PAST THE FAR SEA.
WHOA...
IT STOLE YOUR HEART THAT SWEET, WARM NIGHT, AND THAT WAS WHEN I LOST THEE.
TRUE MAGIC NEEDS FORCE OF FEELING AND FORCE OF WILL TO COME OUT RIGHT.
ANYONE WITH DETERMINATION AND A REASONABLE AMOUNT OF HEARTACHE CAN MUSTER UP THE FEELING.
IT TAKES A TRUE BARD TO SHAPE THE MAGIC WITH THEIR WILL. OTHERWISE YOU'RE JUST SHOOTING PRETTY SPARKS.
BUT I'VE BEEN WORKING ON MY WILL. I CAN'T GET IT TO COME OUT HOW YOURS DOES.
IT'S BEEN A LONG TIME SINCE I'VE TAUGHT AN APPRENTICE, ALTO, BUT I'LL TELL YOU WHAT I TOLD THEM—

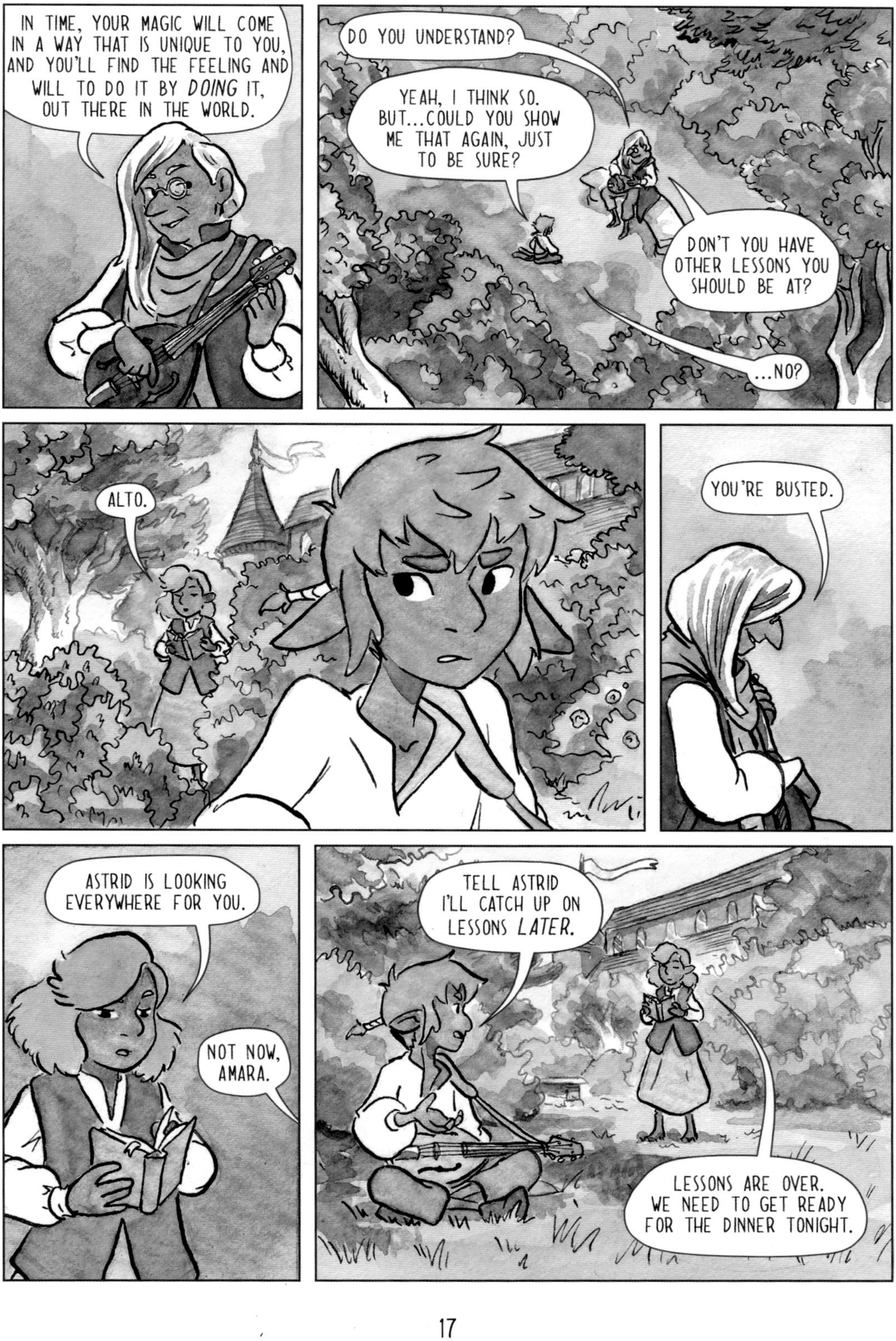
IN TIME, YOUR MAGIC WILL COME IN A WAY THAT IS UNIQUE TO YOU, AND YOU'LL FIND THE FEELING AND WILL TO DO IT BY *DOING* IT, OUT THERE IN THE WORLD.
DO YOU UNDERSTAND?
YEAH, I THINK SO. BUT...COULD YOU SHOW ME THAT AGAIN, JUST TO BE SURE?
DON'T YOU HAVE OTHER LESSONS YOU SHOULD BE AT?
...NO?
ALTO.
YOU'RE BUSTED.
ASTRID IS LOOKING EVERYWHERE FOR YOU.
NOT NOW, AMARA.
TELL ASTRID I'LL CATCH UP ON LESSONS *LATER*.
LESSONS ARE OVER. WE NEED TO GET READY FOR THE DINNER TONIGHT.

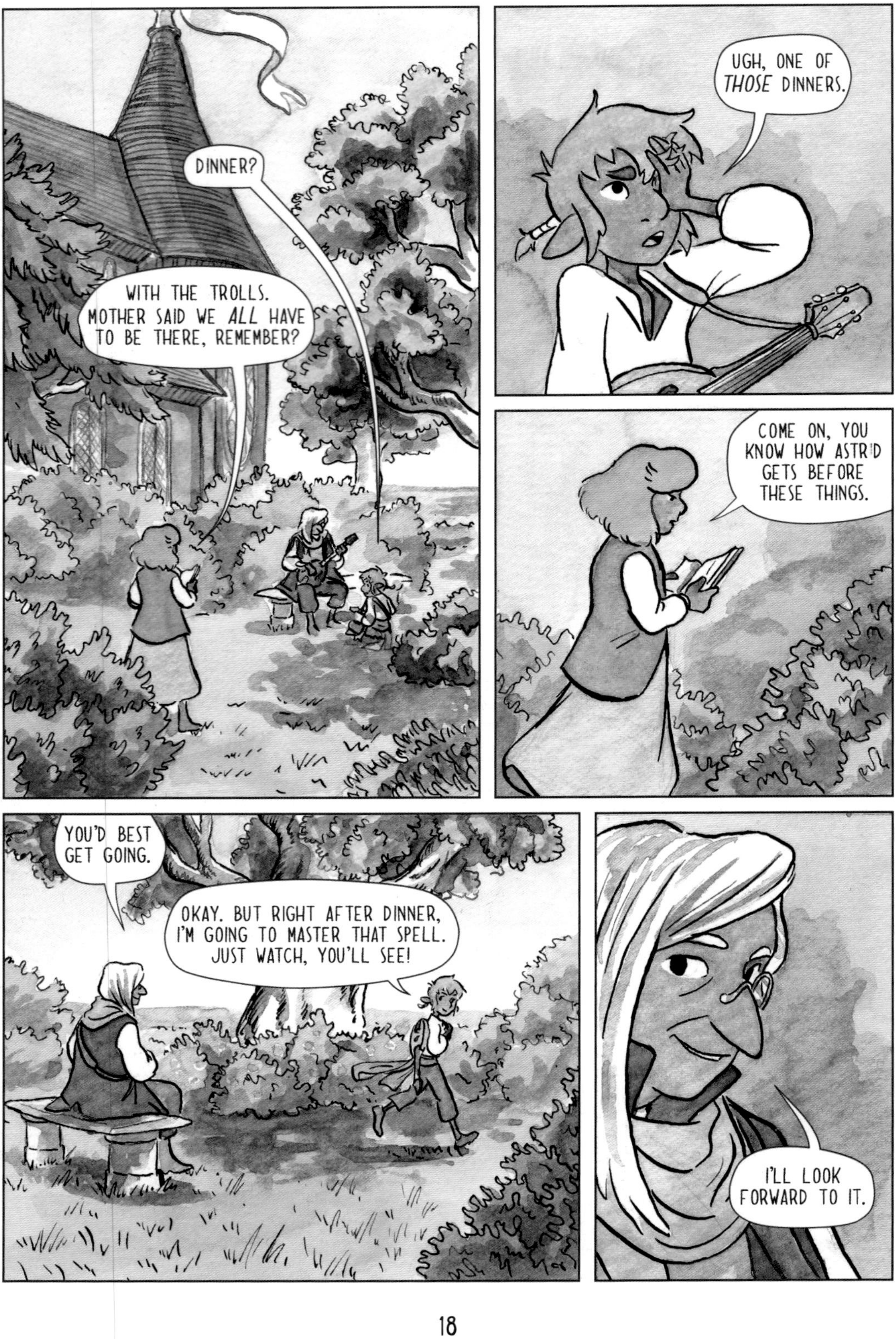
DINNER?
WITH THE TROLLS. MOTHER SAID WE *ALL* HAVE TO BE THERE, REMEMBER?
UGH, ONE OF *THOSE* DINNERS.
COME ON, YOU KNOW HOW ASTRID GETS BEFORE THESE THINGS.
YOU'D BEST GET GOING.
OKAY. BUT RIGHT AFTER DINNER, I'M GOING TO MASTER THAT SPELL. JUST WATCH, YOU'LL SEE!
I'LL LOOK FORWARD TO IT.

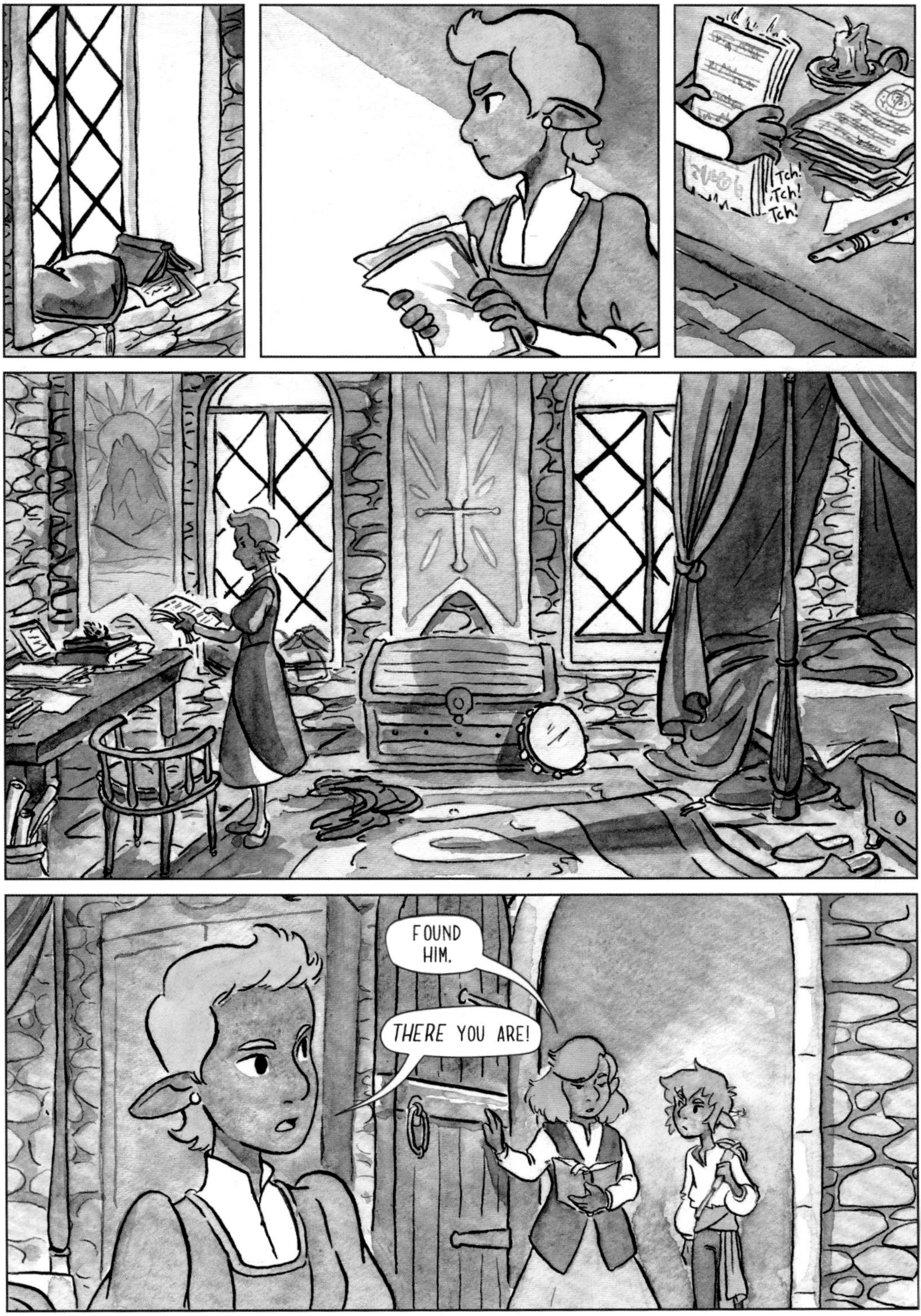
Tch!
Tch!
Tch!
FOUND HIM.
THERE YOU ARE!

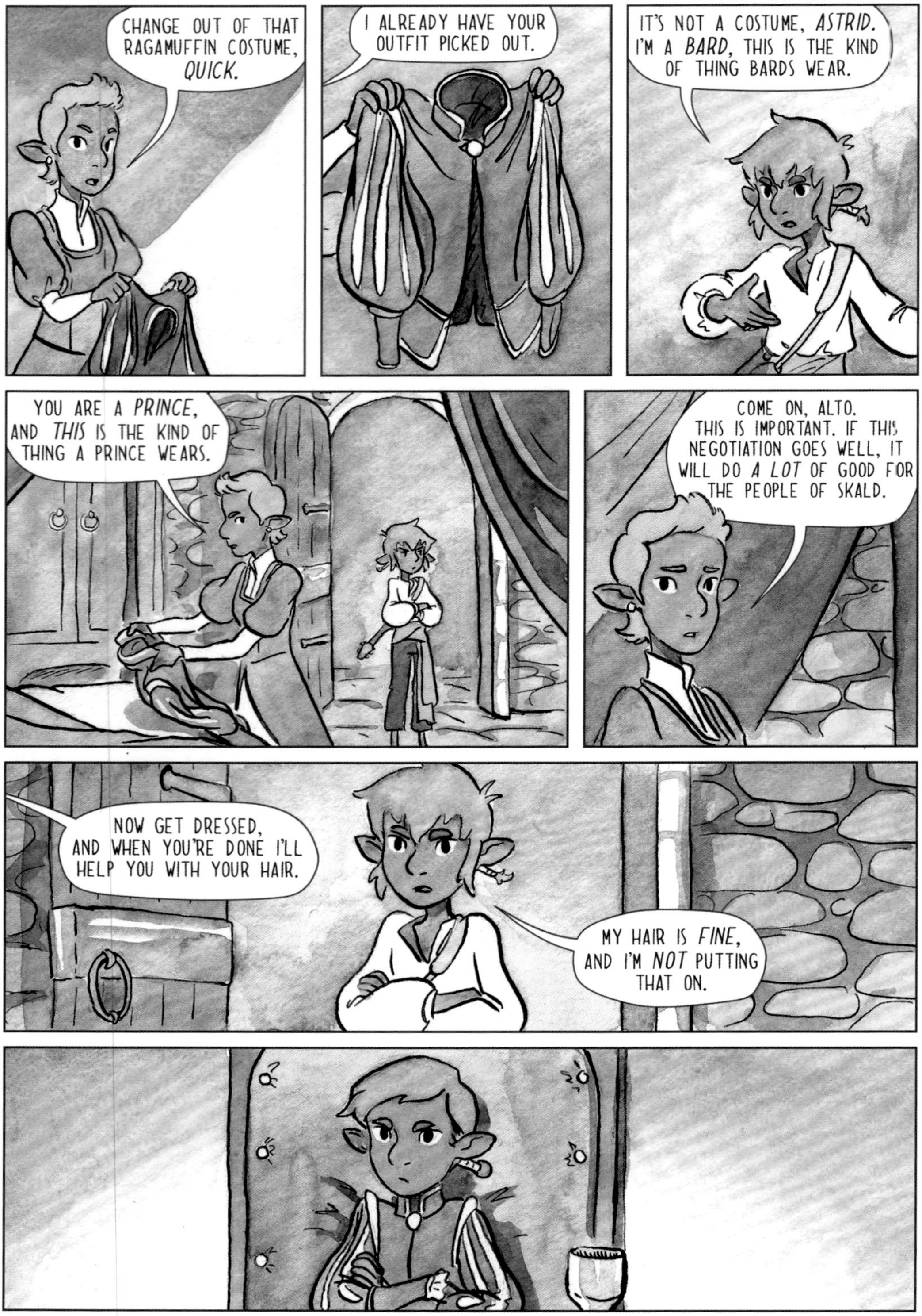
CHANGE OUT OF THAT RAGAMUFFIN COSTUME, QUICK.
I ALREADY HAVE YOUR OUTFIT PICKED OUT.
IT'S NOT A COSTUME, ASTRID. I'M A BARD, THIS IS THE KIND OF THING BARDS WEAR.
YOU ARE A PRINCE, AND THIS IS THE KIND OF THING A PRINCE WEARS.
COME ON, ALTO. THIS IS IMPORTANT. IF THIS NEGOTIATION GOES WELL, IT WILL DO A LOT OF GOOD FOR THE PEOPLE OF SKALD.
NOW GET DRESSED, AND WHEN YOU'RE DONE I'LL HELP YOU WITH YOUR HAIR.
MY HAIR IS FINE, AND I'M NOT PUTTING THAT ON.

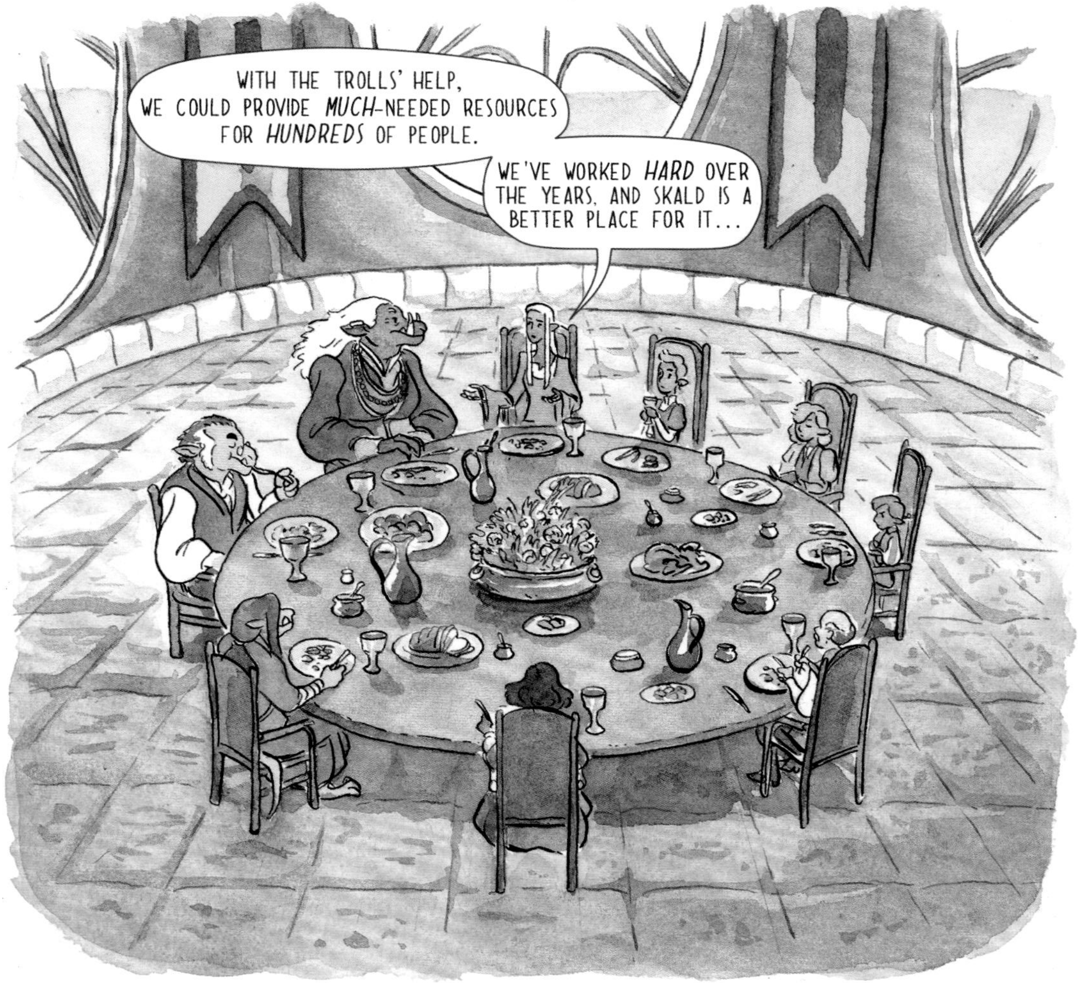
WITH THE TROLLS' HELP, WE COULD PROVIDE *MUCH*-NEEDED RESOURCES FOR *HUNDREDS* OF PEOPLE.
WE'VE WORKED *HARD* OVER THE YEARS, AND SKALD IS A BETTER PLACE FOR IT...

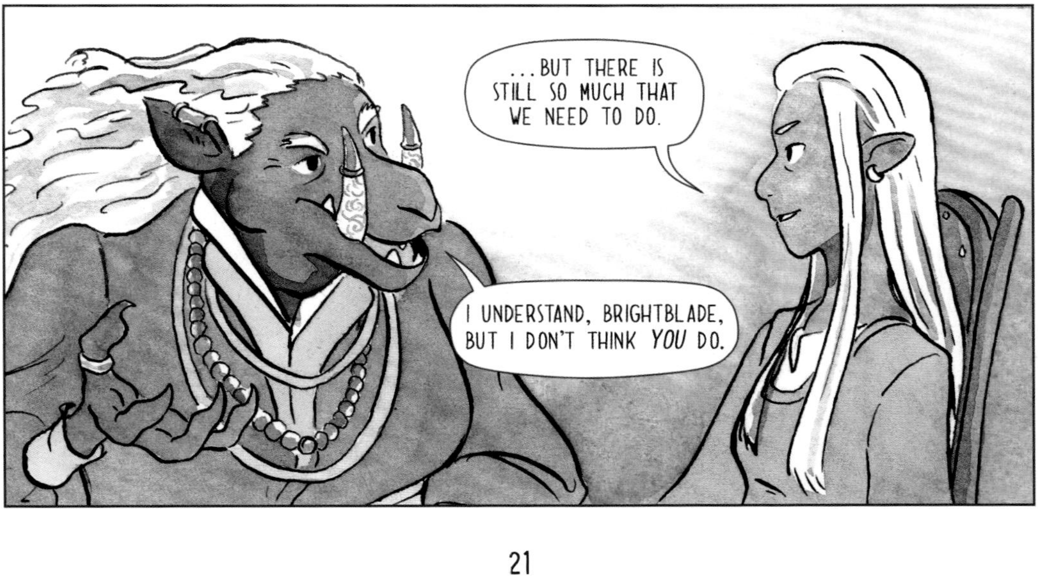
...BUT THERE IS STILL SO MUCH THAT WE NEED TO DO.
I UNDERSTAND, BRIGHTBLADE, BUT I DON'T THINK *YOU* DO.

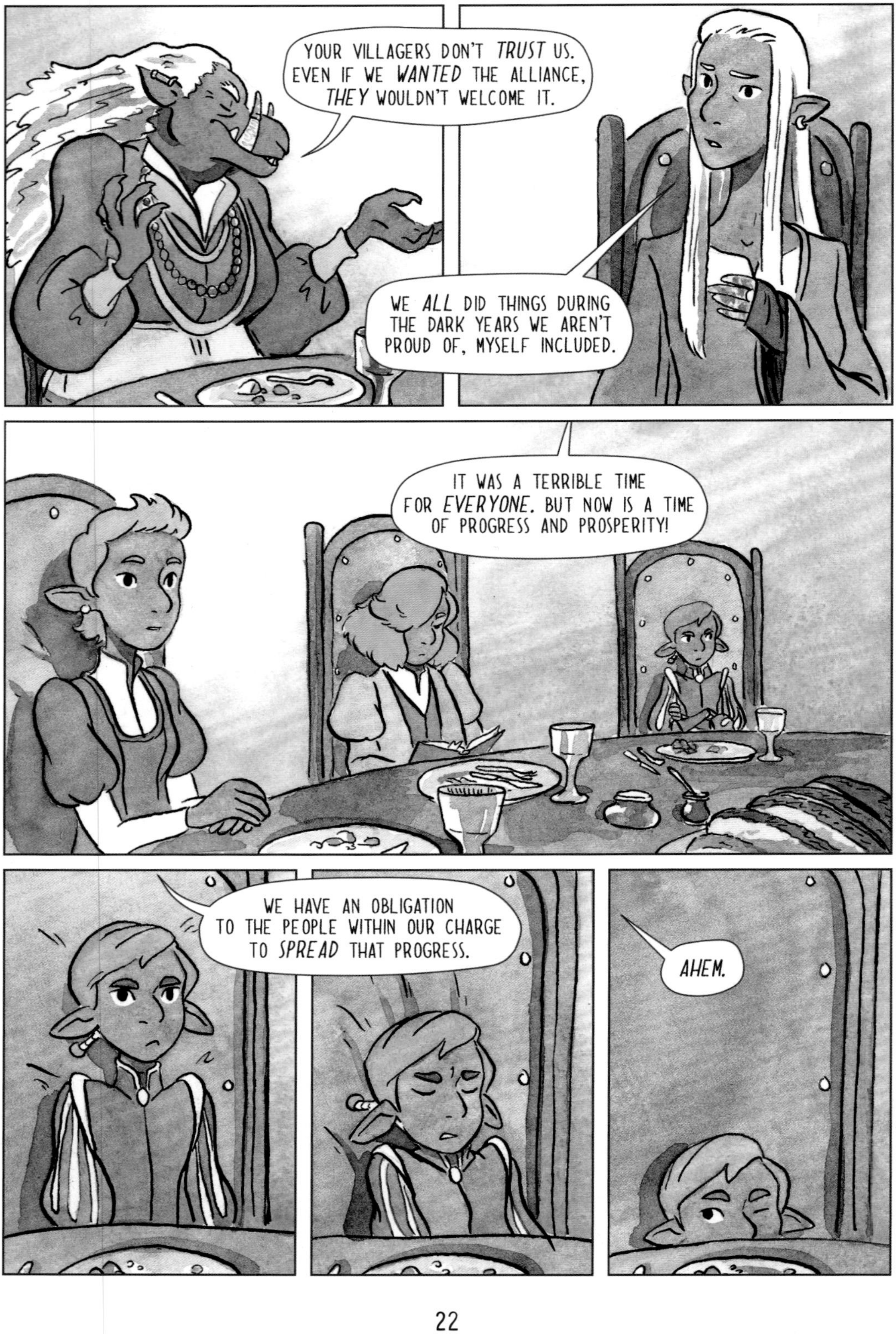
YOUR VILLAGERS DON'T TRUST US. EVEN IF WE WANTED THE ALLIANCE, THEY WOULDN'T WELCOME IT.
WE ALL DID THINGS DURING THE DARK YEARS WE AREN'T PROUD OF, MYSELF INCLUDED.
IT WAS A TERRIBLE TIME FOR EVERYONE. BUT NOW IS A TIME OF PROGRESS AND PROSPERITY!
WE HAVE AN OBLIGATION TO THE PEOPLE WITHIN OUR CHARGE TO SPREAD THAT PROGRESS.
AHEM.

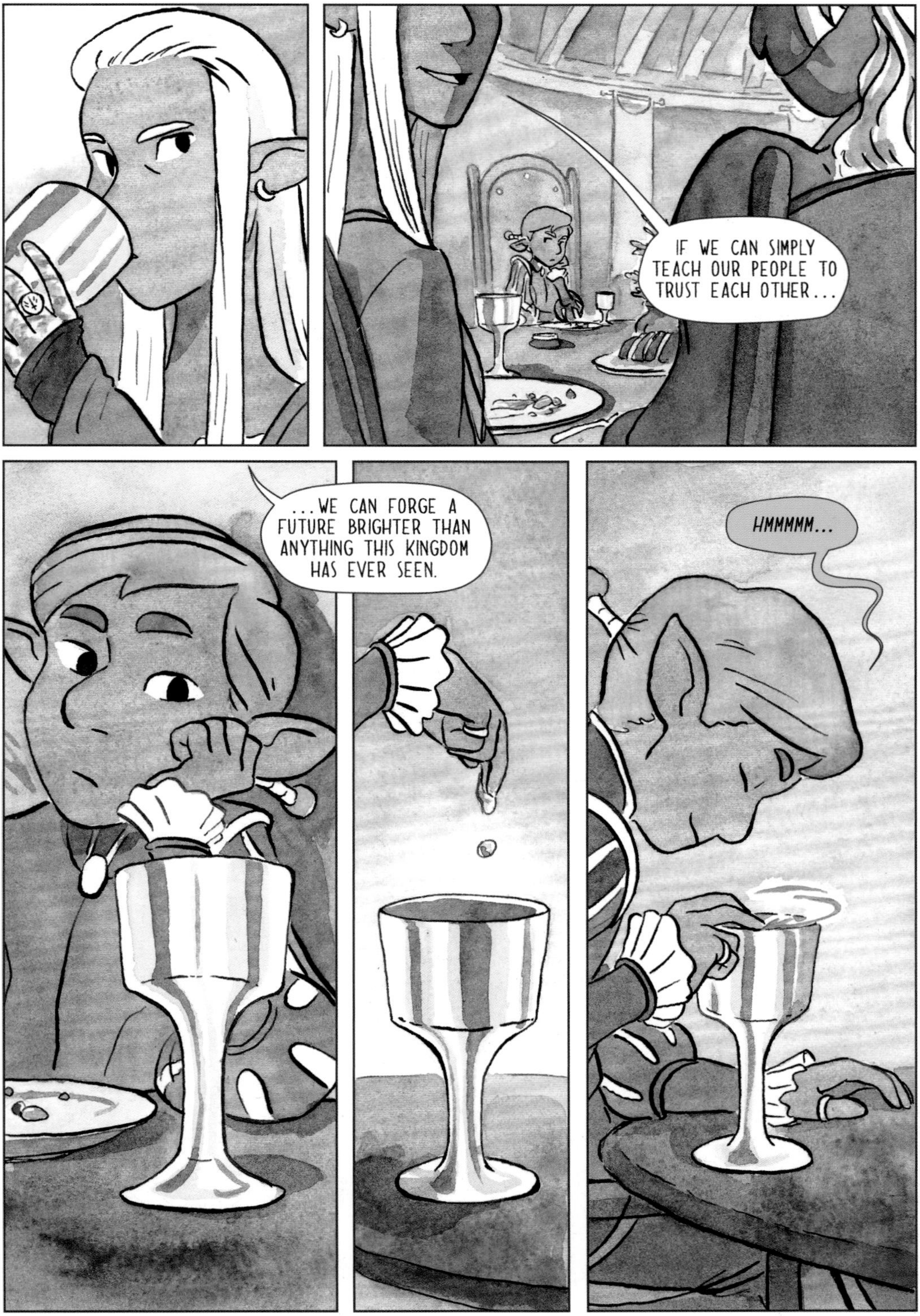
IF WE CAN SIMPLY TEACH OUR PEOPLE TO TRUST EACH OTHER...
...WE CAN FORGE A FUTURE BRIGHTER THAN ANYTHING THIS KINGDOM HAS EVER SEEN.
HMMMMM...

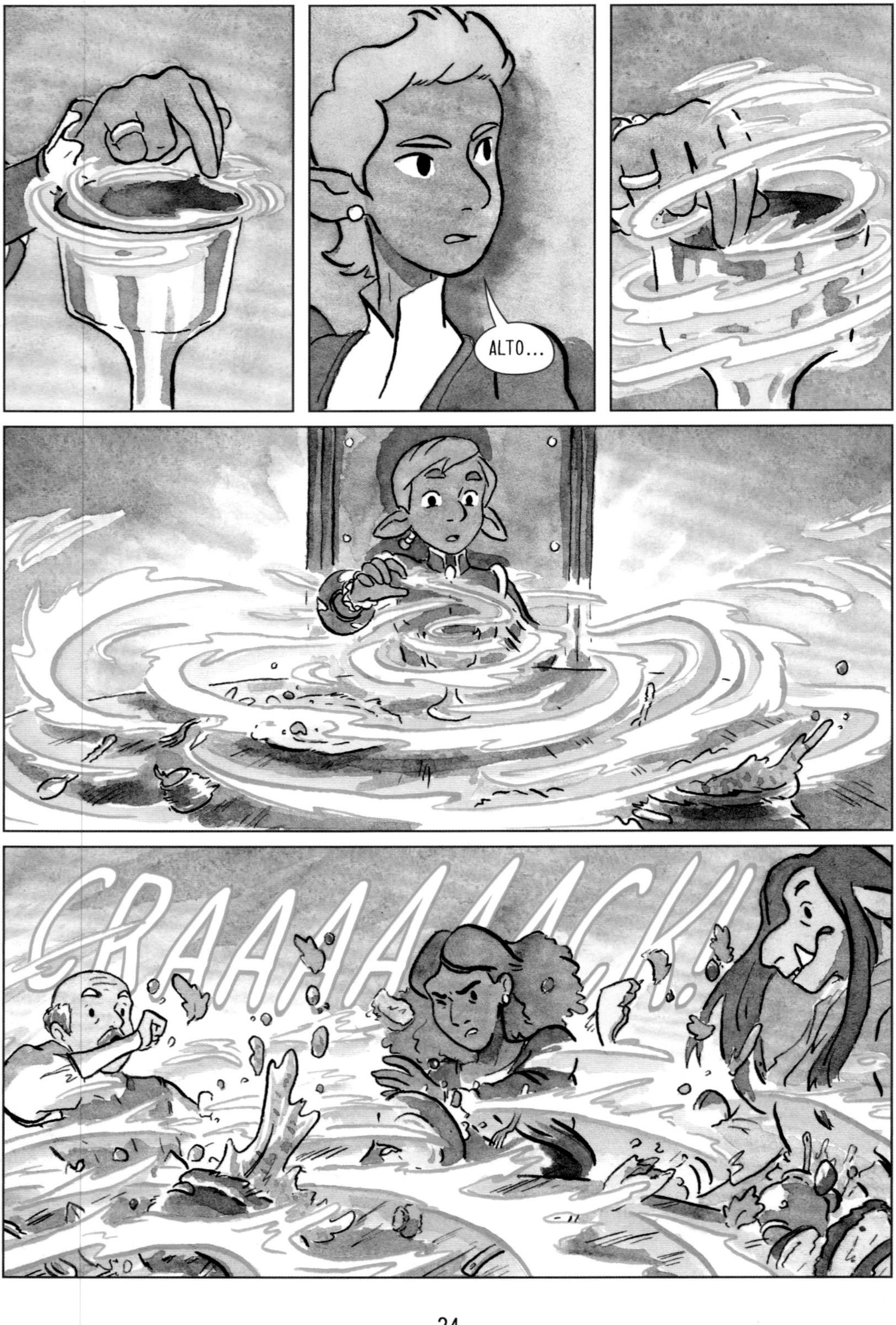
ALTO...
CRAAAAACK!!

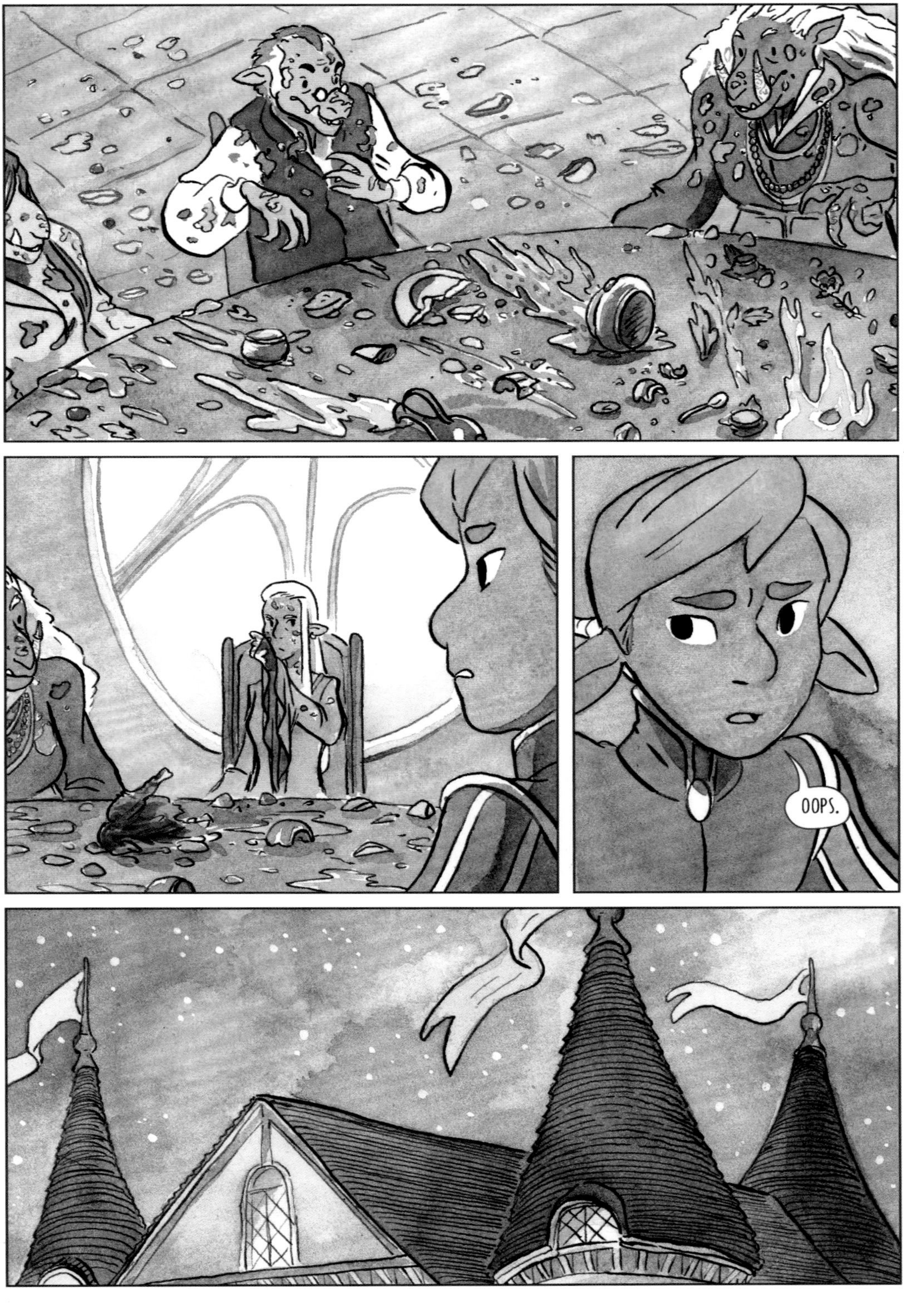
OOPS.

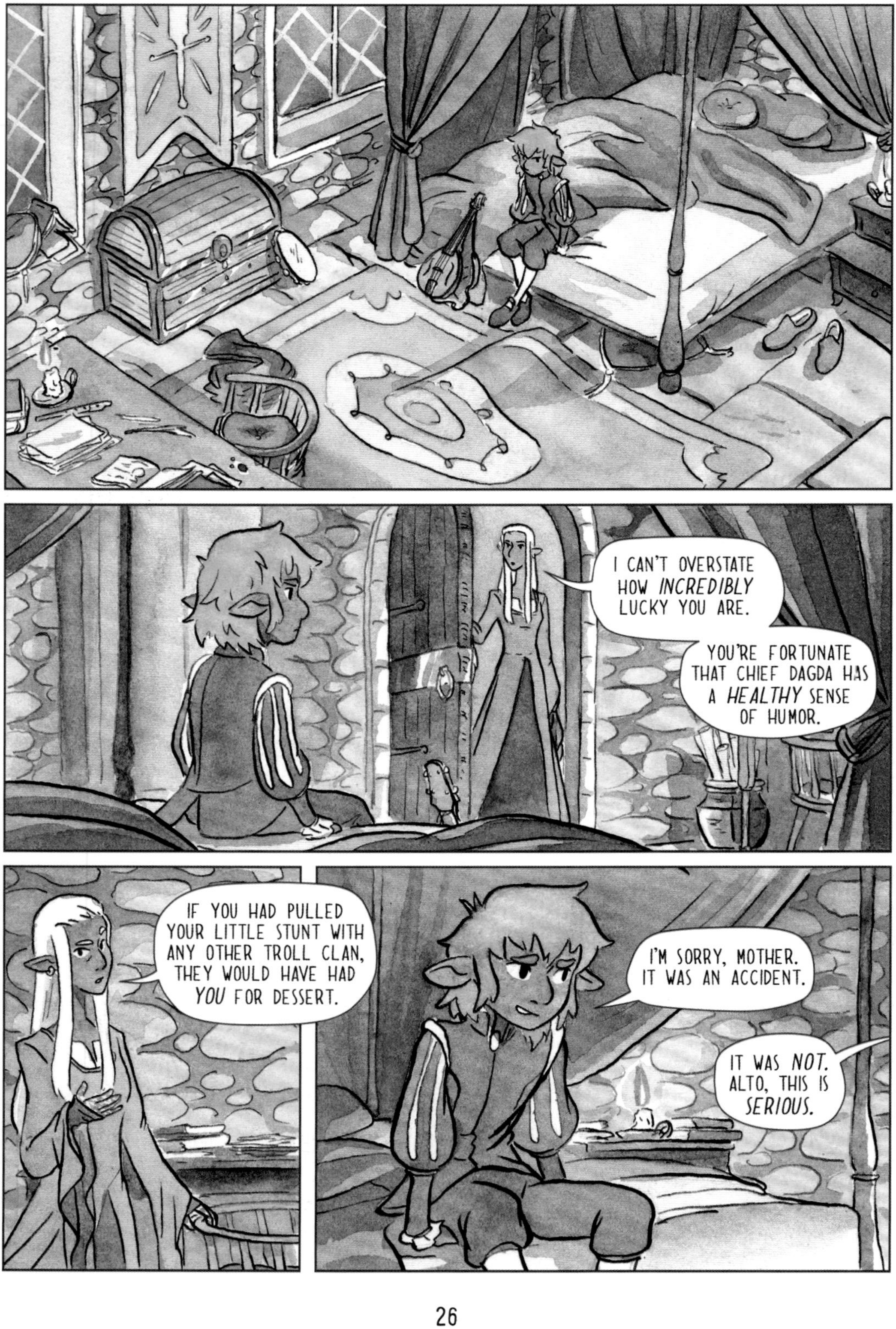
I CAN'T OVERSTATE HOW *INCREDIBLY* LUCKY YOU ARE.
YOU'RE FORTUNATE THAT CHIEF DAGDA HAS A *HEALTHY* SENSE OF HUMOR.
IF YOU HAD PULLED YOUR LITTLE STUNT WITH ANY OTHER TROLL CLAN, THEY WOULD HAVE HAD *YOU* FOR DESSERT.
I'M SORRY, MOTHER. IT WAS AN ACCIDENT.
IT WAS *NOT*. ALTO, THIS IS *SERIOUS*.

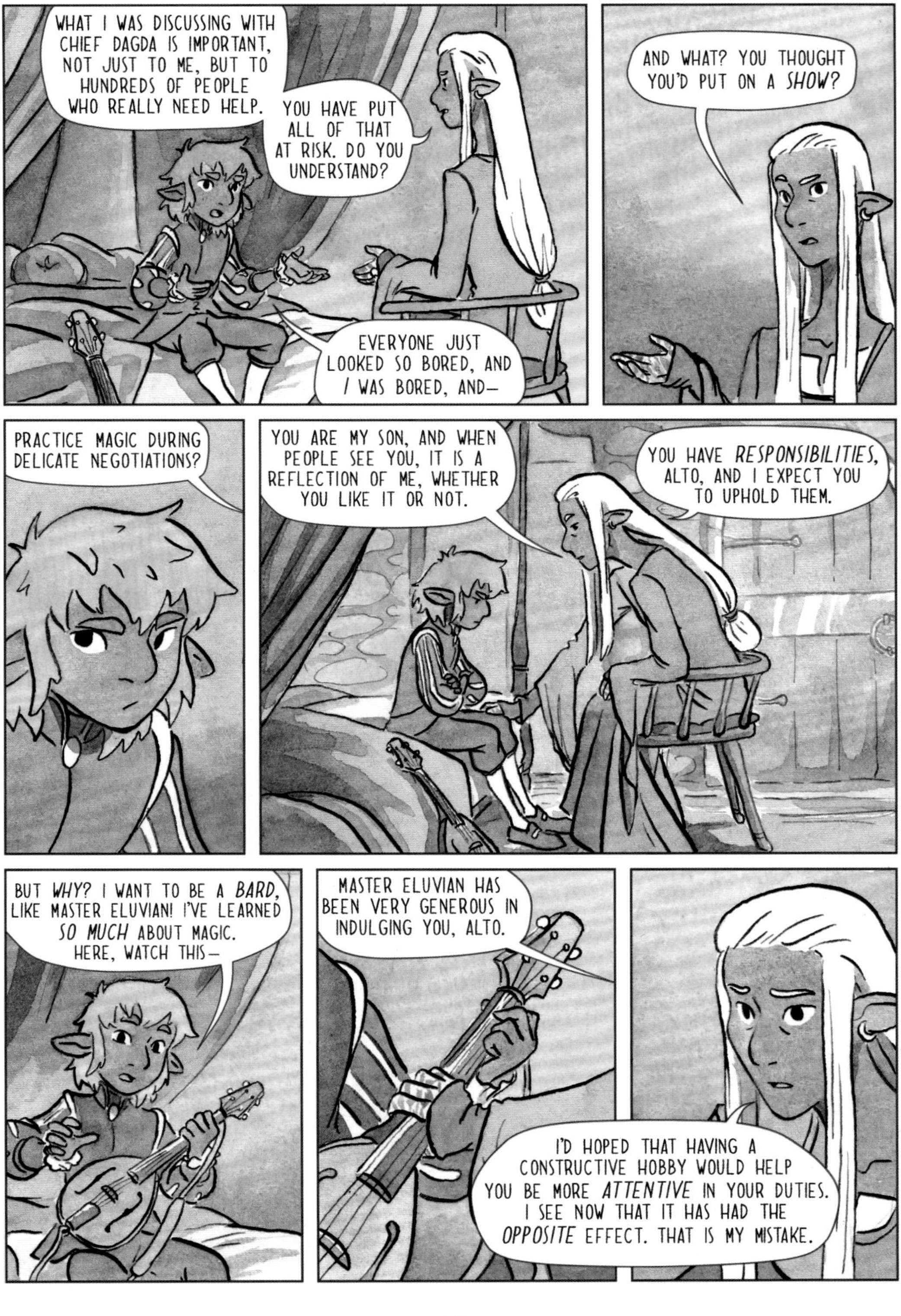
WHAT I WAS DISCUSSING WITH CHIEF DAGDA IS IMPORTANT, NOT JUST TO ME, BUT TO HUNDREDS OF PEOPLE WHO REALLY NEED HELP.
YOU HAVE PUT ALL OF THAT AT RISK. DO YOU UNDERSTAND?
EVERYONE JUST LOOKED SO BORED, AND I WAS BORED, AND—
AND WHAT? YOU THOUGHT YOU'D PUT ON A *SHOW*?
PRACTICE MAGIC DURING DELICATE NEGOTIATIONS?
YOU ARE MY SON, AND WHEN PEOPLE SEE YOU, IT IS A REFLECTION OF ME, WHETHER YOU LIKE IT OR NOT.
YOU HAVE *RESPONSIBILITIES*, ALTO, AND I EXPECT YOU TO UPHOLD THEM.
BUT *WHY*? I WANT TO BE A *BARD*, LIKE MASTER ELUVIAN! I'VE LEARNED *SO MUCH* ABOUT MAGIC. HERE, WATCH THIS—
MASTER ELUVIAN HAS BEEN VERY GENEROUS IN INDULGING YOU, ALTO.
I'D HOPED THAT HAVING A CONSTRUCTIVE HOBBY WOULD HELP YOU BE MORE *ATTENTIVE* IN YOUR DUTIES. I SEE NOW THAT IT HAS HAD THE *OPPOSITE* EFFECT. THAT IS MY MISTAKE.

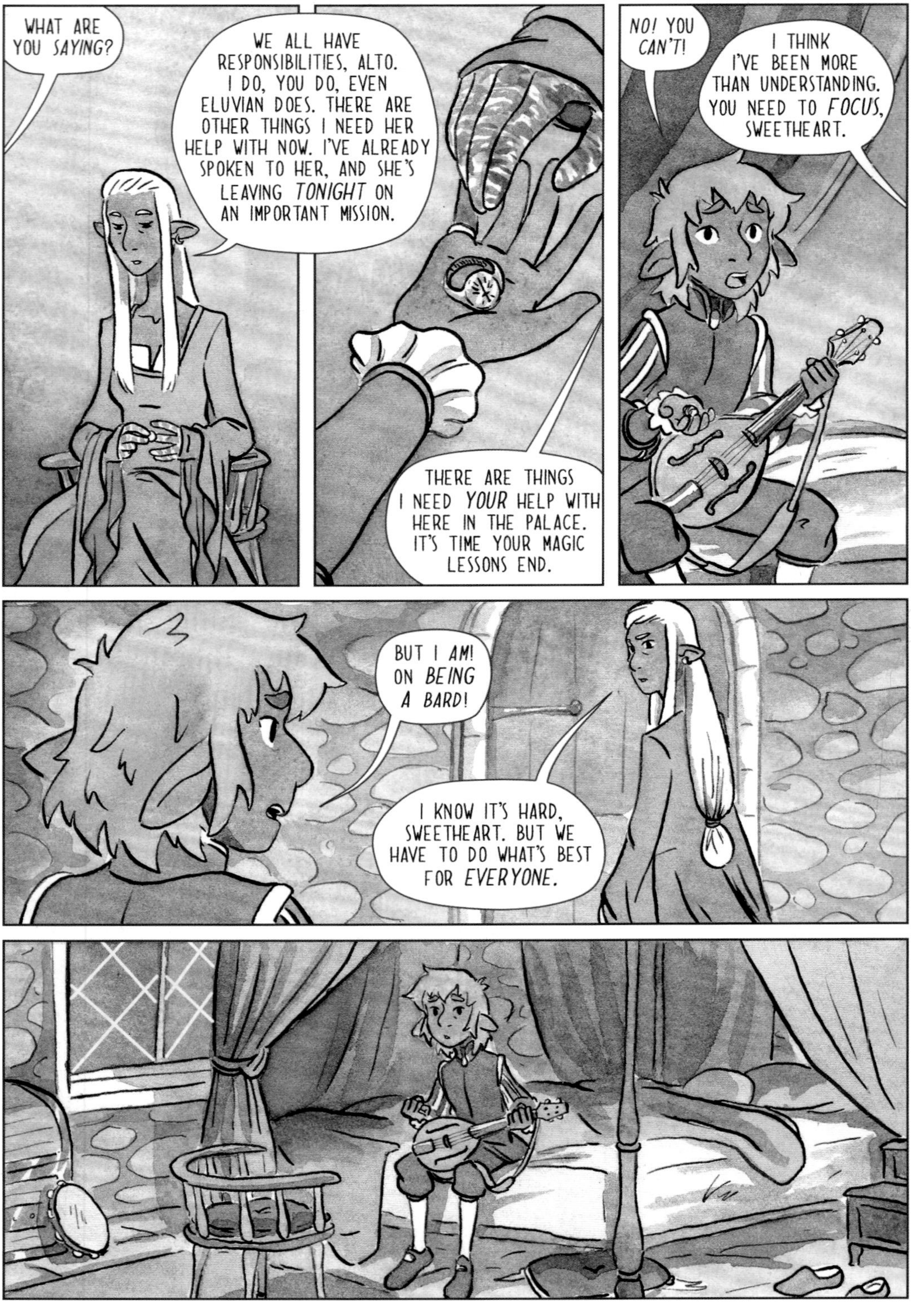
WHAT ARE YOU SAYING?
WE ALL HAVE RESPONSIBILITIES, ALTO. I DO, YOU DO, EVEN ELUVIAN DOES. THERE ARE OTHER THINGS I NEED HER HELP WITH NOW. I'VE ALREADY SPOKEN TO HER, AND SHE'S LEAVING TONIGHT ON AN IMPORTANT MISSION.
THERE ARE THINGS I NEED YOUR HELP WITH HERE IN THE PALACE. IT'S TIME YOUR MAGIC LESSONS END.
NO! YOU CAN'T!
I THINK I'VE BEEN MORE THAN UNDERSTANDING. YOU NEED TO FOCUS, SWEETHEART.
BUT I AM! ON BEING A BARD!
I KNOW IT'S HARD, SWEETHEART. BUT WE HAVE TO DO WHAT'S BEST FOR EVERYONE.

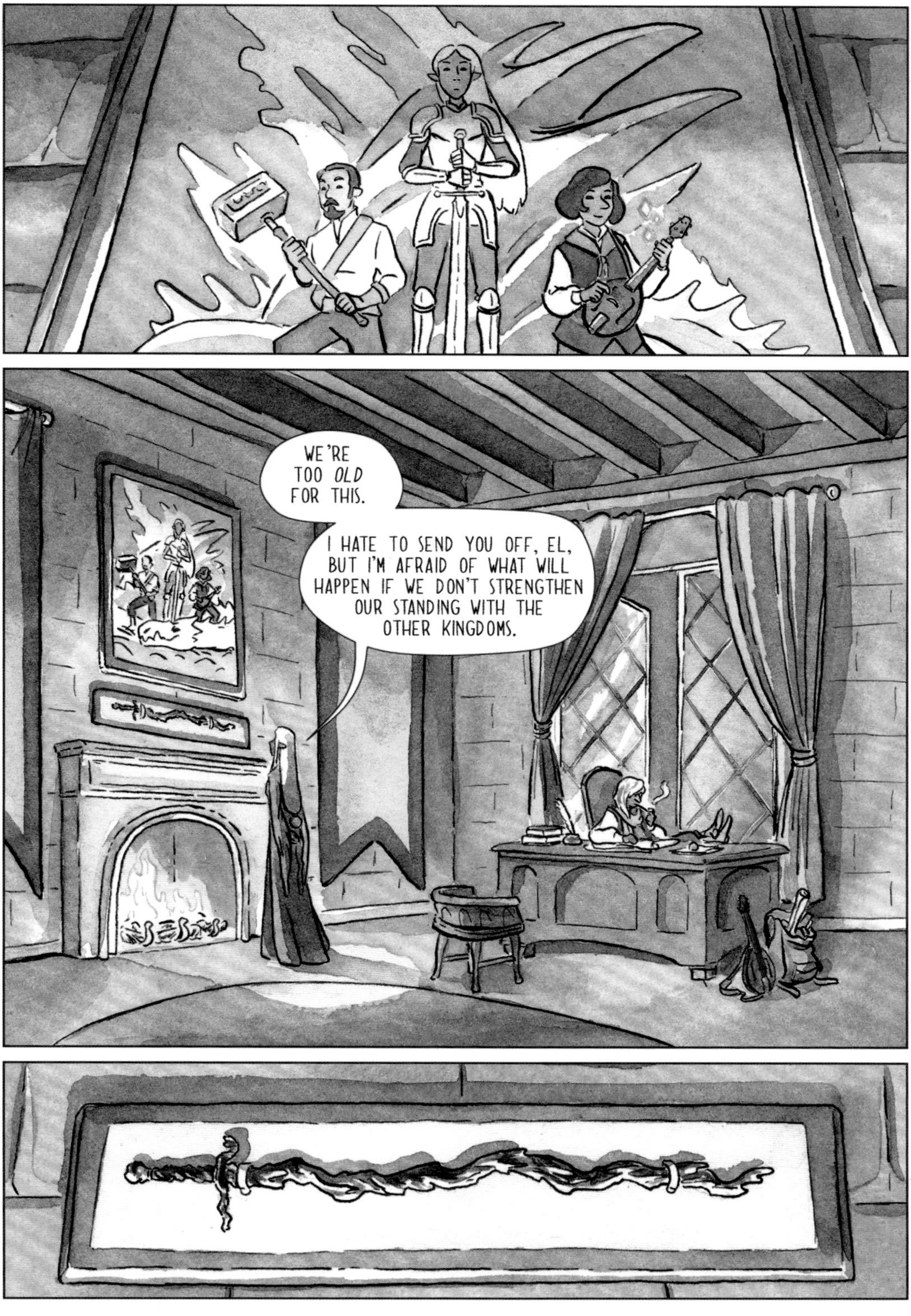
WE'RE TOO *OLD* FOR THIS.
I HATE TO SEND YOU OFF, EL, BUT I'M AFRAID OF WHAT WILL HAPPEN IF WE DON'T STRENGTHEN OUR STANDING WITH THE OTHER KINGDOMS.

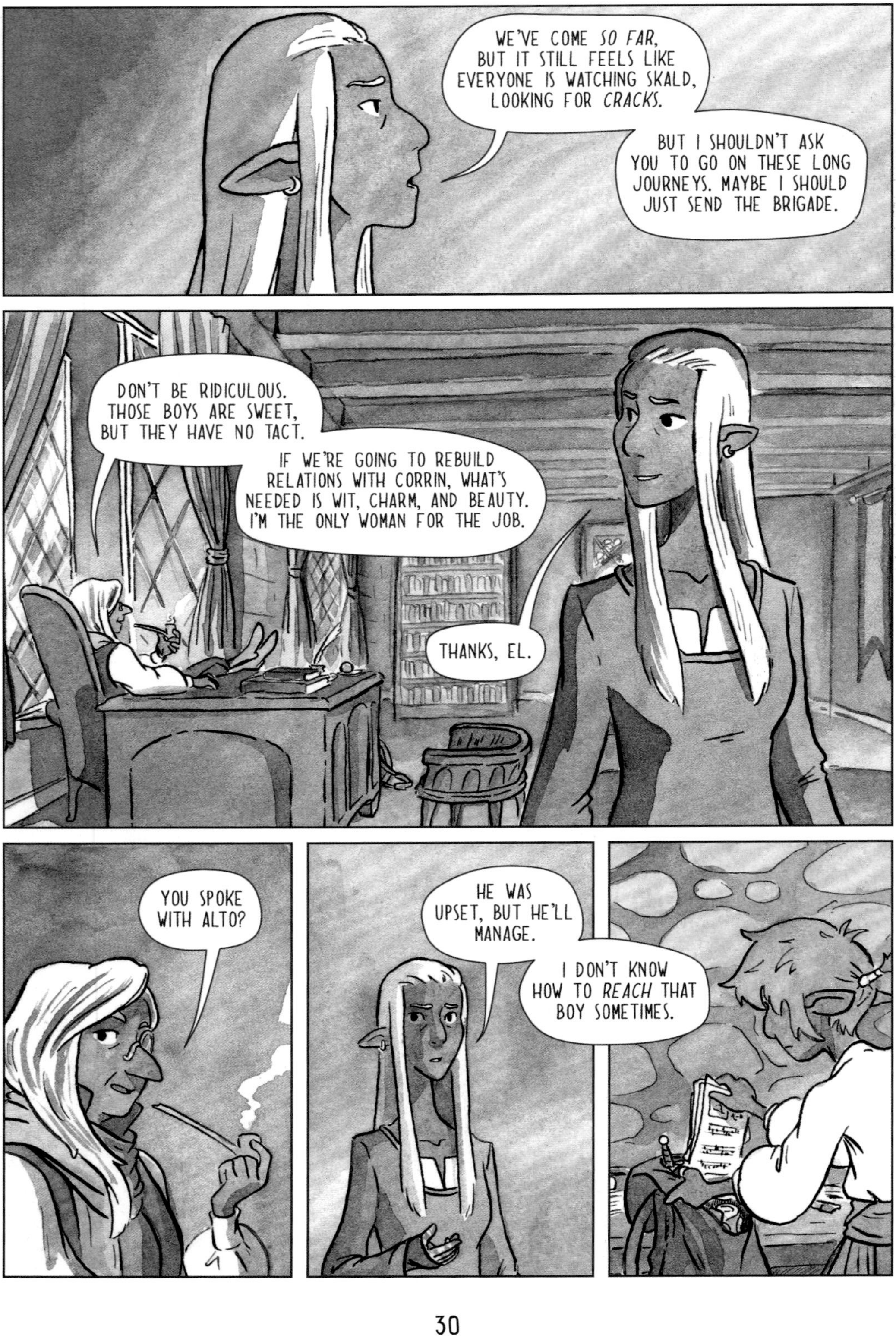
WE'VE COME *SO FAR*, BUT IT STILL FEELS LIKE EVERYONE IS WATCHING SKALD, LOOKING FOR *CRACKS*.
BUT I SHOULDN'T ASK YOU TO GO ON THESE LONG JOURNEYS. MAYBE I SHOULD JUST SEND THE BRIGADE.
DON'T BE RIDICULOUS. THOSE BOYS ARE SWEET, BUT THEY HAVE NO TACT.
IF WE'RE GOING TO REBUILD RELATIONS WITH CORRIN, WHAT'S NEEDED IS WIT, CHARM, AND BEAUTY. I'M THE ONLY WOMAN FOR THE JOB.
THANKS, EL.
YOU SPOKE WITH ALTO?
HE WAS UPSET, BUT HE'LL MANAGE.
I DON'T KNOW HOW TO *REACH* THAT BOY SOMETIMES.

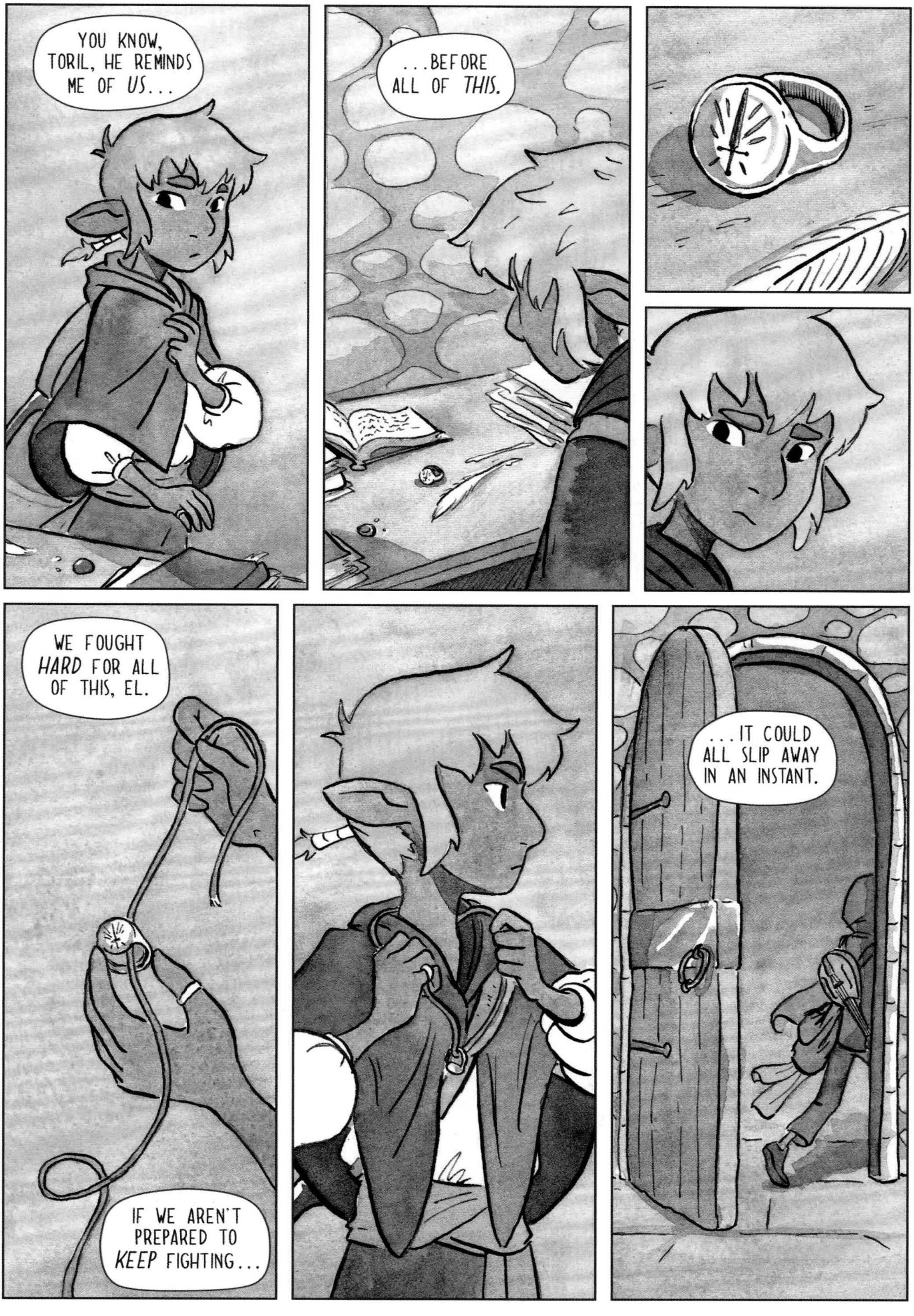
YOU KNOW, TORIL, HE REMINDS ME OF *US*...
...BEFORE ALL OF *THIS*.
WE FOUGHT *HARD* FOR ALL OF THIS, EL.
IF WE AREN'T PREPARED TO *KEEP* FIGHTING...
...IT COULD ALL SLIP AWAY IN AN INSTANT.

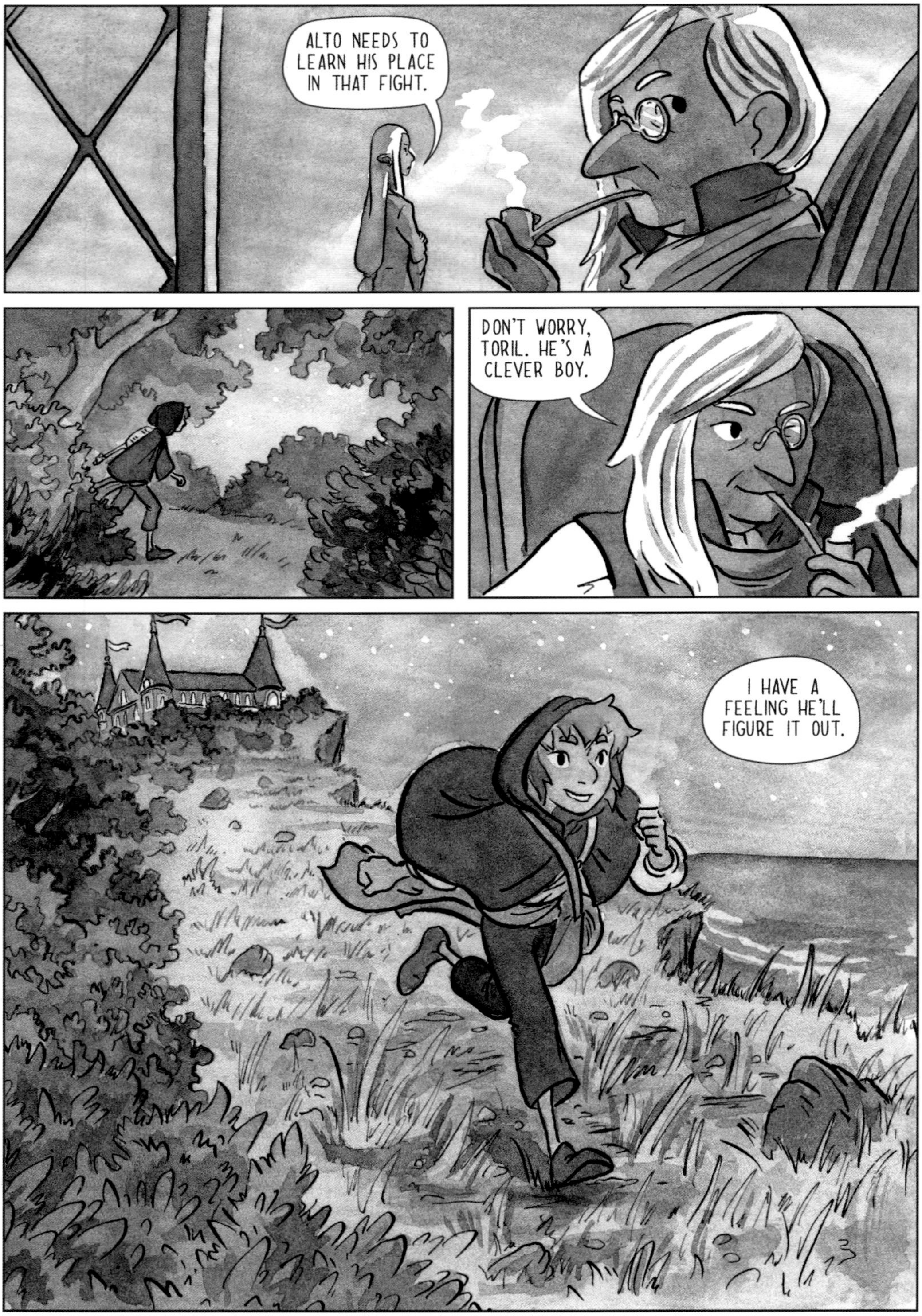
ALTO NEEDS TO LEARN HIS PLACE IN THAT FIGHT.
DON'T WORRY, TORIL. HE'S A CLEVER BOY.
I HAVE A FEELING HE'LL FIGURE IT OUT.

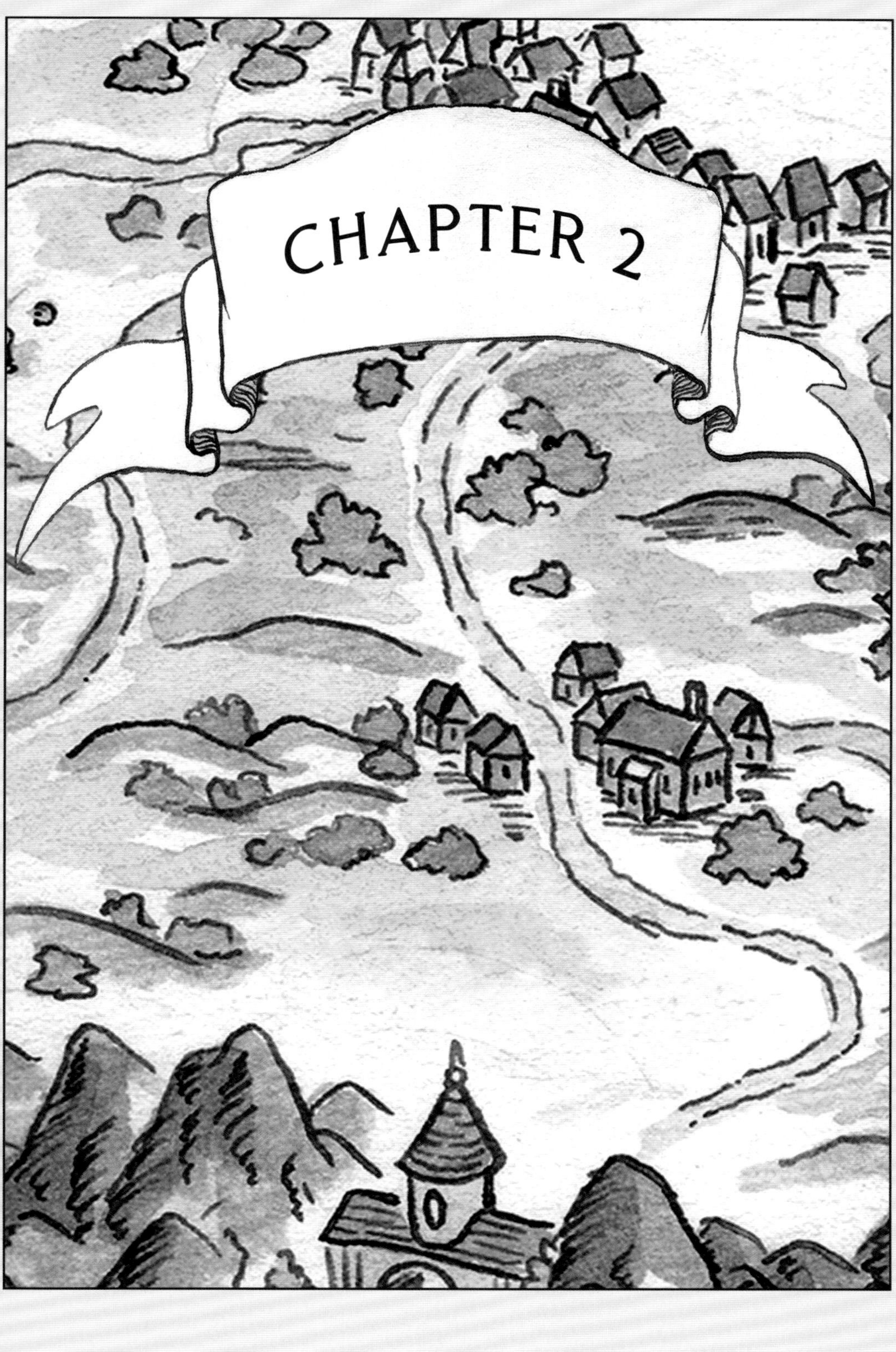
CHAPTER 2

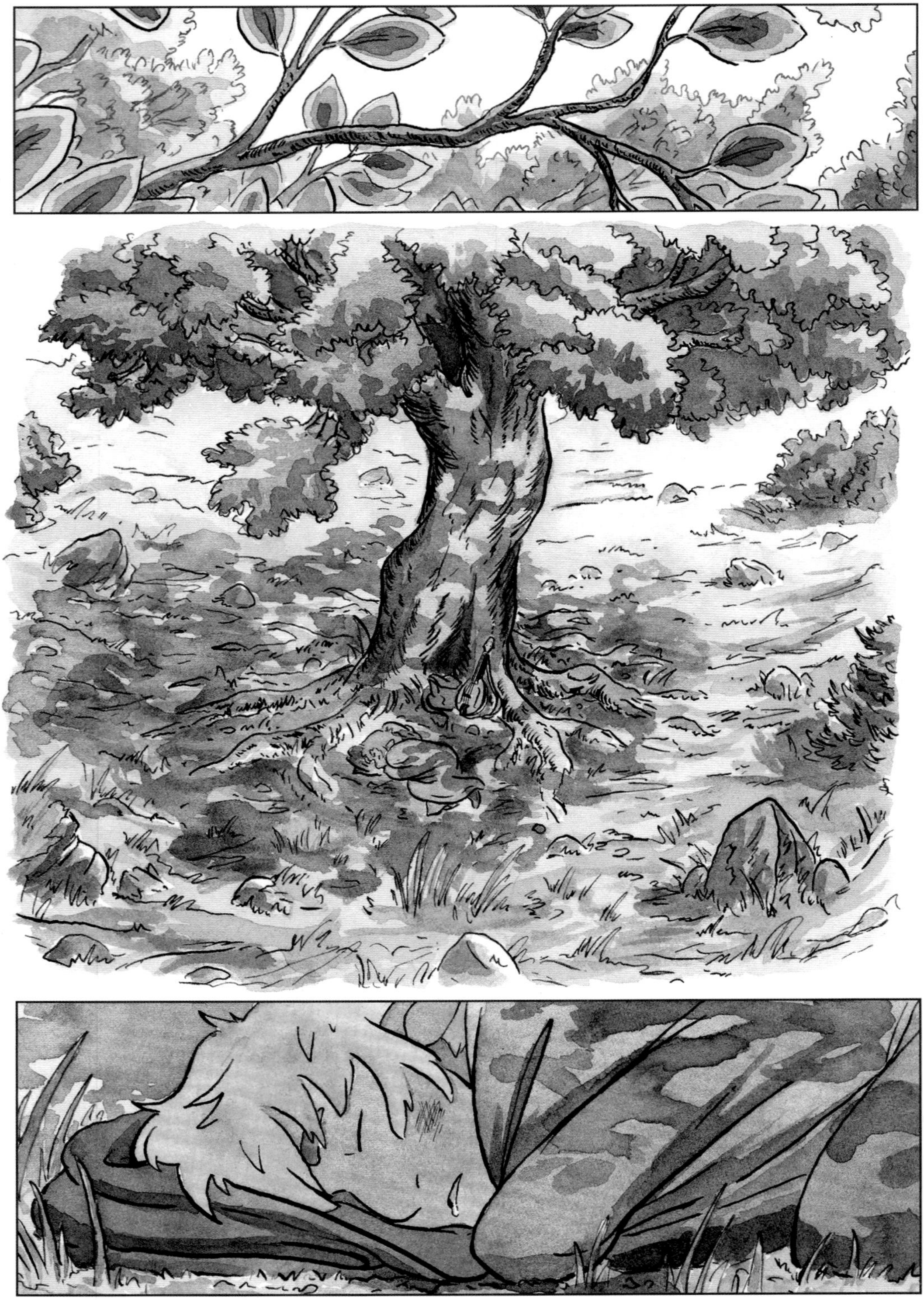

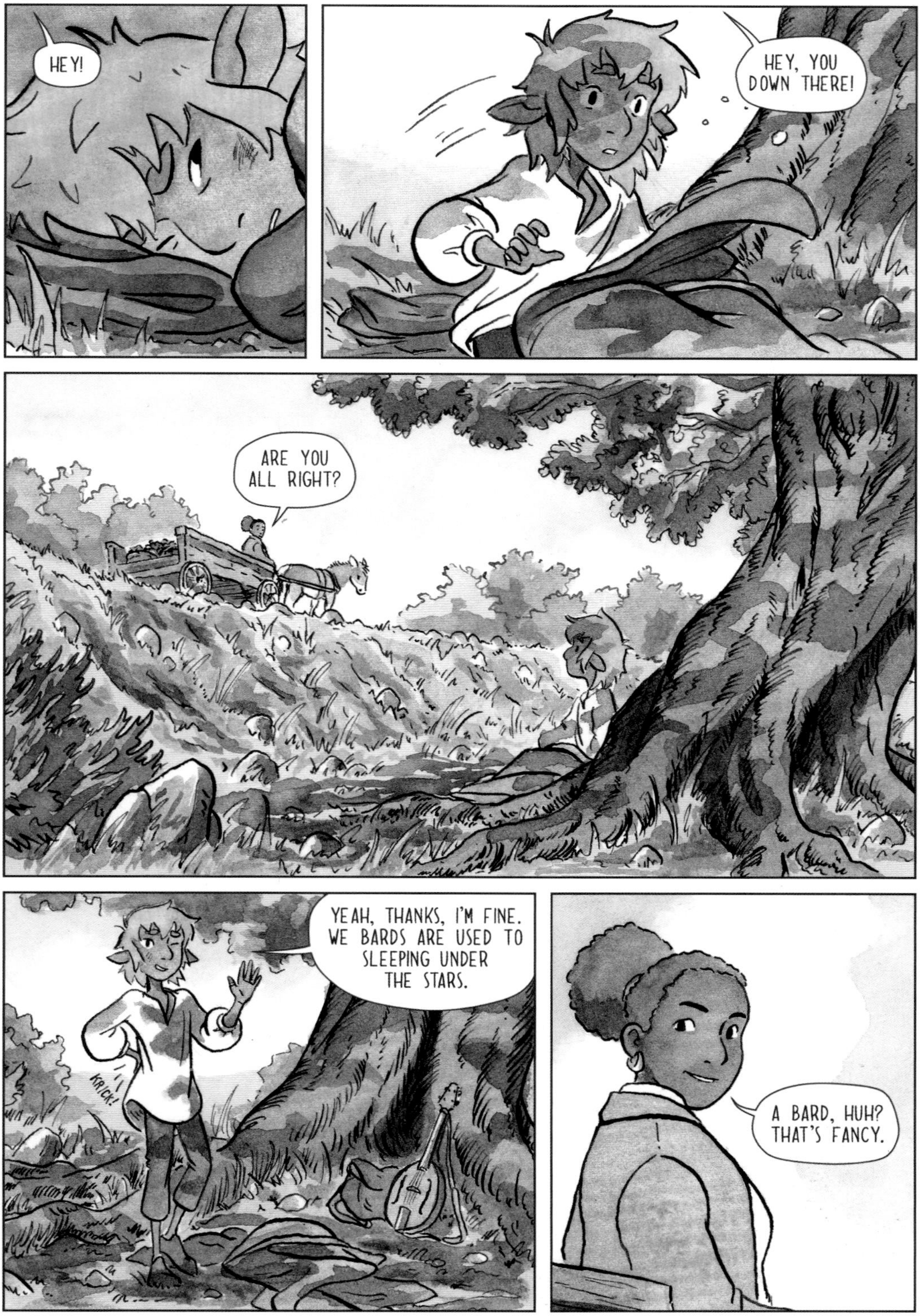
HEY!
HEY, YOU DOWN THERE!
ARE YOU ALL RIGHT?
YEAH, THANKS, I'M FINE. WE BARDS ARE USED TO SLEEPING UNDER THE STARS.
KRICK!
A BARD, HUH? THAT'S FANCY.

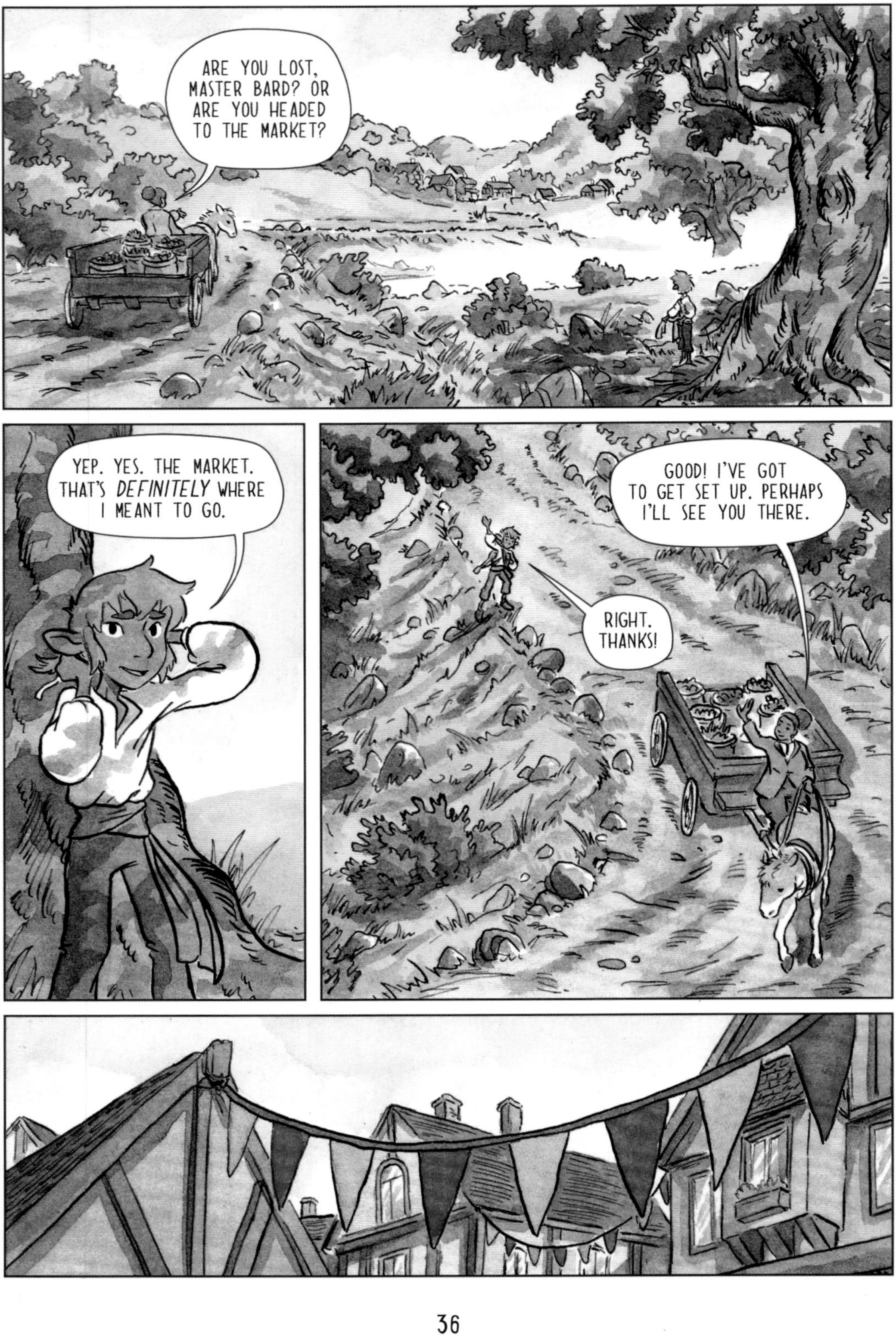
ARE YOU LOST, MASTER BARD? OR ARE YOU HEADED TO THE MARKET?
YEP. YES. THE MARKET. THAT'S *DEFINITELY* WHERE I MEANT TO GO.
GOOD! I'VE GOT TO GET SET UP. PERHAPS I'LL SEE YOU THERE.
RIGHT. THANKS!

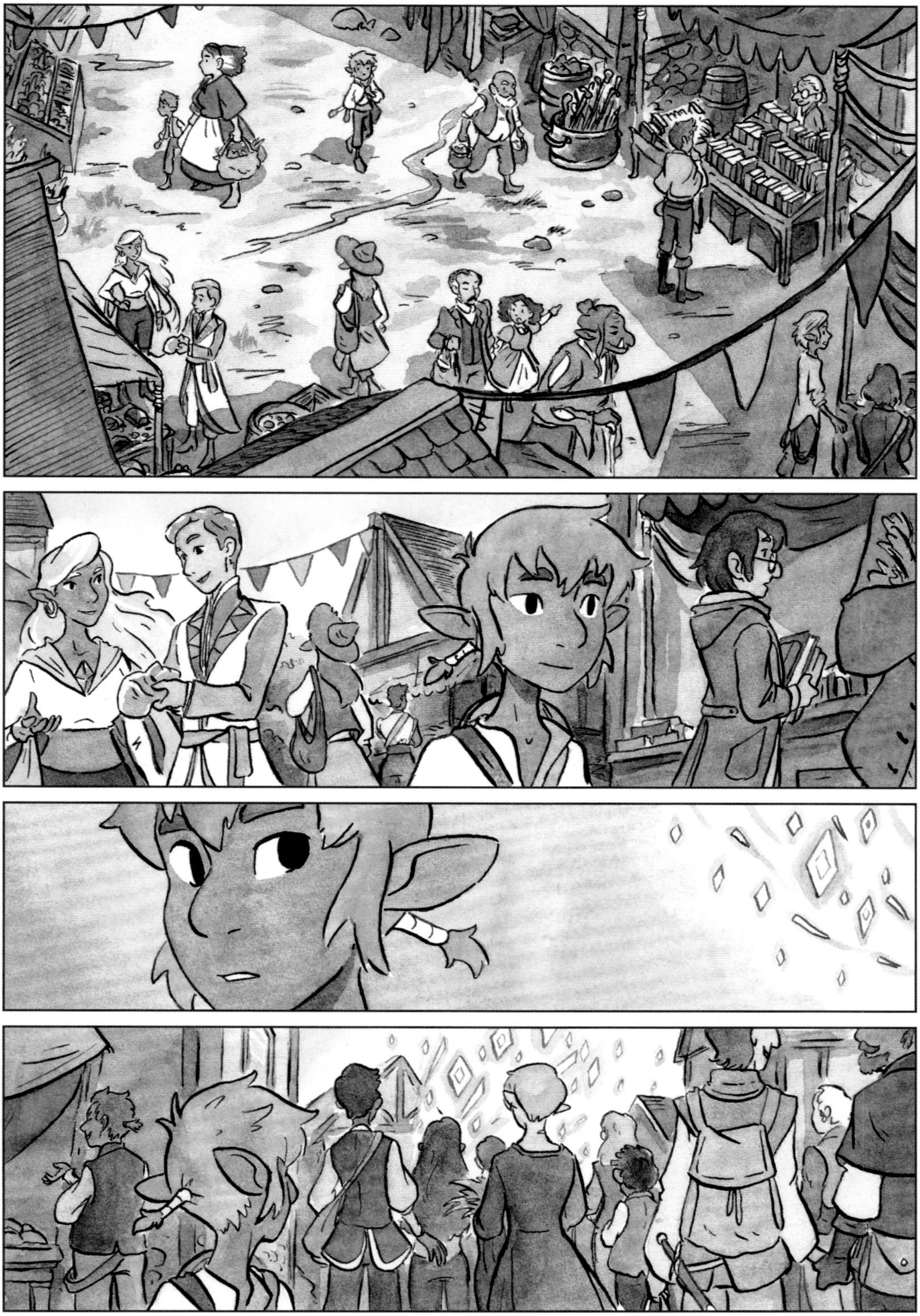

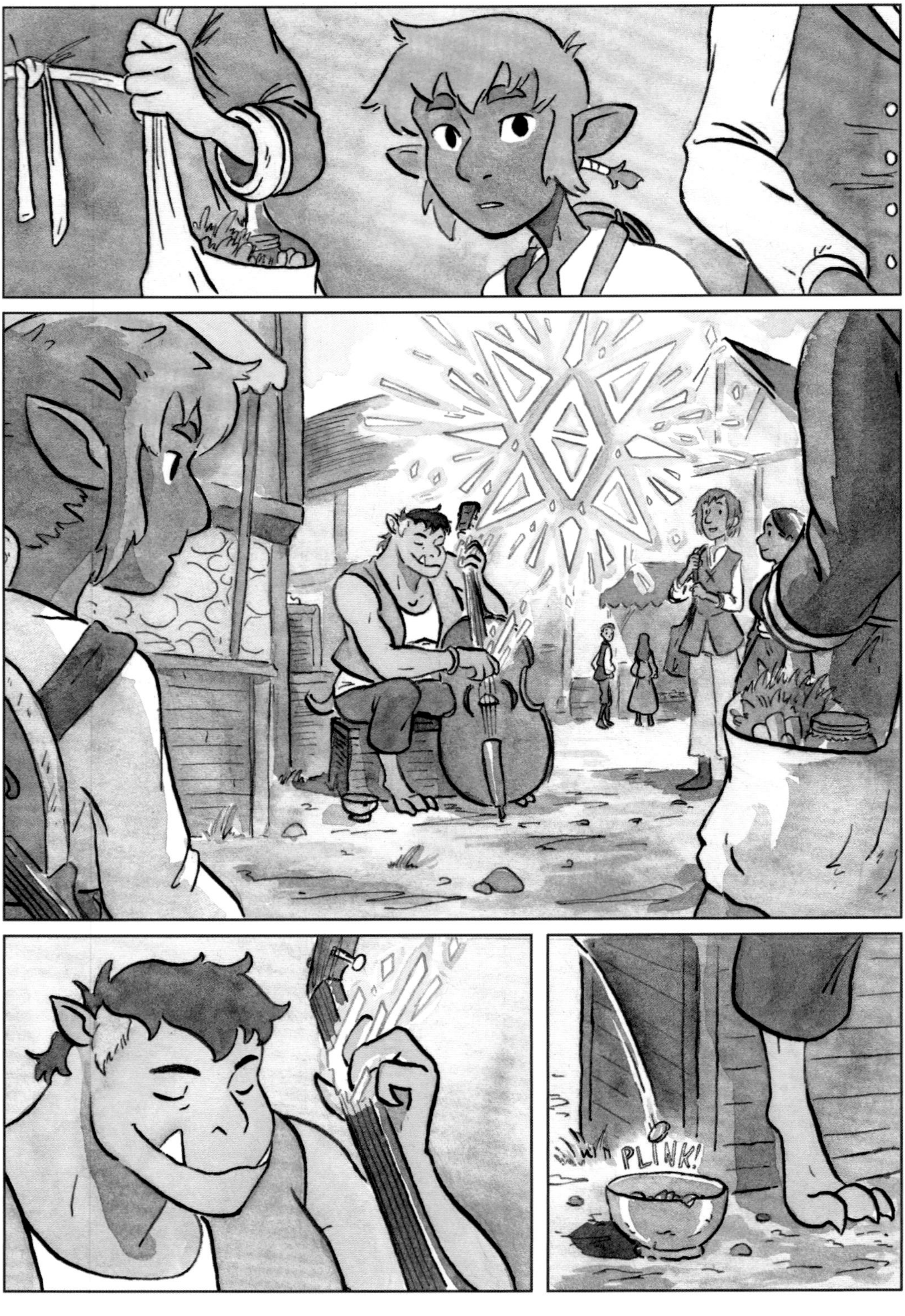
PLINK!

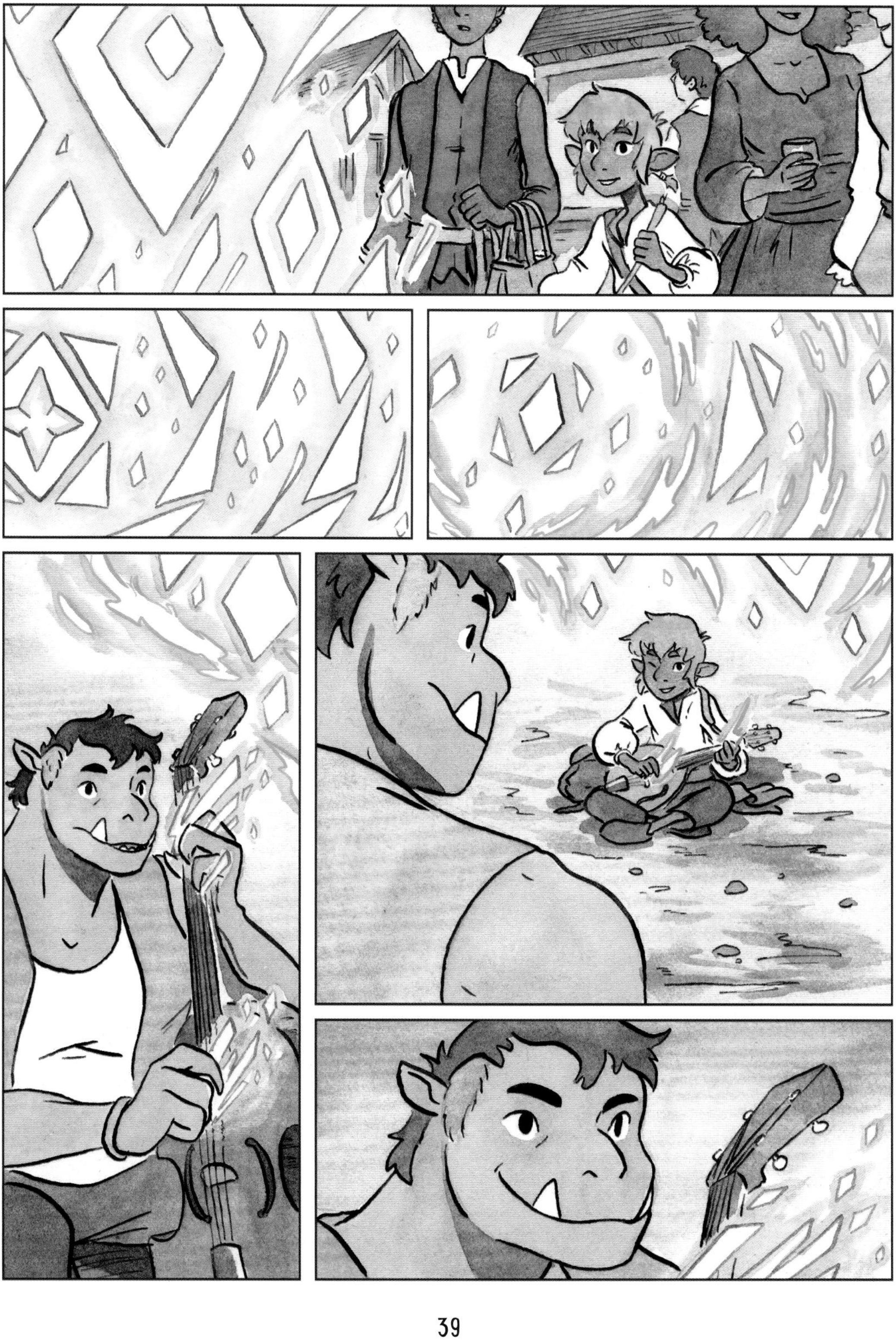

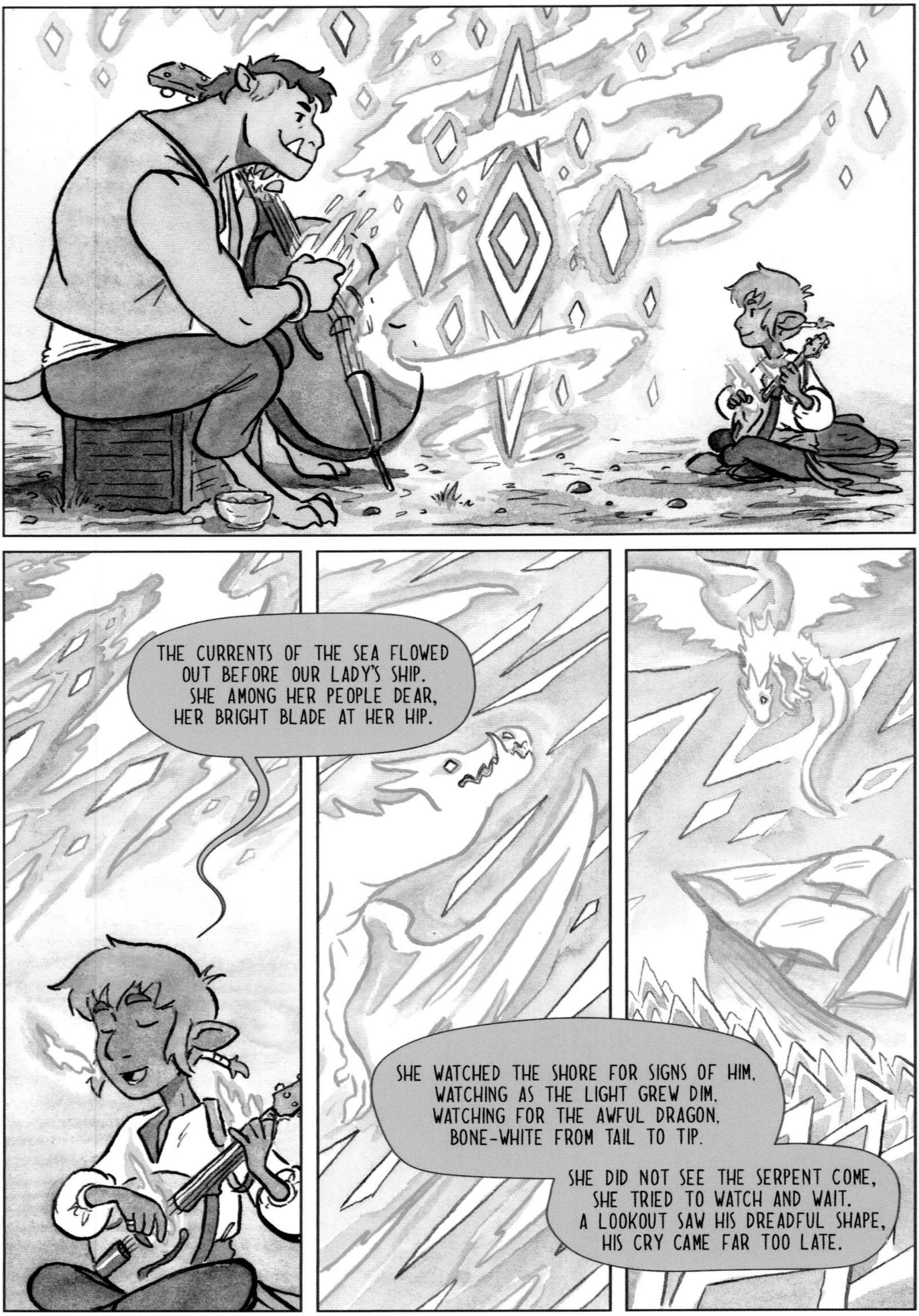
THE CURRENTS OF THE SEA FLOWED OUT BEFORE OUR LADY'S SHIP. SHE AMONG HER PEOPLE DEAR, HER BRIGHT BLADE AT HER HIP.
SHE WATCHED THE SHORE FOR SIGNS OF HIM, WATCHING AS THE LIGHT GREW DIM, WATCHING FOR THE AWFUL DRAGON, BONE-WHITE FROM TAIL TO TIP.
SHE DID NOT SEE THE SERPENT COME, SHE TRIED TO WATCH AND WAIT. A LOOKOUT SAW HIS DREADFUL SHAPE, HIS CRY CAME FAR TOO LATE.

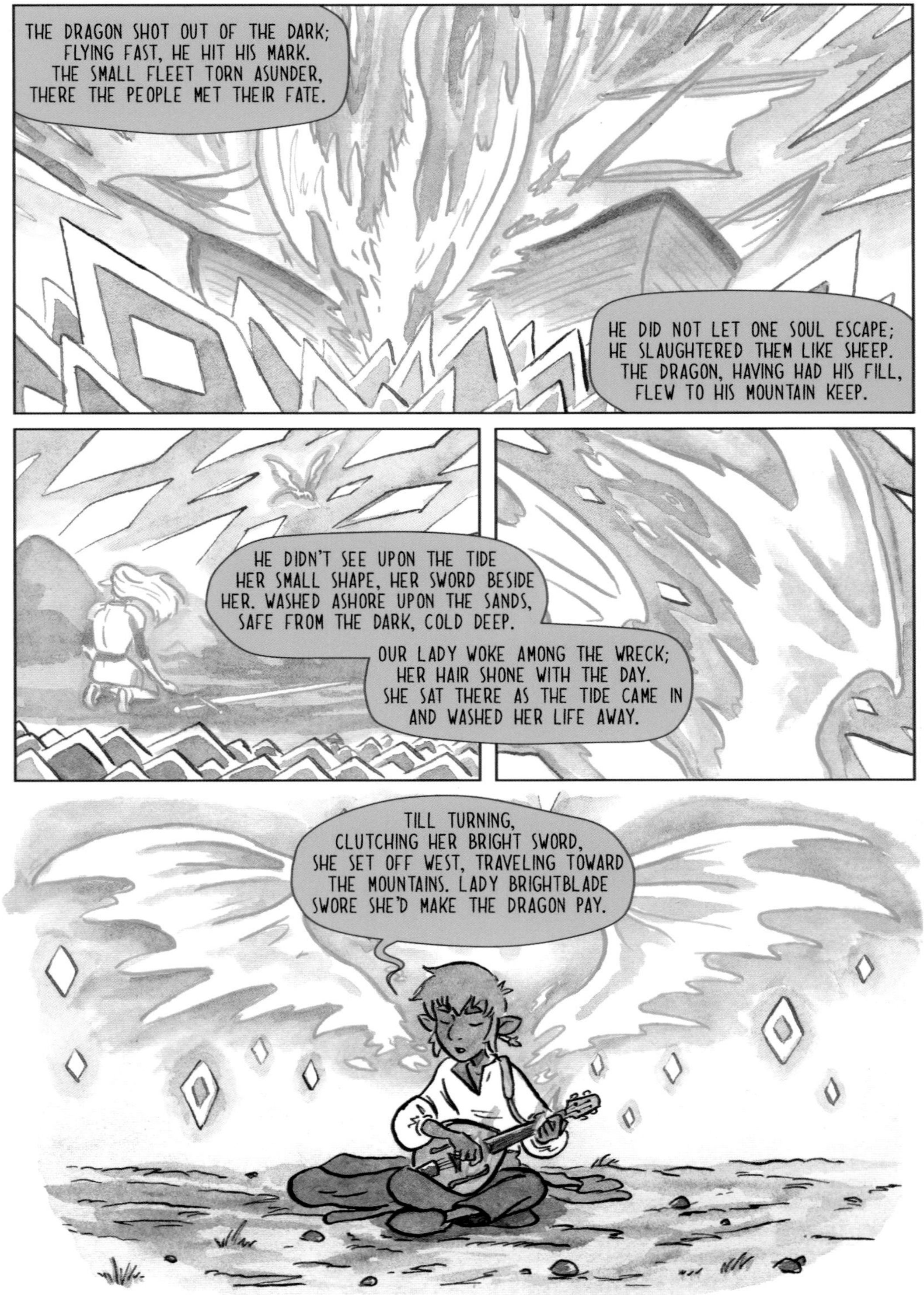
THE DRAGON SHOT OUT OF THE DARK; FLYING FAST, HE HIT HIS MARK. THE SMALL FLEET TORN ASUNDER, THERE THE PEOPLE MET THEIR FATE.
HE DID NOT LET ONE SOUL ESCAPE; HE SLAUGHTERED THEM LIKE SHEEP. THE DRAGON, HAVING HAD HIS FILL, FLEW TO HIS MOUNTAIN KEEP.
HE DIDN'T SEE UPON THE TIDE HER SMALL SHAPE, HER SWORD BESIDE HER. WASHED ASHORE UPON THE SANDS, SAFE FROM THE DARK, COLD DEEP.
OUR LADY WOKE AMONG THE WRECK; HER HAIR SHONE WITH THE DAY. SHE SAT THERE AS THE TIDE CAME IN AND WASHED HER LIFE AWAY.
TILL TURNING, CLUTCHING HER BRIGHT SWORD, SHE SET OFF WEST, TRAVELING TOWARD THE MOUNTAINS. LADY BRIGHTBLADE SWORE SHE'D MAKE THE DRAGON PAY.

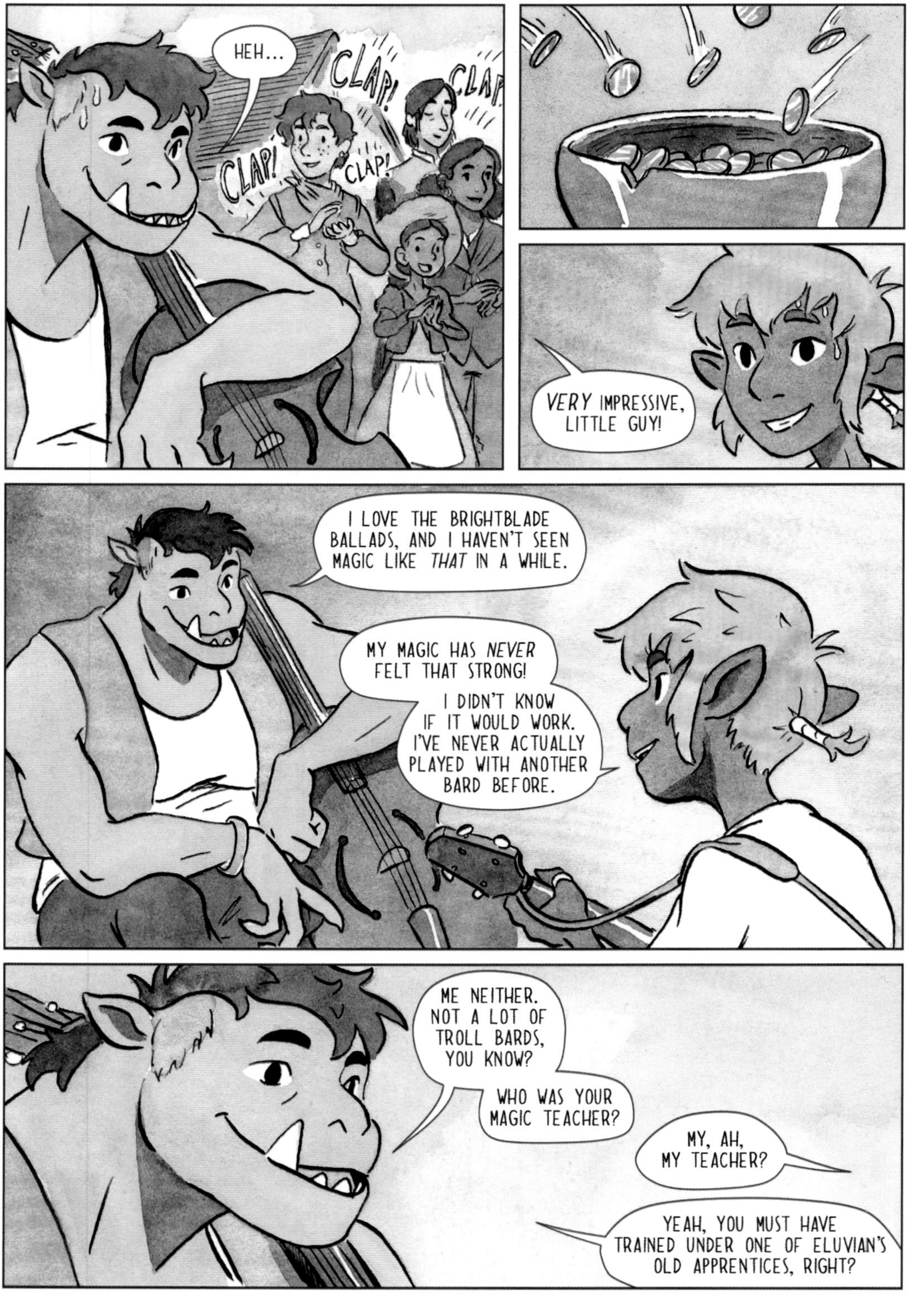
HEH...
CLAP! CLAP!
CLAP!
CLAP!
VERY IMPRESSIVE, LITTLE GUY!
I LOVE THE BRIGHTBLADE BALLADS, AND I HAVEN'T SEEN MAGIC LIKE THAT IN A WHILE.
MY MAGIC HAS NEVER FELT THAT STRONG!
I DIDN'T KNOW IF IT WOULD WORK. I'VE NEVER ACTUALLY PLAYED WITH ANOTHER BARD BEFORE.
ME NEITHER. NOT A LOT OF TROLL BARDS, YOU KNOW?
WHO WAS YOUR MAGIC TEACHER?
MY, AH, MY TEACHER?
YEAH, YOU MUST HAVE TRAINED UNDER ONE OF ELUVIAN'S OLD APPRENTICES, RIGHT?

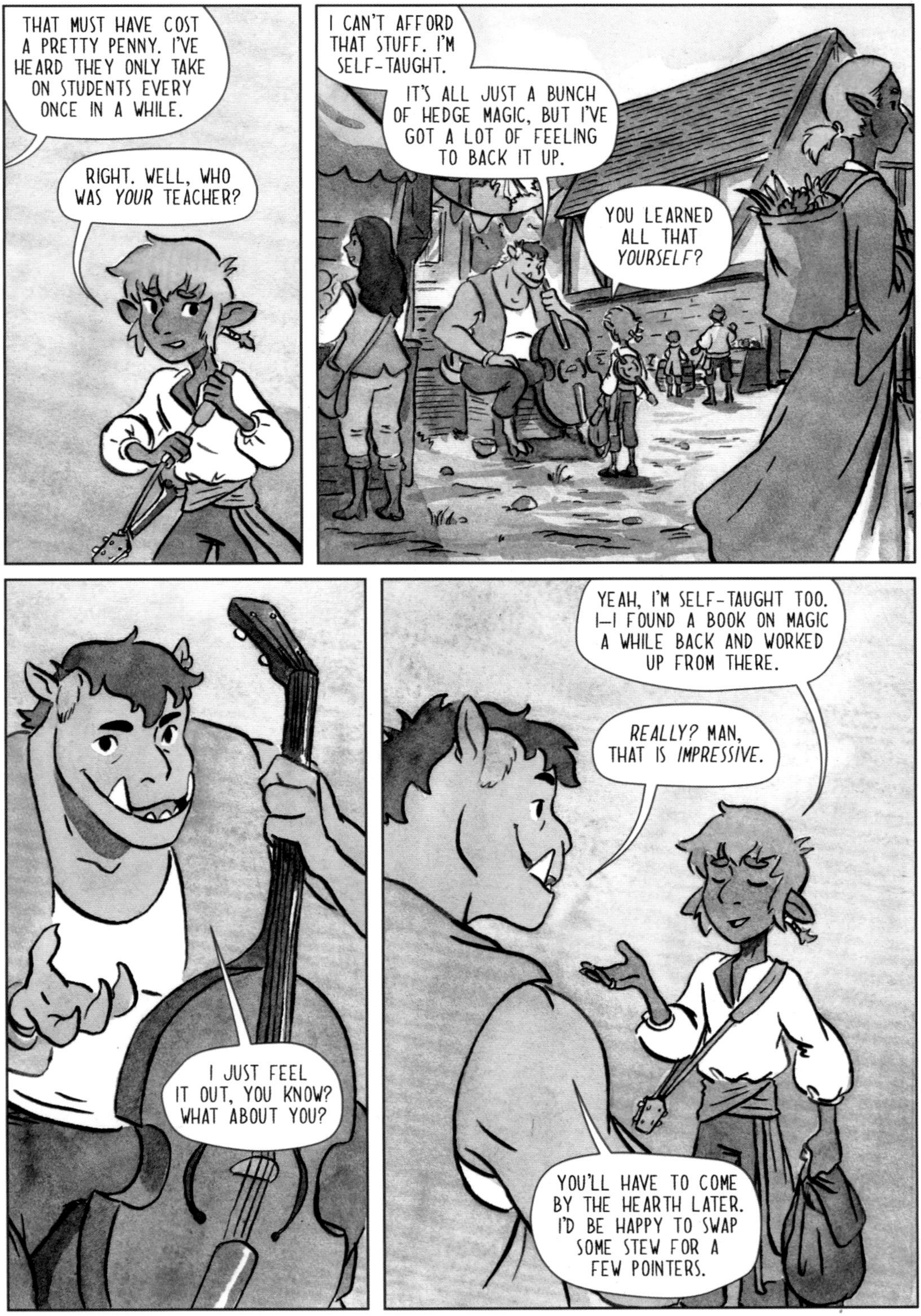
THAT MUST HAVE COST A PRETTY PENNY. I'VE HEARD THEY ONLY TAKE ON STUDENTS EVERY ONCE IN A WHILE.
RIGHT. WELL, WHO WAS *YOUR* TEACHER?
I CAN'T AFFORD THAT STUFF. I'M SELF-TAUGHT.
IT'S ALL JUST A BUNCH OF HEDGE MAGIC, BUT I'VE GOT A LOT OF FEELING TO BACK IT UP.
YOU LEARNED ALL THAT *YOURSELF*?
I JUST FEEL IT OUT, YOU KNOW? WHAT ABOUT YOU?
YEAH, I'M SELF-TAUGHT TOO. I—I FOUND A BOOK ON MAGIC A WHILE BACK AND WORKED UP FROM THERE.
REALLY? MAN, THAT IS *IMPRESSIVE.*
YOU'LL HAVE TO COME BY THE HEARTH LATER. I'D BE HAPPY TO SWAP SOME STEW FOR A FEW POINTERS.

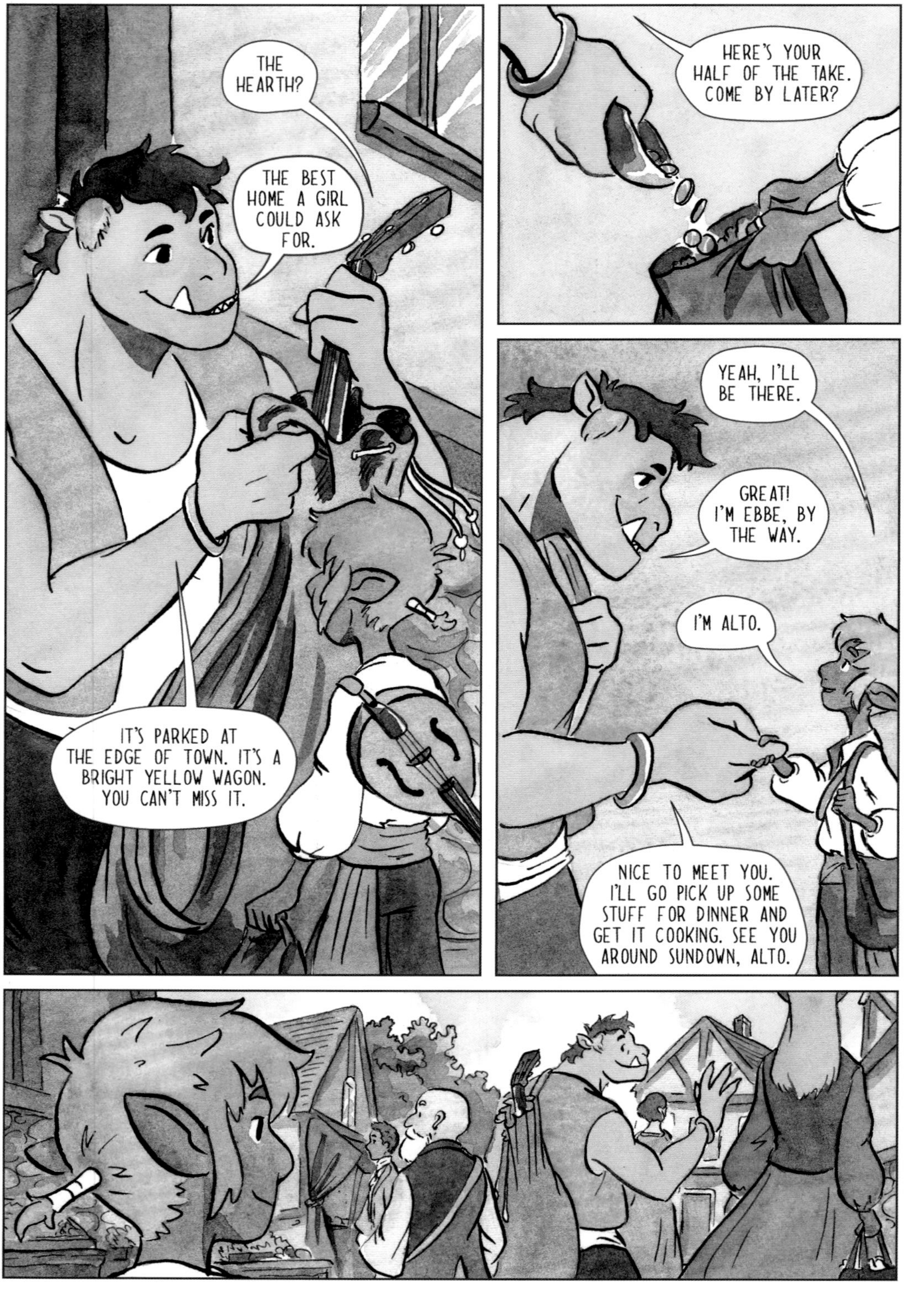
THE HEARTH?
THE BEST HOME A GIRL COULD ASK FOR.
IT'S PARKED AT THE EDGE OF TOWN. IT'S A BRIGHT YELLOW WAGON. YOU CAN'T MISS IT.
HERE'S YOUR HALF OF THE TAKE. COME BY LATER?
YEAH, I'LL BE THERE.
GREAT! I'M EBBE, BY THE WAY.
I'M ALTO.
NICE TO MEET YOU. I'LL GO PICK UP SOME STUFF FOR DINNER AND GET IT COOKING. SEE YOU AROUND SUNDOWN, ALTO.

CHAPTER 3

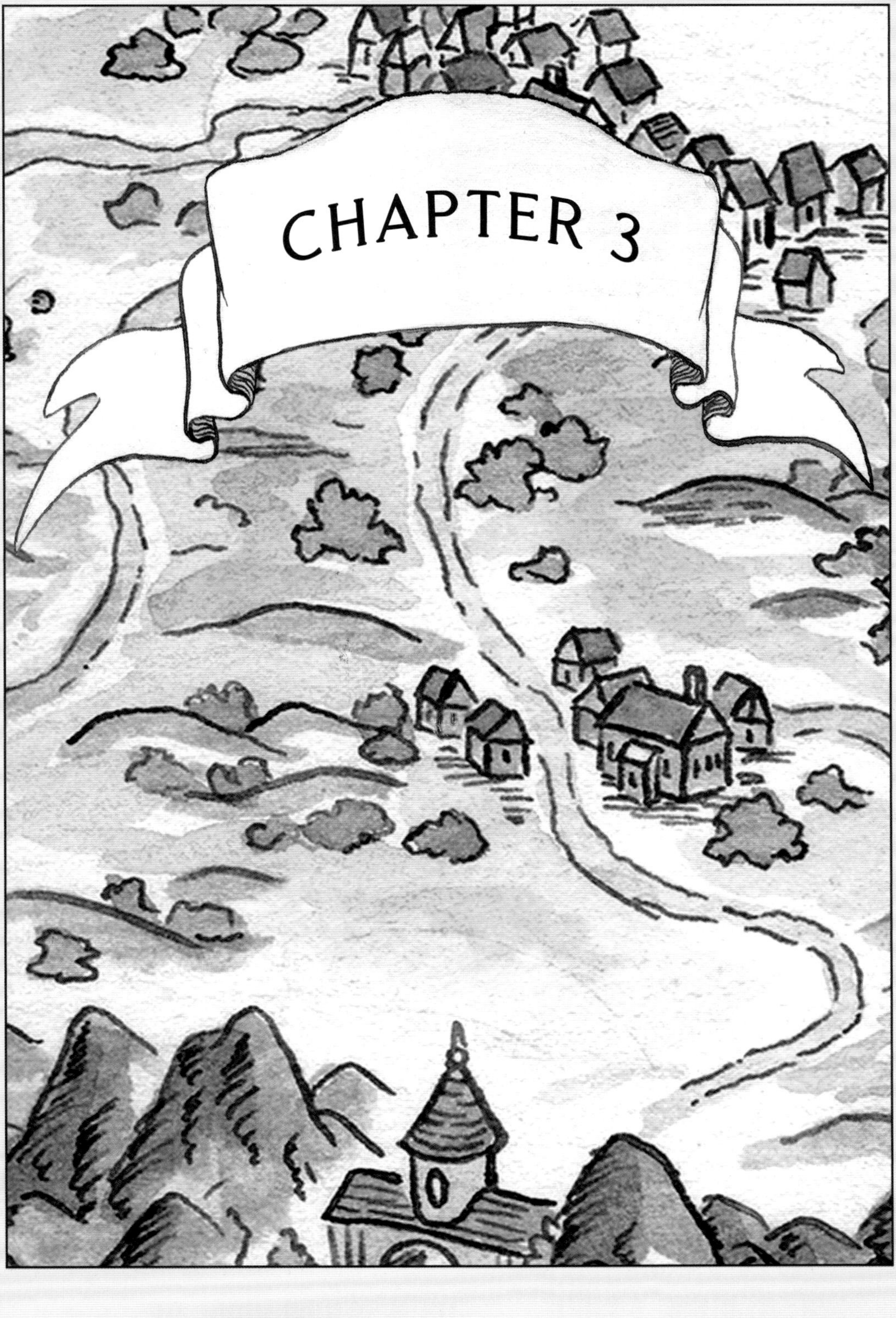

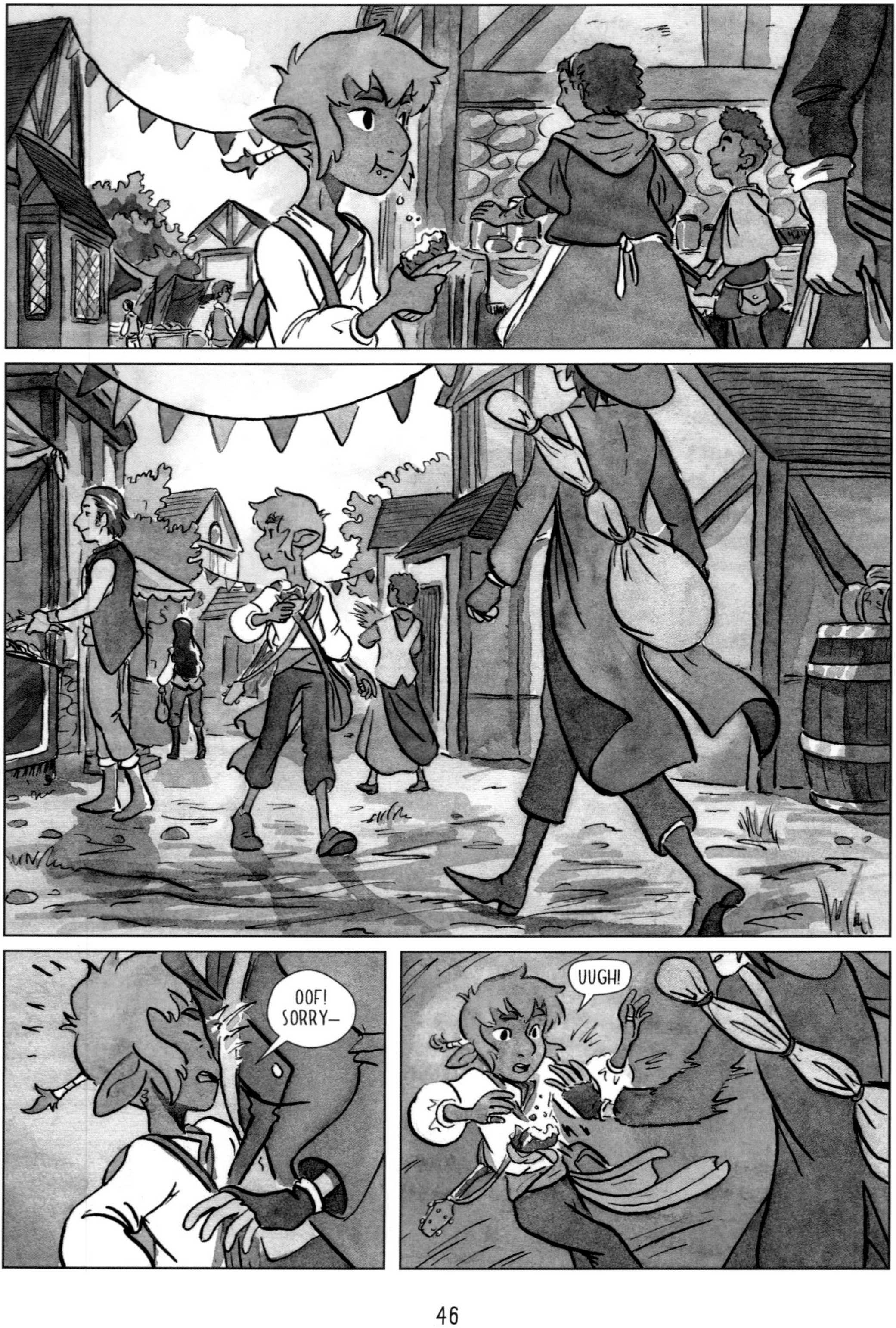
OOF! SORRY—
UUGH!

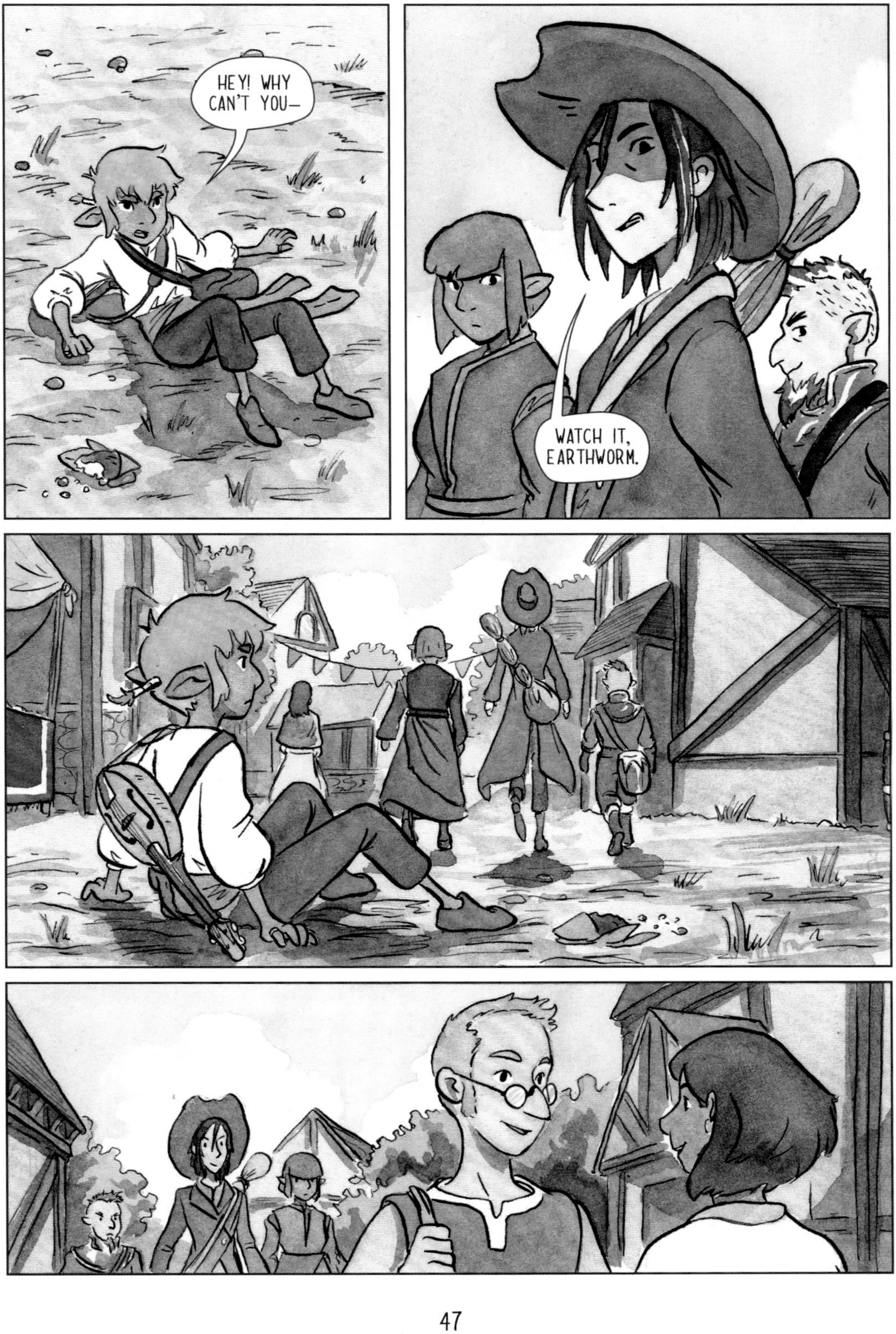
HEY! WHY CAN'T YOU—
WATCH IT, EARTHWORM.

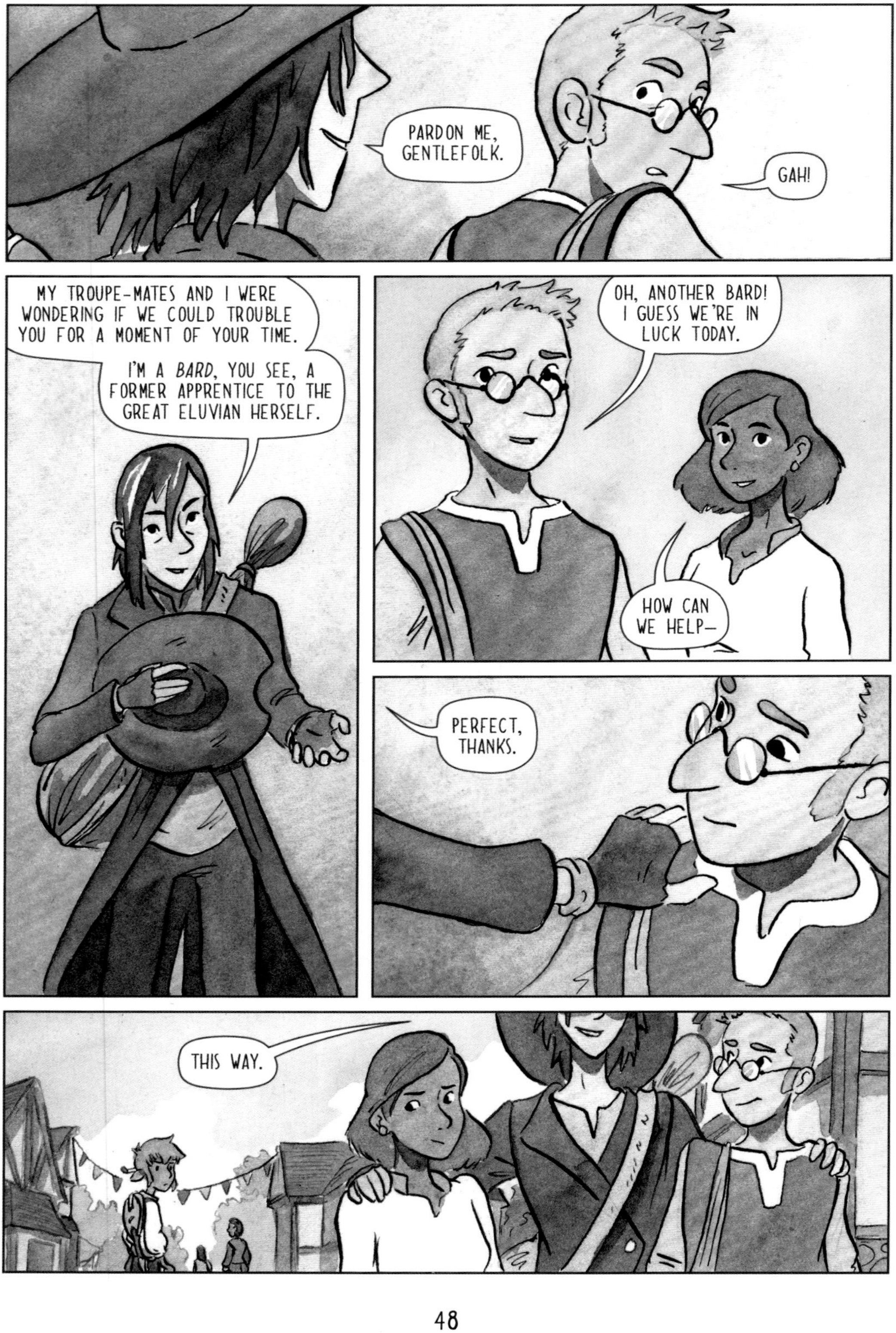
PARDON ME, GENTLEFOLK.
GAH!
MY TROUPE-MATES AND I WERE WONDERING IF WE COULD TROUBLE YOU FOR A MOMENT OF YOUR TIME.
I'M A *BARD*, YOU SEE, A FORMER APPRENTICE TO THE GREAT ELUVIAN HERSELF.
OH, ANOTHER BARD! I GUESS WE'RE IN LUCK TODAY.
HOW CAN WE HELP—
PERFECT, THANKS.
THIS WAY.

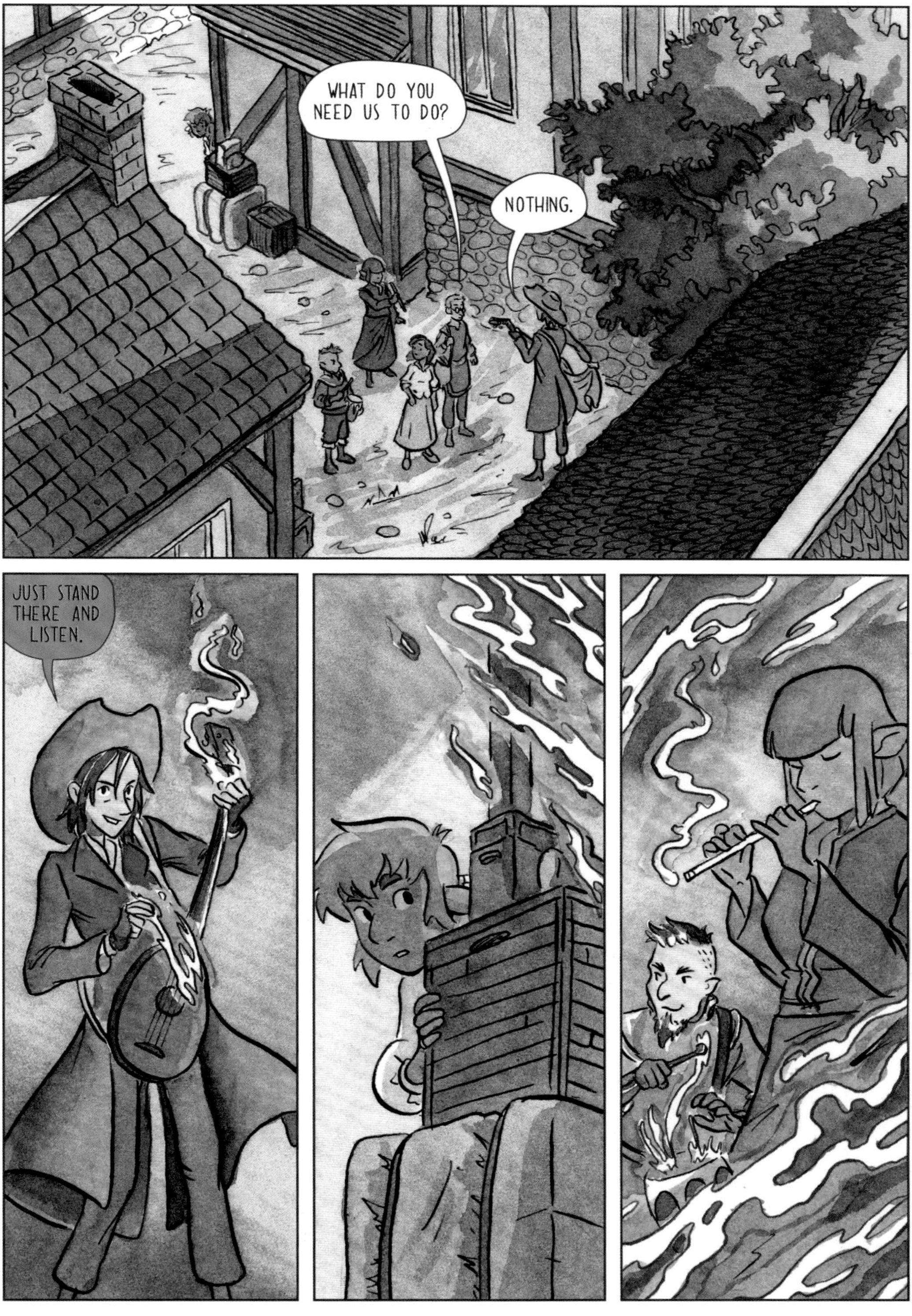
WHAT DO YOU NEED US TO DO?
NOTHING.
JUST STAND THERE AND LISTEN.

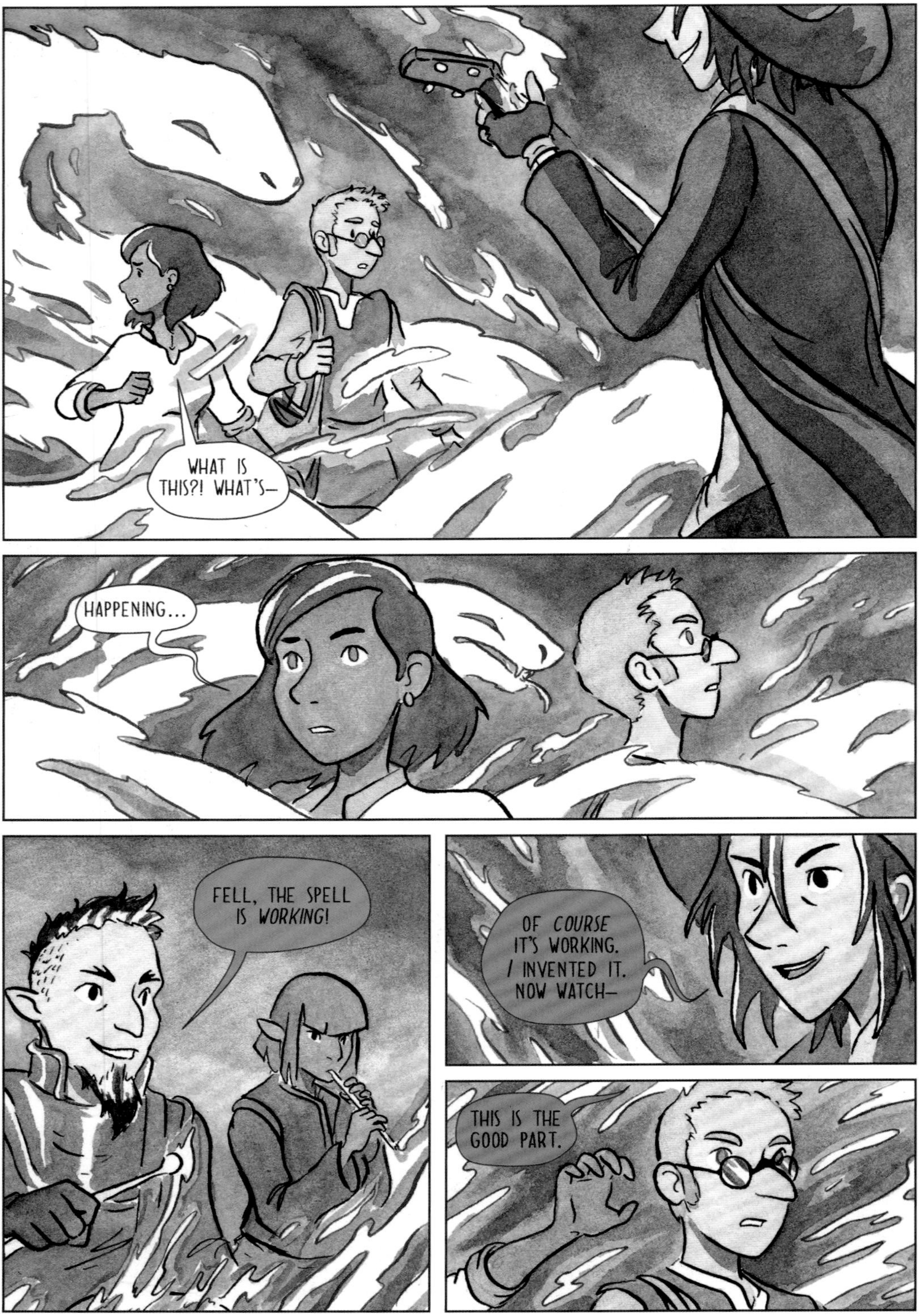
WHAT IS THIS?! WHAT'S—
HAPPENING...
FELL, THE SPELL IS *WORKING*!
OF *COURSE* IT'S WORKING. *I* INVENTED IT. NOW WATCH—
THIS IS THE GOOD PART.

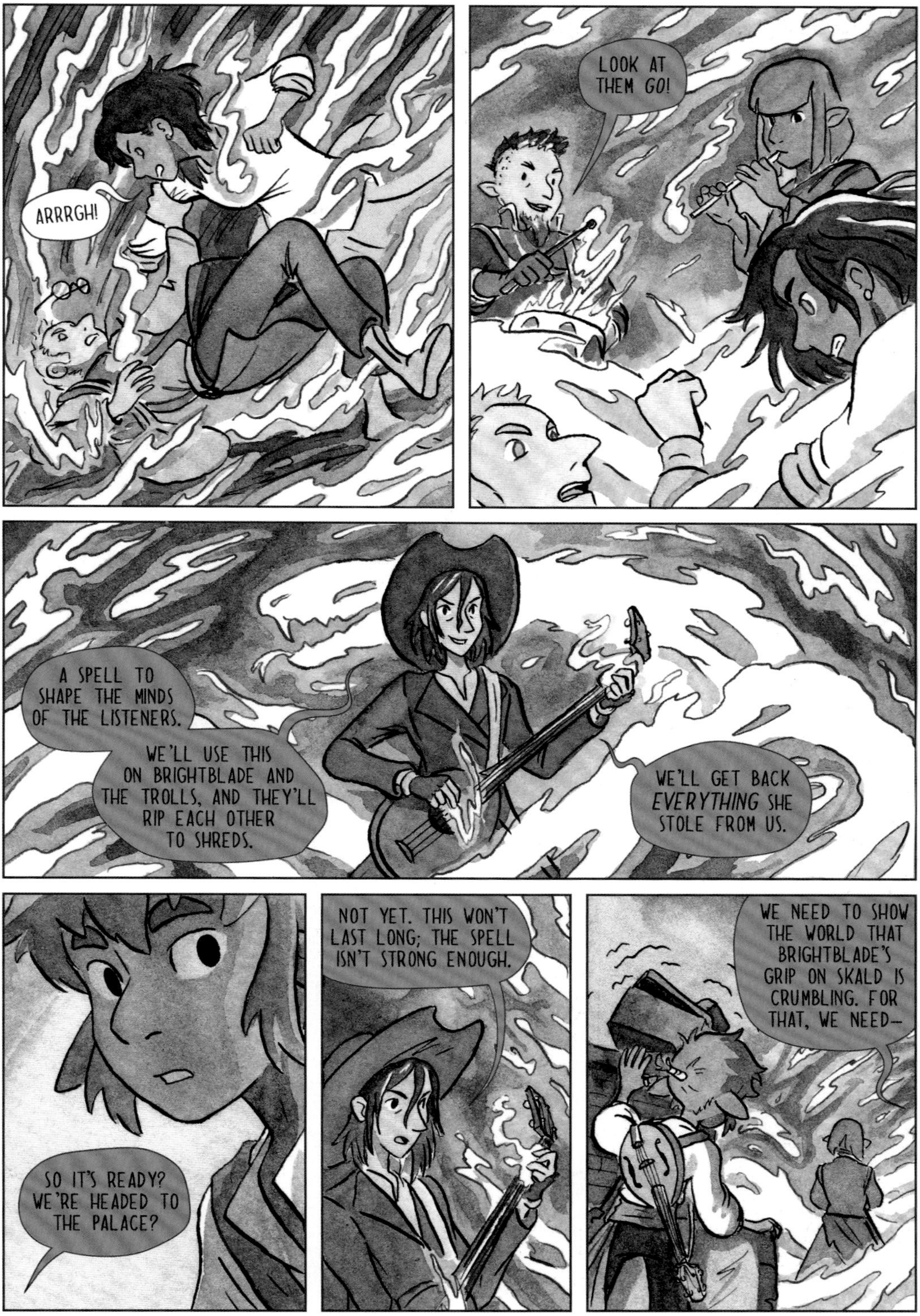
ARRRGH!
LOOK AT THEM GO!
A SPELL TO SHAPE THE MINDS OF THE LISTENERS.
WE'LL USE THIS ON BRIGHTBLADE AND THE TROLLS, AND THEY'LL RIP EACH OTHER TO SHREDS.
WE'LL GET BACK EVERYTHING SHE STOLE FROM US.
SO IT'S READY? WE'RE HEADED TO THE PALACE?
NOT YET. THIS WON'T LAST LONG; THE SPELL ISN'T STRONG ENOUGH.
WE NEED TO SHOW THE WORLD THAT BRIGHTBLADE'S GRIP ON SKALD IS CRUMBLING. FOR THAT, WE NEED—

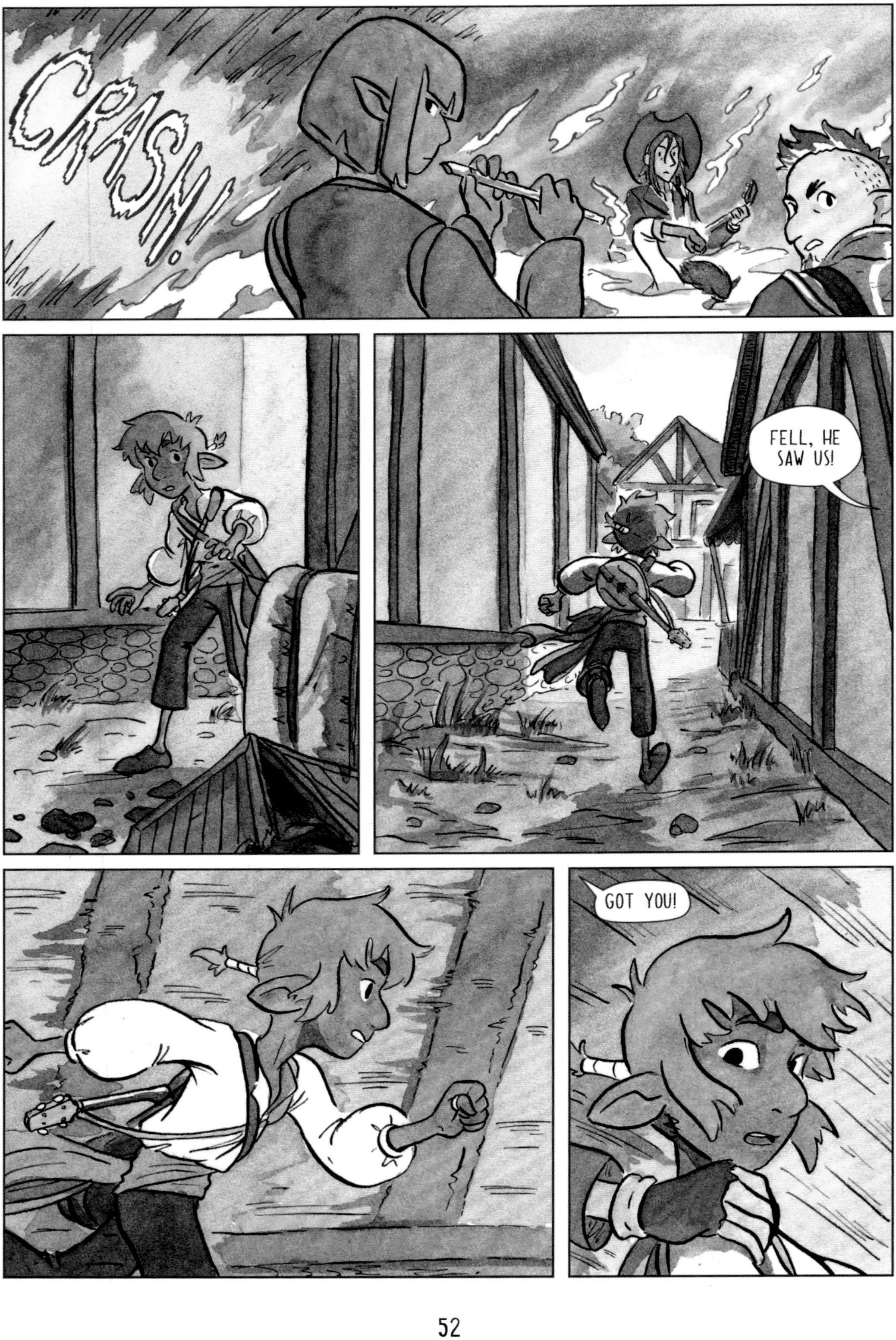
CRASH!
FELL, HE SAW US!
GOT YOU!

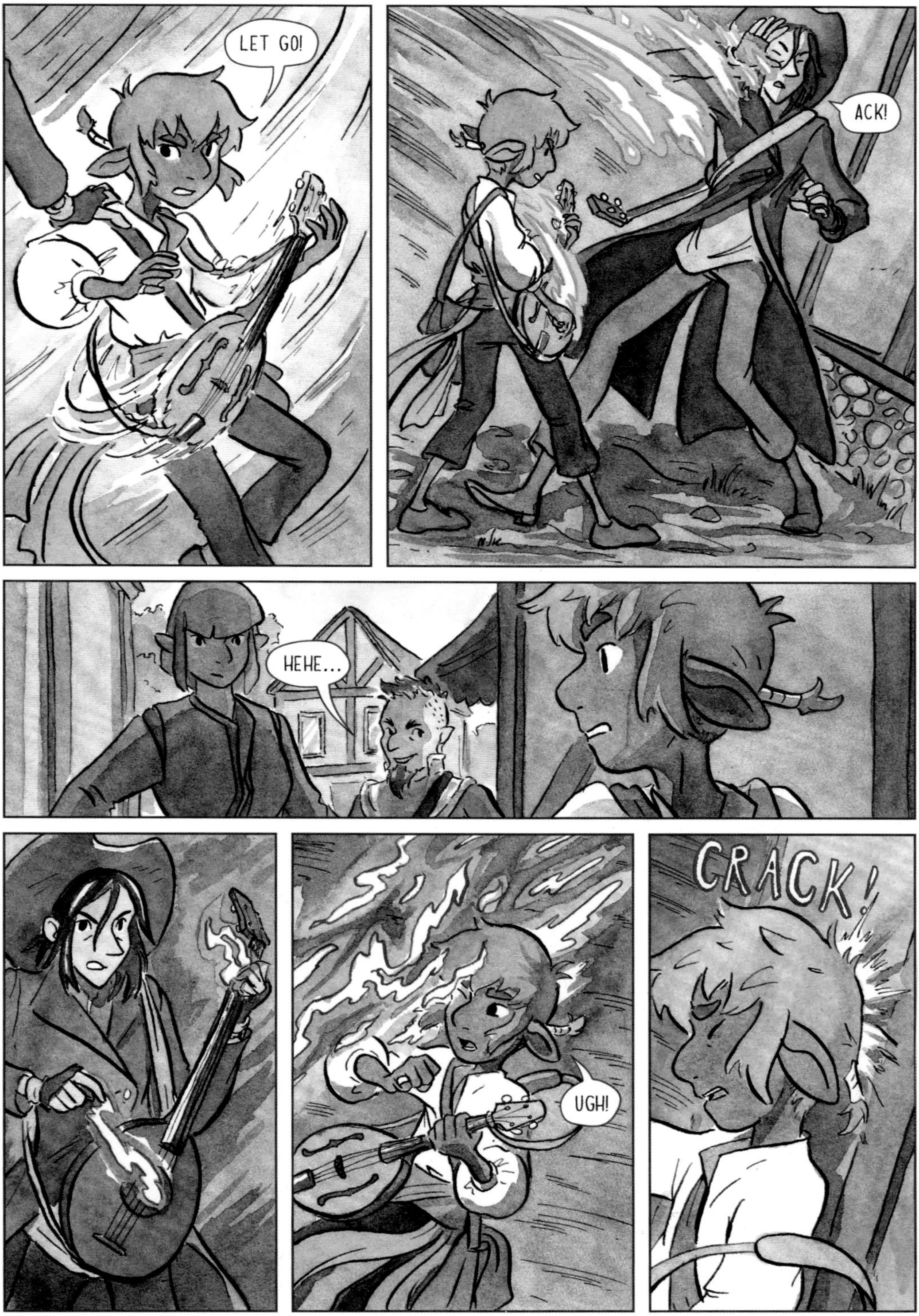
LET GO!
ACK!
HEHE...
UGH!
CRACK!

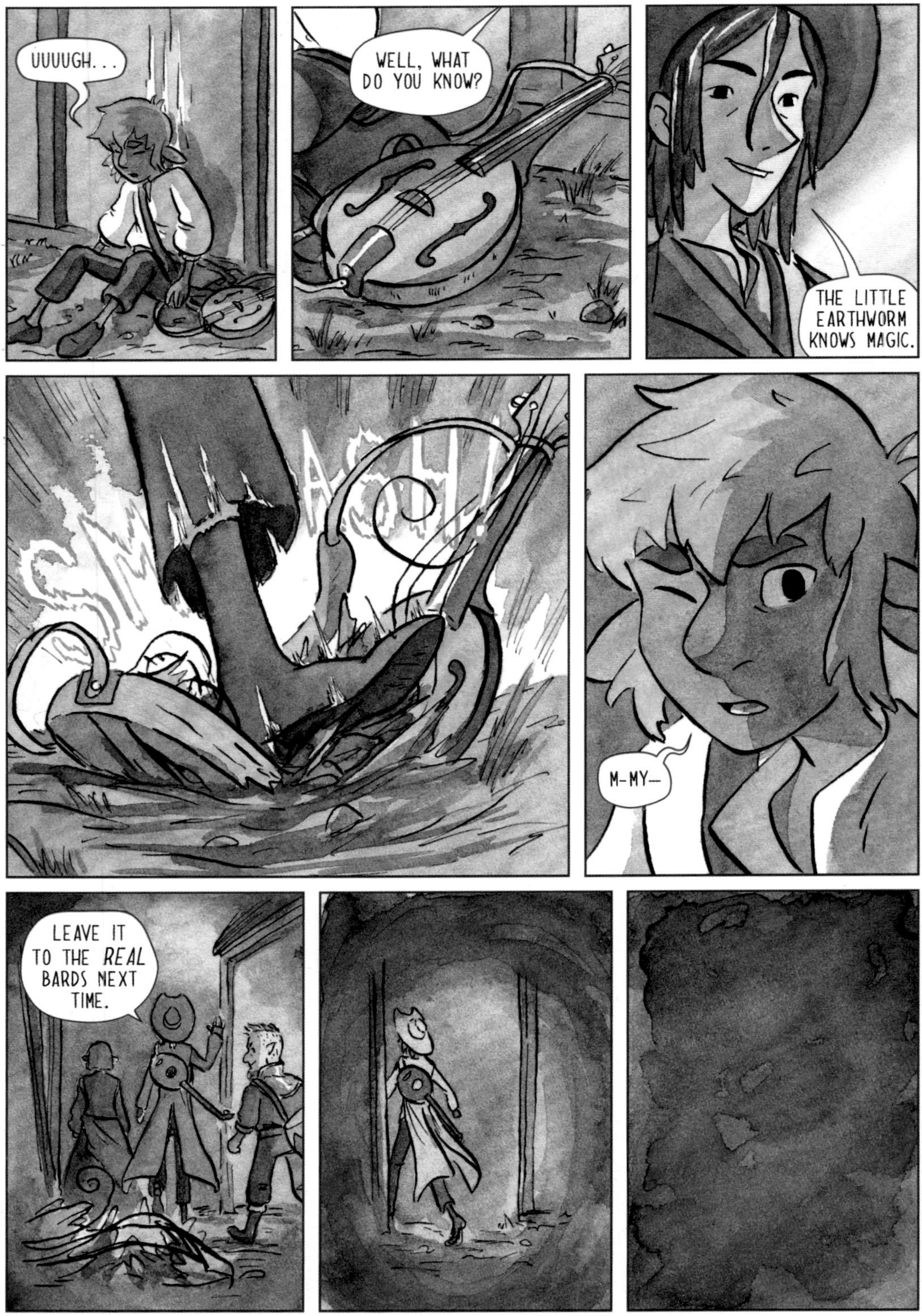
UUUUGH...
WELL, WHAT DO YOU KNOW?
THE LITTLE EARTHWORM KNOWS MAGIC.
M-MY--
LEAVE IT TO THE *REAL* BARDS NEXT TIME.

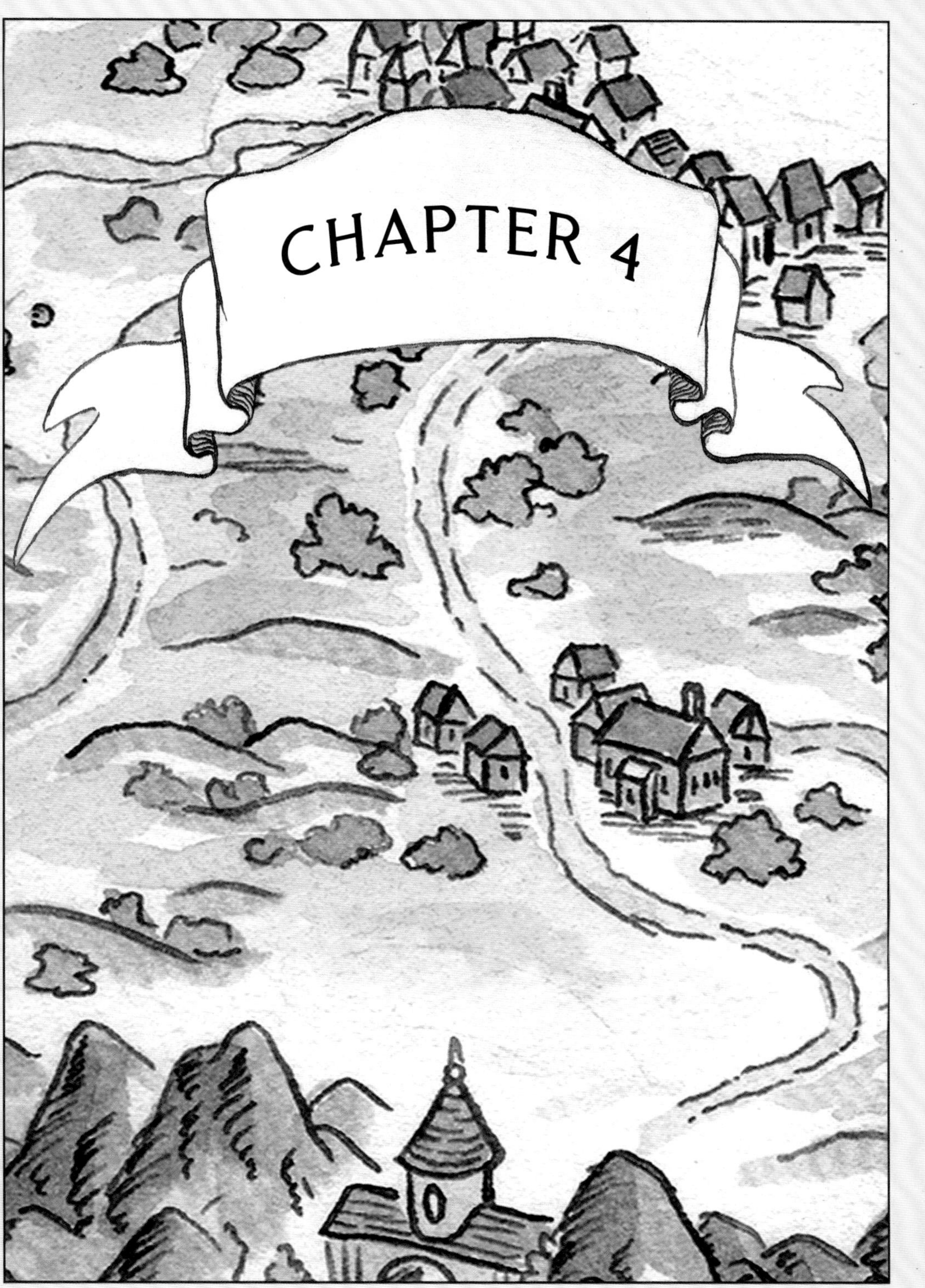
CHAPTER 4

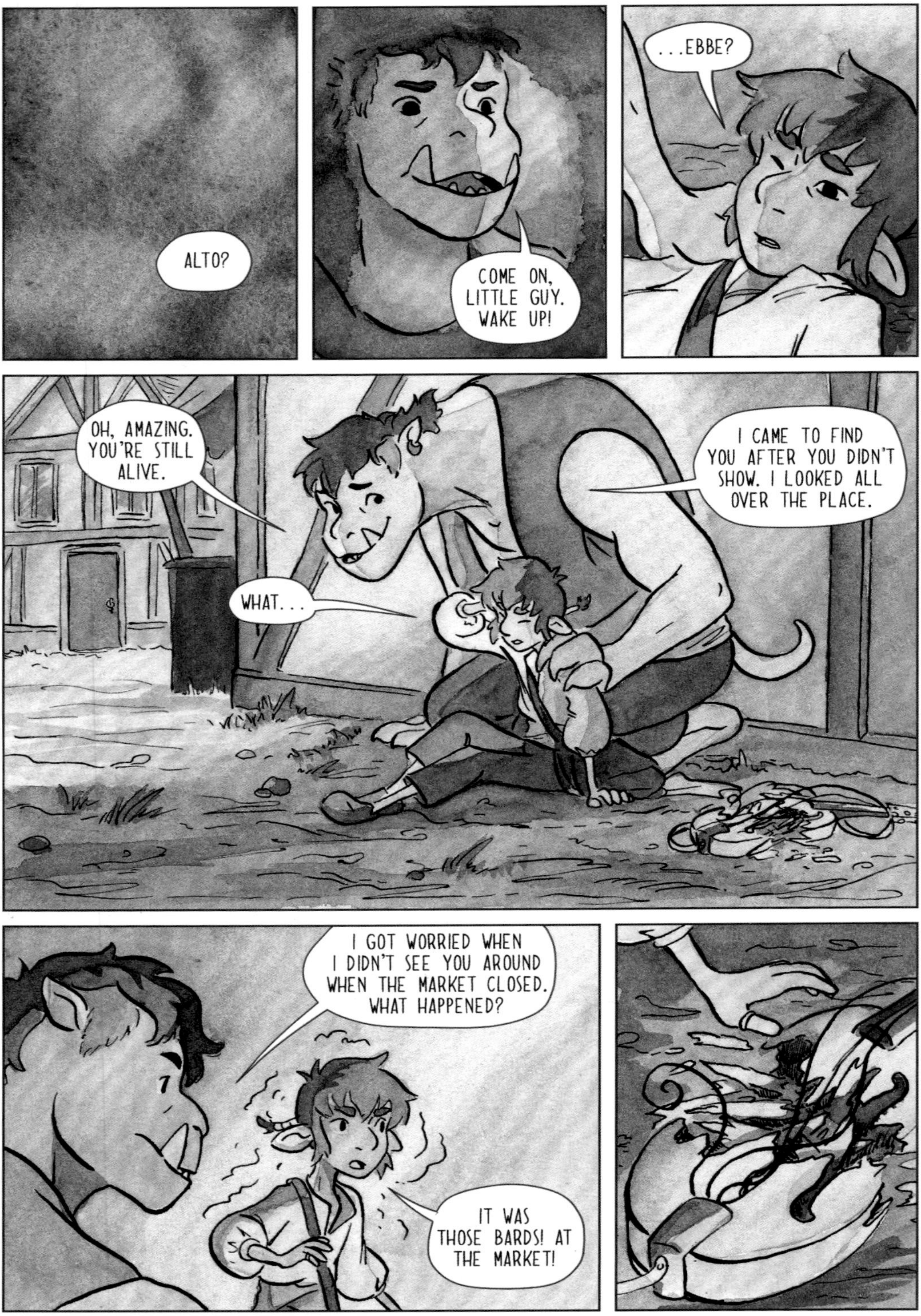
ALTO?
COME ON, LITTLE GUY. WAKE UP!
...EBBE?
OH, AMAZING. YOU'RE STILL ALIVE.
I CAME TO FIND YOU AFTER YOU DIDN'T SHOW. I LOOKED ALL OVER THE PLACE.
WHAT...
I GOT WORRIED WHEN I DIDN'T SEE YOU AROUND WHEN THE MARKET CLOSED. WHAT HAPPENED?
IT WAS THOSE BARDS! AT THE MARKET!

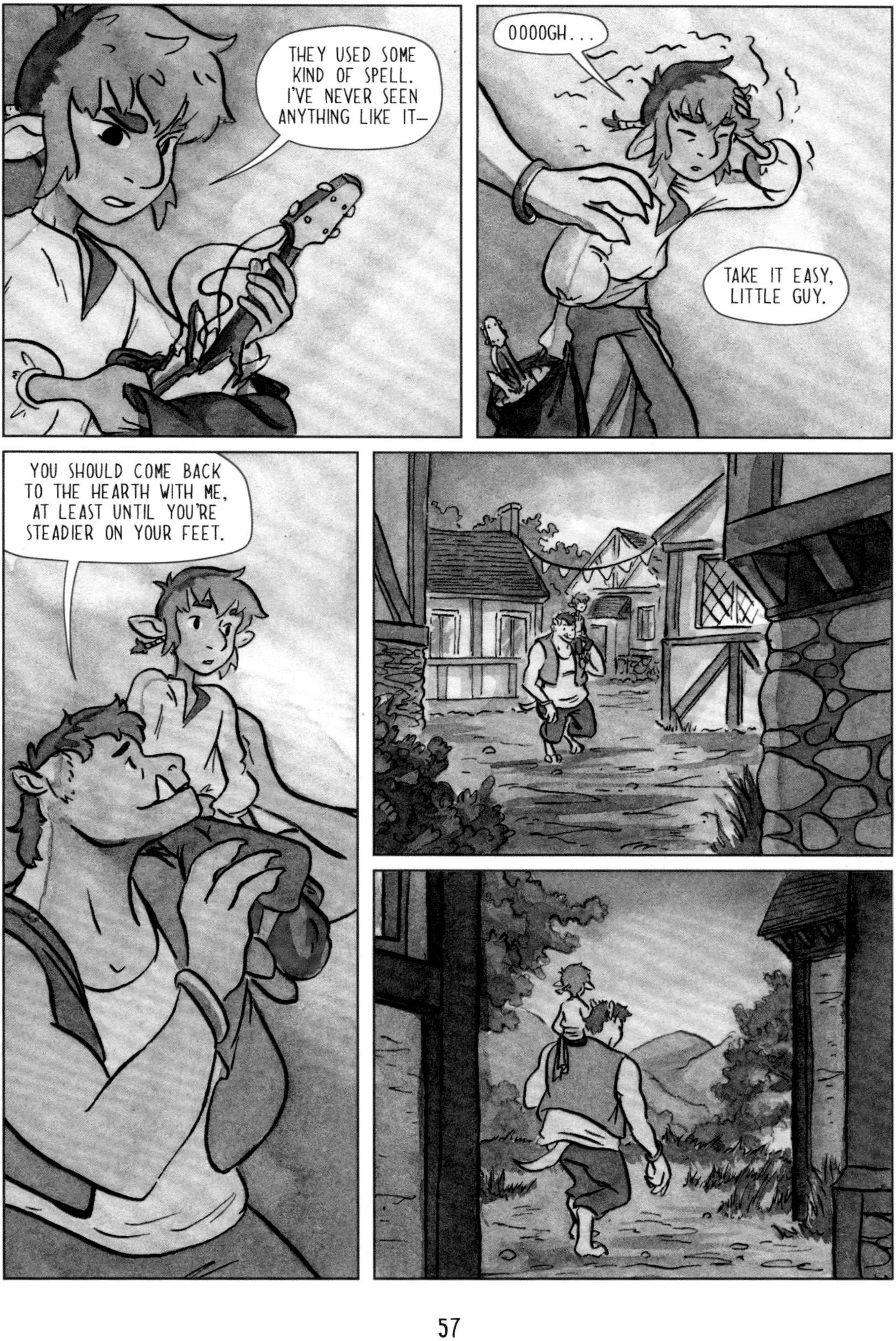
THEY USED SOME KIND OF SPELL. I'VE NEVER SEEN ANYTHING LIKE IT—
OOOOGH...
TAKE IT EASY, LITTLE GUY.
YOU SHOULD COME BACK TO THE HEARTH WITH ME, AT LEAST UNTIL YOU'RE STEADIER ON YOUR FEET.

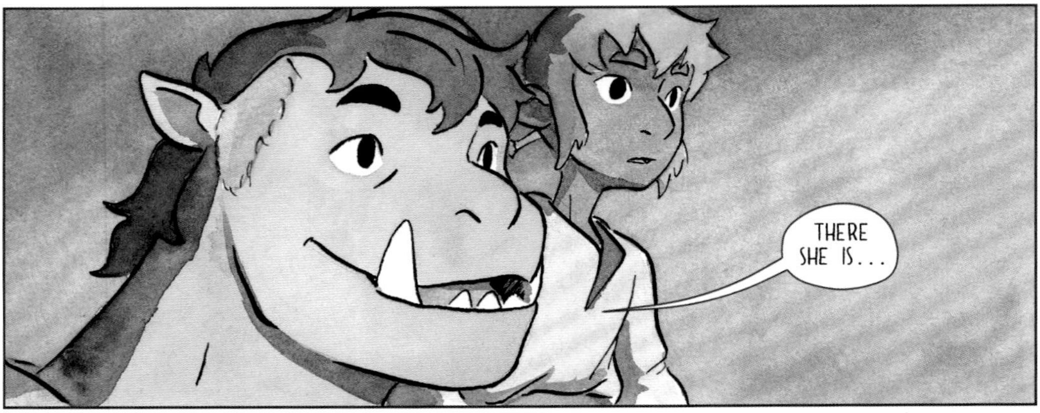
THERE SHE IS...
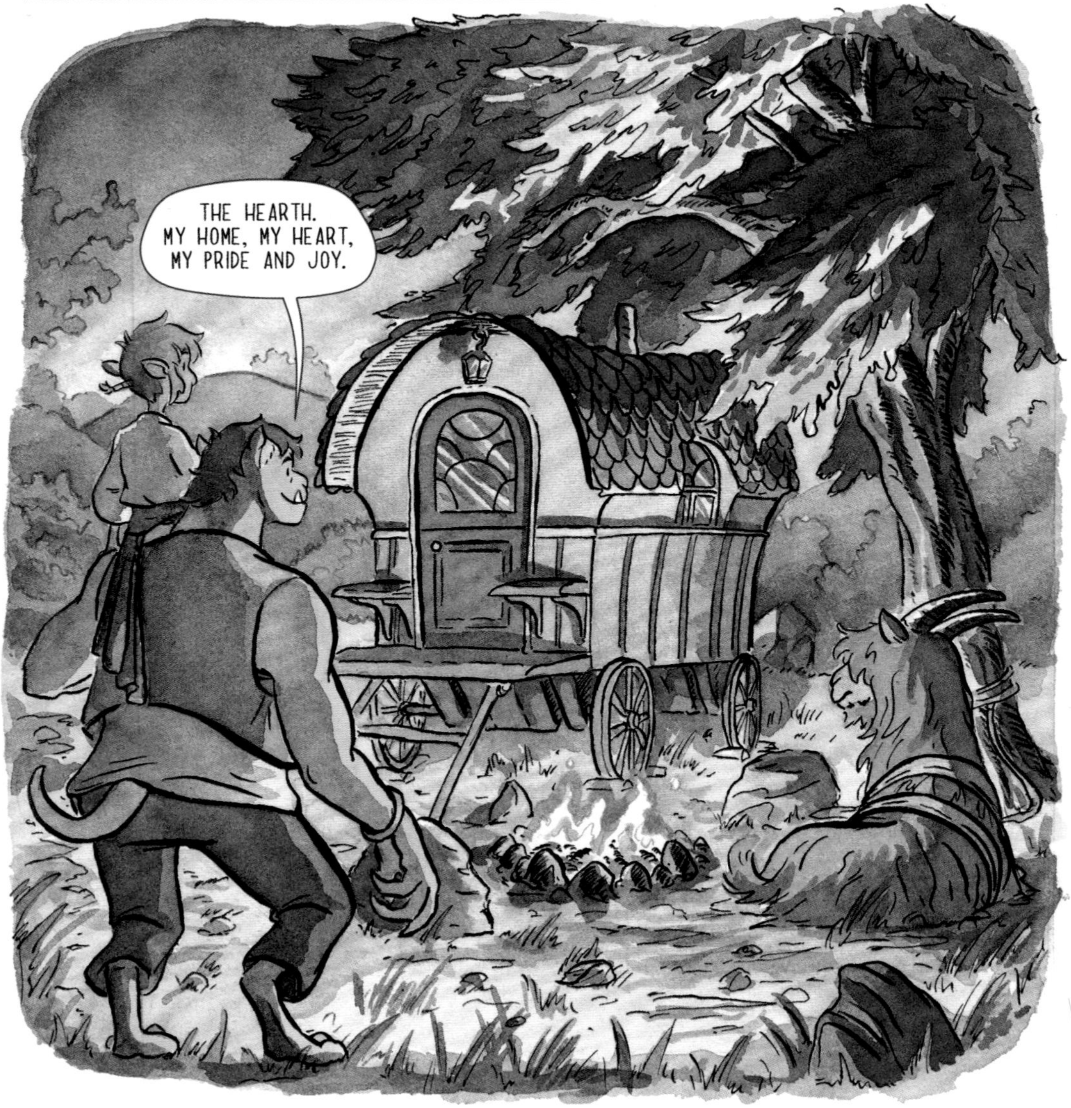
THE HEARTH. MY HOME, MY HEART, MY PRIDE AND JOY.

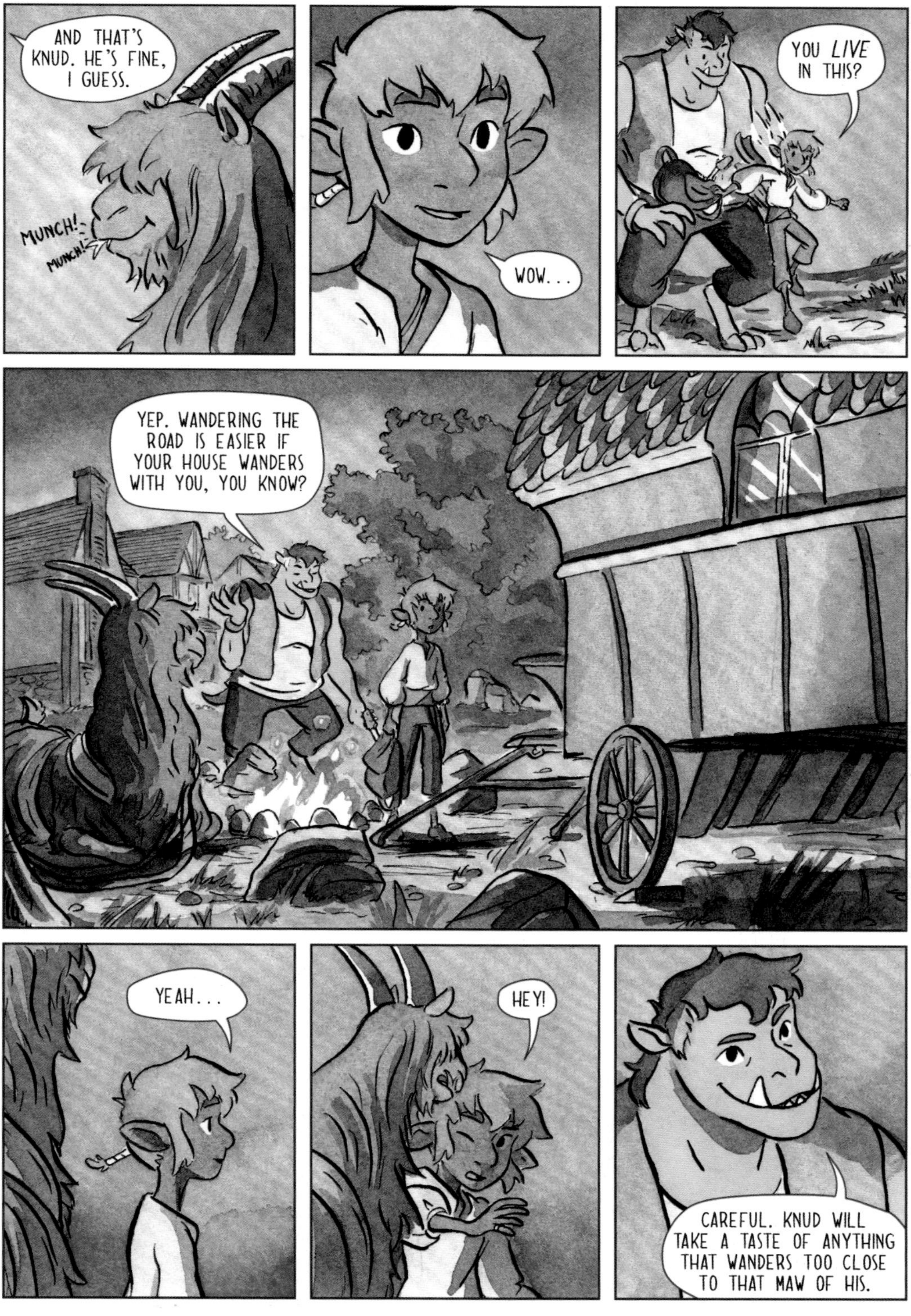
AND THAT'S KNUD. HE'S FINE, I GUESS.
MUNCH! MUNCH!
WOW...
YOU *LIVE* IN THIS?
YEP. WANDERING THE ROAD IS EASIER IF YOUR HOUSE WANDERS WITH YOU, YOU KNOW?
YEAH...
HEY!
CAREFUL. KNUD WILL TAKE A TASTE OF ANYTHING THAT WANDERS TOO CLOSE TO THAT MAW OF HIS.

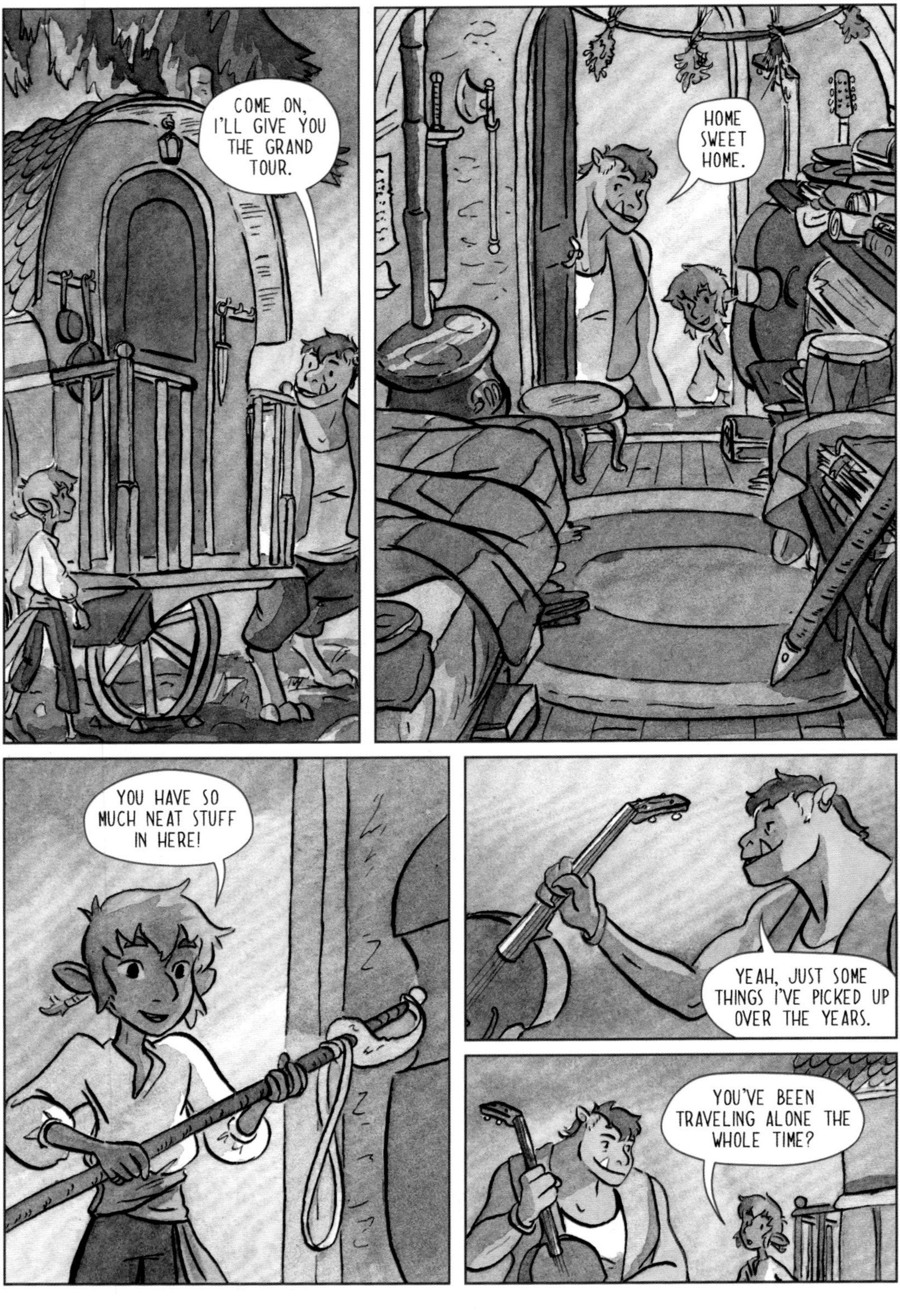
COME ON, I'LL GIVE YOU THE GRAND TOUR.
HOME SWEET HOME.
YOU HAVE SO MUCH NEAT STUFF IN HERE!
YEAH, JUST SOME THINGS I'VE PICKED UP OVER THE YEARS.
YOU'VE BEEN TRAVELING ALONE THE WHOLE TIME?

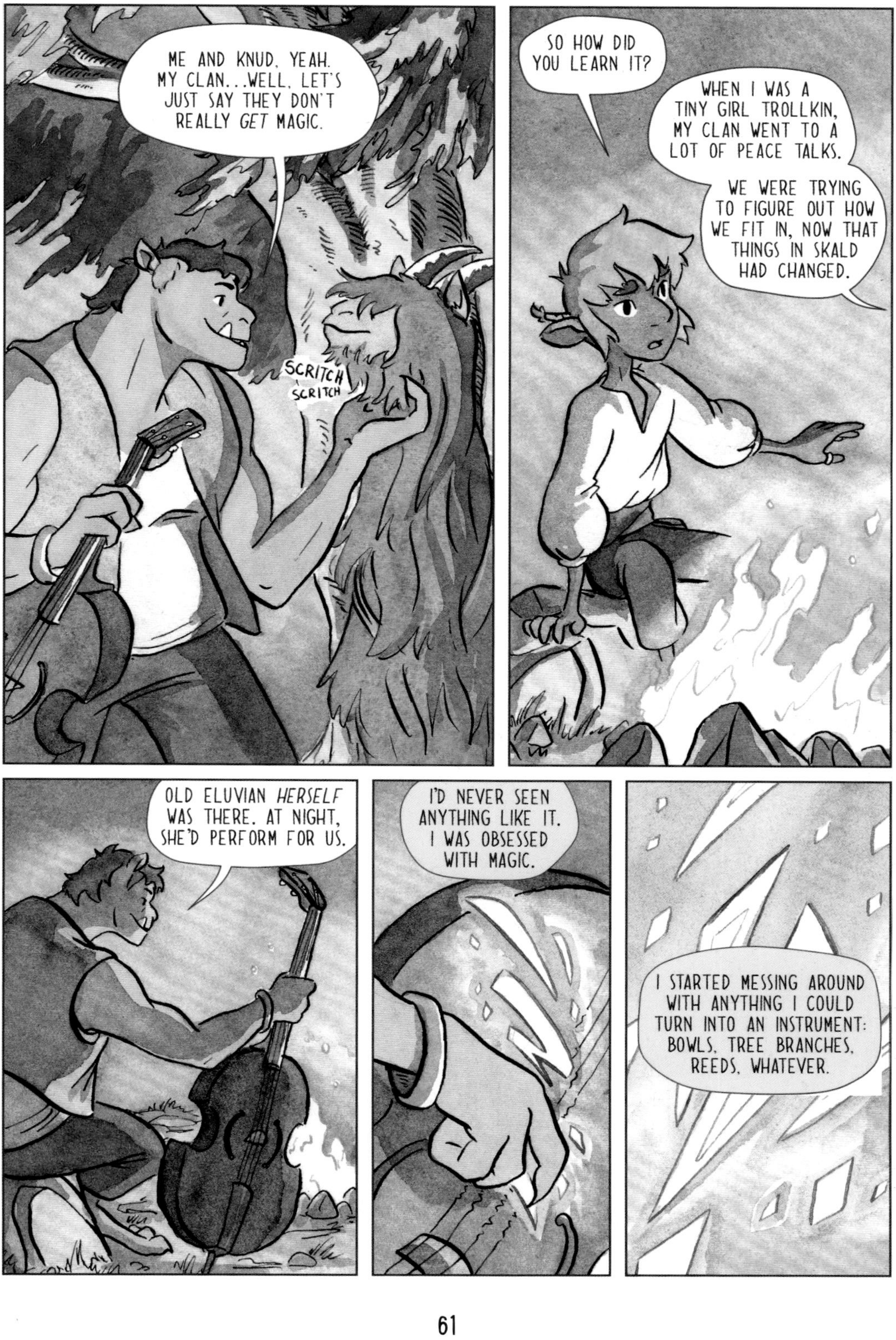
ME AND KNUD, YEAH. MY CLAN...WELL, LET'S JUST SAY THEY DON'T REALLY *GET* MAGIC.
SCRITCH SCRITCH
SO HOW DID YOU LEARN IT?
WHEN I WAS A TINY GIRL TROLLKIN, MY CLAN WENT TO A LOT OF PEACE TALKS.
WE WERE TRYING TO FIGURE OUT HOW WE FIT IN, NOW THAT THINGS IN SKALD HAD CHANGED.
OLD ELUVIAN *HERSELF* WAS THERE. AT NIGHT, SHE'D PERFORM FOR US.
I'D NEVER SEEN ANYTHING LIKE IT. I WAS OBSESSED WITH MAGIC.
I STARTED MESSING AROUND WITH ANYTHING I COULD TURN INTO AN INSTRUMENT: BOWLS, TREE BRANCHES, REEDS, WHATEVER.

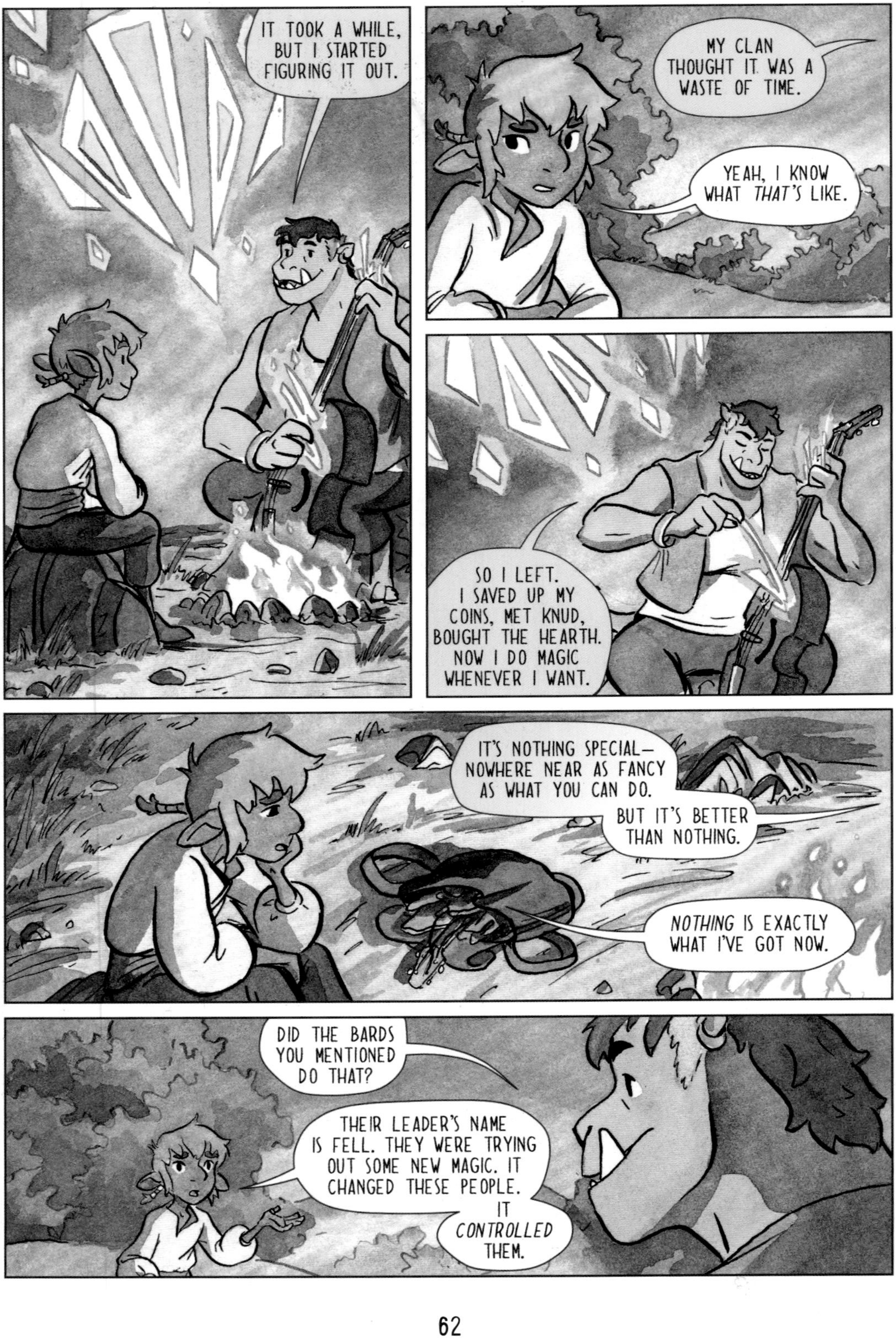
IT TOOK A WHILE, BUT I STARTED FIGURING IT OUT.
MY CLAN THOUGHT IT WAS A WASTE OF TIME.
YEAH, I KNOW WHAT *THAT'S* LIKE.
SO I LEFT. I SAVED UP MY COINS, MET KNUD, BOUGHT THE HEARTH. NOW I DO MAGIC WHENEVER I WANT.
IT'S NOTHING SPECIAL—NOWHERE NEAR AS FANCY AS WHAT YOU CAN DO.
BUT IT'S BETTER THAN NOTHING.
NOTHING IS EXACTLY WHAT I'VE GOT NOW.
DID THE BARDS YOU MENTIONED DO THAT?
THEIR LEADER'S NAME IS FELL. THEY WERE TRYING OUT SOME NEW MAGIC. IT CHANGED THESE PEOPLE.
IT *CONTROLLED* THEM.

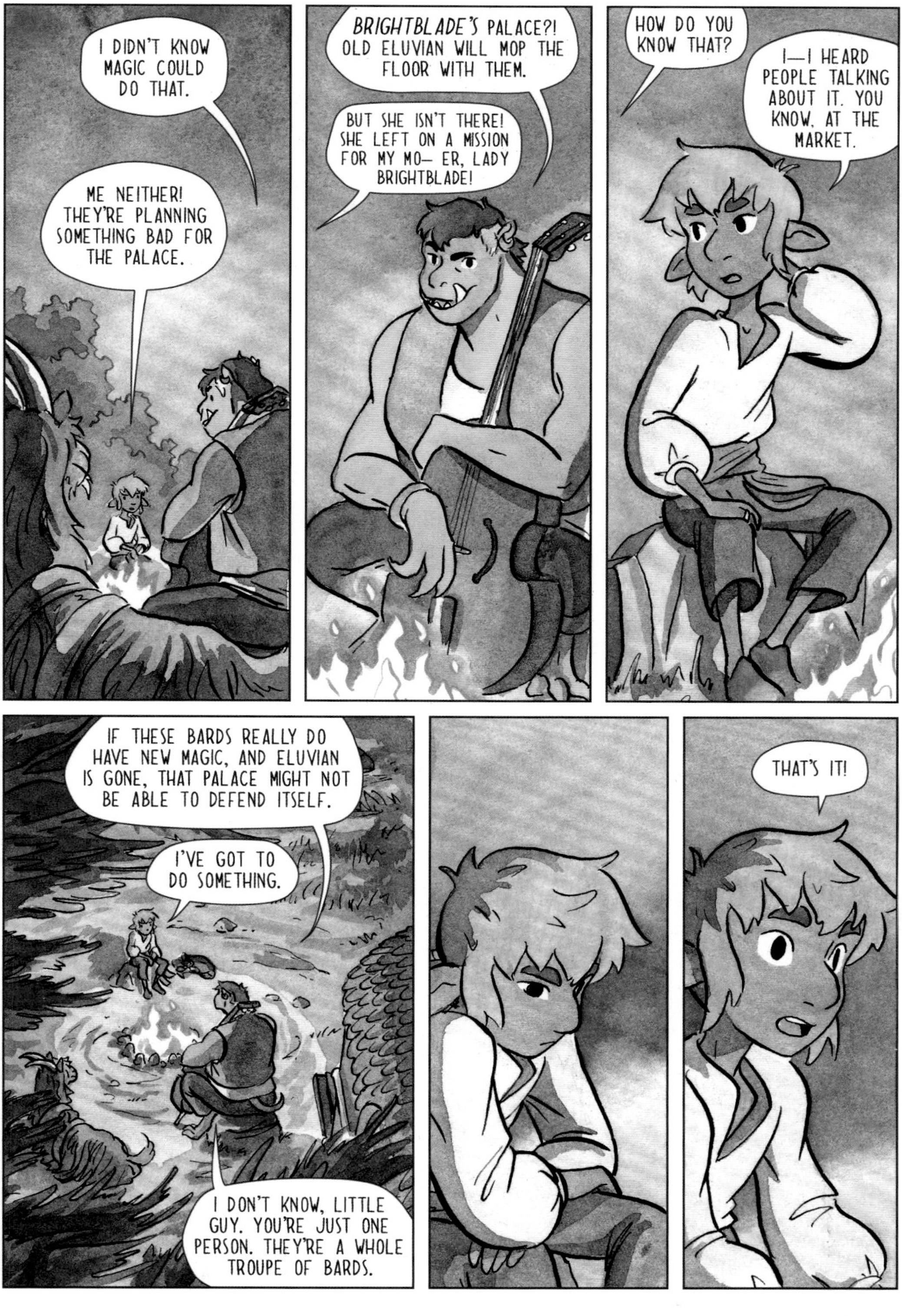
I DIDN'T KNOW MAGIC COULD DO THAT.
ME NEITHER! THEY'RE PLANNING SOMETHING BAD FOR THE PALACE.
BRIGHTBLADE'S PALACE?! OLD ELUVIAN WILL MOP THE FLOOR WITH THEM.
BUT SHE ISN'T THERE! SHE LEFT ON A MISSION FOR MY MO— ER, LADY BRIGHTBLADE!
HOW DO YOU KNOW THAT?
I—I HEARD PEOPLE TALKING ABOUT IT. YOU KNOW, AT THE MARKET.
IF THESE BARDS REALLY DO HAVE NEW MAGIC, AND ELUVIAN IS GONE, THAT PALACE MIGHT NOT BE ABLE TO DEFEND ITSELF.
I'VE GOT TO DO SOMETHING.
I DON'T KNOW, LITTLE GUY. YOU'RE JUST ONE PERSON. THEY'RE A WHOLE TROUPE OF BARDS.
THAT'S IT!

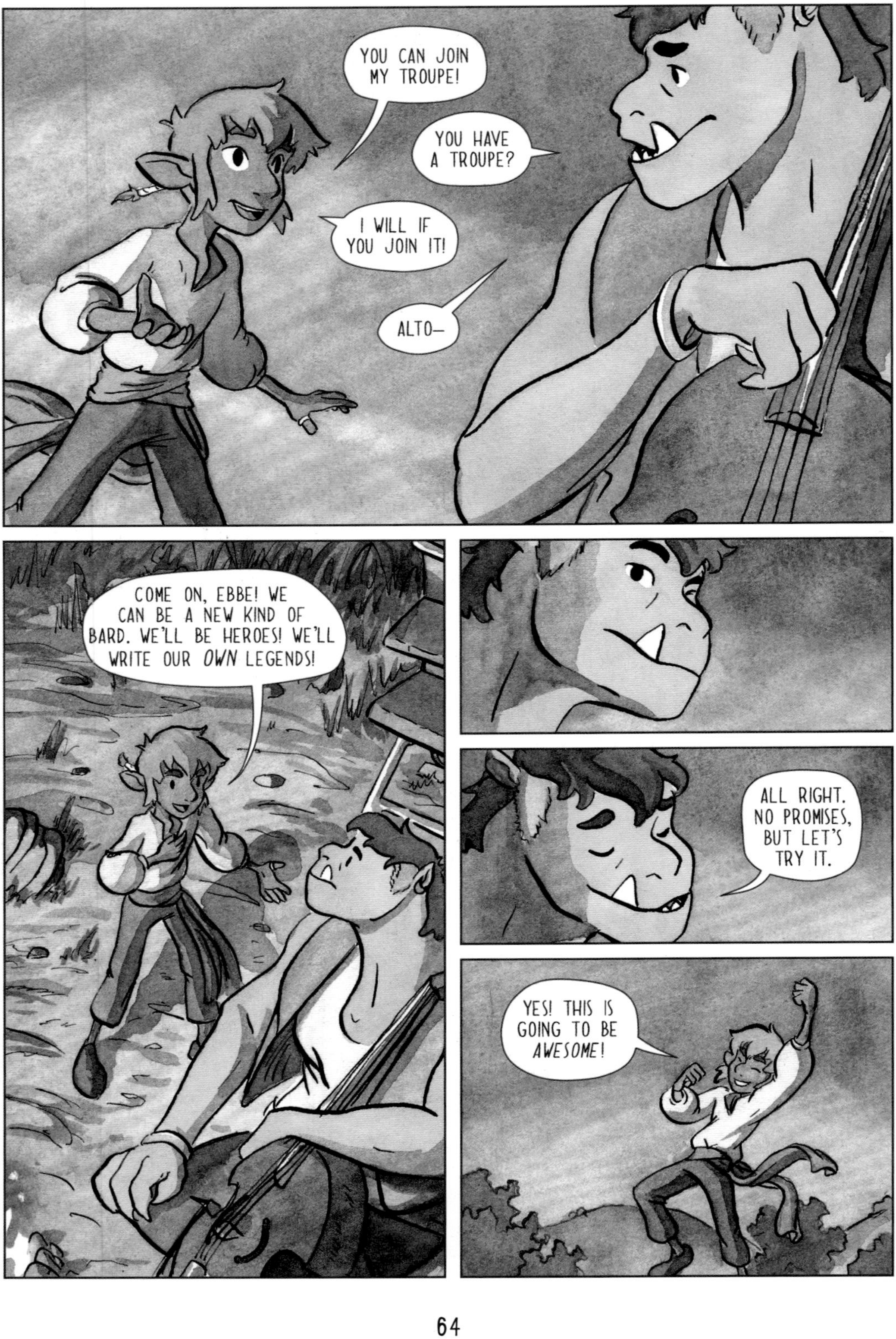
YOU CAN JOIN MY TROUPE!
YOU HAVE A TROUPE?
I WILL IF YOU JOIN IT!
ALTO—
COME ON, EBBE! WE CAN BE A NEW KIND OF BARD. WE'LL BE HEROES! WE'LL WRITE OUR *OWN* LEGENDS!
ALL RIGHT. NO PROMISES, BUT LET'S TRY IT.
YES! THIS IS GOING TO BE *AWESOME*!

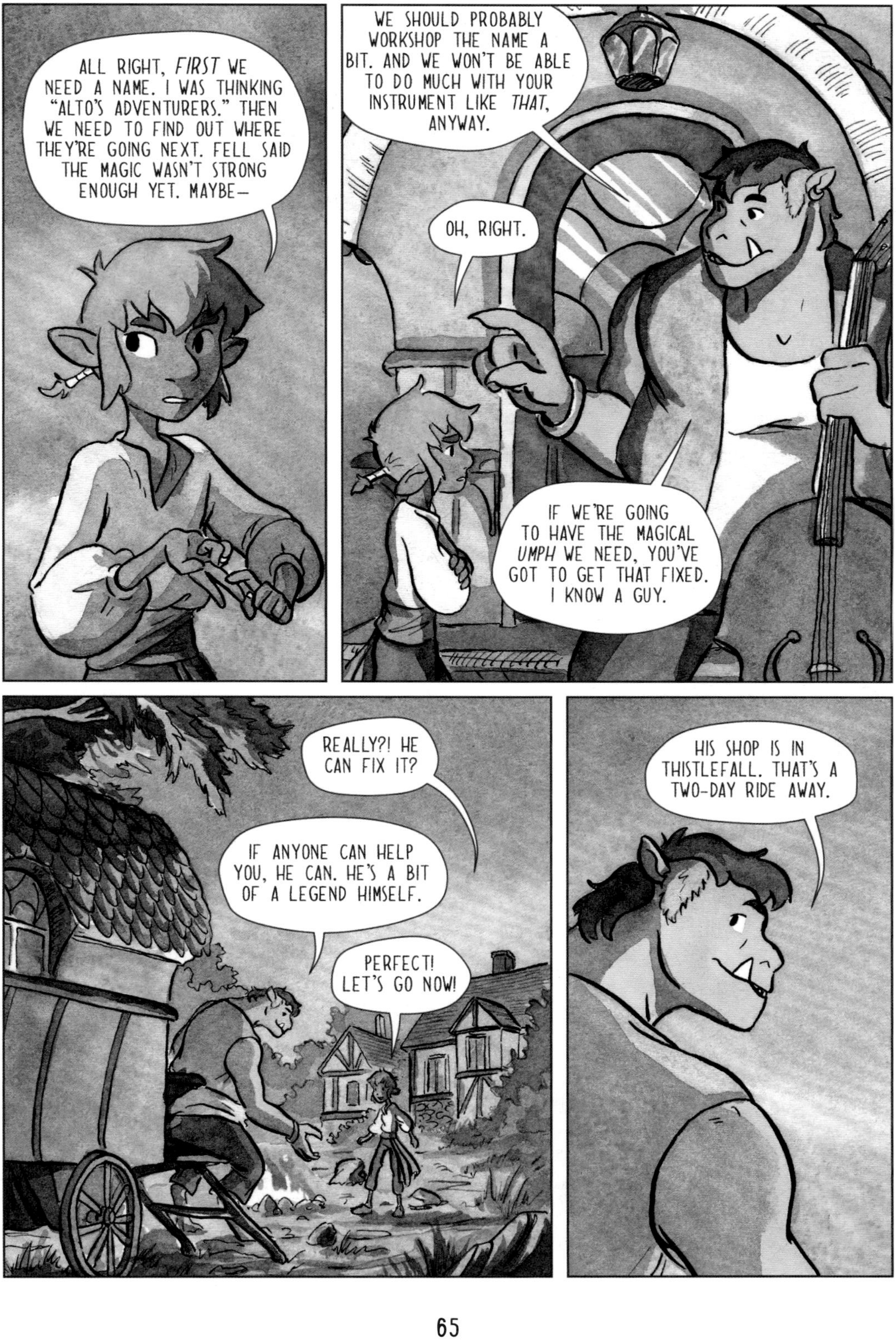
ALL RIGHT, *FIRST* WE NEED A NAME. I WAS THINKING "ALTO'S ADVENTURERS." THEN WE NEED TO FIND OUT WHERE THEY'RE GOING NEXT. FELL SAID THE MAGIC WASN'T STRONG ENOUGH YET. MAYBE—
WE SHOULD PROBABLY WORKSHOP THE NAME A BIT. AND WE WON'T BE ABLE TO DO MUCH WITH YOUR INSTRUMENT LIKE *THAT*, ANYWAY.
OH, RIGHT.
IF WE'RE GOING TO HAVE THE MAGICAL *UMPH* WE NEED, YOU'VE GOT TO GET THAT FIXED. I KNOW A GUY.
REALLY?! HE CAN FIX IT?
IF ANYONE CAN HELP YOU, HE CAN. HE'S A BIT OF A LEGEND HIMSELF.
PERFECT! LET'S GO NOW!
HIS SHOP IS IN THISTLEFALL. THAT'S A TWO-DAY RIDE AWAY.

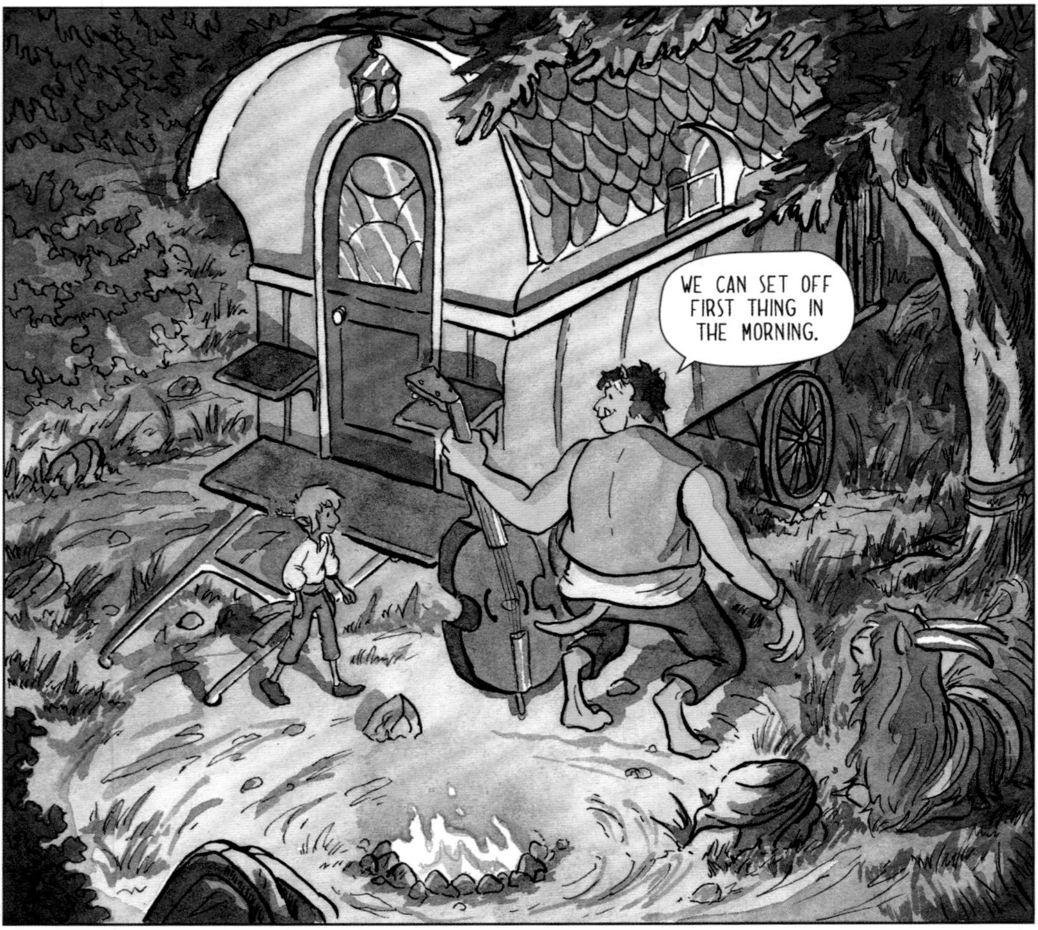
WE CAN SET OFF FIRST THING IN THE MORNING.

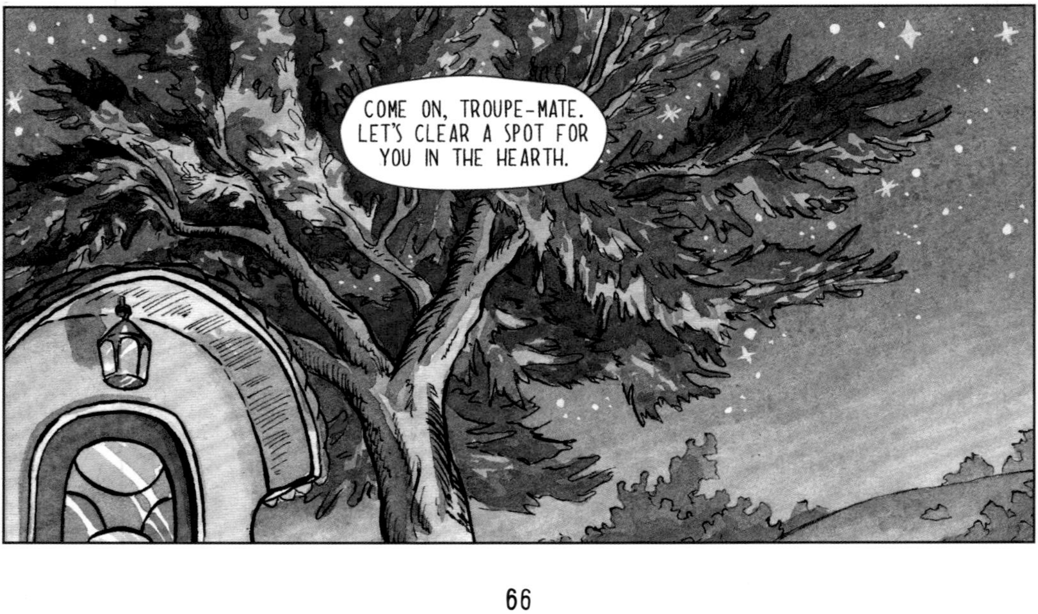
COME ON, TROUPE-MATE. LET'S CLEAR A SPOT FOR YOU IN THE HEARTH.

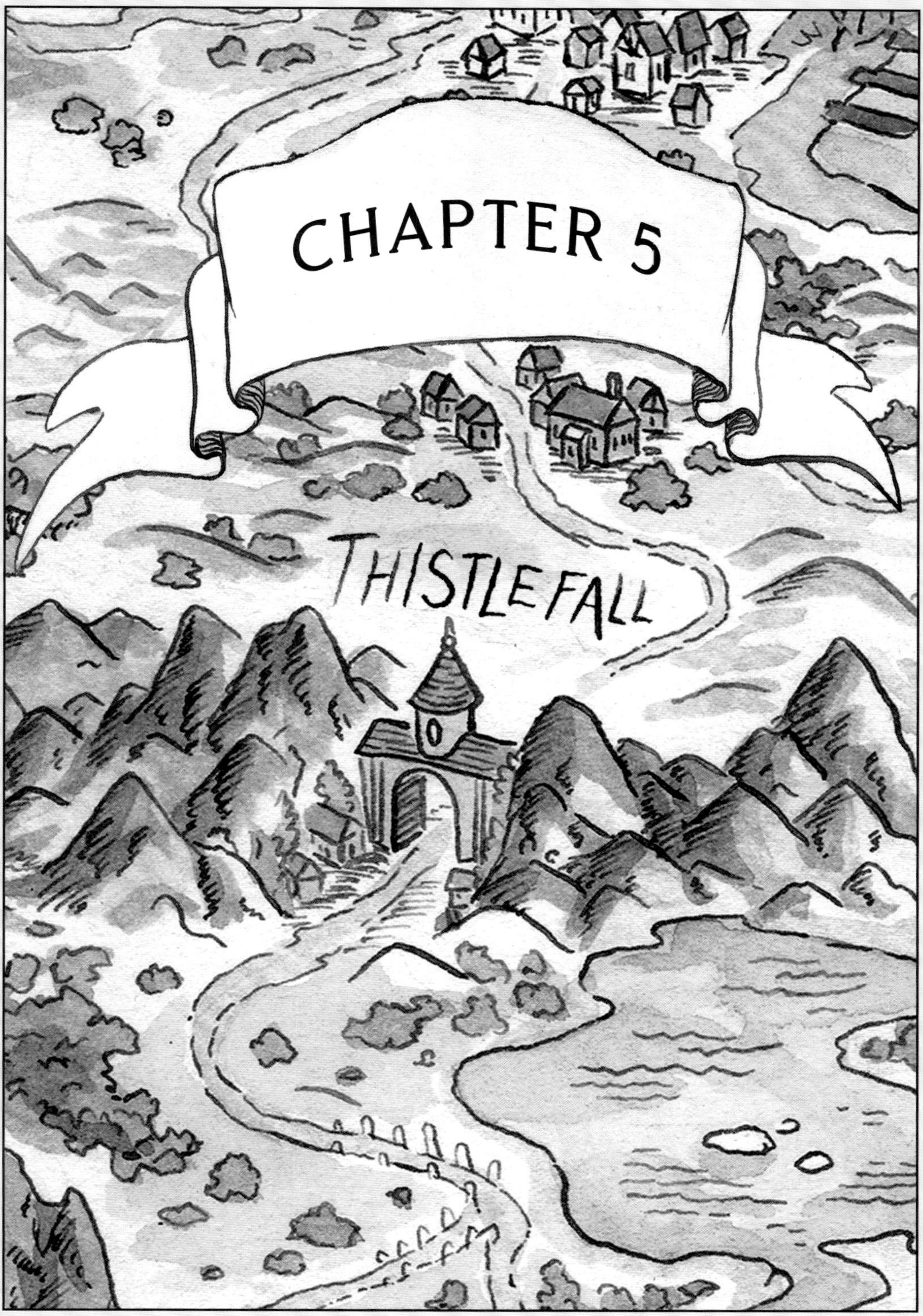
CHAPTER 5
THISTLEFALL

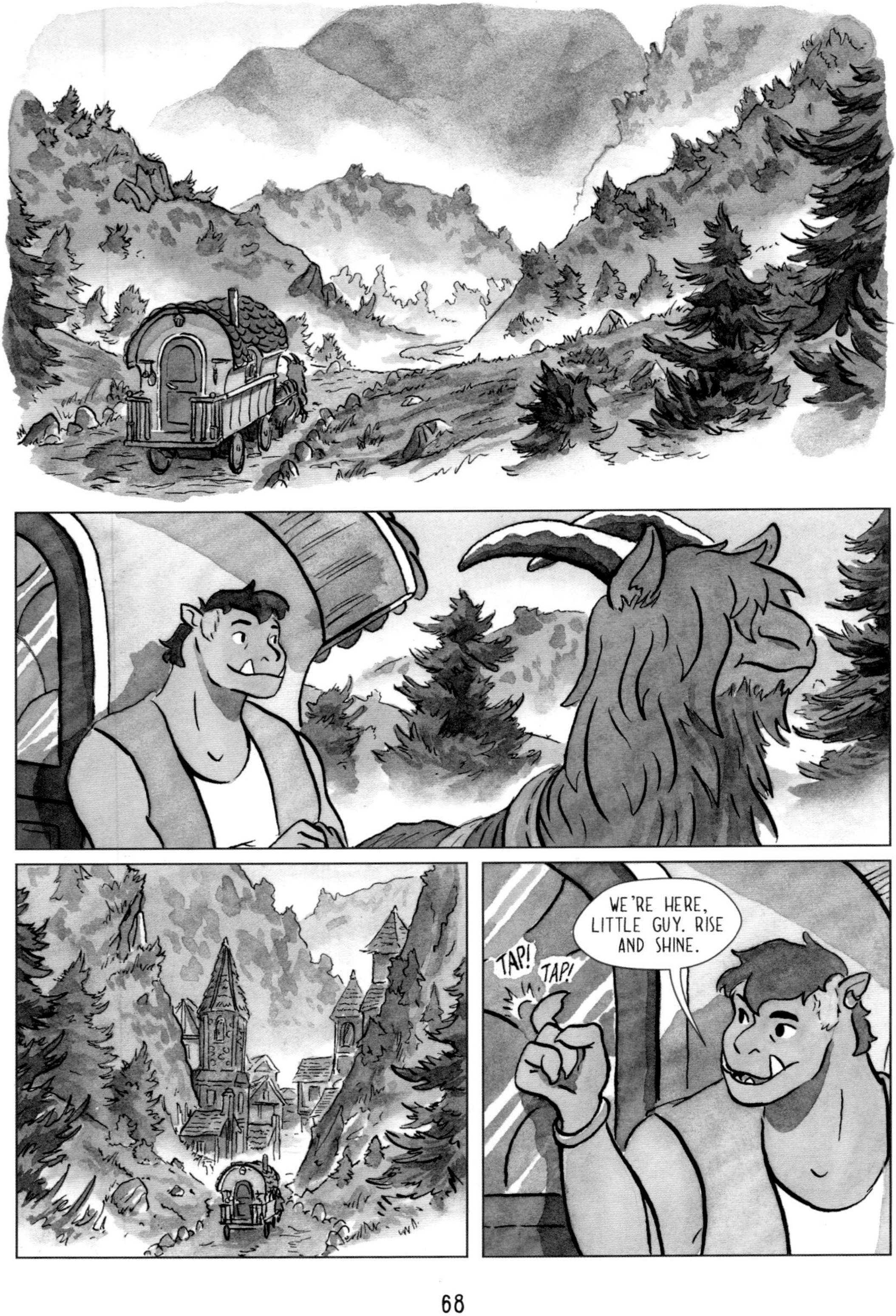
WE'RE HERE, LITTLE GUY. RISE AND SHINE.
TAP! TAP!

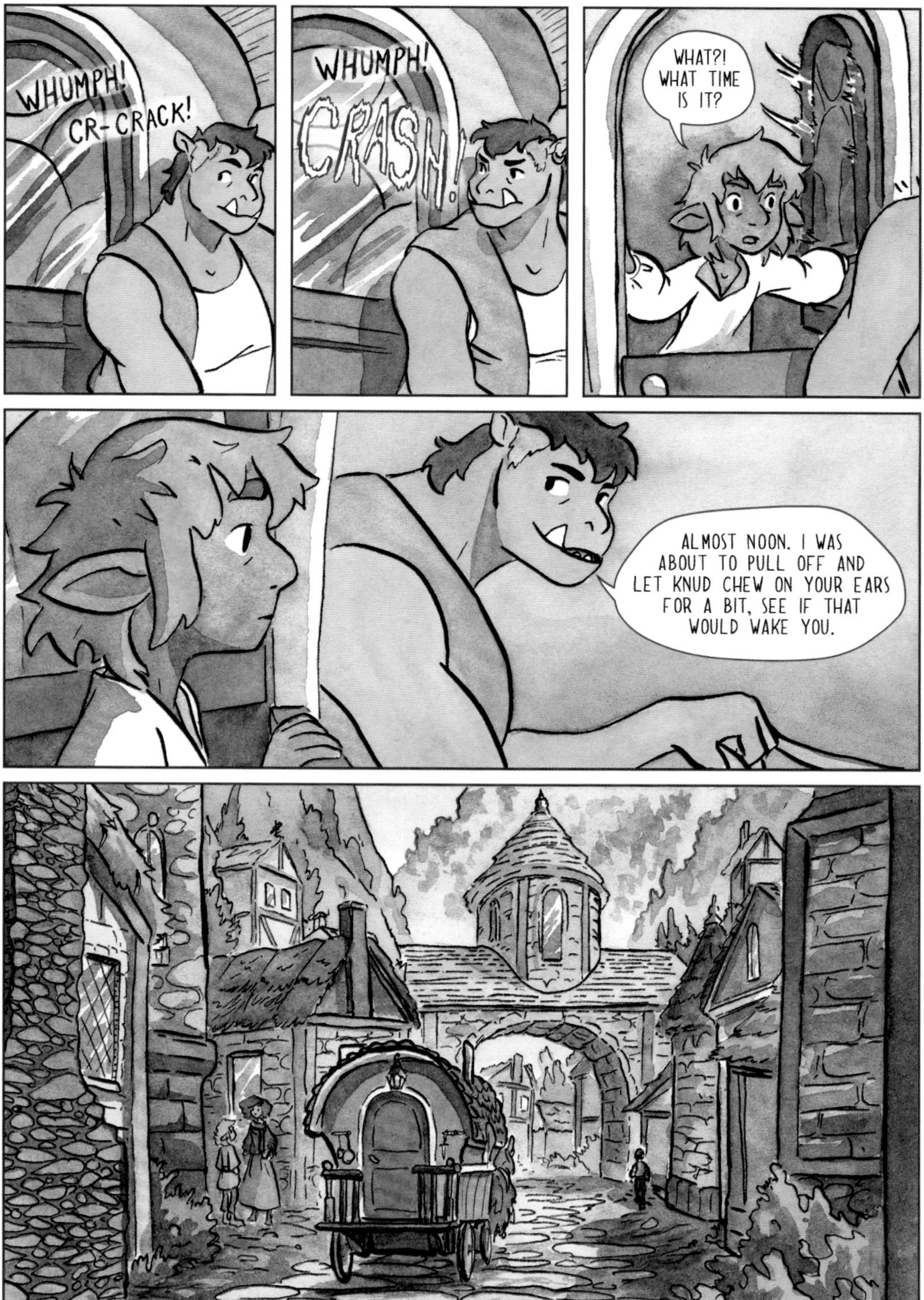
WHUMPH!
CR-CRACK!
WHUMPH!
CRASH!
WHAT?! WHAT TIME IS IT?
ALMOST NOON. I WAS ABOUT TO PULL OFF AND LET KNUD CHEW ON YOUR EARS FOR A BIT, SEE IF THAT WOULD WAKE YOU.

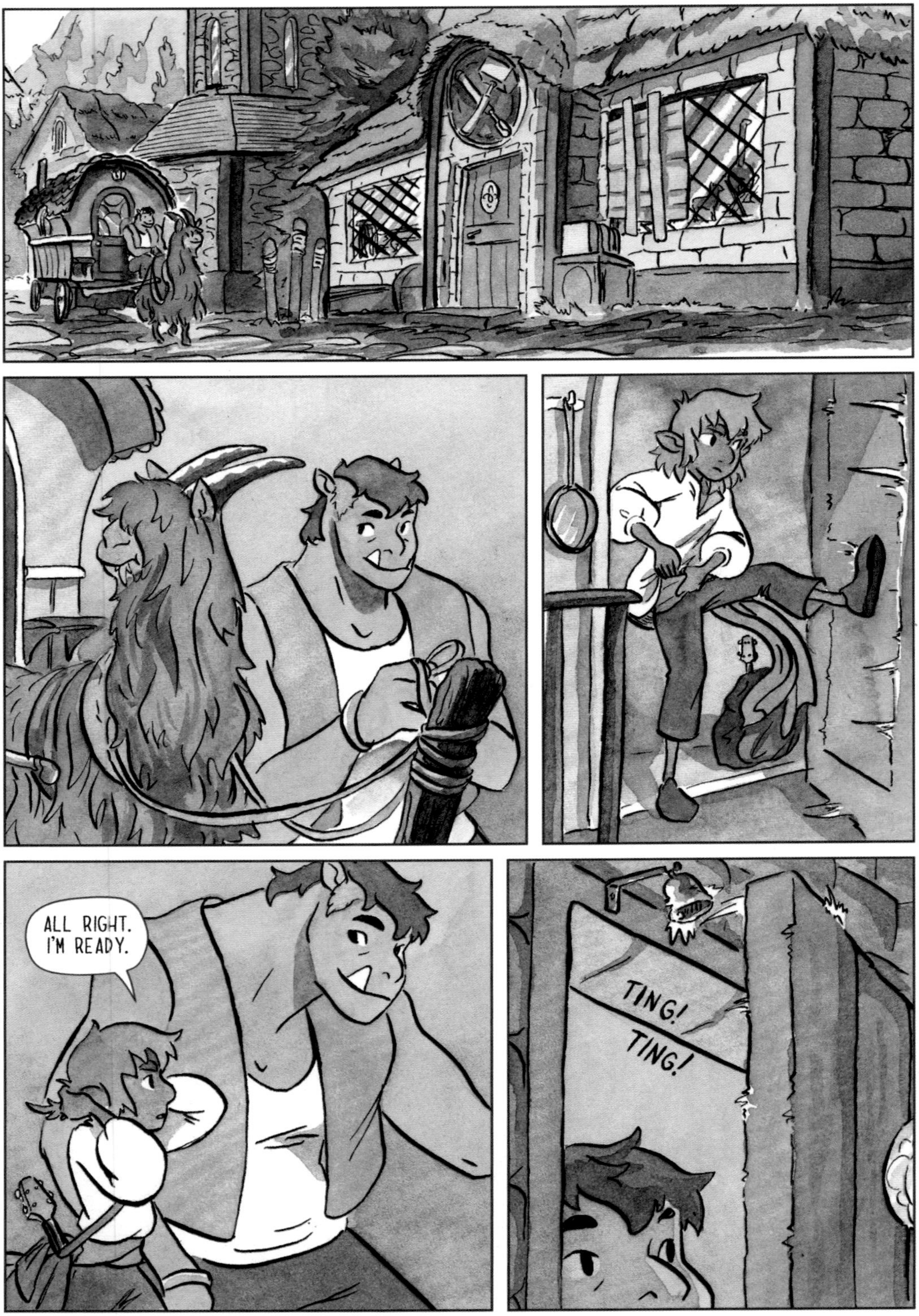
ALL RIGHT.
I'M READY.
TING!
TING!

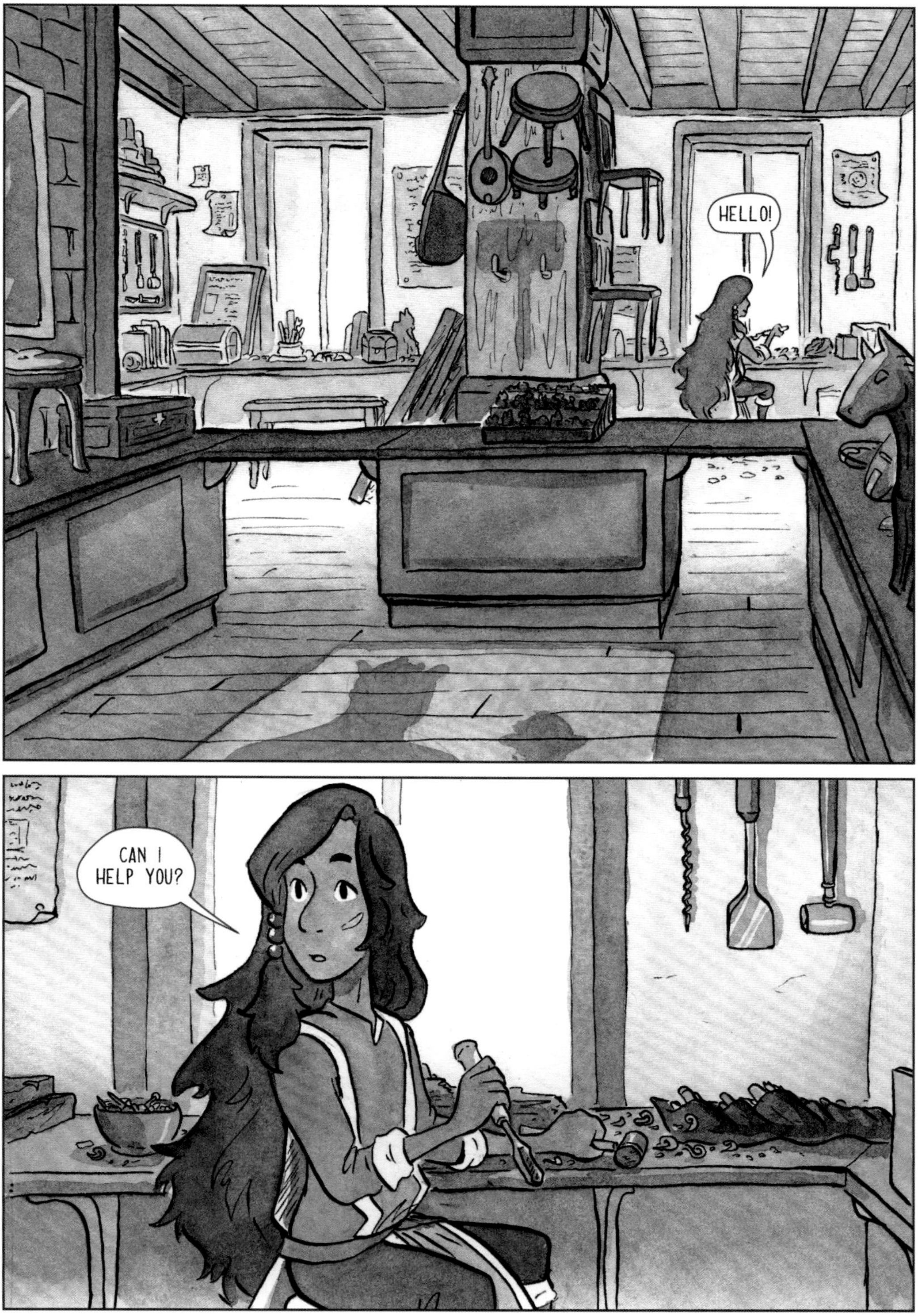
HELLO!
CAN I HELP YOU?

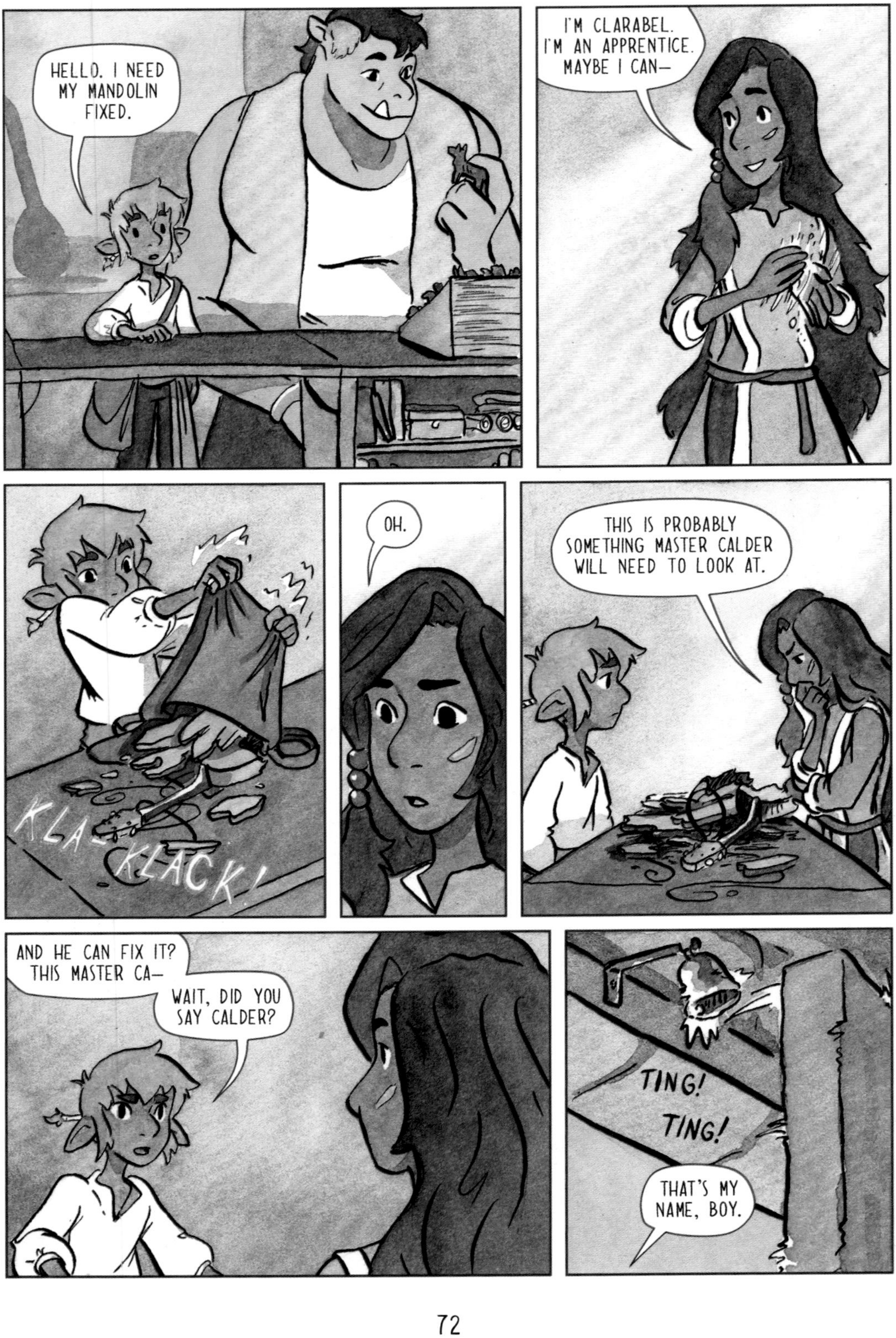
HELLO. I NEED MY MANDOLIN FIXED.
I'M CLARABEL. I'M AN APPRENTICE. MAYBE I CAN—
KLA-KLACK!
OH.
THIS IS PROBABLY SOMETHING MASTER CALDER WILL NEED TO LOOK AT.
AND HE CAN FIX IT? THIS MASTER CA—
WAIT, DID YOU SAY CALDER?
TING!
TING!
THAT'S MY NAME, BOY.

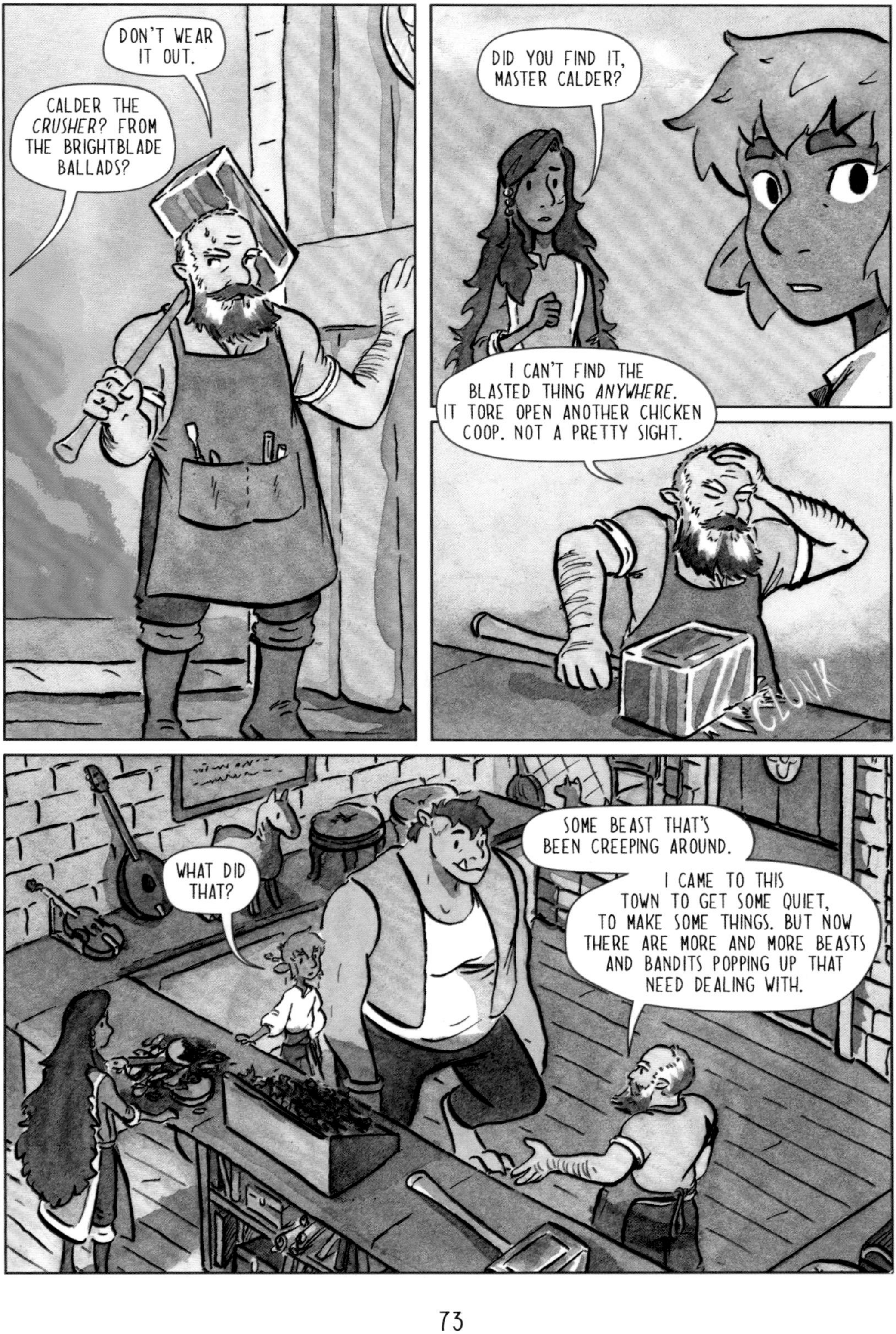
CALDER THE *CRUSHER*? FROM THE BRIGHTBLADE BALLADS?
DON'T WEAR IT OUT.
DID YOU FIND IT, MASTER CALDER?
I CAN'T FIND THE BLASTED THING *ANYWHERE*. IT TORE OPEN ANOTHER CHICKEN COOP. NOT A PRETTY SIGHT.
CLUNK
WHAT DID THAT?
SOME BEAST THAT'S BEEN CREEPING AROUND.
I CAME TO THIS TOWN TO GET SOME QUIET, TO MAKE SOME THINGS. BUT NOW THERE ARE MORE AND MORE BEASTS AND BANDITS POPPING UP THAT NEED DEALING WITH.

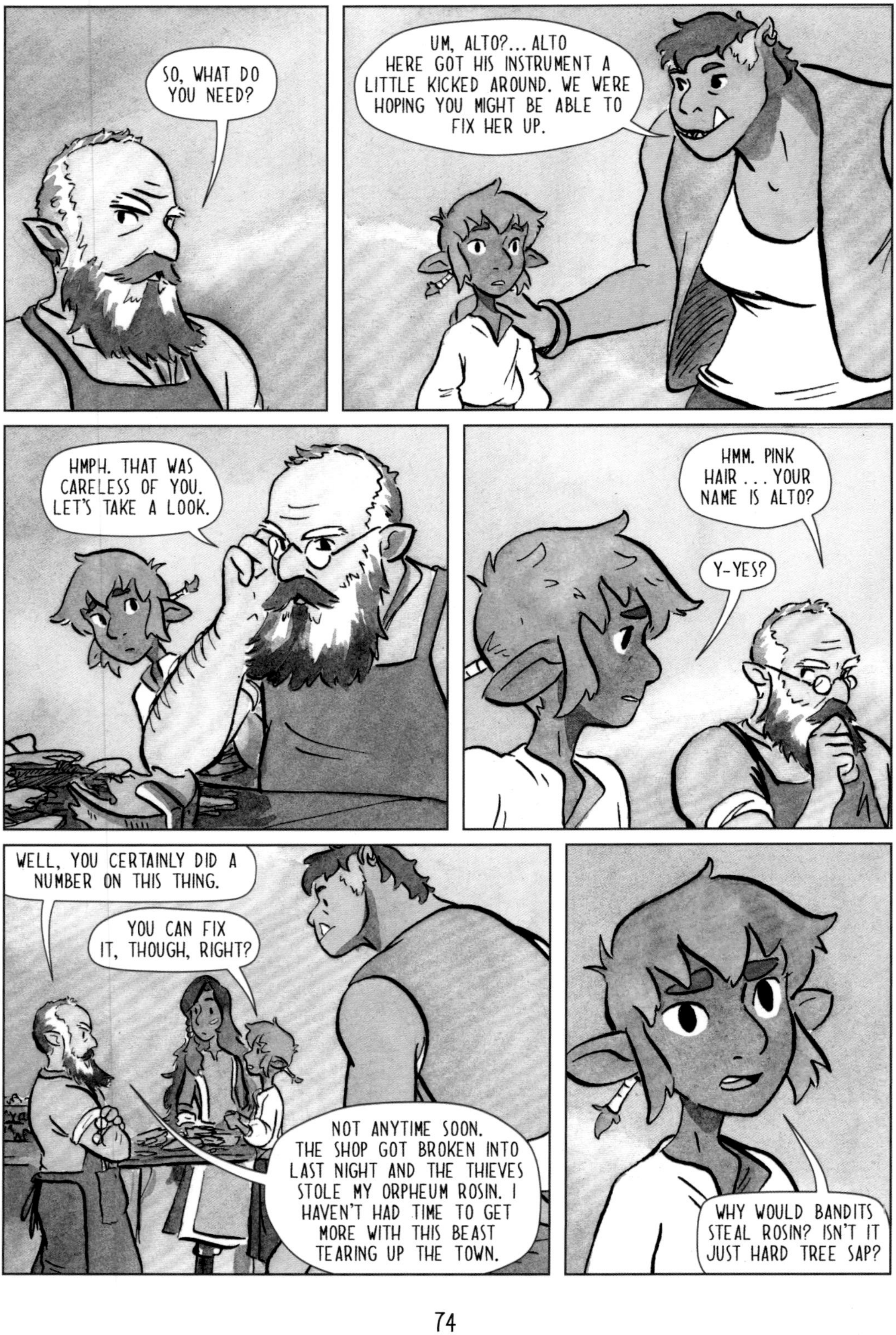
SO, WHAT DO YOU NEED?
UM, ALTO?... ALTO HERE GOT HIS INSTRUMENT A LITTLE KICKED AROUND. WE WERE HOPING YOU MIGHT BE ABLE TO FIX HER UP.
HMPH. THAT WAS CARELESS OF YOU. LET'S TAKE A LOOK.
HMM. PINK HAIR . . . YOUR NAME IS ALTO?
Y-YES?
WELL, YOU CERTAINLY DID A NUMBER ON THIS THING.
YOU CAN FIX IT, THOUGH, RIGHT?
NOT ANYTIME SOON. THE SHOP GOT BROKEN INTO LAST NIGHT AND THE THIEVES STOLE MY ORPHEUM ROSIN. I HAVEN'T HAD TIME TO GET MORE WITH THIS BEAST TEARING UP THE TOWN.
WHY WOULD BANDITS STEAL ROSIN? ISN'T IT JUST HARD TREE SAP?

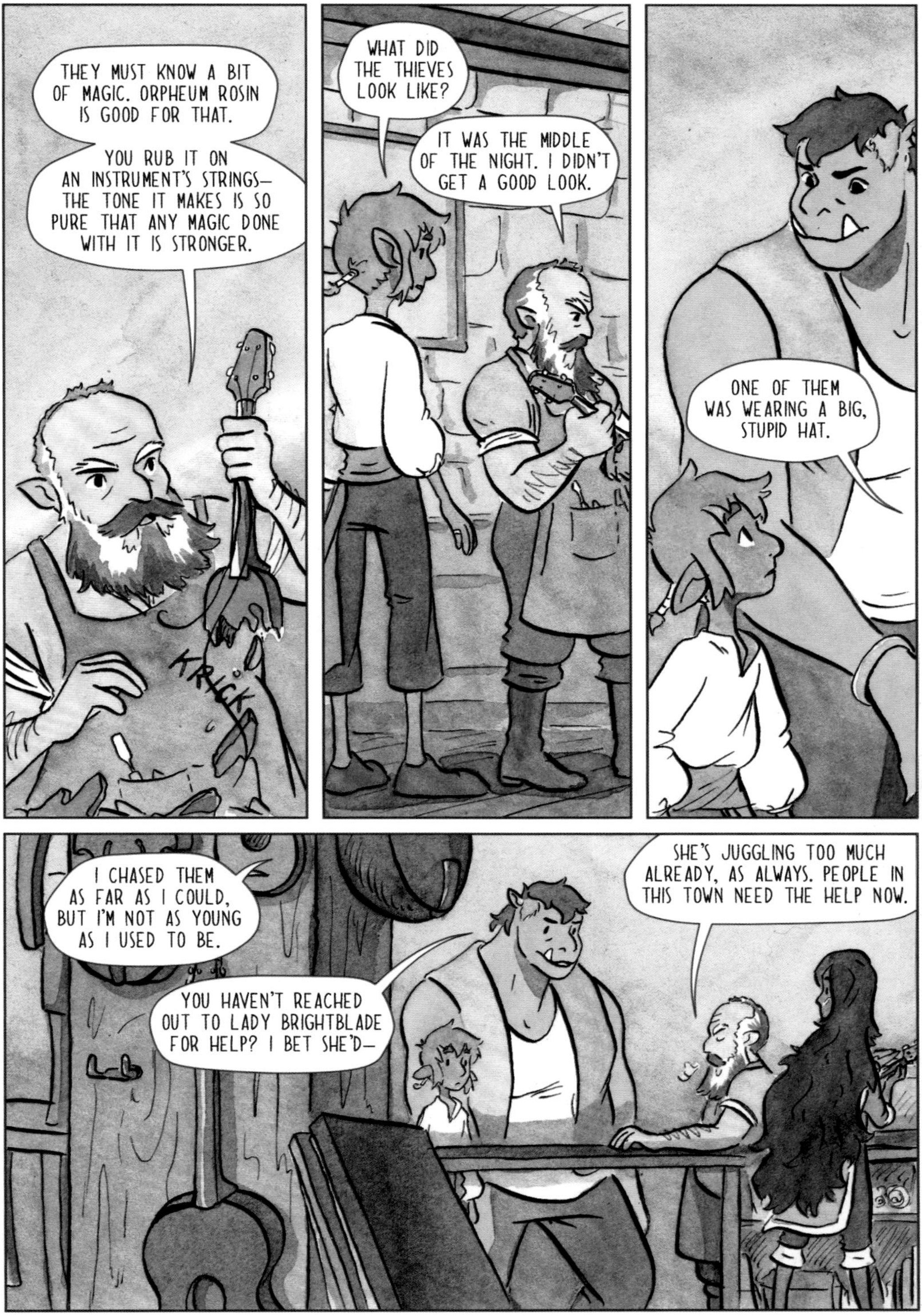
THEY MUST KNOW A BIT OF MAGIC. ORPHEUM ROSIN IS GOOD FOR THAT.
YOU RUB IT ON AN INSTRUMENT'S STRINGS—THE TONE IT MAKES IS SO PURE THAT ANY MAGIC DONE WITH IT IS STRONGER.
KRICK
WHAT DID THE THIEVES LOOK LIKE?
IT WAS THE MIDDLE OF THE NIGHT. I DIDN'T GET A GOOD LOOK.
ONE OF THEM WAS WEARING A BIG, STUPID HAT.
I CHASED THEM AS FAR AS I COULD, BUT I'M NOT AS YOUNG AS I USED TO BE.
YOU HAVEN'T REACHED OUT TO LADY BRIGHTBLADE FOR HELP? I BET SHE'D—
SHE'S JUGGLING TOO MUCH ALREADY, AS ALWAYS. PEOPLE IN THIS TOWN NEED THE HELP NOW.

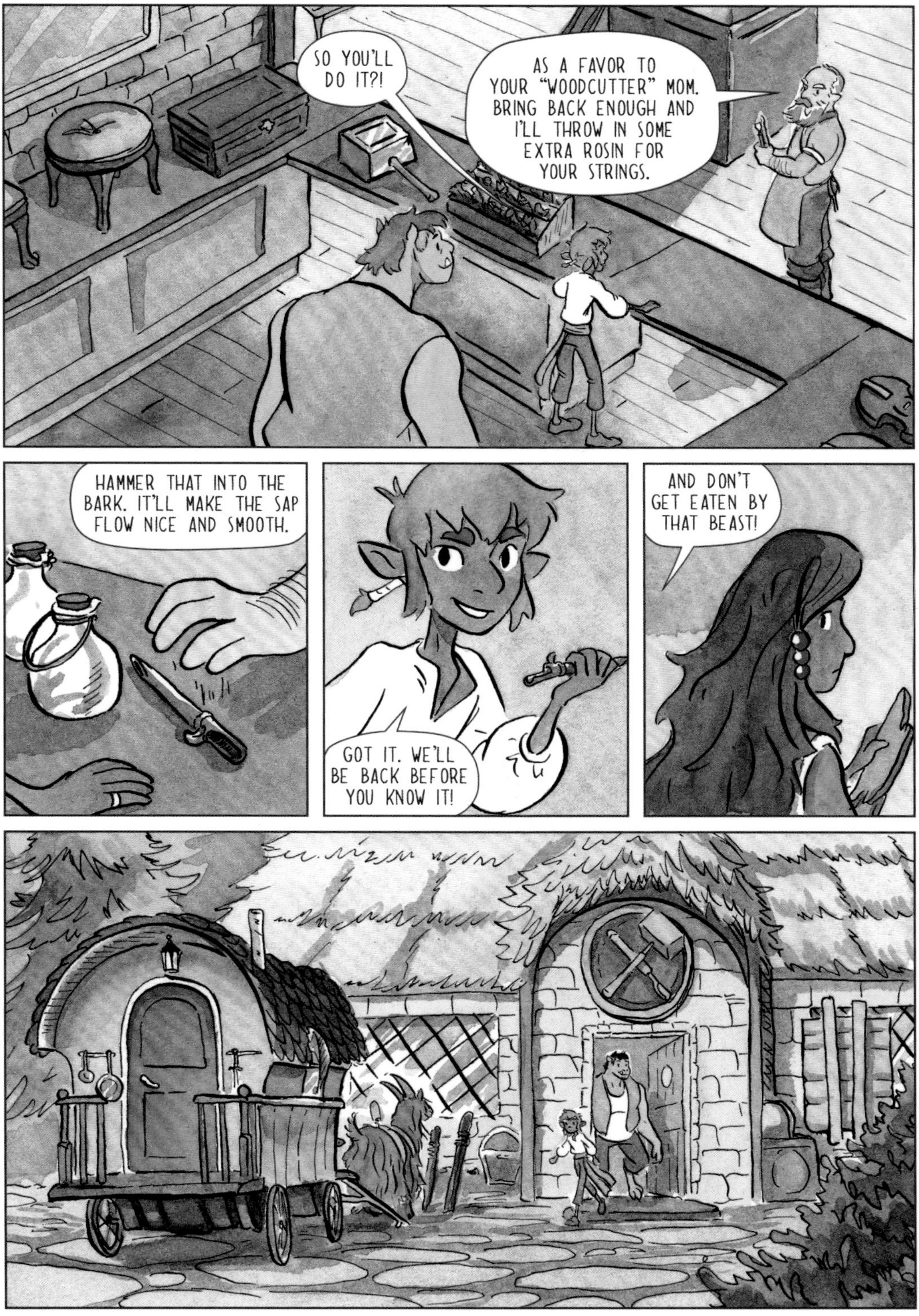
SO YOU'LL DO IT?!
AS A FAVOR TO YOUR "WOODCUTTER" MOM. BRING BACK ENOUGH AND I'LL THROW IN SOME EXTRA ROSIN FOR YOUR STRINGS.
HAMMER THAT INTO THE BARK. IT'LL MAKE THE SAP FLOW NICE AND SMOOTH.
GOT IT. WE'LL BE BACK BEFORE YOU KNOW IT!
AND DON'T GET EATEN BY THAT BEAST!

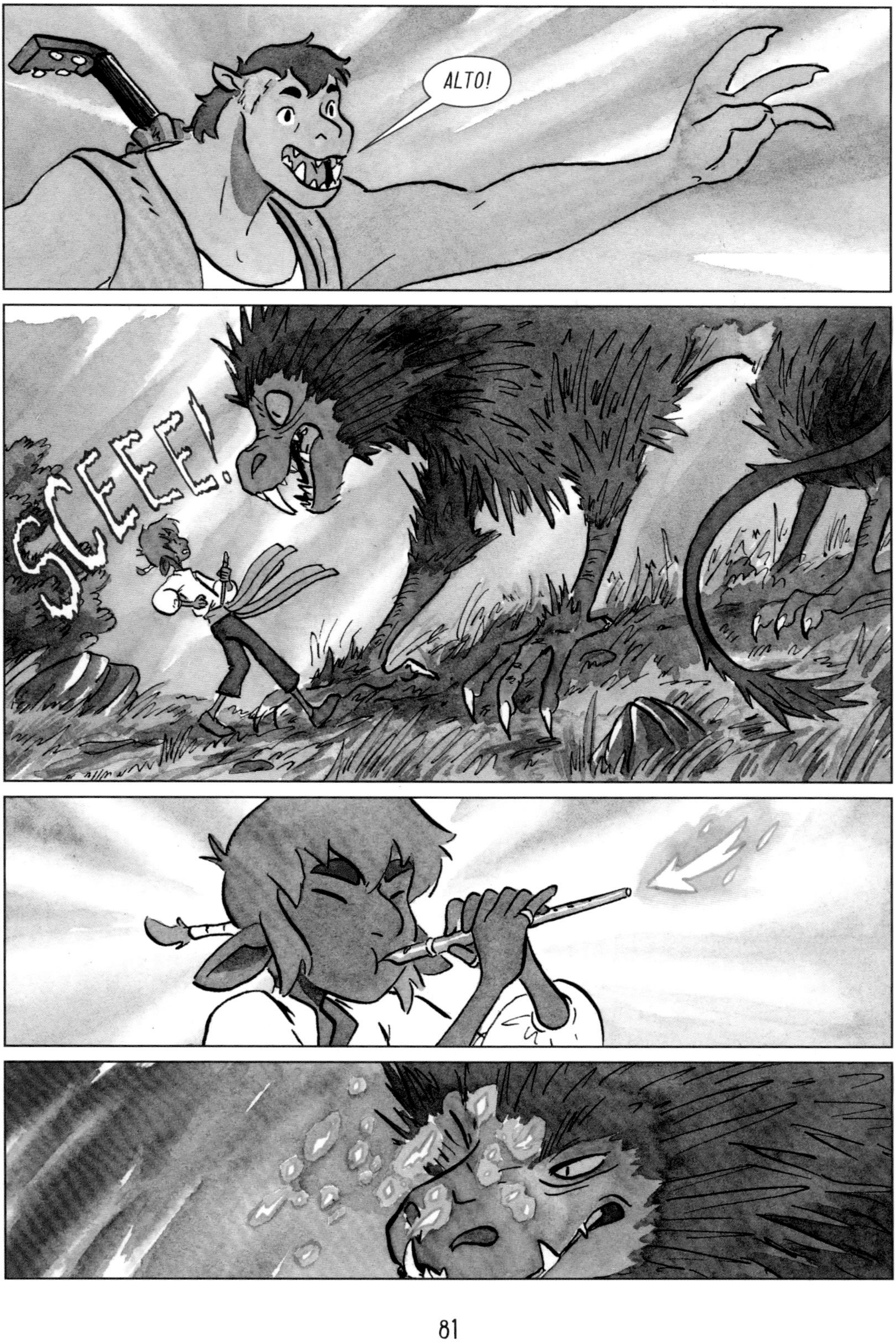
ALTO!
SCEEE!

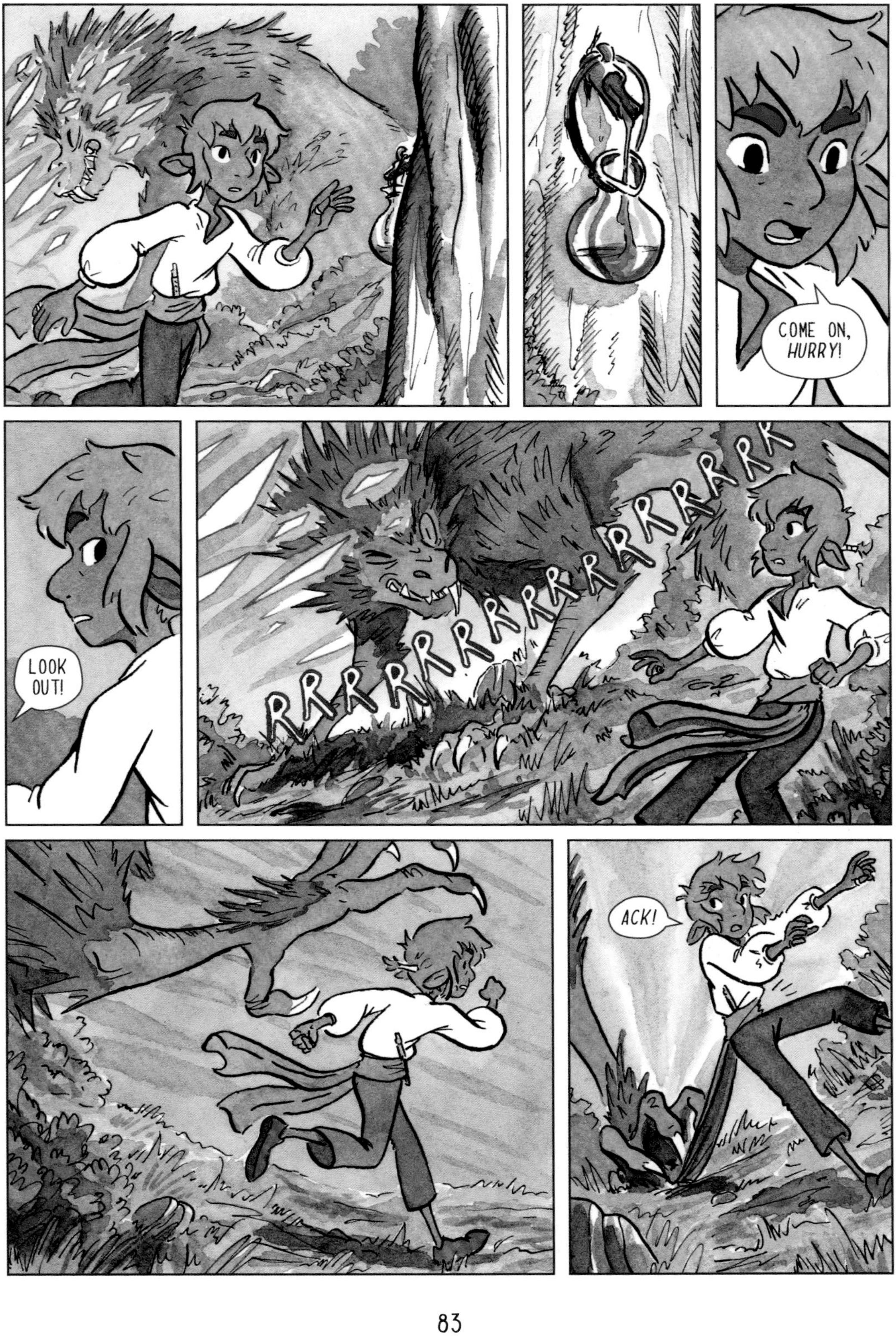
COME ON, HURRY!
LOOK OUT!
RRRRRRRRRRRRRRRRR
ACK!

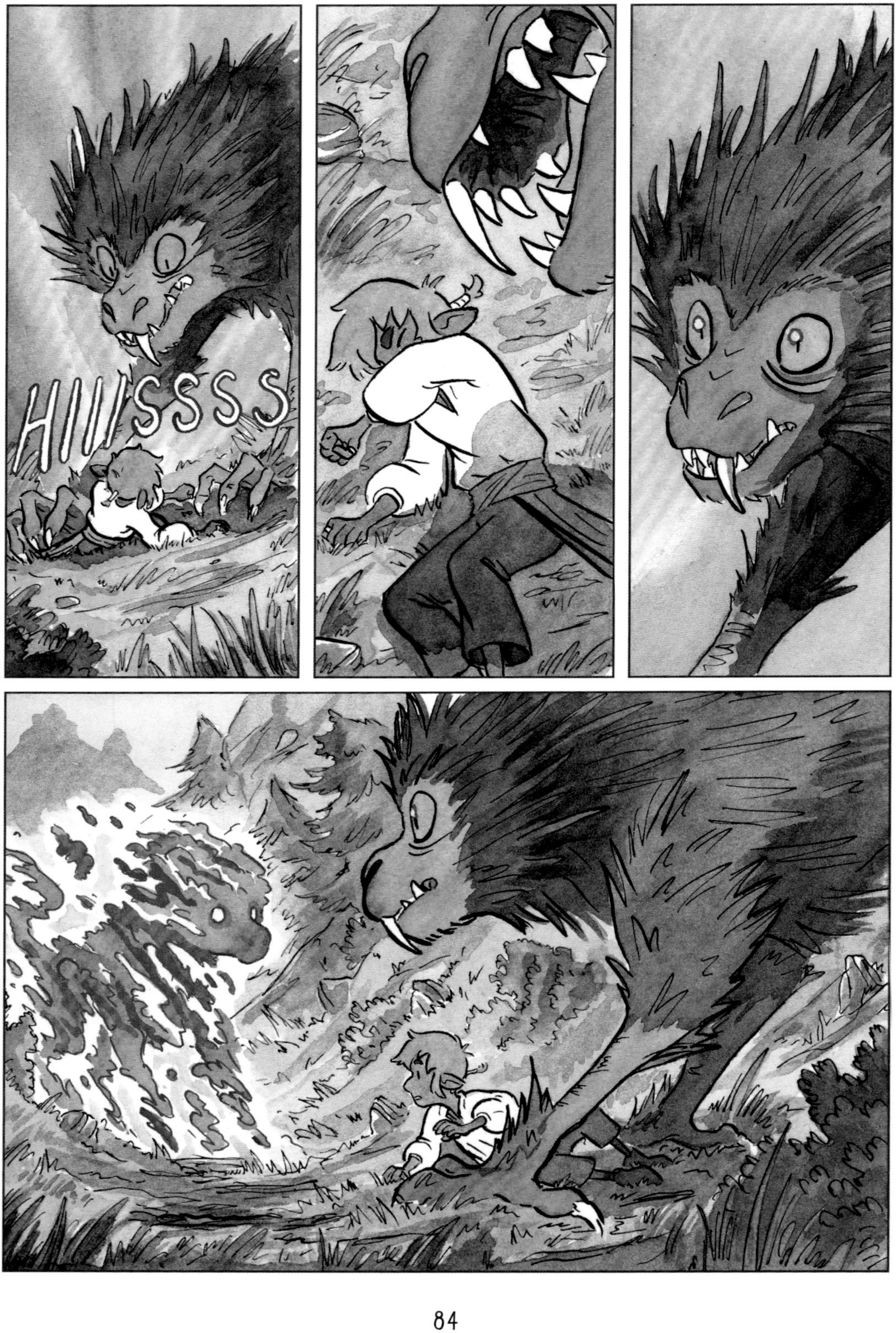
HIIISSSS

85

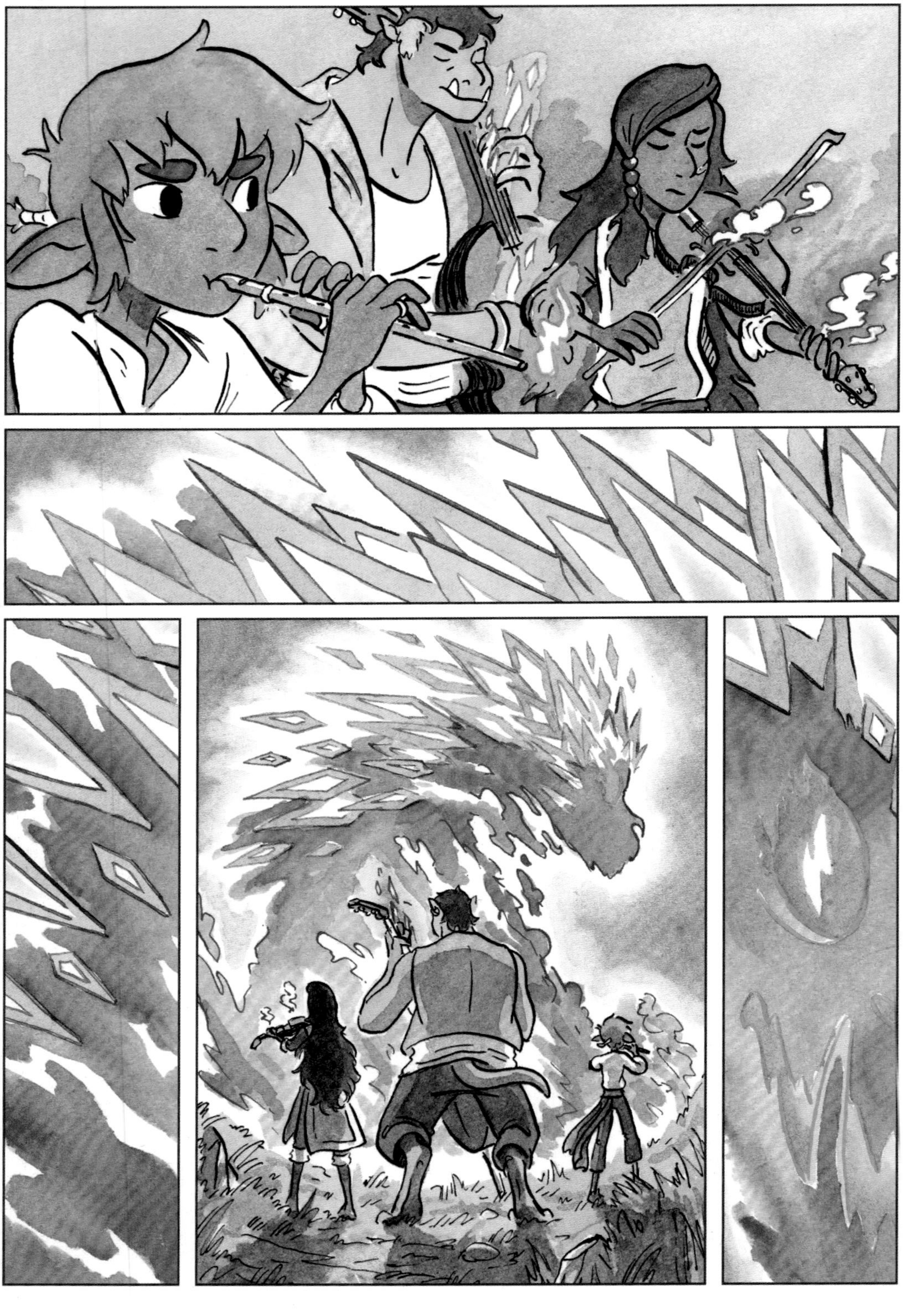

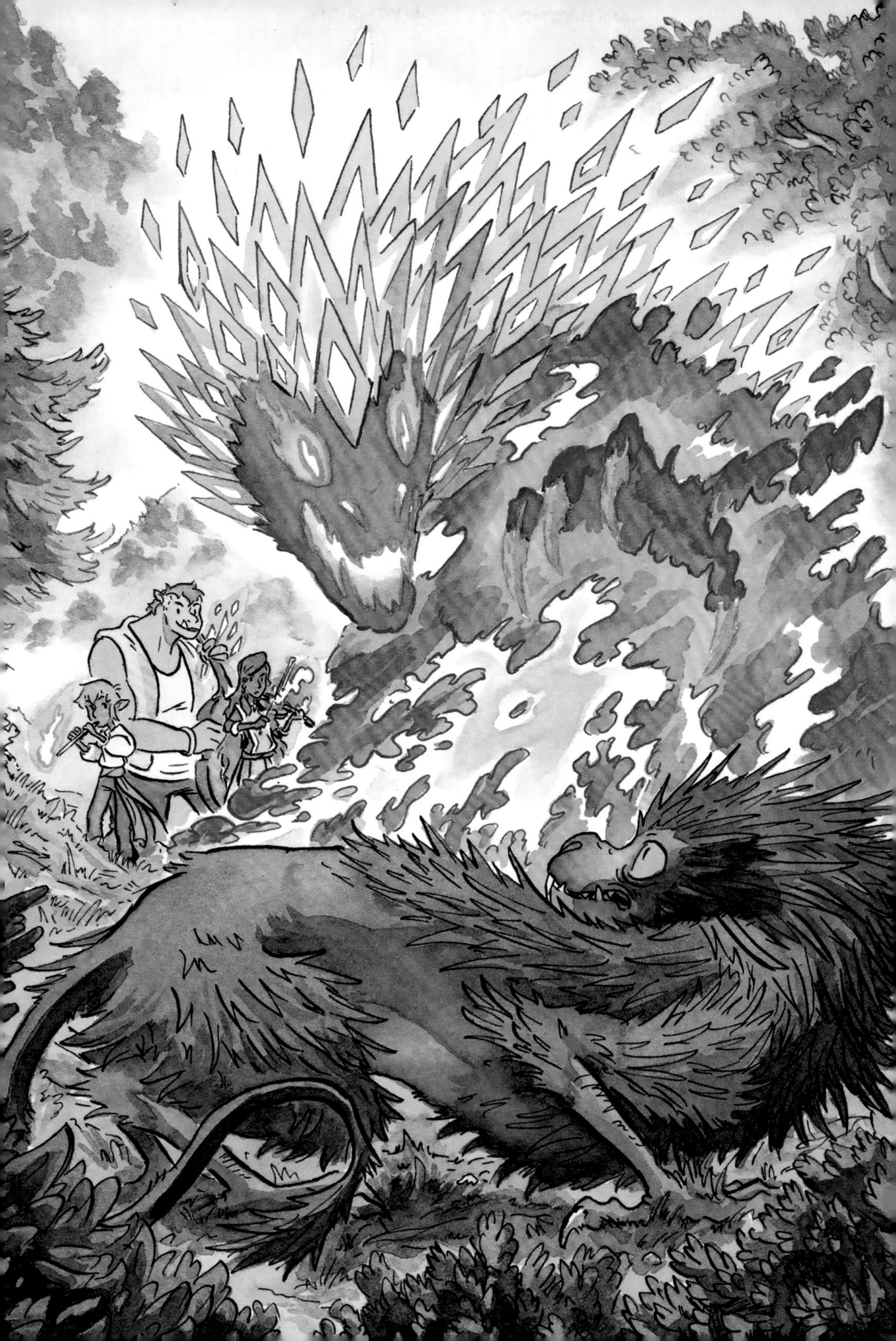

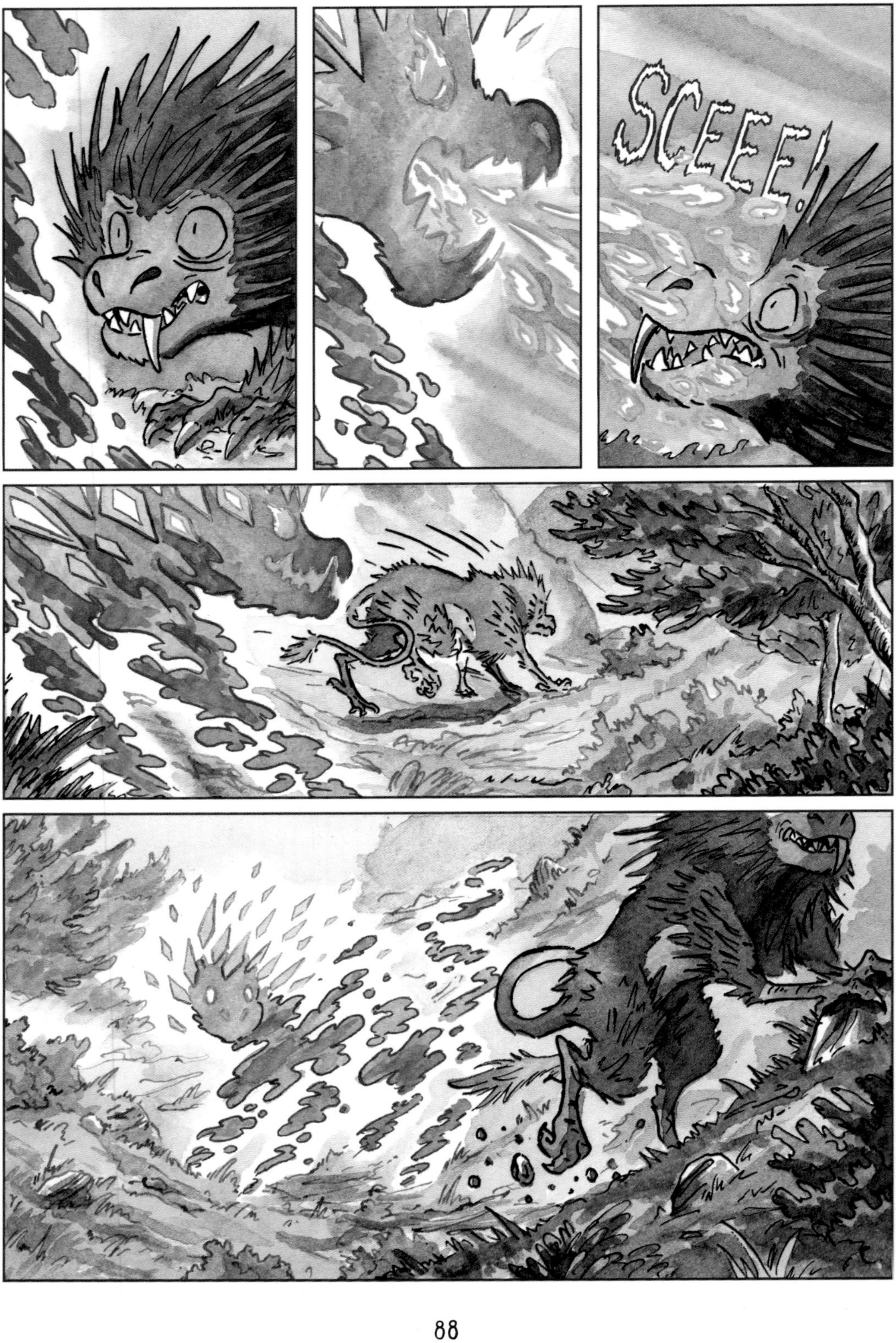
SCEEE!

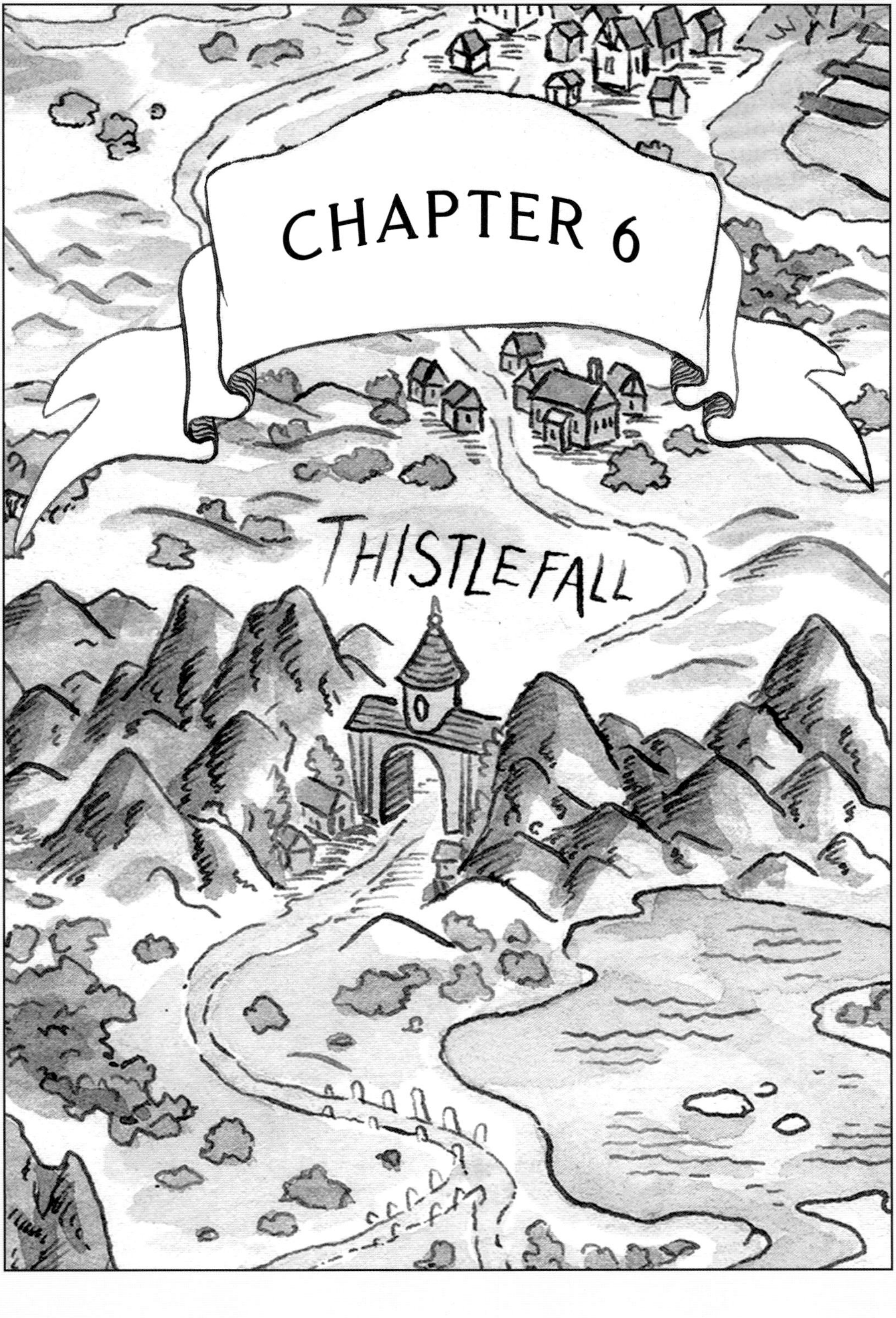
CHAPTER 6
THISTLEFALL

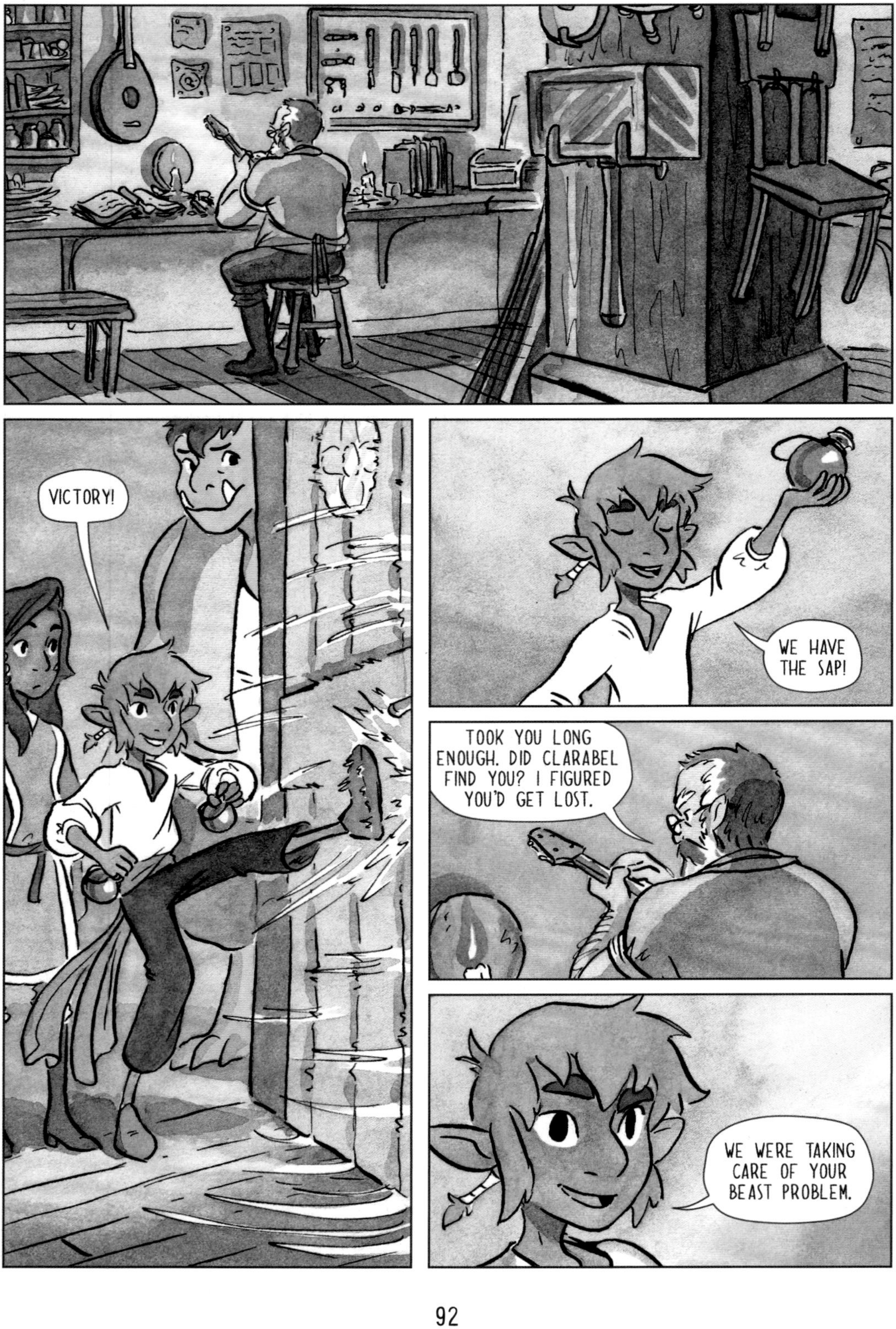
VICTORY!
WE HAVE THE SAP!
TOOK YOU LONG ENOUGH. DID CLARABEL FIND YOU? I FIGURED YOU'D GET LOST.
WE WERE TAKING CARE OF YOUR BEAST PROBLEM.

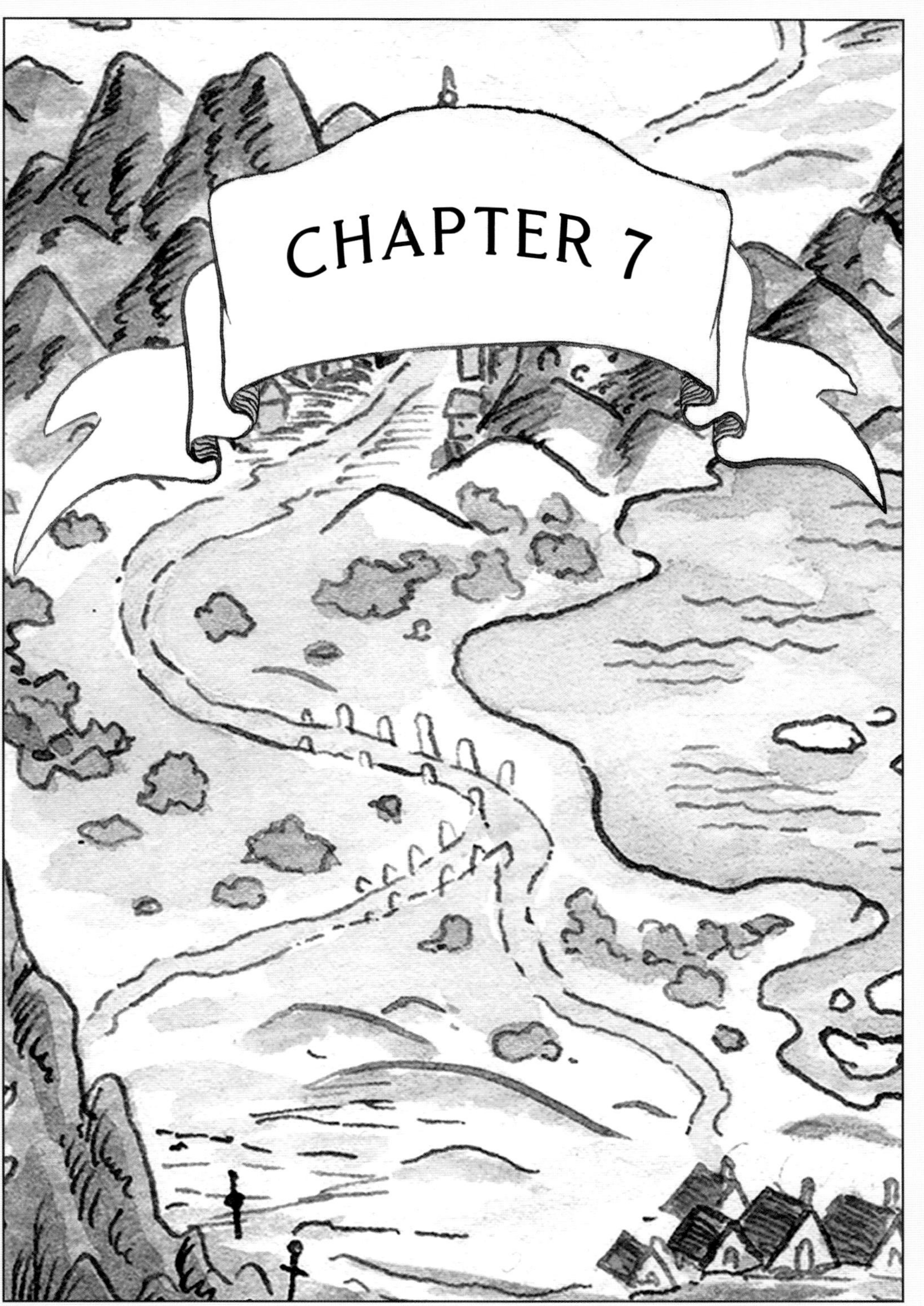
CHAPTER 7

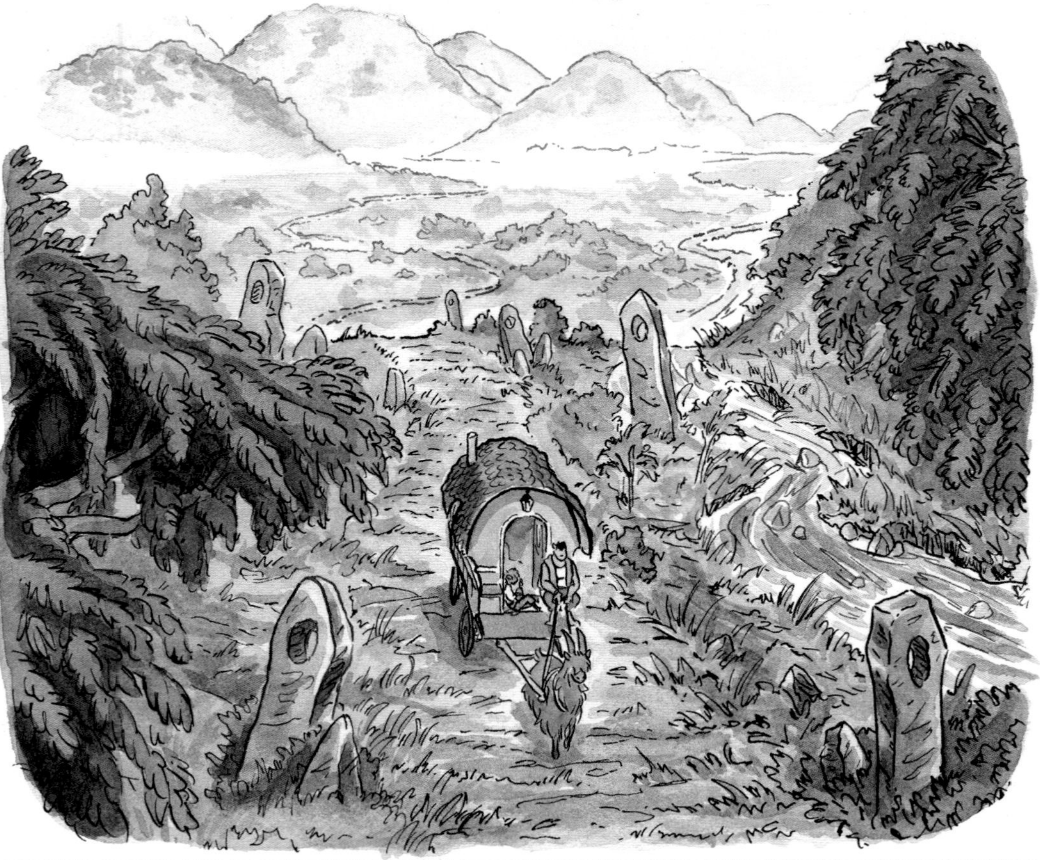

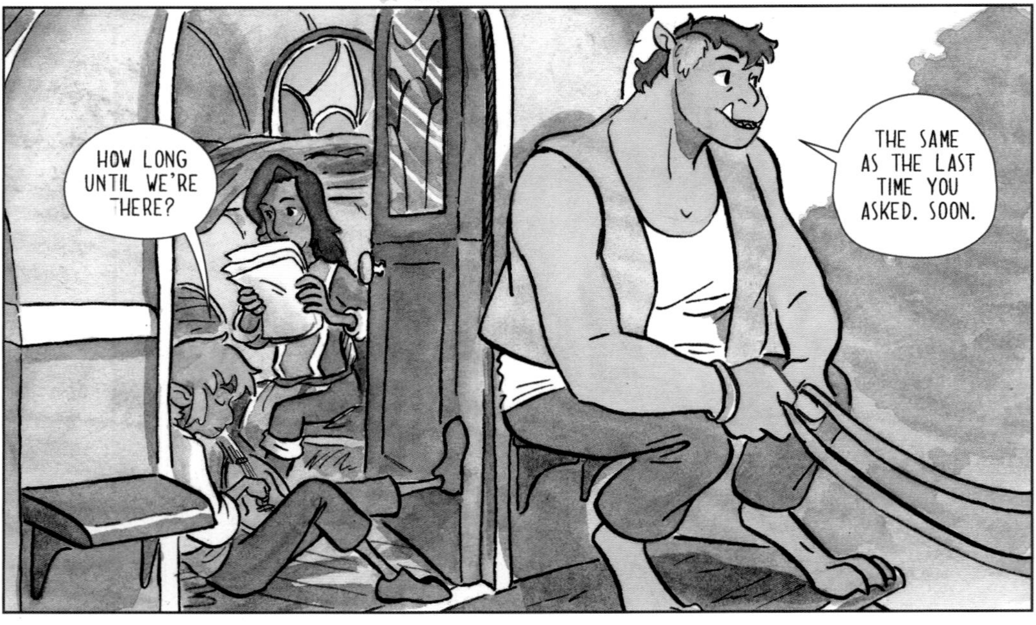
HOW LONG UNTIL WE'RE THERE?
THE SAME AS THE LAST TIME YOU ASKED. SOON.

105

106

107

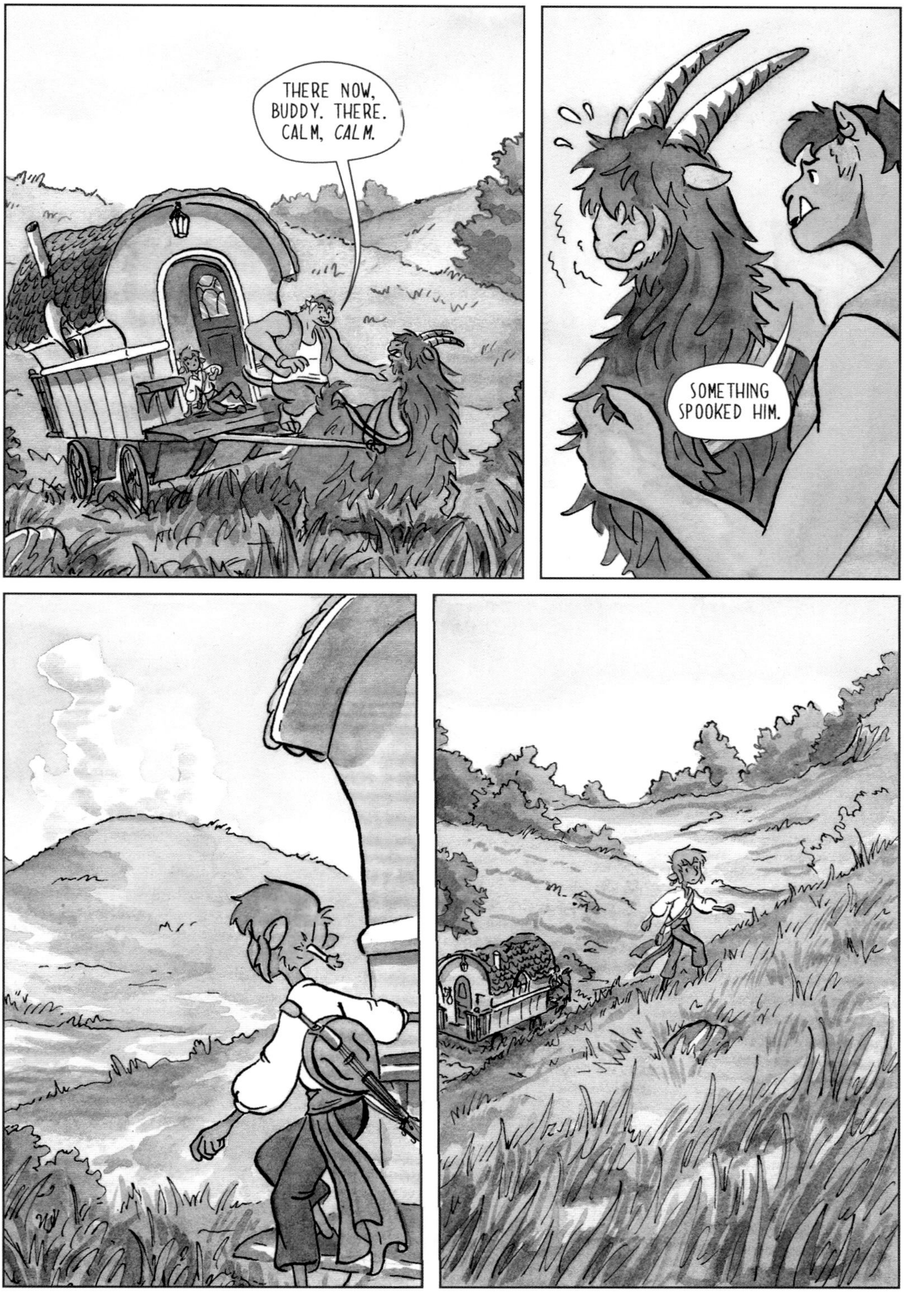
THERE NOW, BUDDY. THERE. CALM, *CALM.*
SOMETHING SPOOKED HIM.

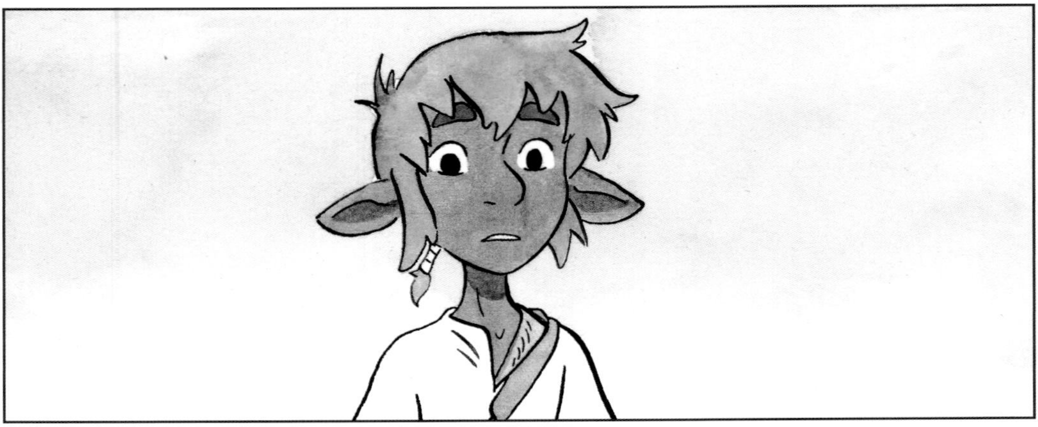

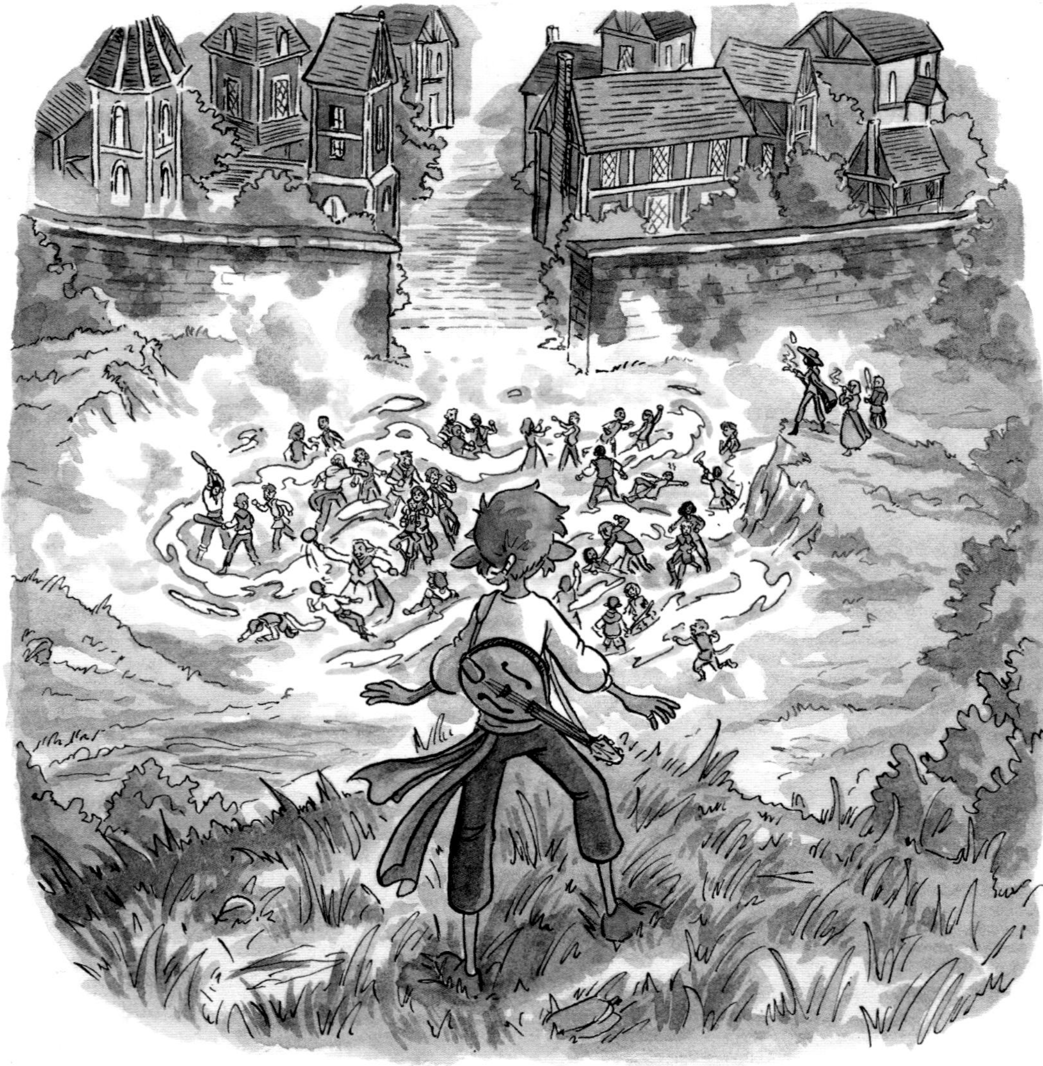

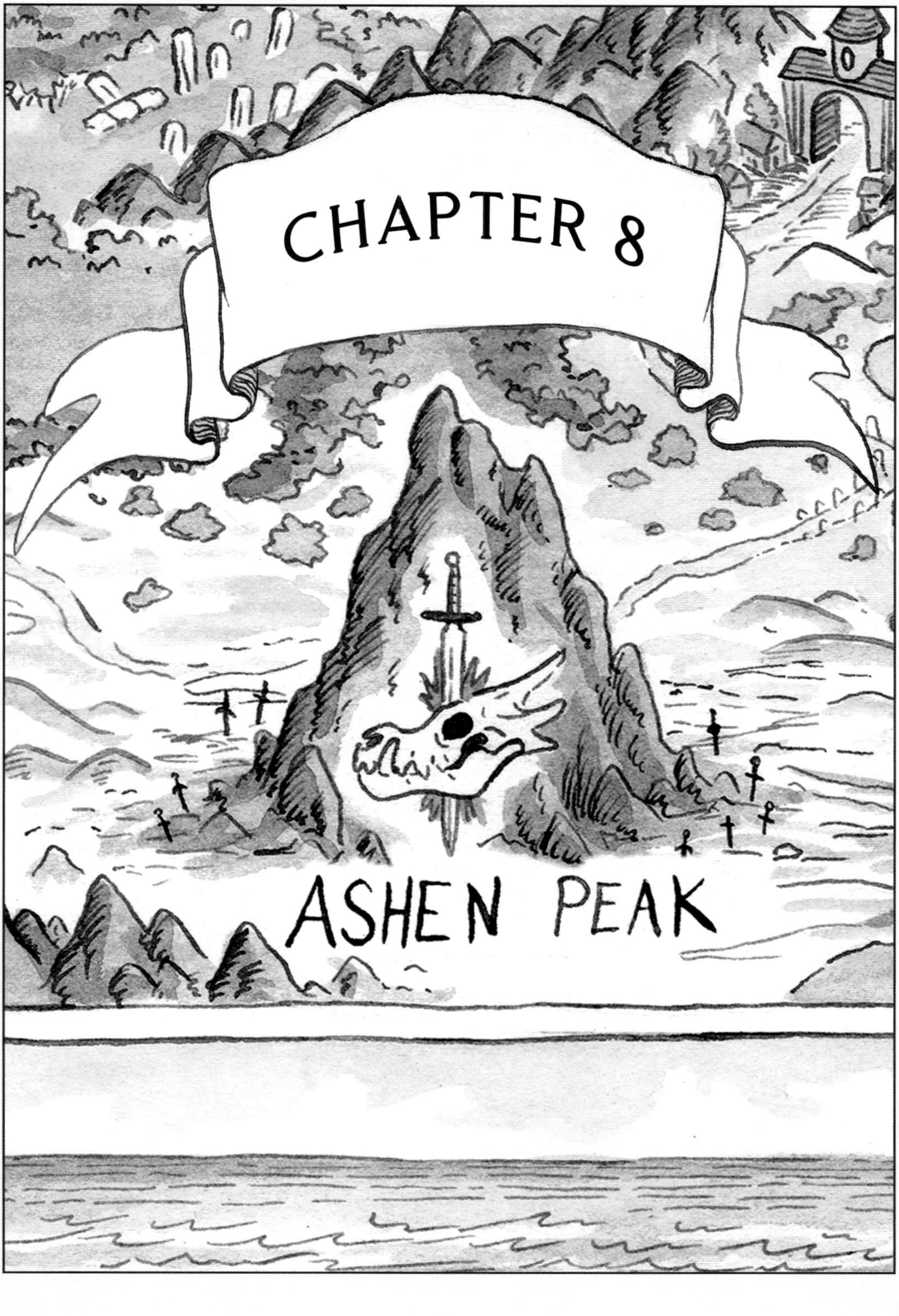
CHAPTER 8
ASHEN PEAK

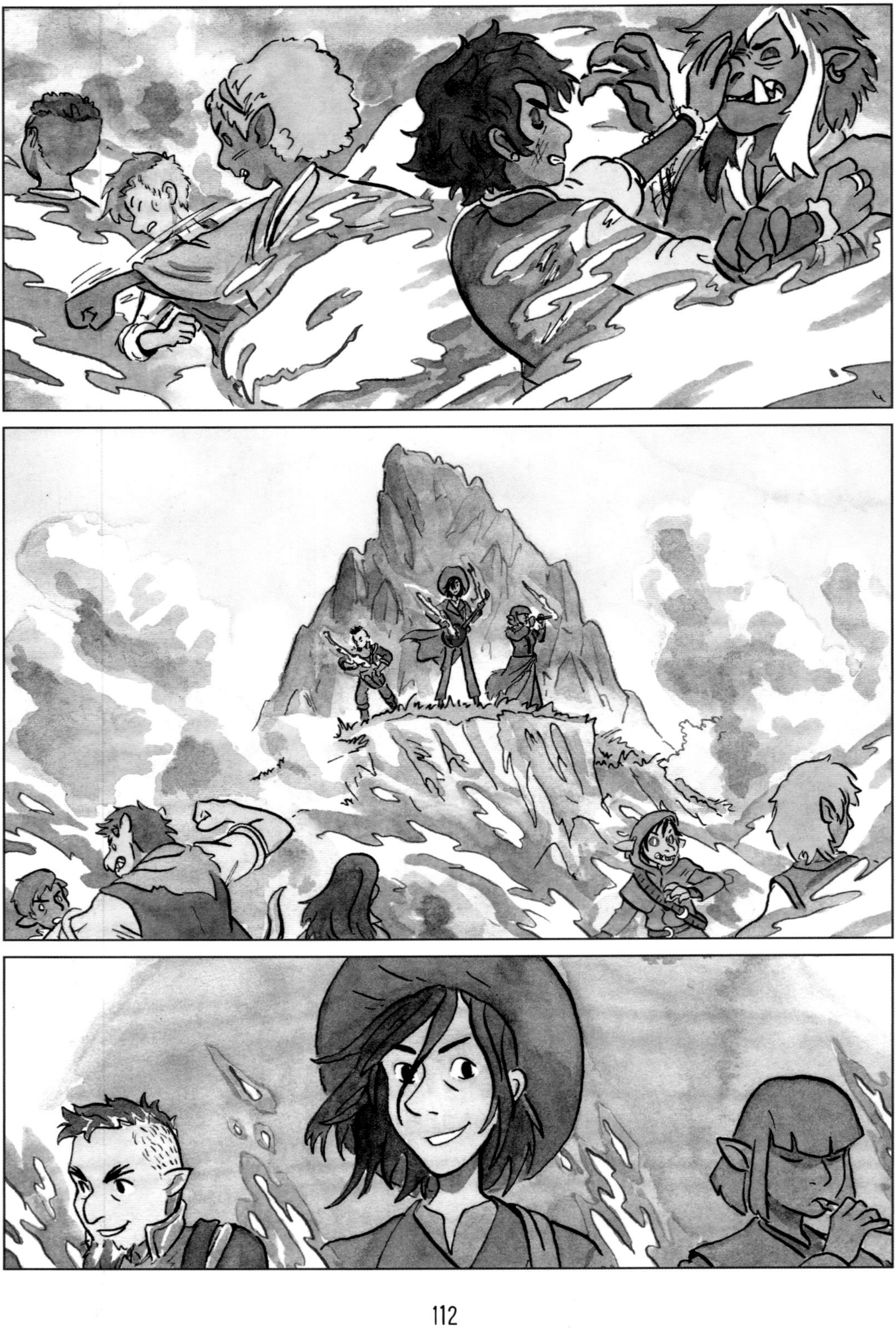

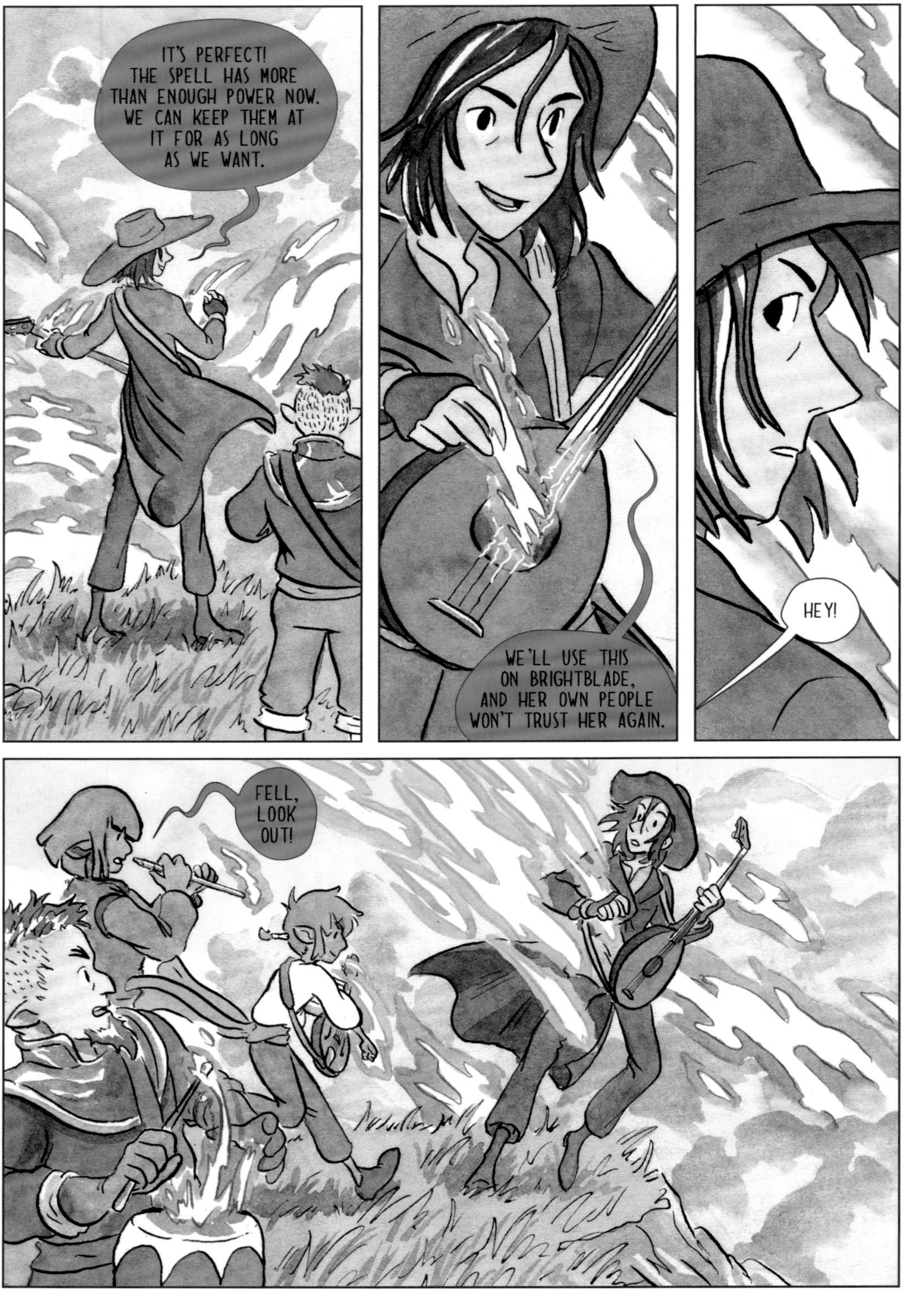
IT'S PERFECT! THE SPELL HAS MORE THAN ENOUGH POWER NOW. WE CAN KEEP THEM AT IT FOR AS LONG AS WE WANT.
WE'LL USE THIS ON BRIGHTBLADE, AND HER OWN PEOPLE WON'T TRUST HER AGAIN.
HEY!
FELL, LOOK OUT!

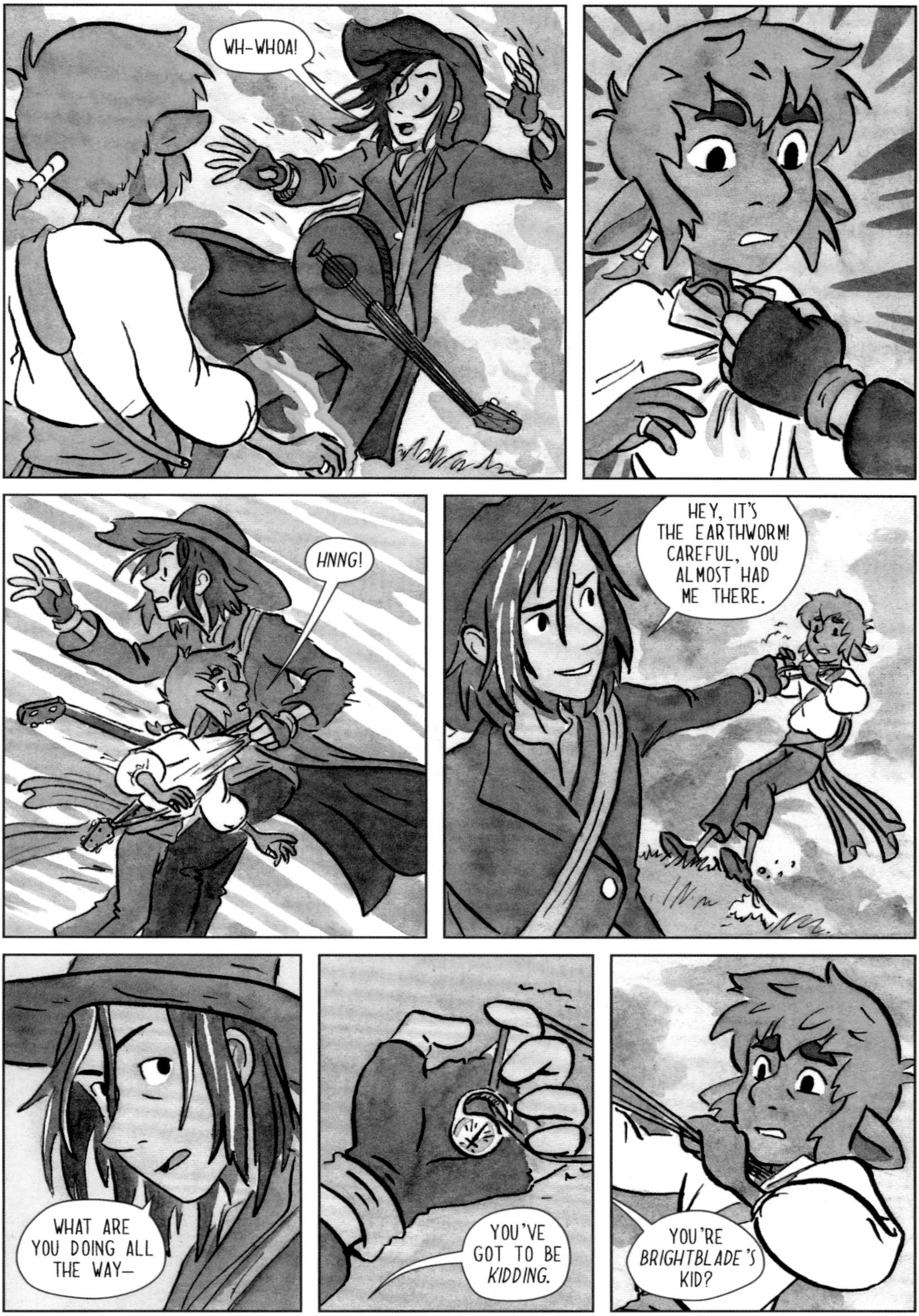
WH-WHOA!
HNNG!
HEY, IT'S THE EARTHWORM! CAREFUL, YOU ALMOST HAD ME THERE.
WHAT ARE YOU DOING ALL THE WAY—
YOU'VE GOT TO BE *KIDDING*.
YOU'RE *BRIGHTBLADE'S* KID?

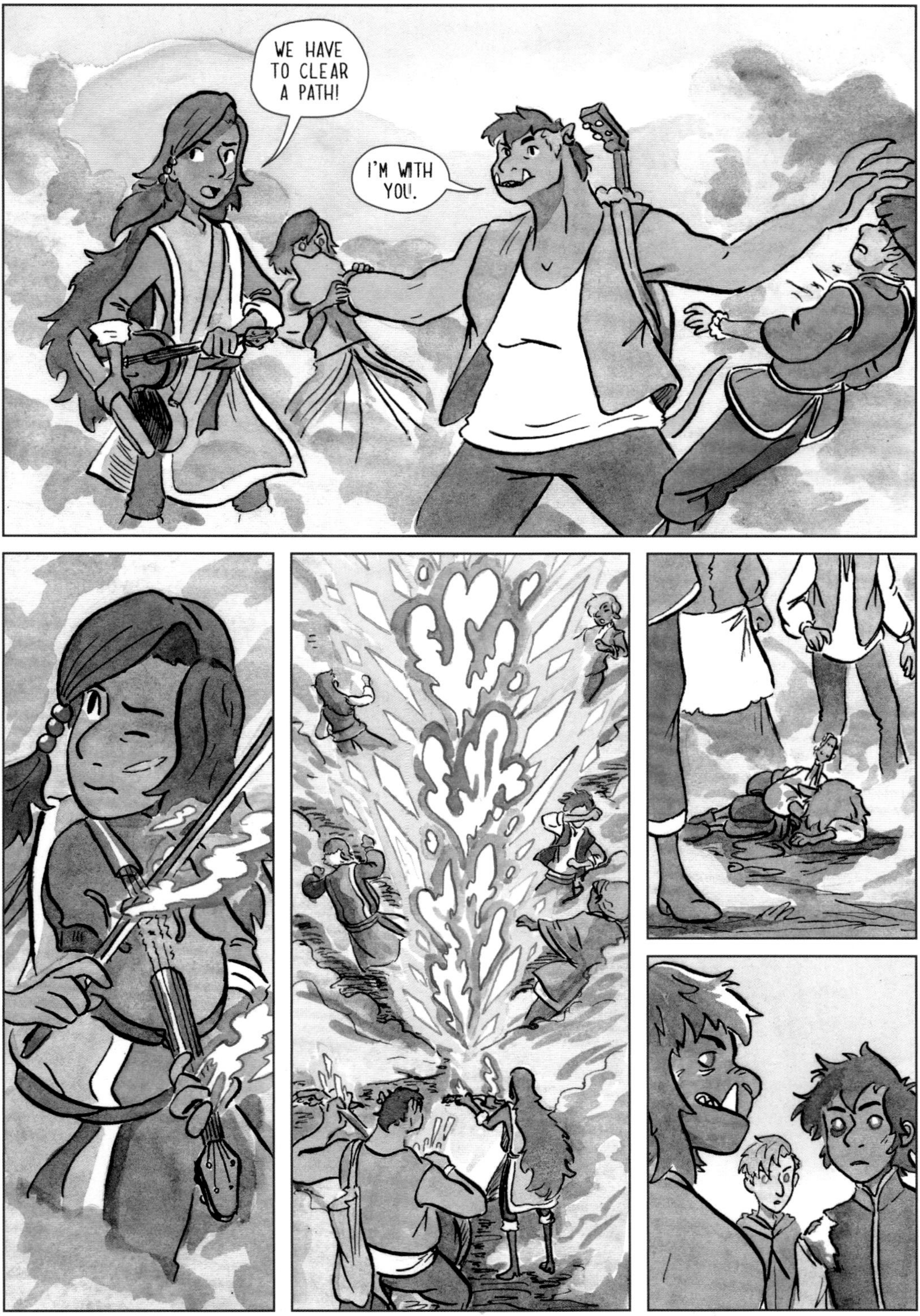
WE HAVE TO CLEAR A PATH!
I'M WITH YOU.

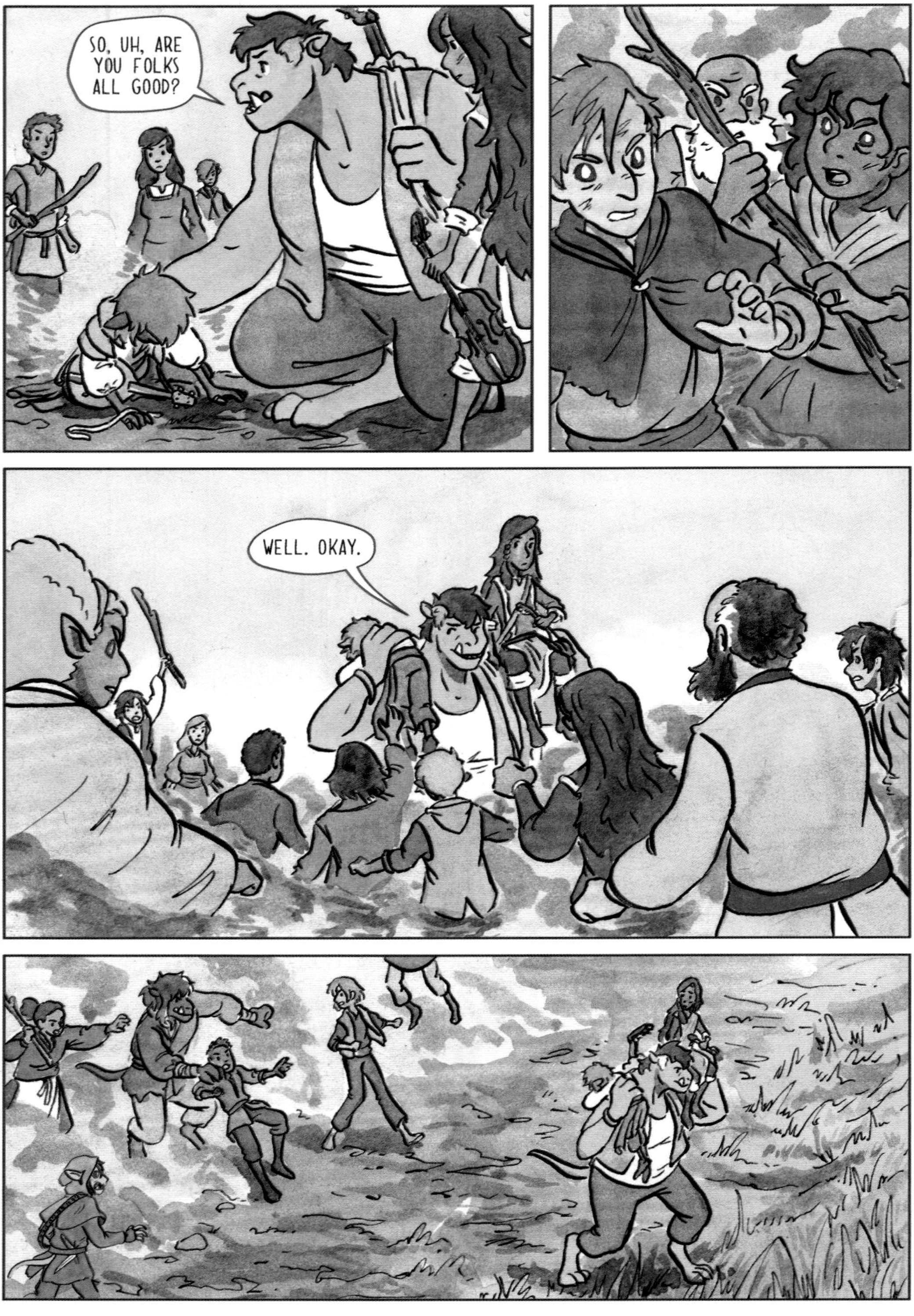
SO, UH, ARE YOU FOLKS ALL GOOD?
WELL. OKAY.

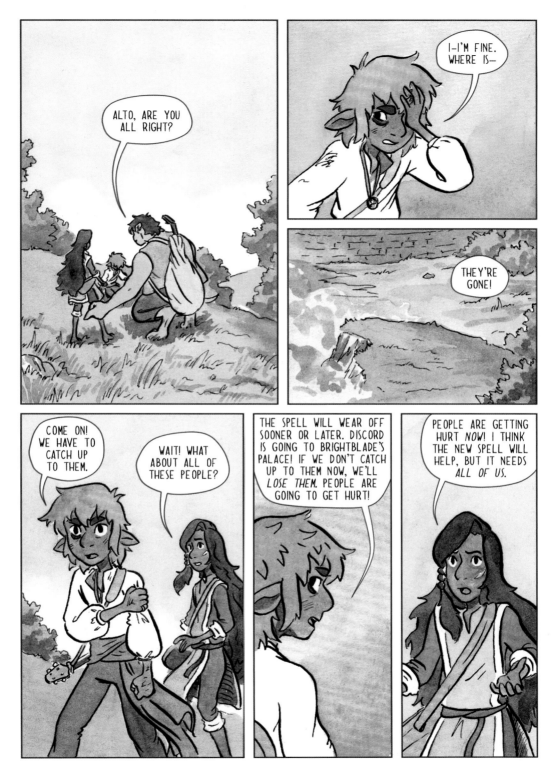

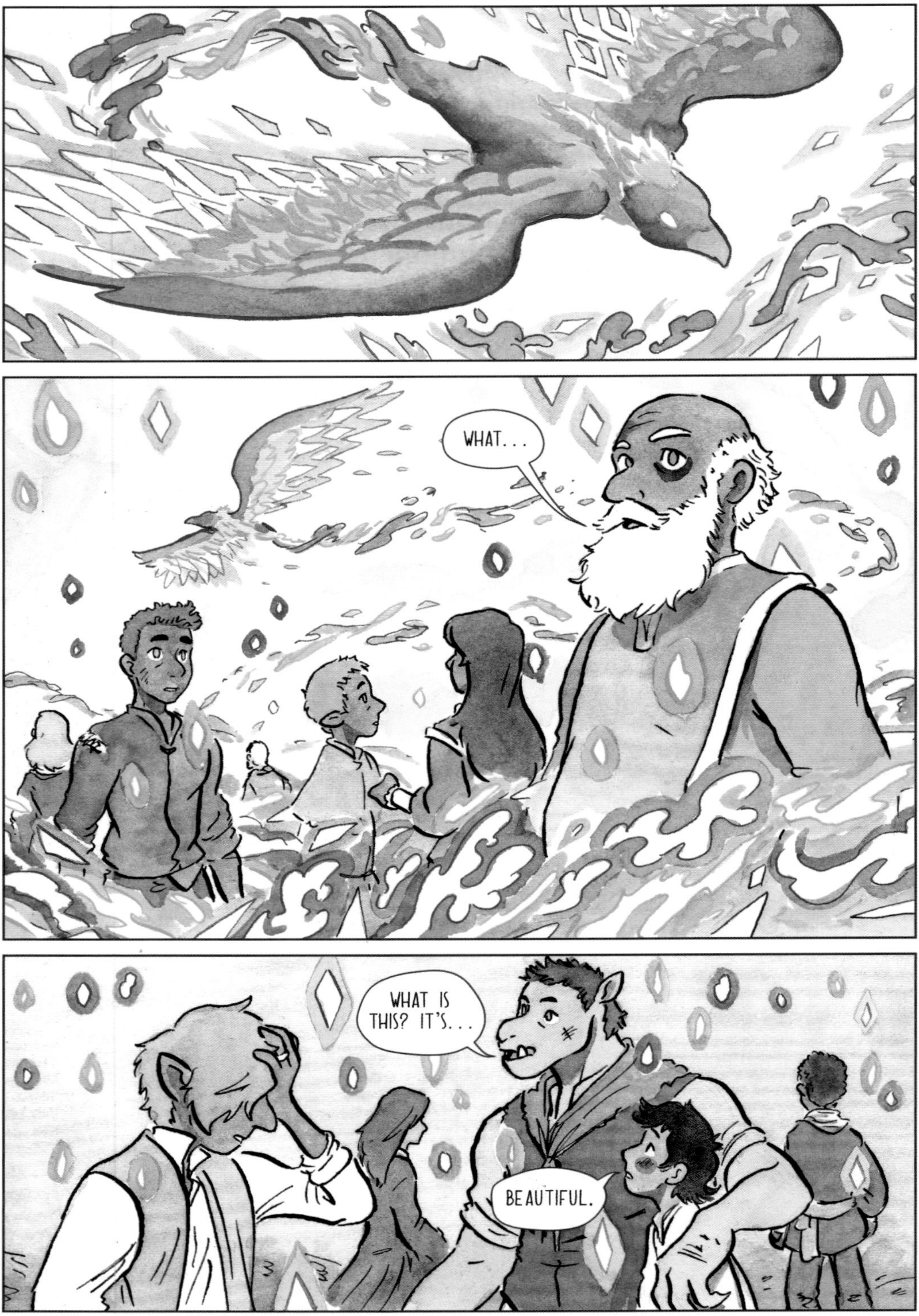
WHAT...
WHAT IS THIS? IT'S...
BEAUTIFUL.

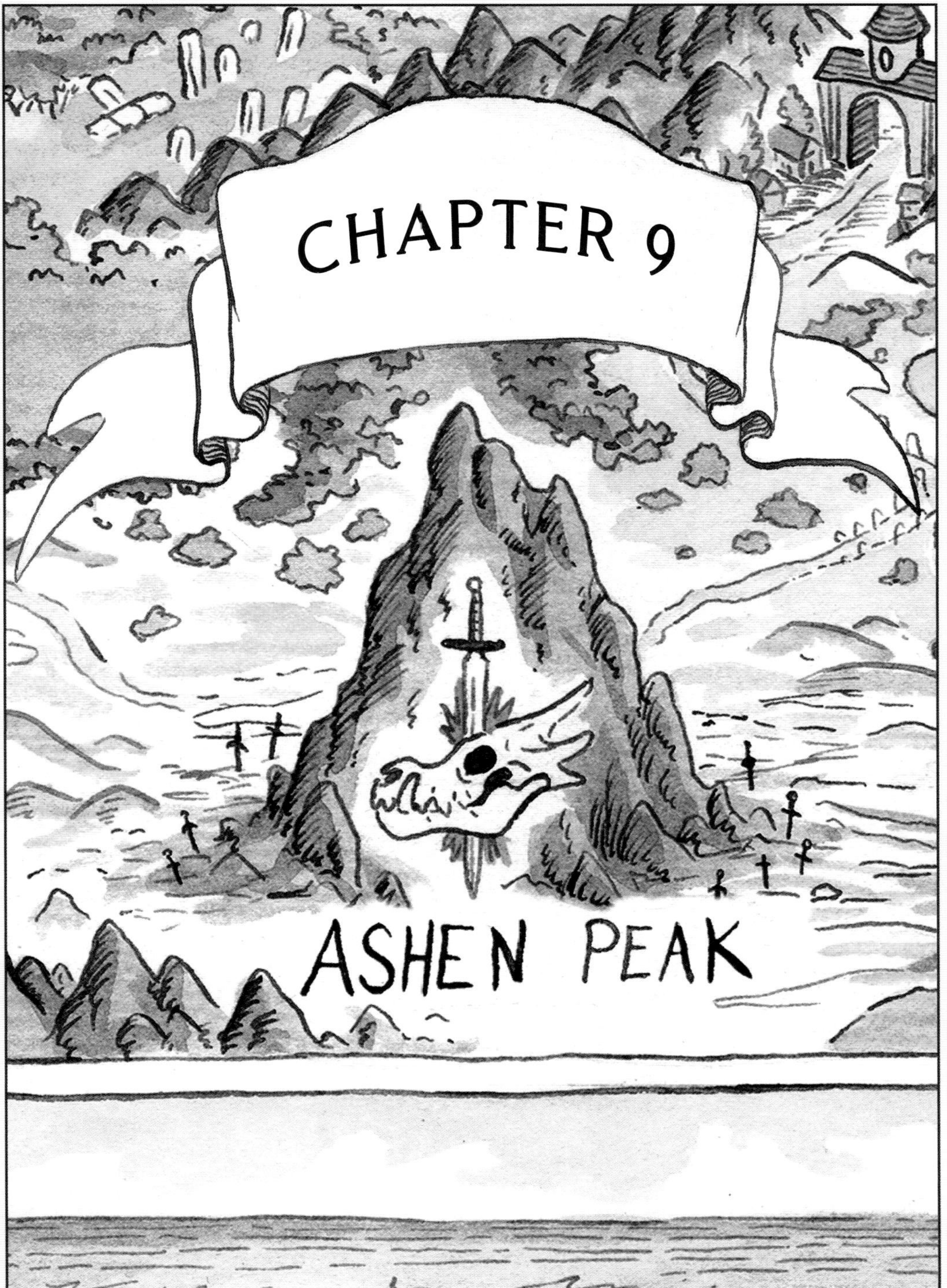
CHAPTER 9
ASHEN PEAK

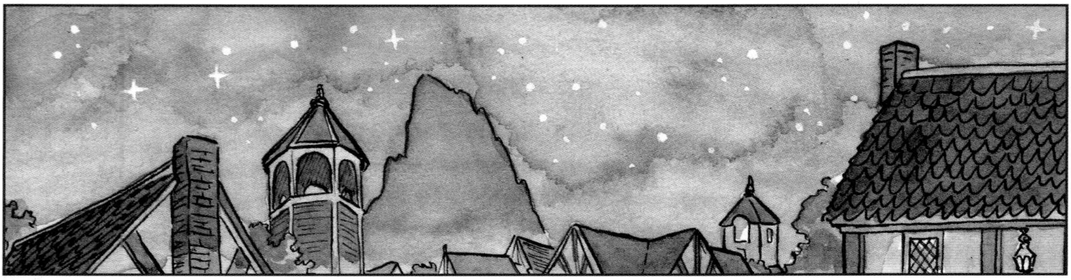

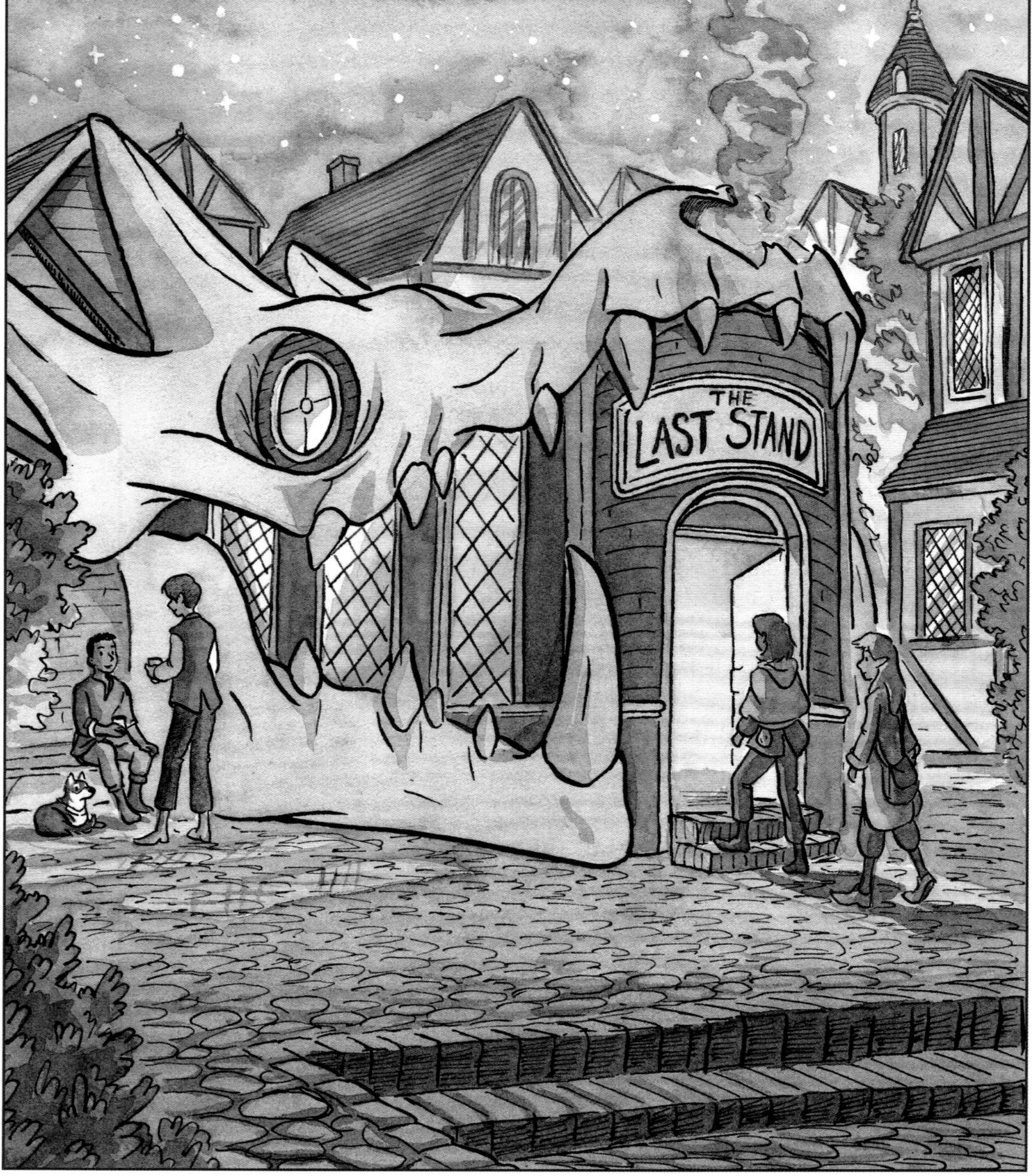
THE LAST STAND

132

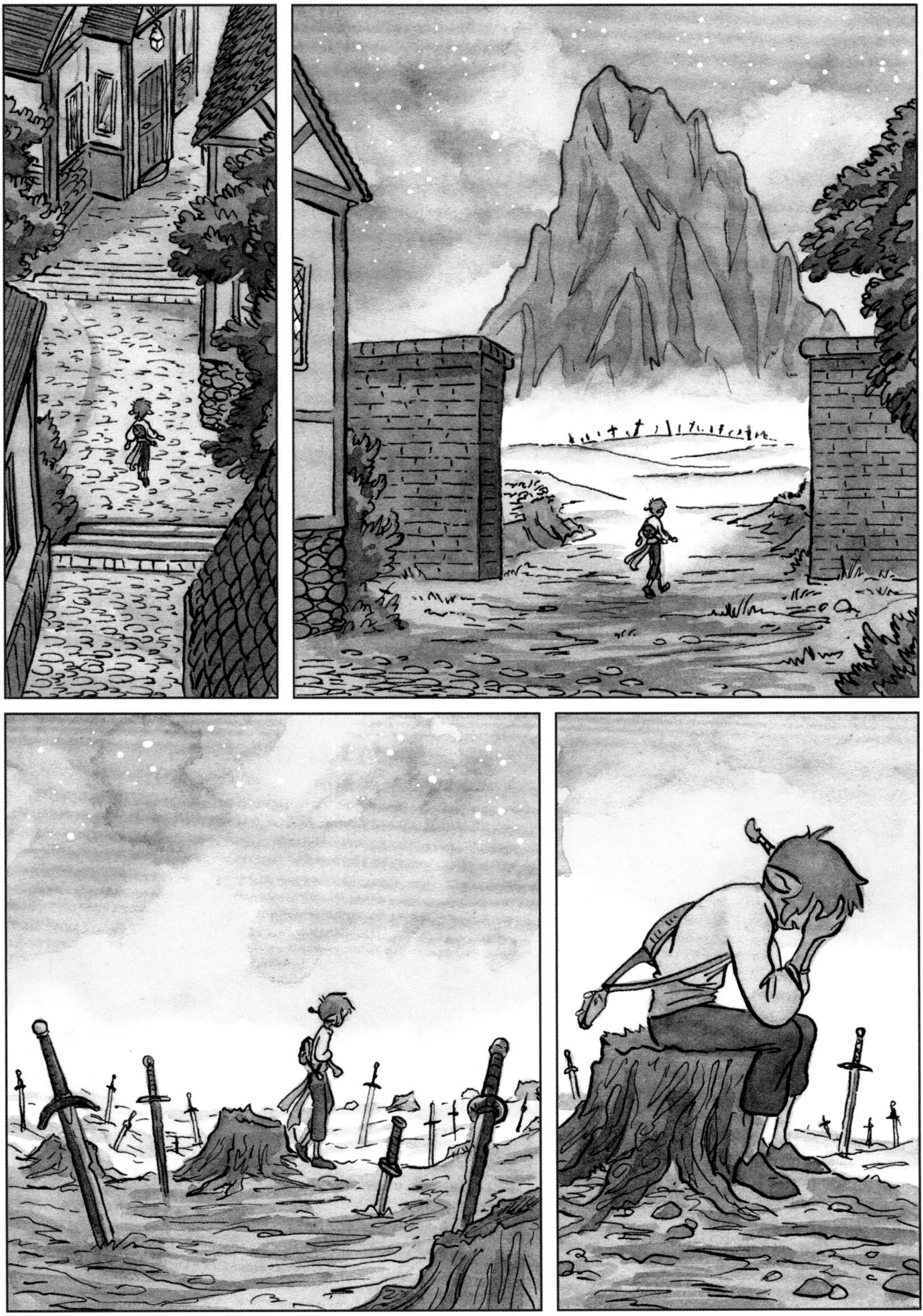

135

136

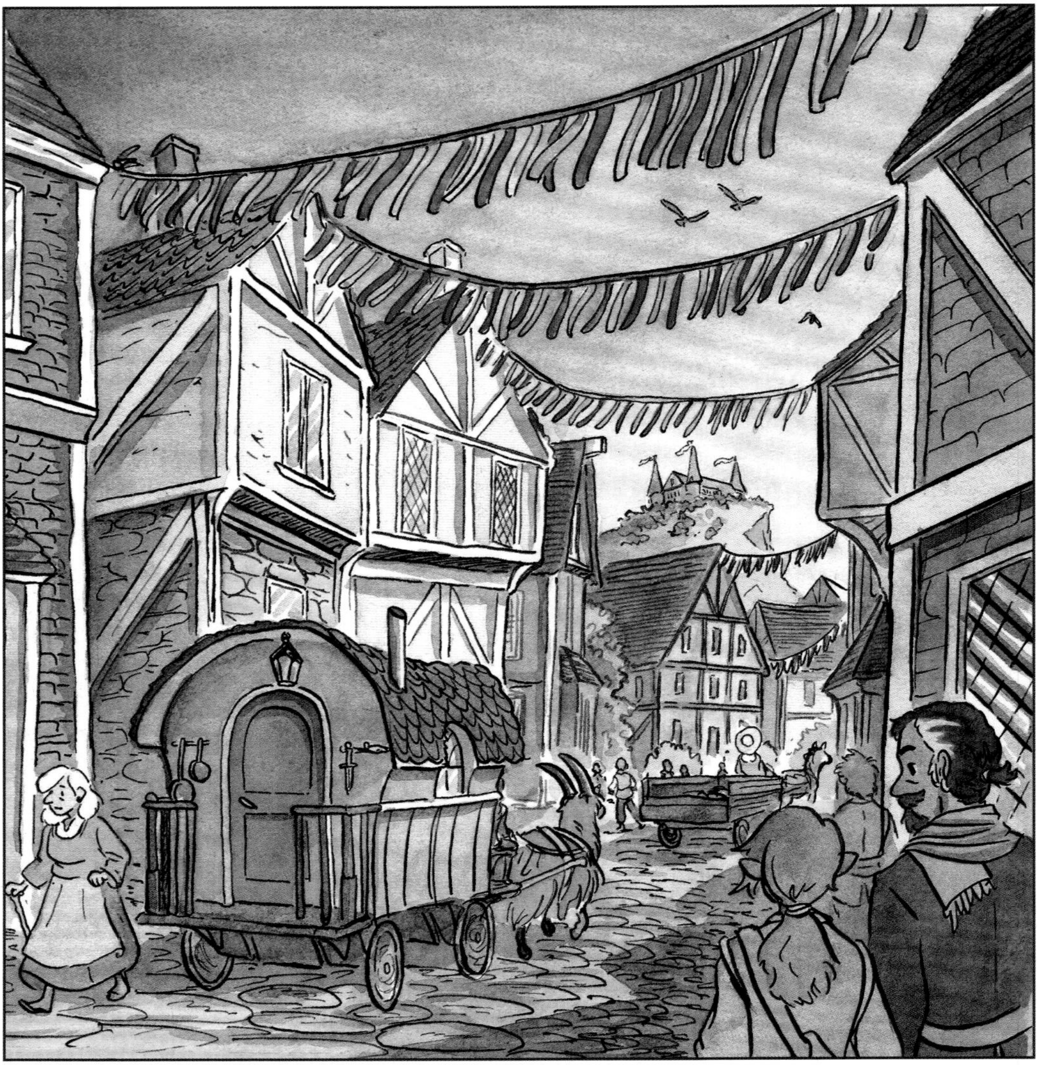

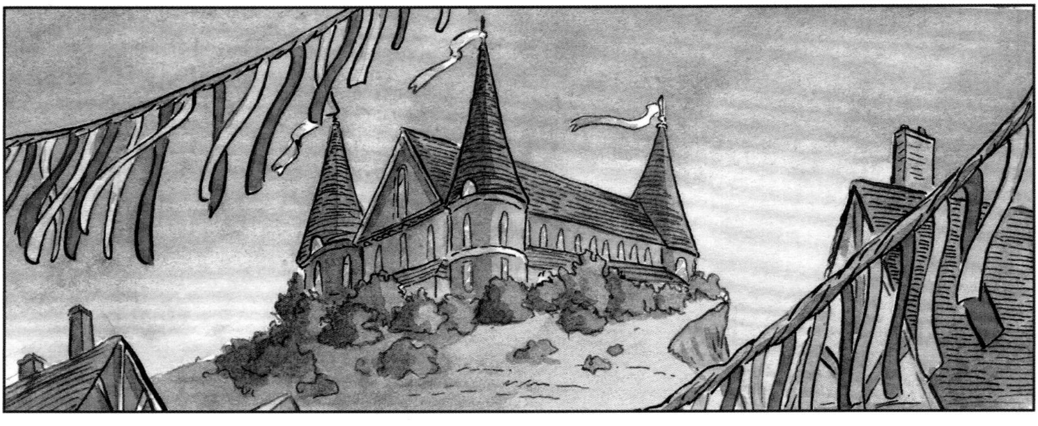

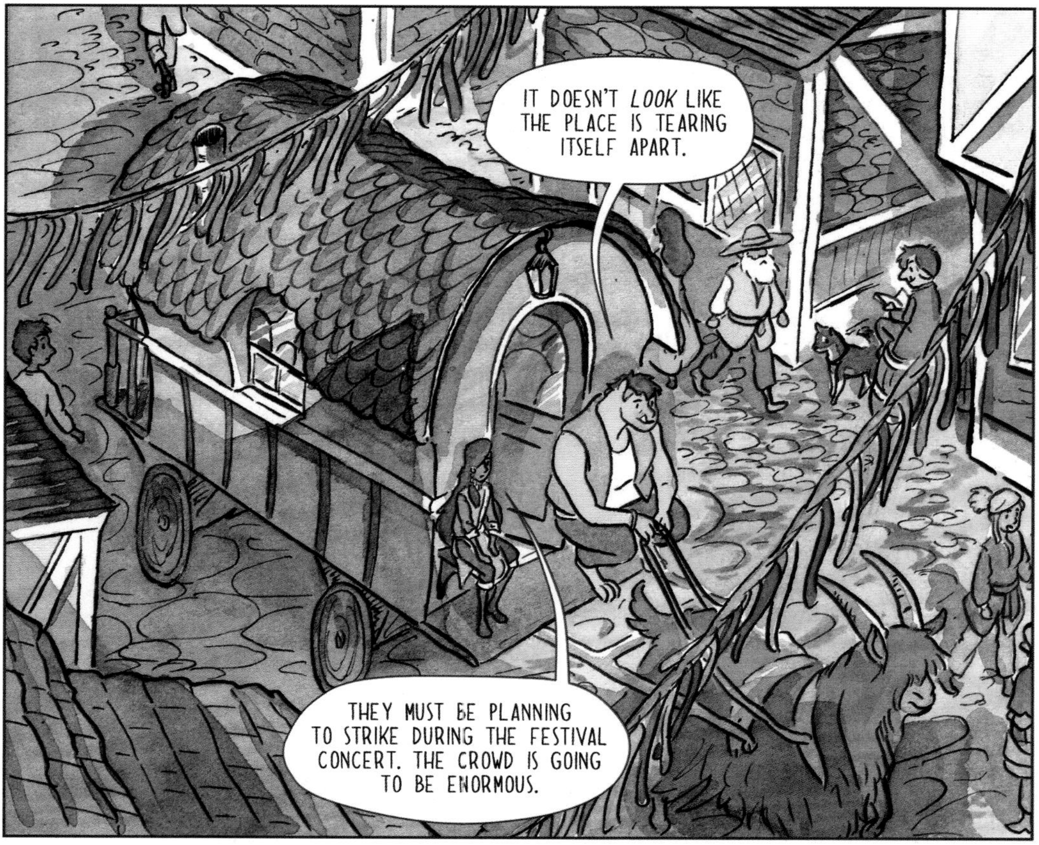
IT DOESN'T *LOOK* LIKE THE PLACE IS TEARING ITSELF APART.
THEY MUST BE PLANNING TO STRIKE DURING THE FESTIVAL CONCERT. THE CROWD IS GOING TO BE ENORMOUS.

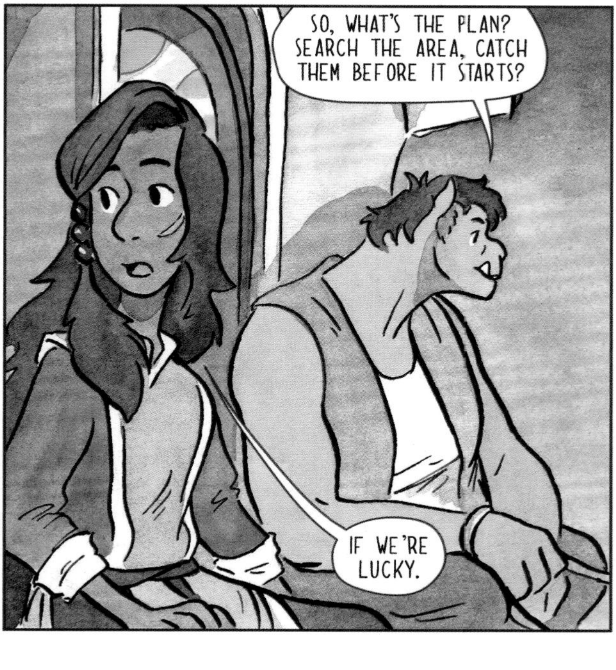
SO, WHAT'S THE PLAN? SEARCH THE AREA, CATCH THEM BEFORE IT STARTS?
IF WE'RE LUCKY.

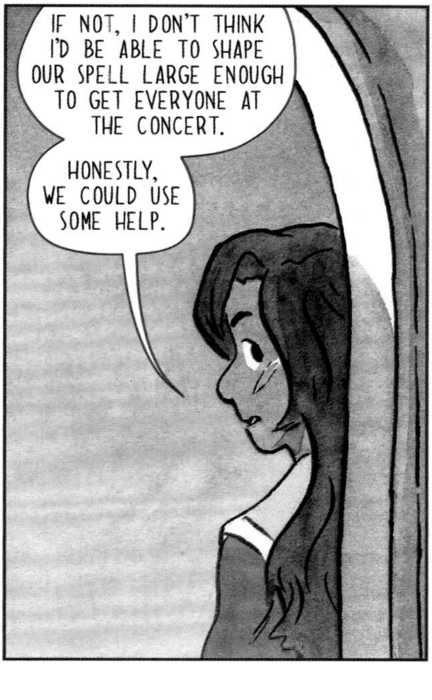
IF NOT, I DON'T THINK I'D BE ABLE TO SHAPE OUR SPELL LARGE ENOUGH TO GET EVERYONE AT THE CONCERT.
HONESTLY, WE COULD USE SOME HELP.

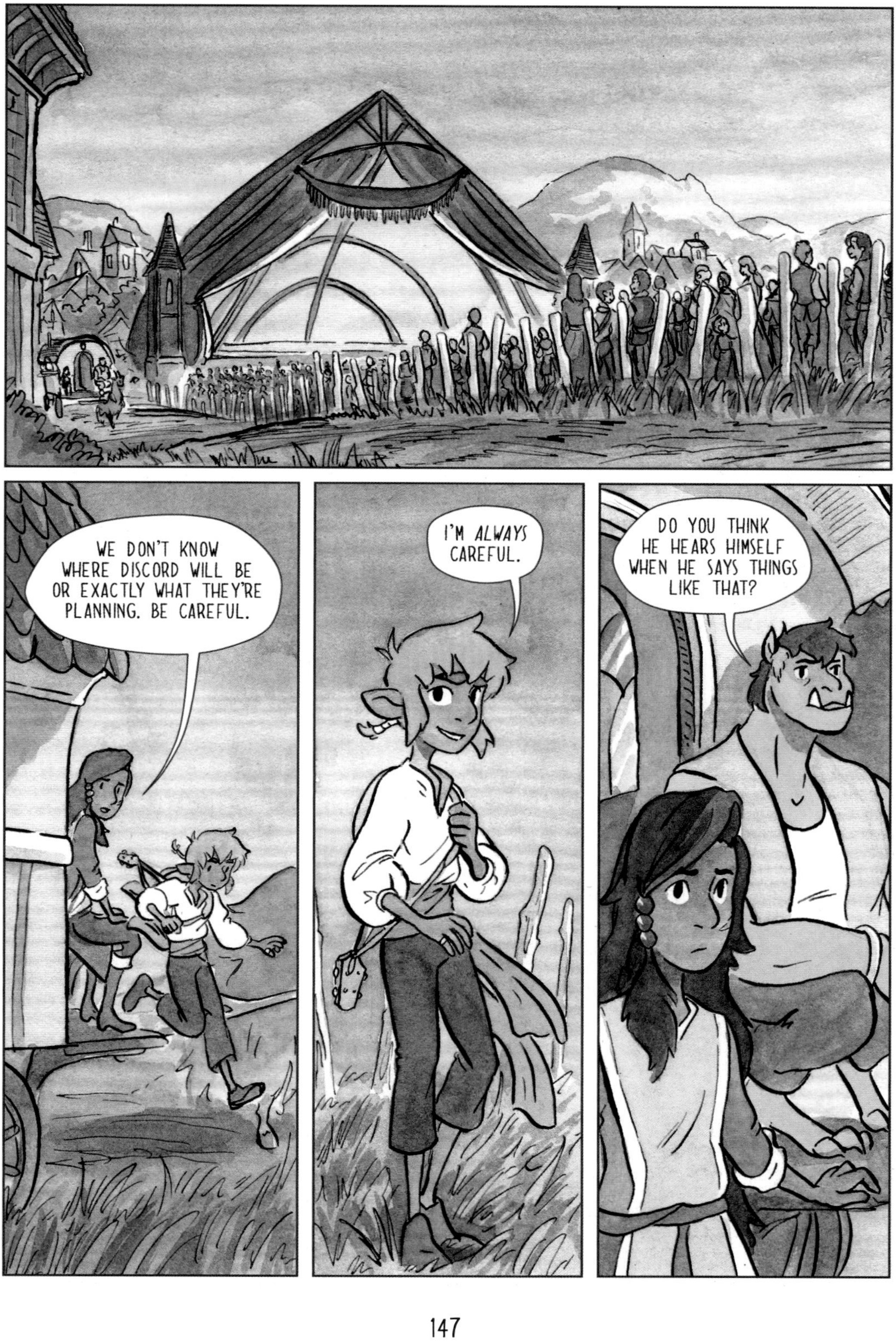
WE DON'T KNOW WHERE DISCORD WILL BE OR EXACTLY WHAT THEY'RE PLANNING. BE CAREFUL.
I'M *ALWAYS* CAREFUL.
DO YOU THINK HE HEARS HIMSELF WHEN HE SAYS THINGS LIKE THAT?

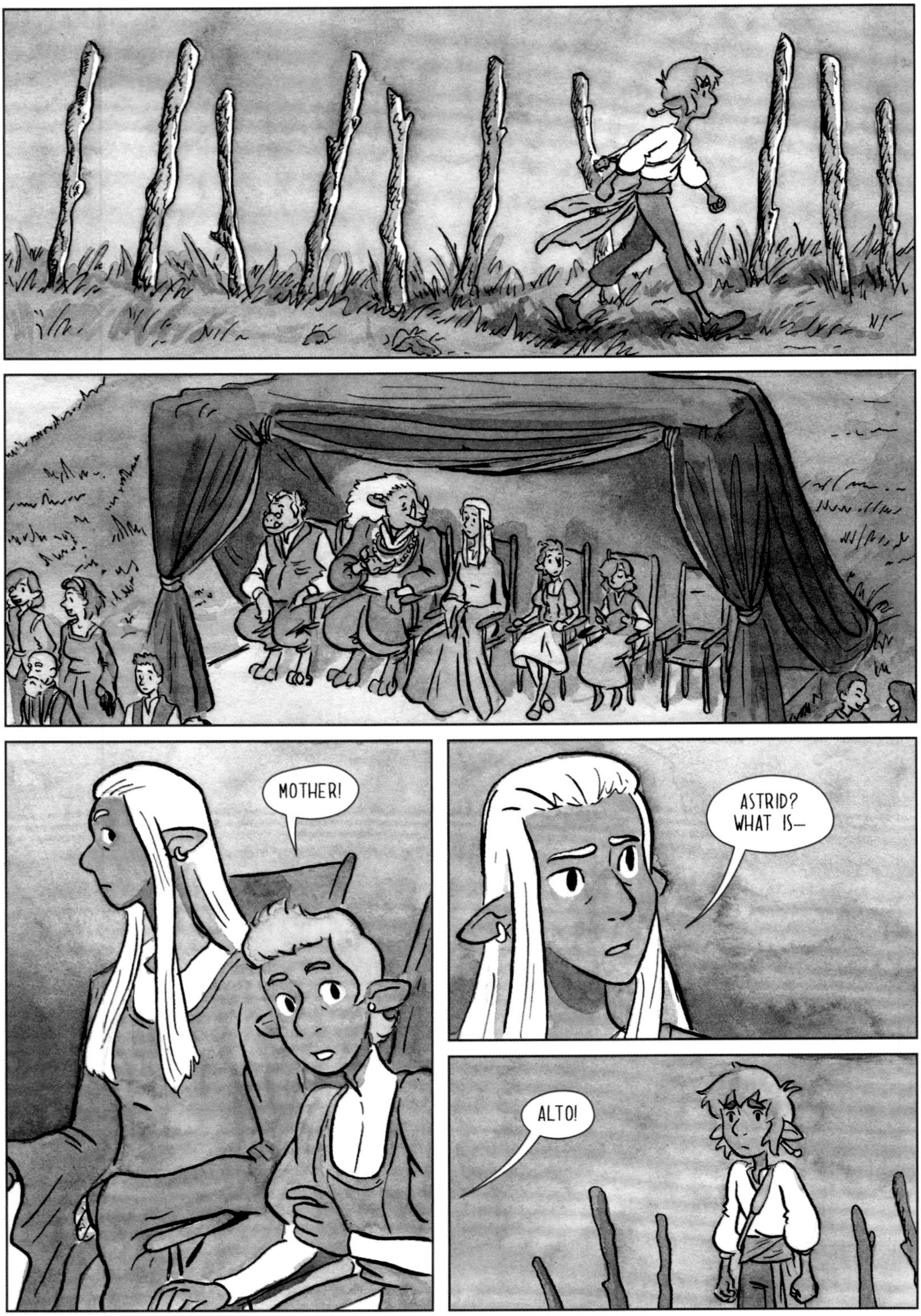
MOTHER!
ASTRID?
WHAT IS—
ALTO!

151

153

CHAPTER 11

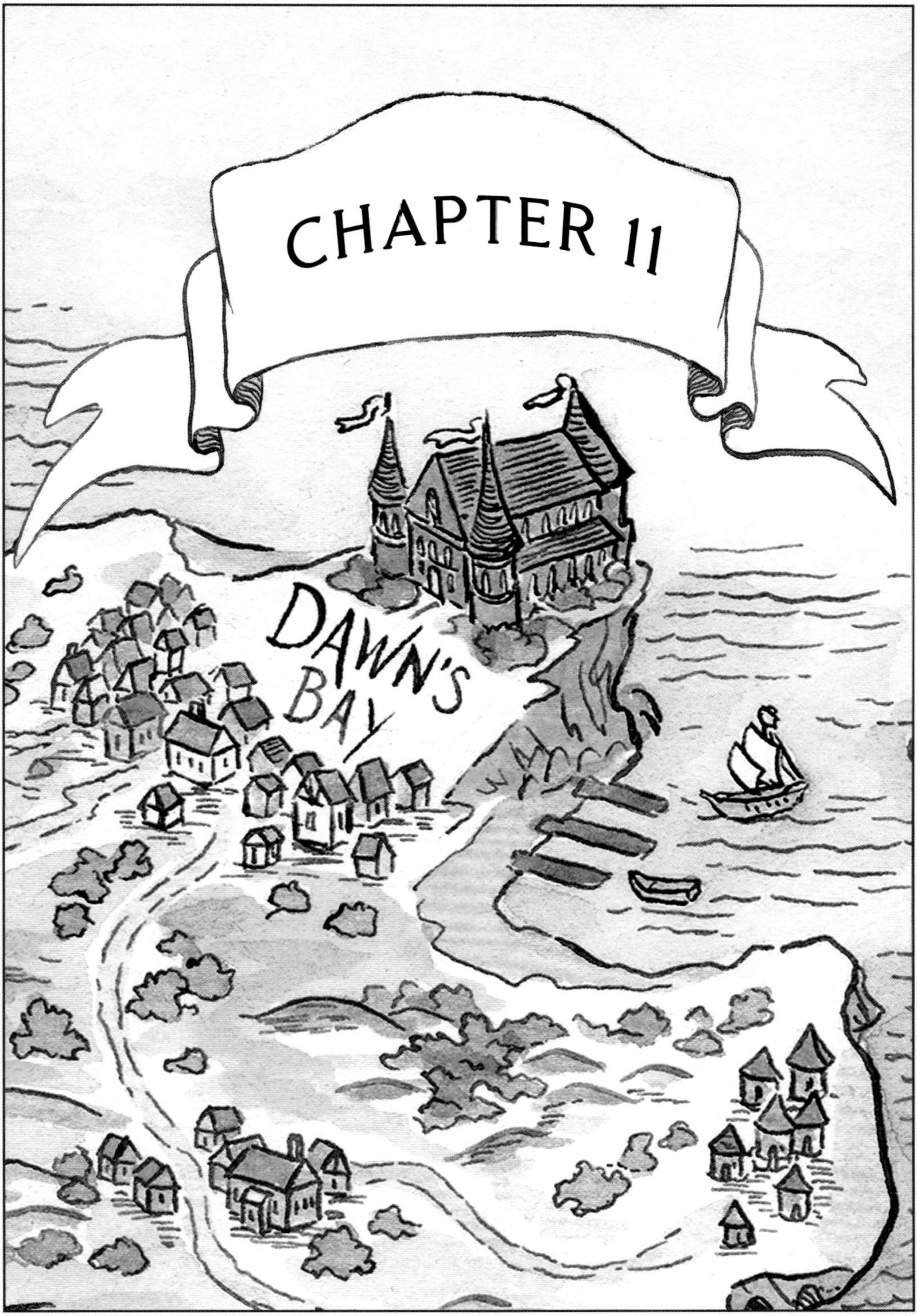
DAWN'S BAY

159

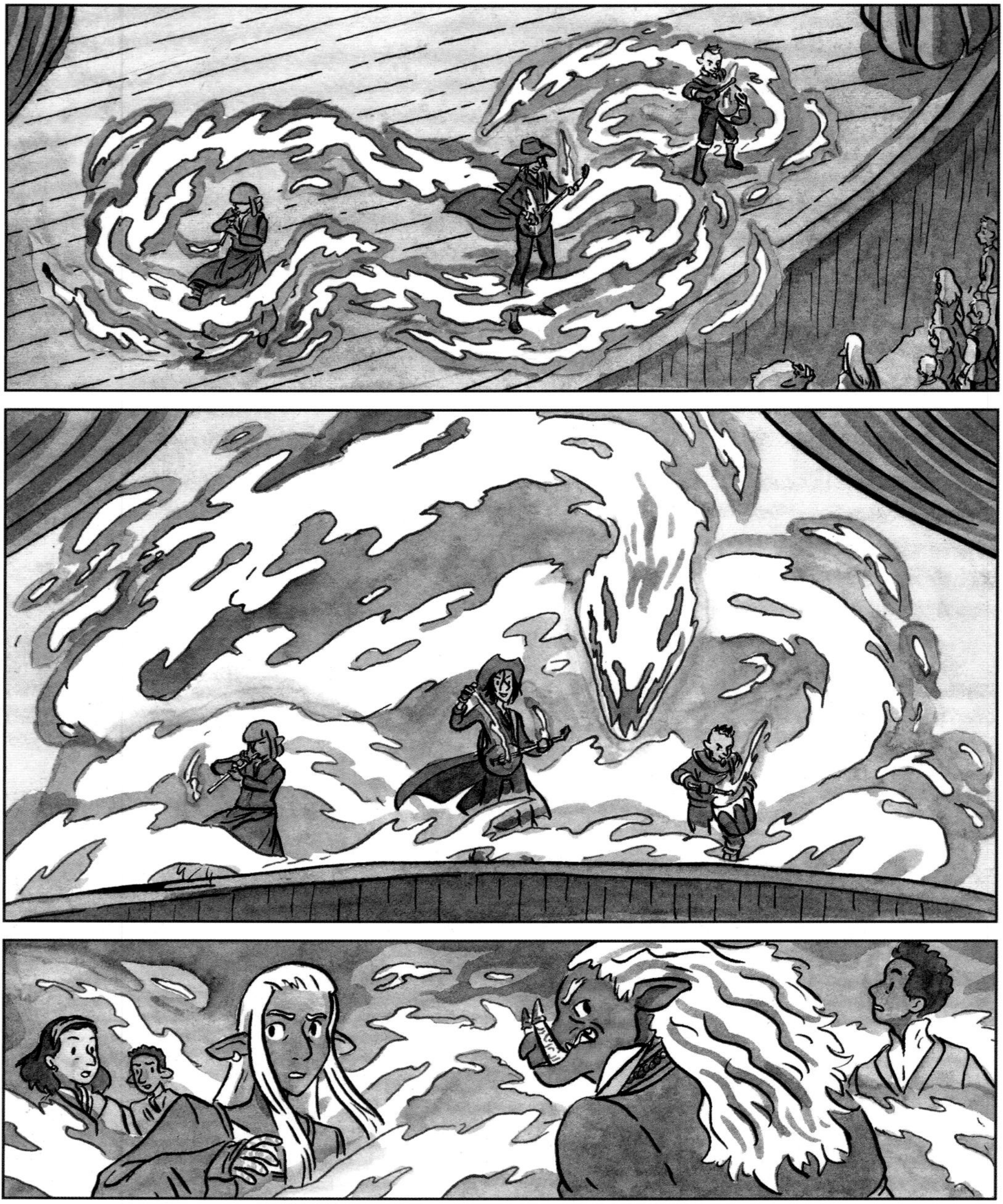

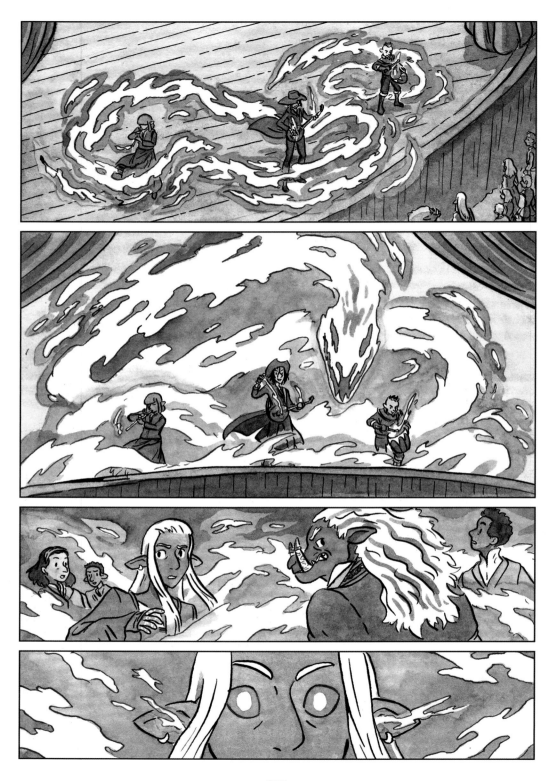

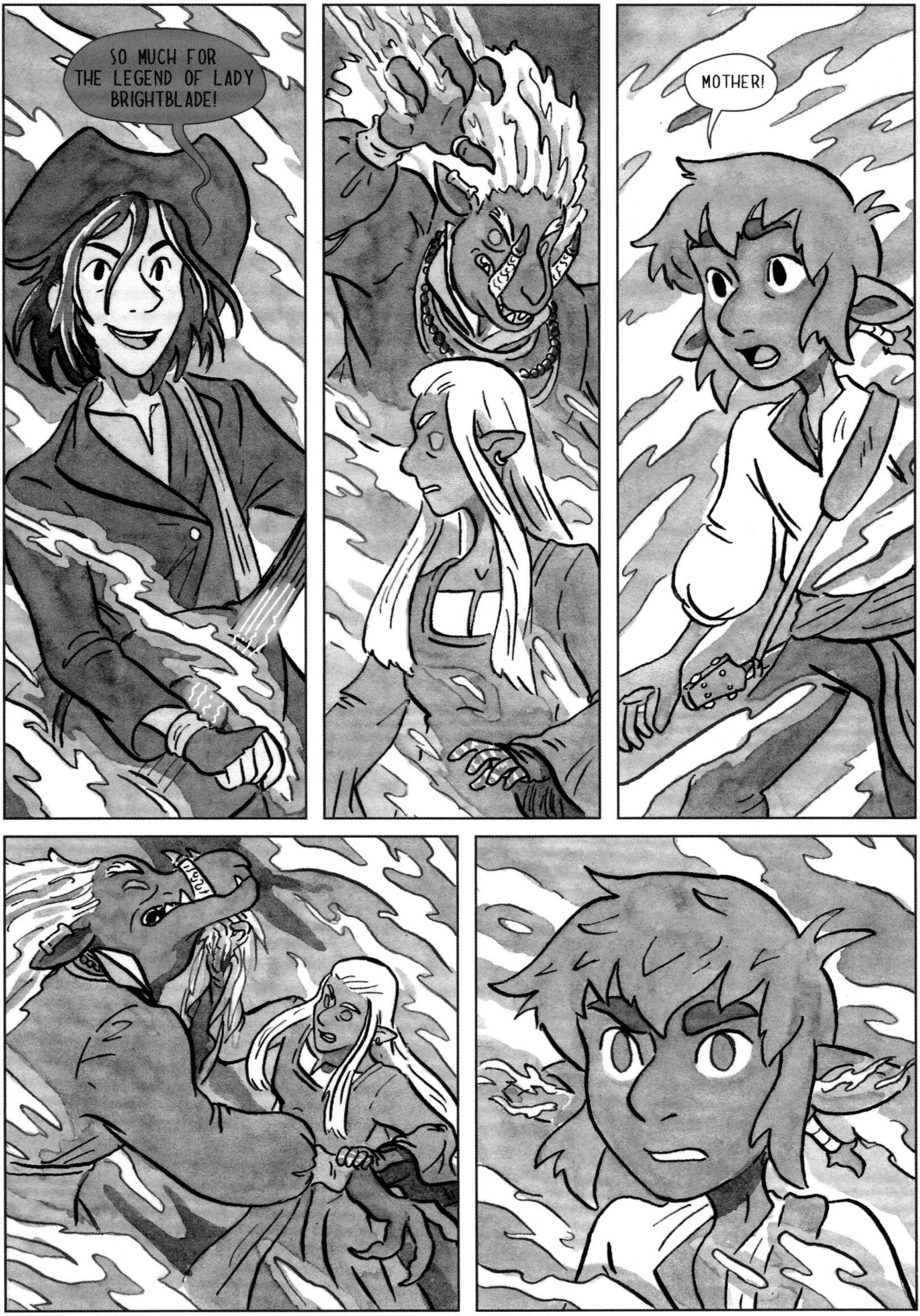
SO MUCH FOR THE LEGEND OF LADY BRIGHTBLADE!
MOTHER!

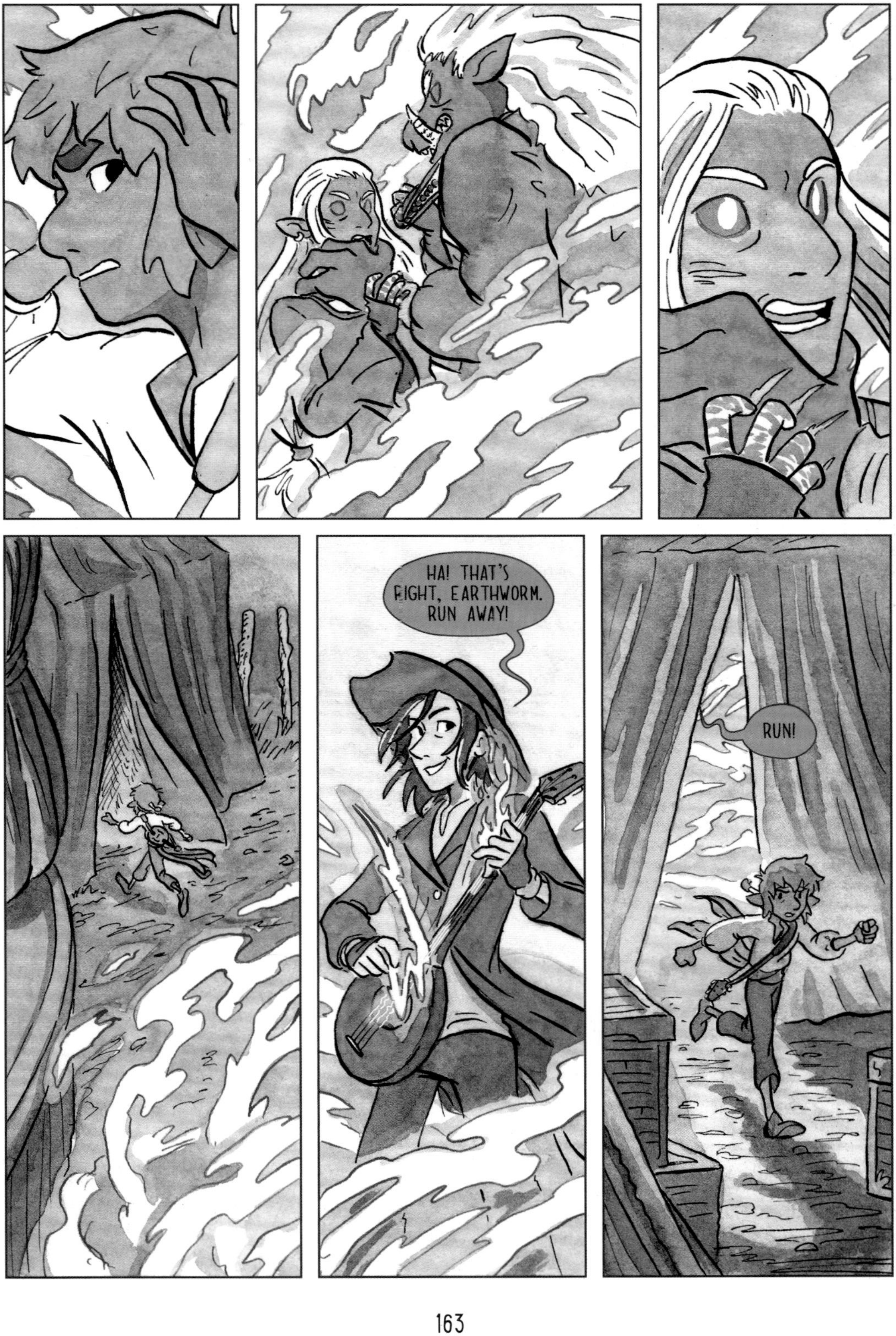
HA! THAT'S RIGHT, EARTHWORM. RUN AWAY!
RUN!

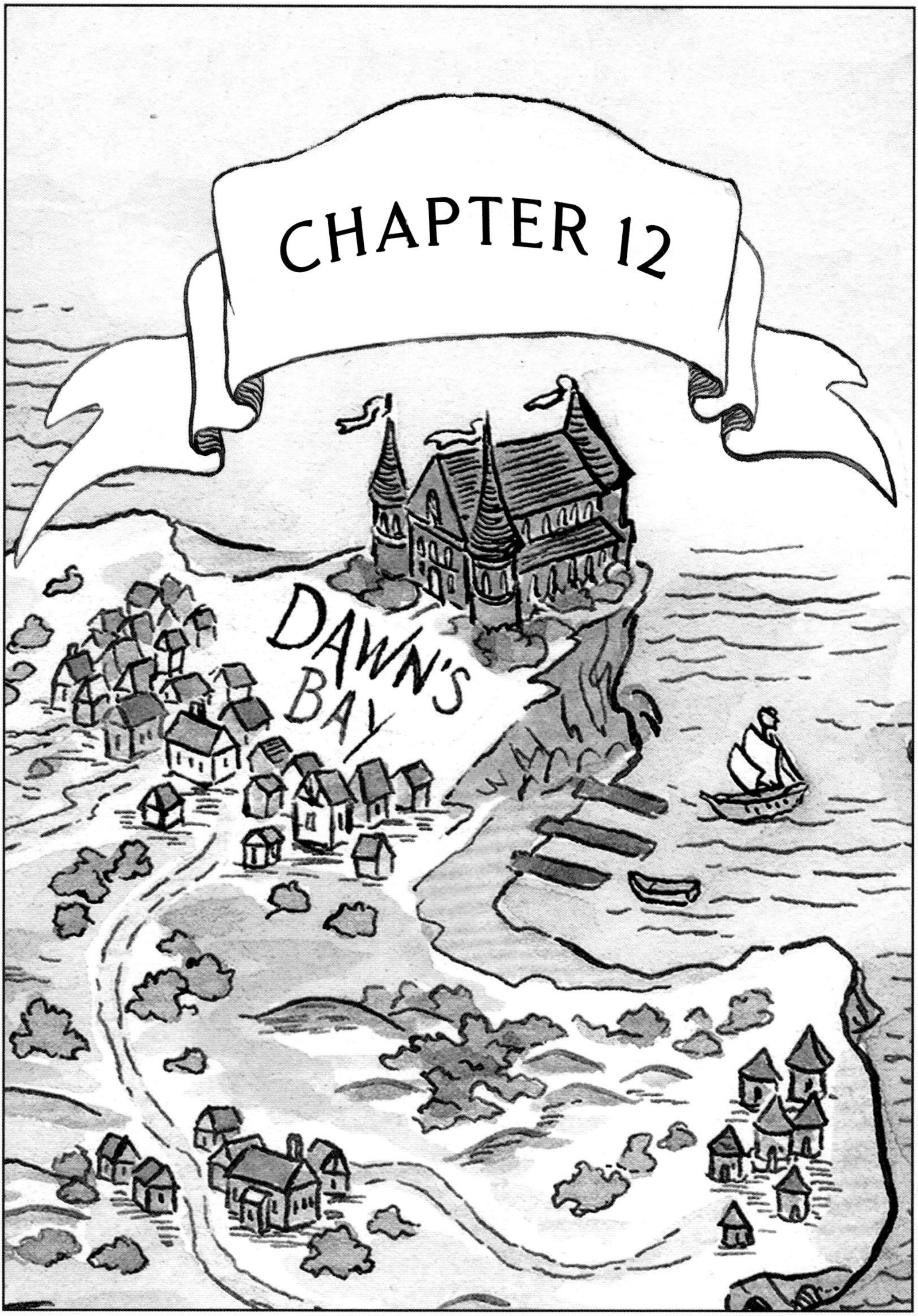
CHAPTER 12
DAWN'S BAY

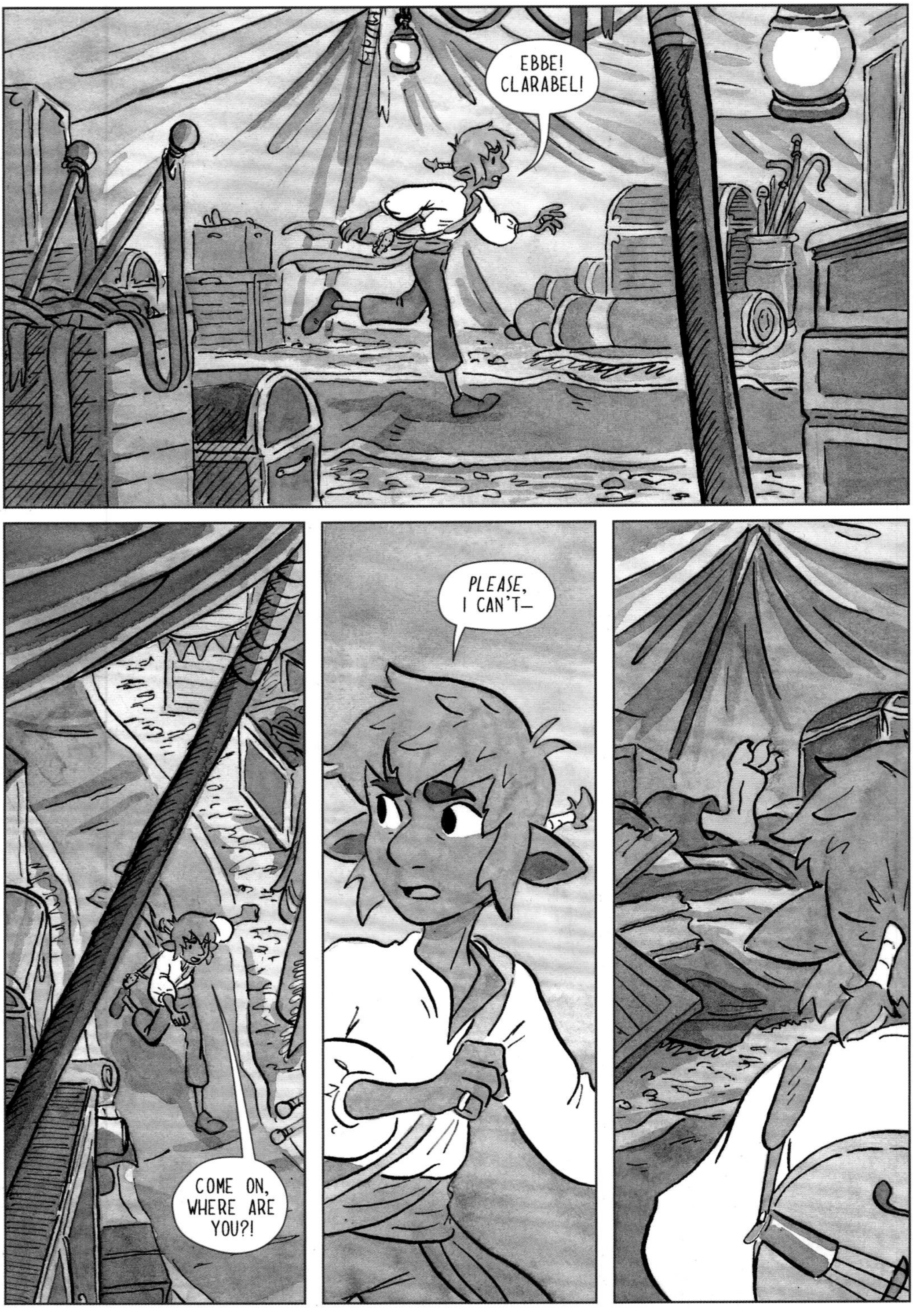
EBBE! CLARABEL!
COME ON, WHERE ARE YOU?!
PLEASE, I CAN'T—

168

169

173

174

178

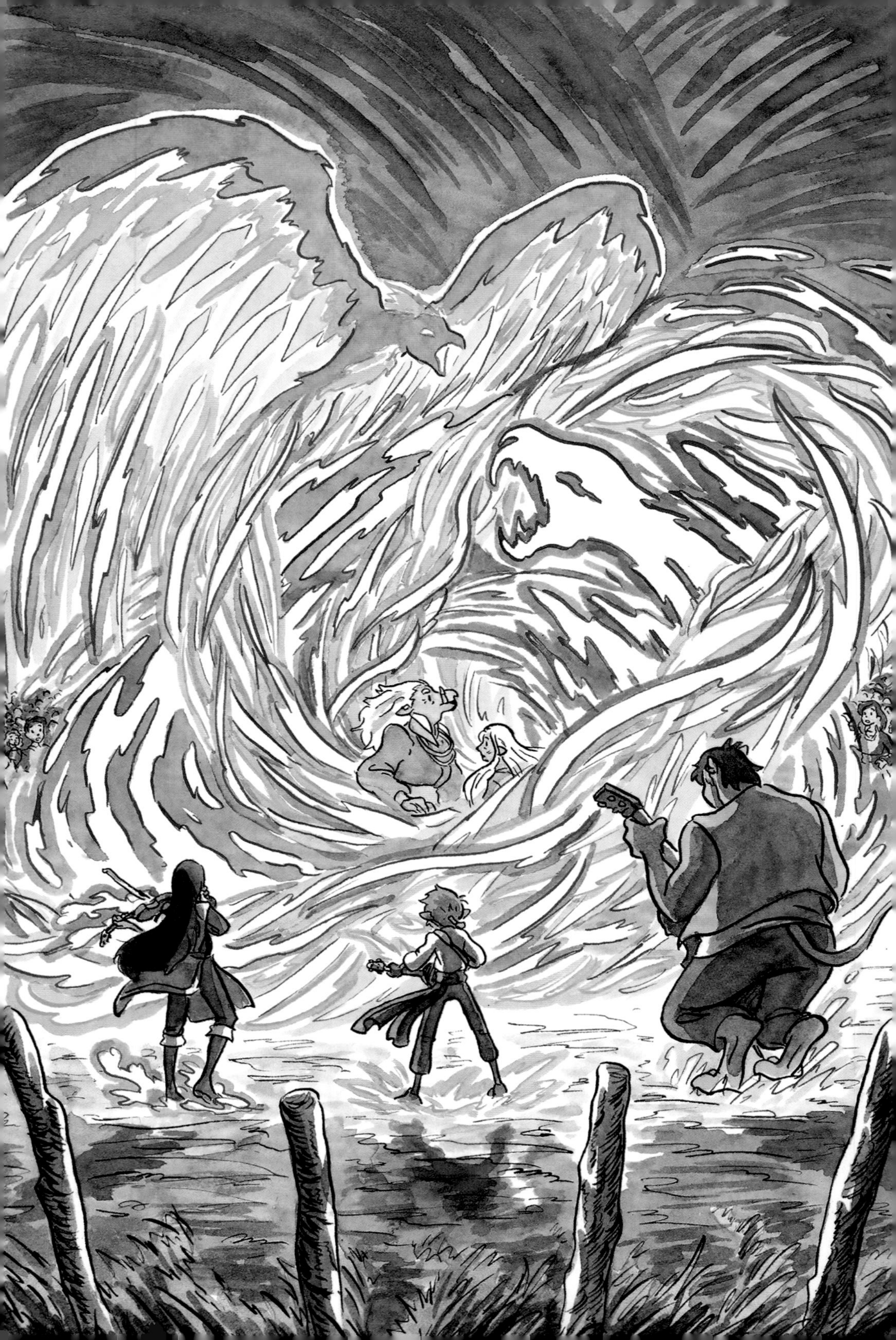

181

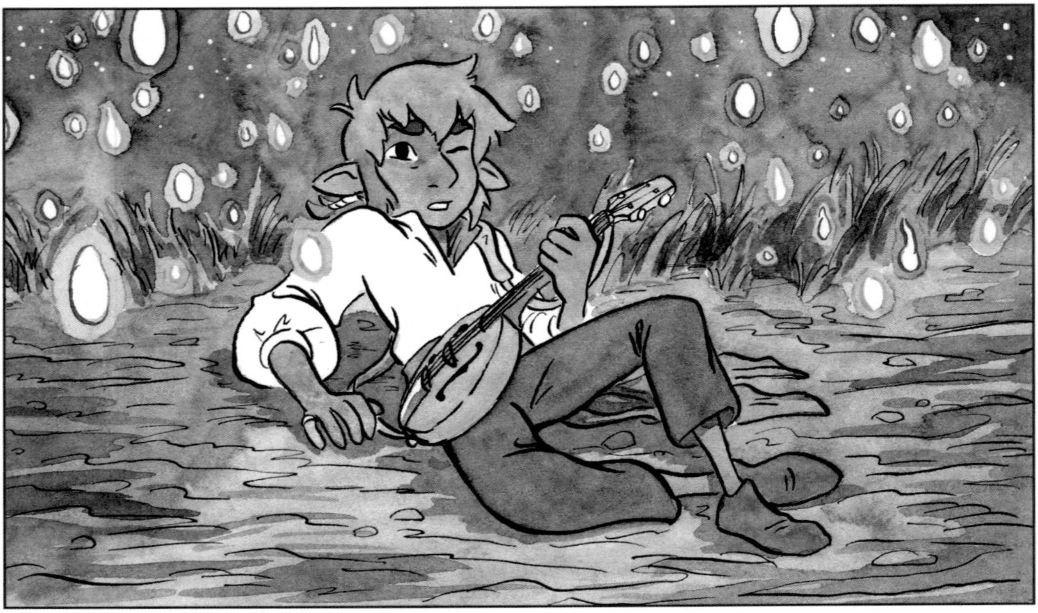

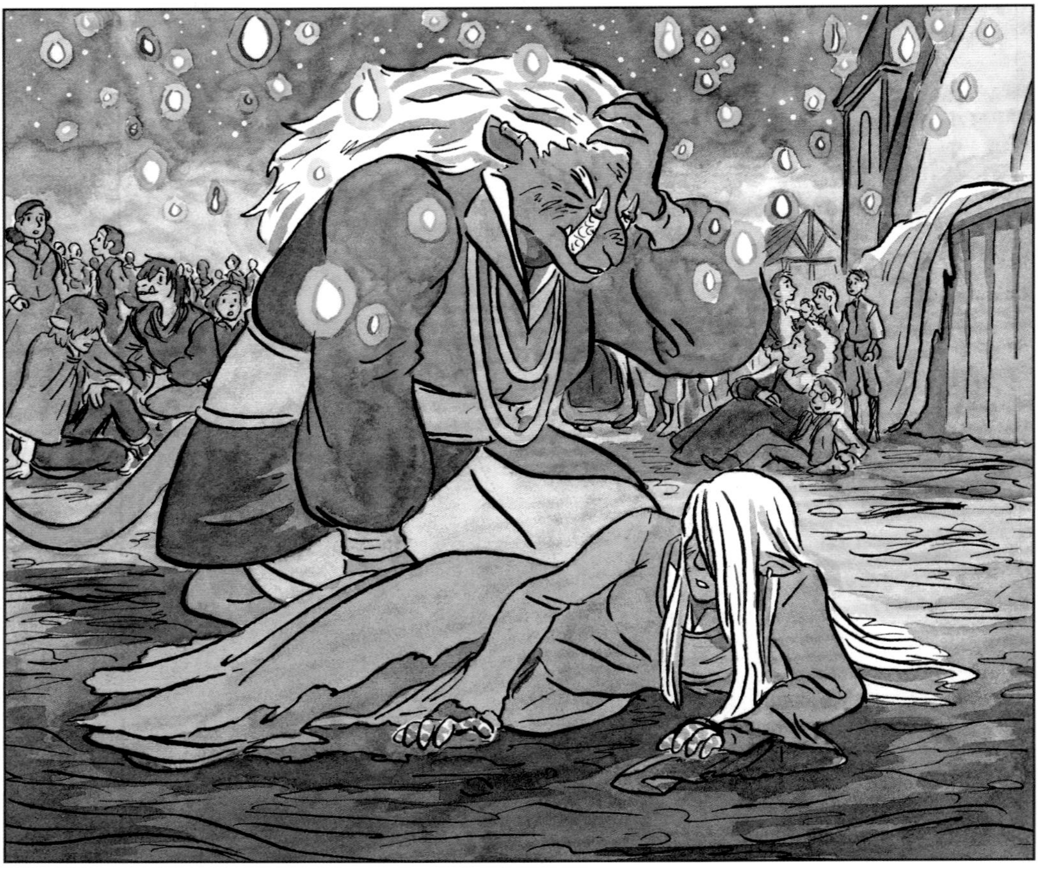

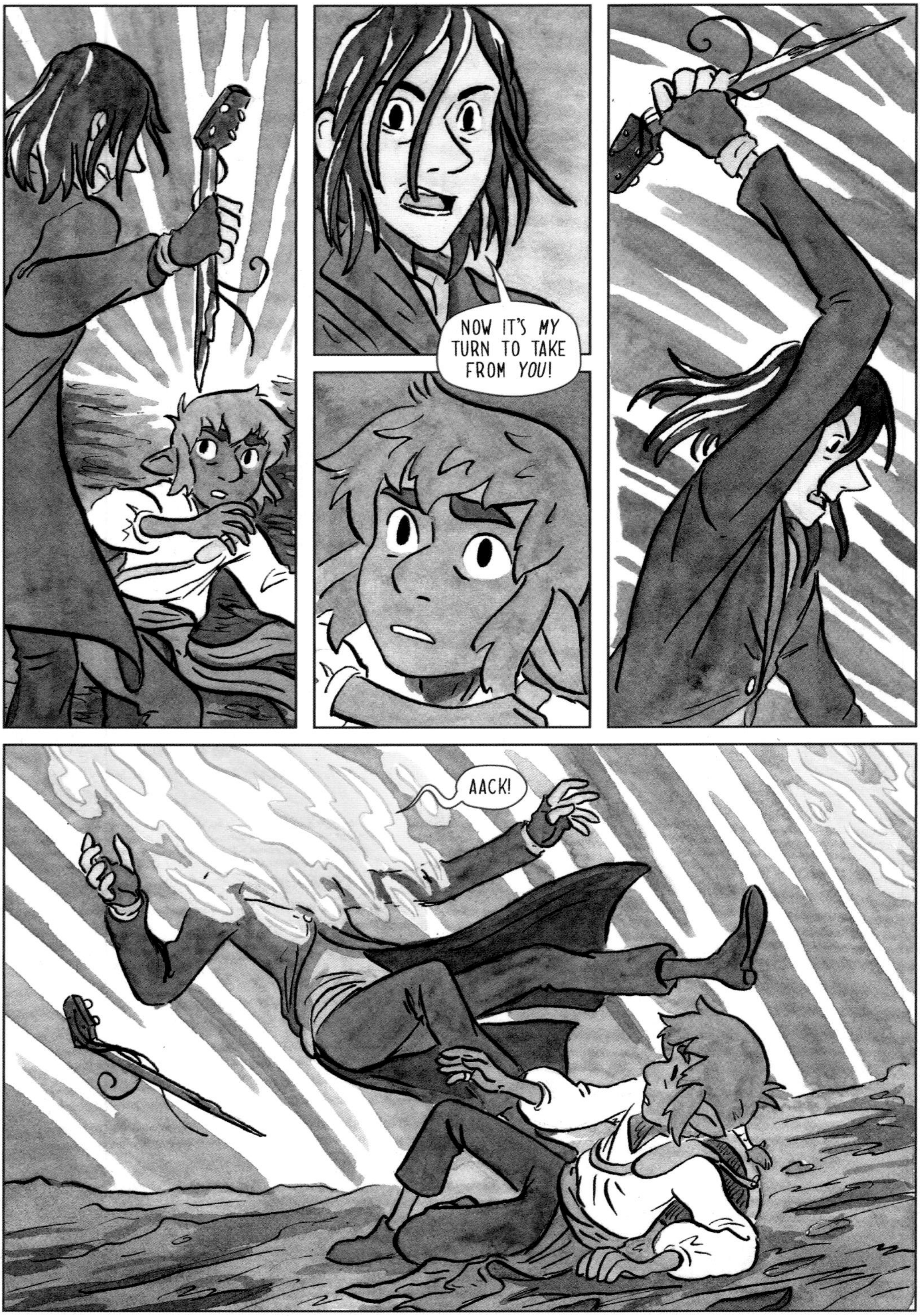
NOW IT'S MY TURN TO TAKE FROM YOU!
AACK!

186

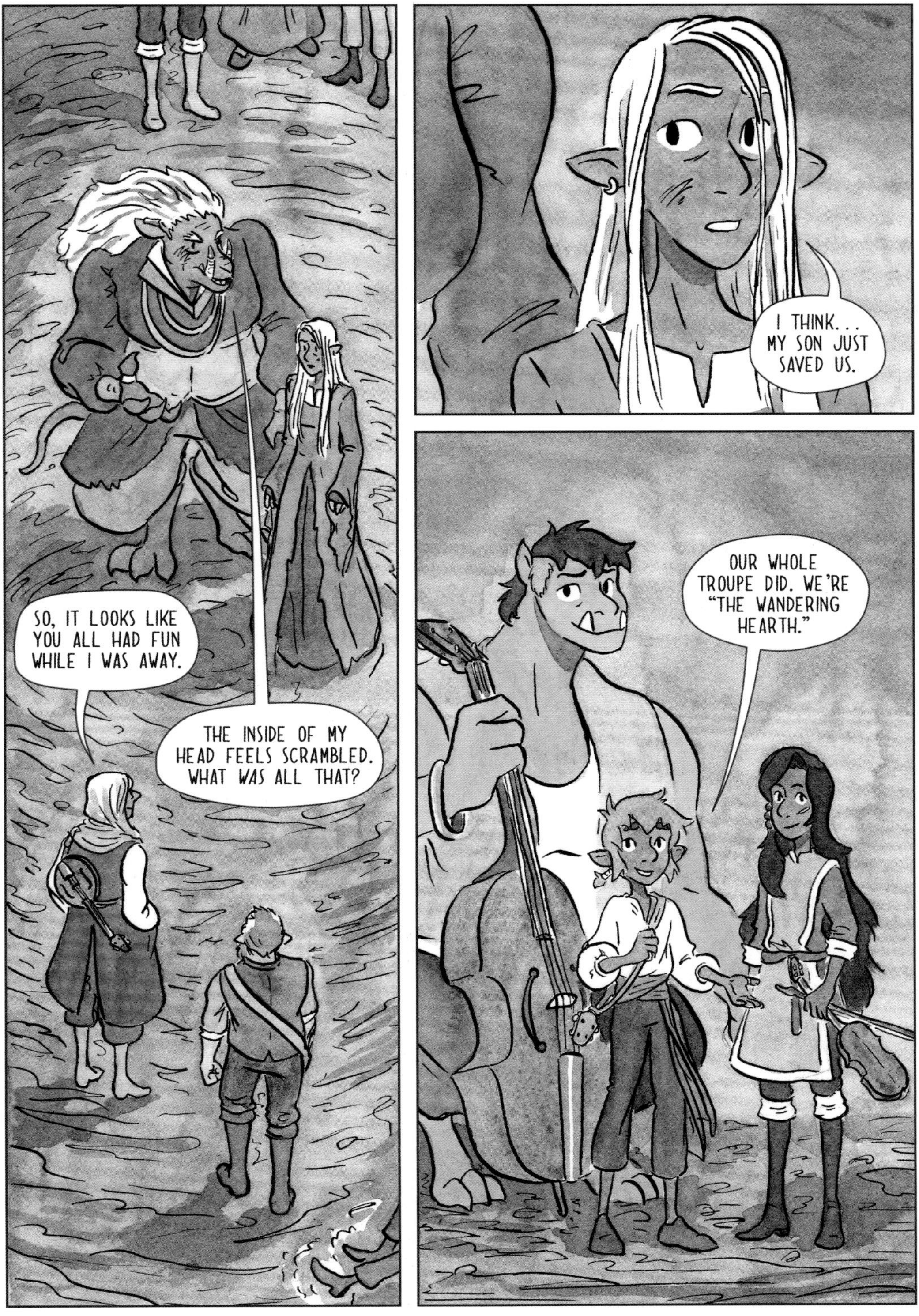
SO, IT LOOKS LIKE YOU ALL HAD FUN WHILE I WAS AWAY.
THE INSIDE OF MY HEAD FEELS SCRAMBLED. WHAT WAS ALL THAT?
I THINK. . . MY SON JUST SAVED US.
OUR WHOLE TROUPE DID. WE'RE "THE WANDERING HEARTH."

188

189

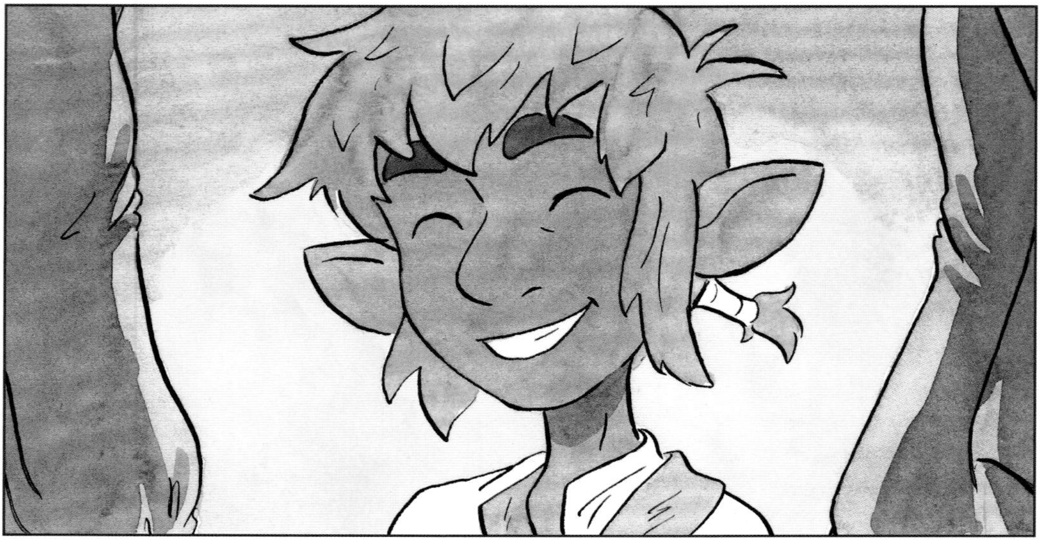

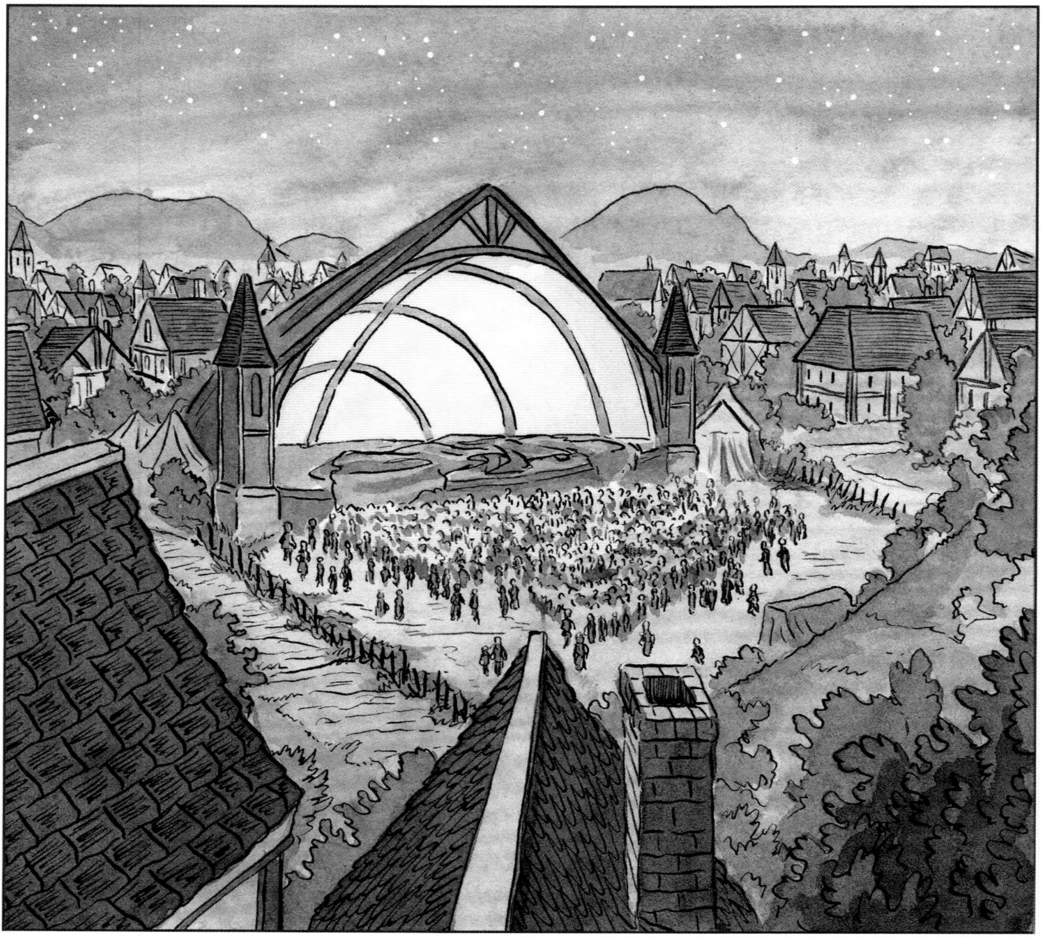

EPILOGUE

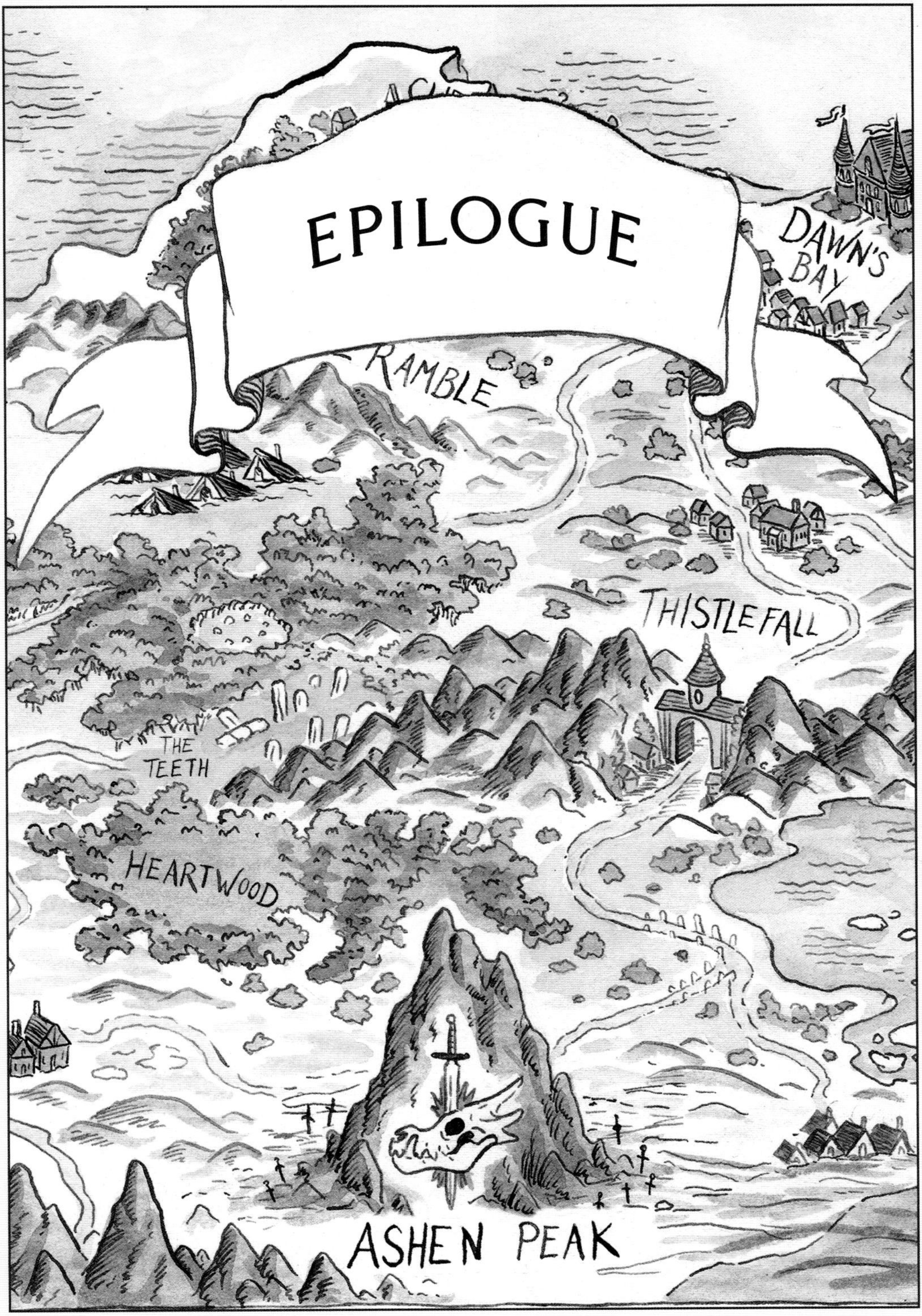
DAWN'S BAY
RAMBLE
THISTLEFALL
THE TEETH
HEARTWOOD
ASHEN PEAK

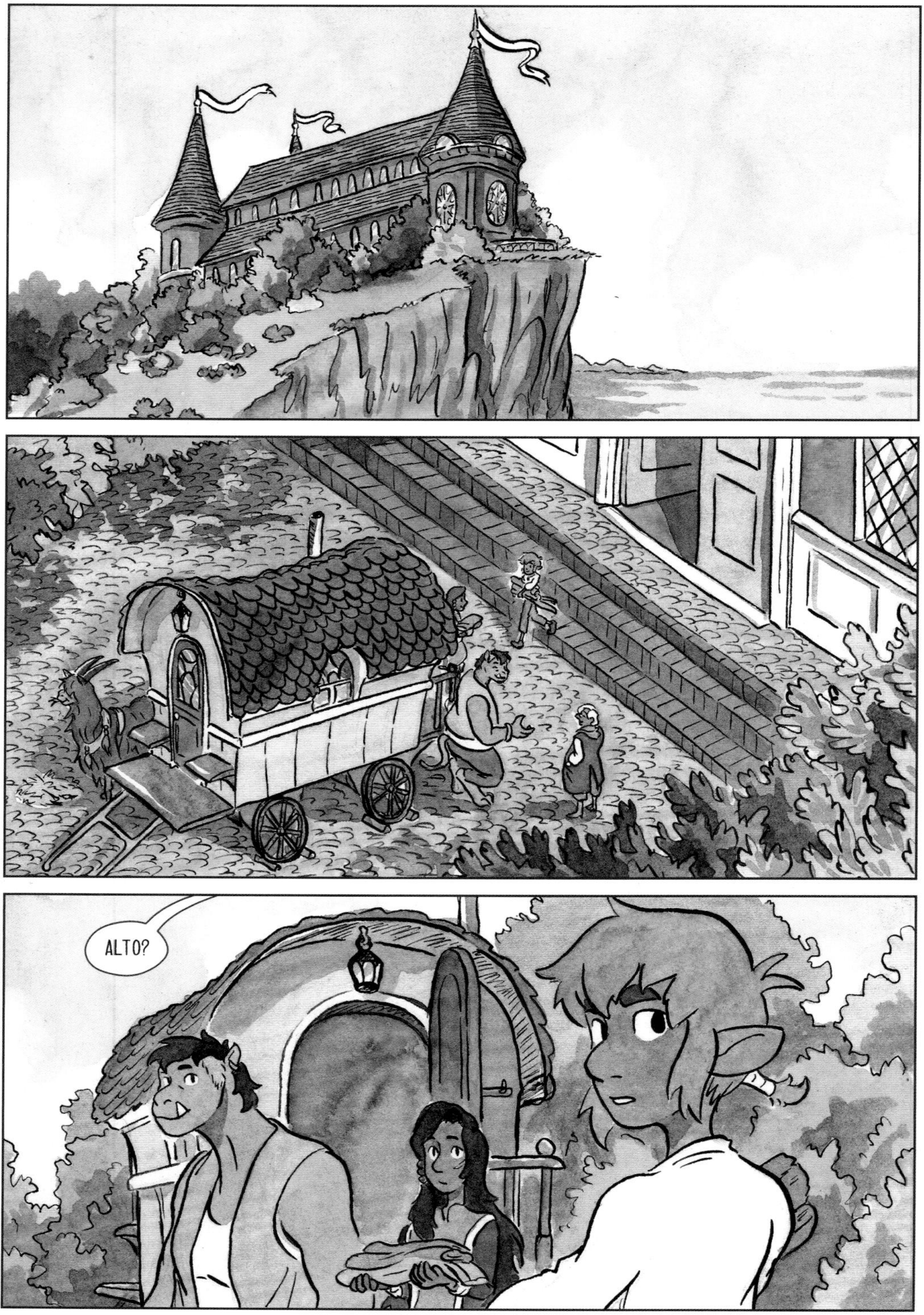
ALTO?

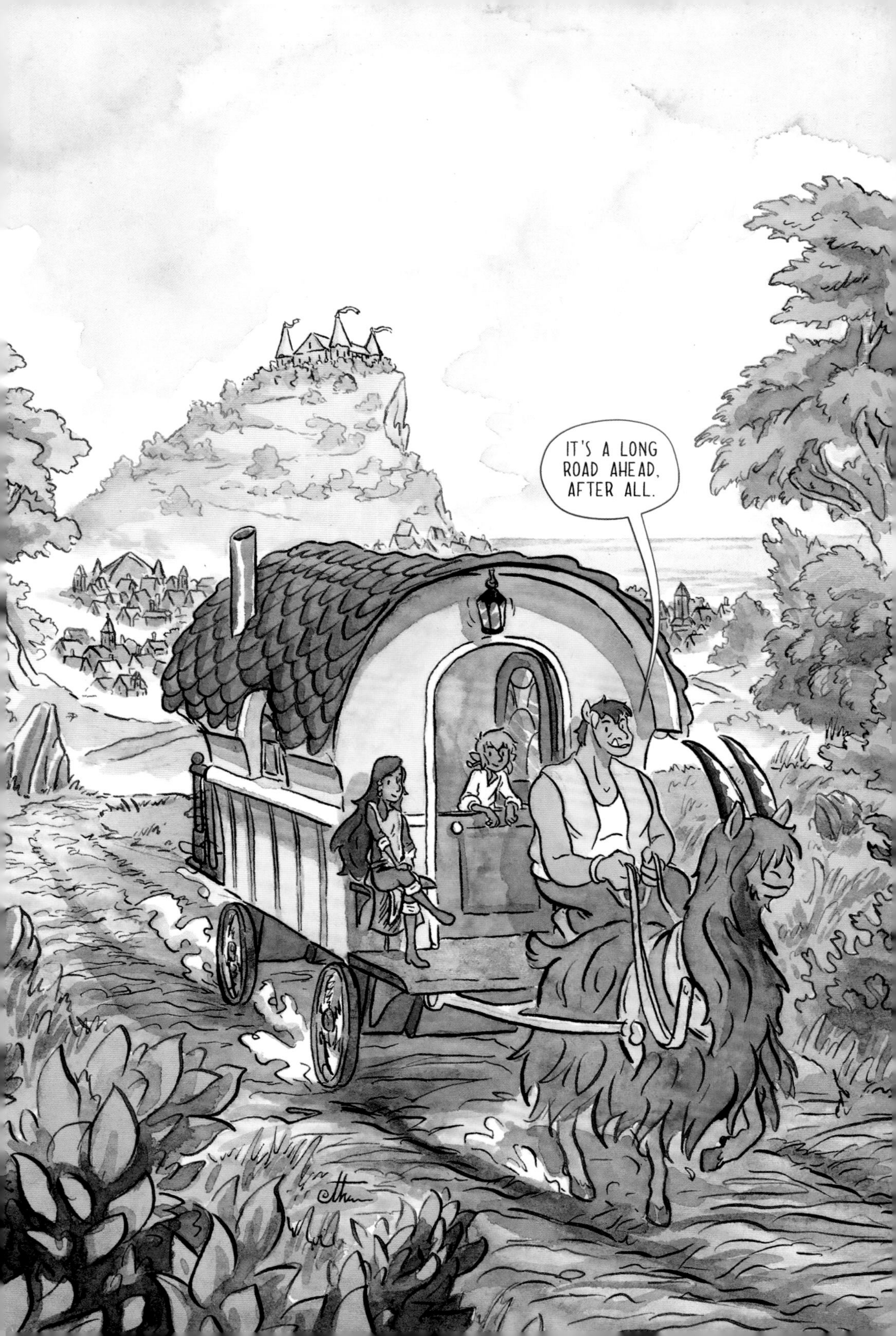
IT'S A LONG ROAD AHEAD, AFTER ALL.

ACKNOWLEDGMENTS

This book, like all books, was made with the help and support of many. First and always, thanks to my parents, Brad and Julia, and my siblings and their spouses, for nodding enthusiastically as I tried to explain the initial fragments of this story, and for always checking if my books are in stock whenever they're in a bookstore.

Thank you to Andrew Eliopulos for his faith in this story, and for doing so much to make it what it is. To Karen Chaplin, whose enthusiasm and expertise helped craft this story into something book-shaped. To Erin Fitzsimmons, Molly Fehr, Allison Weintraub, Shona McCarthy, Maria Whelan, and the rest of the team at Harper-Collins and Inkwell Management, for all of their hard work and skill. Their dedication to making beautiful books is an inspiration.

To Paul, Mikael, John, Alec, and Dexter, for telling interesting stories that never go the way I think they will.

The Legend of Brightblade was drawn and painted during the Covid-19 pandemic lockdowns, so a special thank-you to the doctors and nurses, the city, grocery, and delivery workers, and all other frontline workers who kept the world running as best they could.

The biggest thank-you to my husband, Matthew, for his wisdom, keen insight, and steadying support. His influence is threaded all throughout this book, for which I am incredibly grateful.